A DARKER TRUTH

A CADY MADDIX MYSTERY

KYLIE BRANT

For sweet and sassy Della Jaye

PRAISE FOR KYLIE BRANT

"Kylie Brant is destined to become a star!"
—Cindy Gerard, *New York Times* and *USA TODAY* bestselling author

"A complex, page-turning mystery plus a heartfelt romance blend into a fast-paced story that kept me reading until the wee hours."
—Allison Brennan, *New York Times* bestselling author of *Make Them Pay* on *Deadly Dreams*

"Dark and compelling suspense."
—Anne Frasier, author of *The Body Reader*

"*Pretty Girls Dancing* is a complex and character-driven mystery that will keep you turning pages until late at night."
—Kendra Elliot, Daphne du Maurier Award- winning author of *A Merciful Truth*

"*Pretty Girls Dancing* is Kylie Brant at her chilling best as she delivers a compelling thriller with a shocking twist."

—Loreth Anne White, author of *A Dark Lure*

ALSO BY KYLIE BRANT

The Cady Maddix Mysteries
Cold Dark Places
Down the Darkest Road
A Darker Truth

The Circle of Evil Trilogy
Chasing Evil
Touching Evil
Facing Evil

The Mindhunters
Deep as the Dead
What the Dead Know
Secrets of the Dead
Deadly Sins
Deadly Dreams
Deadly Intent
Waking the Dead
Waking Evil
Waking Nightmare

Other Works
Pretty Girls Dancing

Terms of Attraction

Terms of Engagement

Terms of Surrender

The Last Warrior

The Business of Strangers

Close to the Edge

In Sight of the Enemy

Dangerous Deception

Truth or Lies Entrapment

Alias Smith and Jones

Hard to Tame

Hard to Resist

Hard to Handle

Born in Secret

Undercover Bride

Falling Hard and Fast

Heartbreak Ranch

Undercover Lover

Friday's Child

Bringing Benjy Home

Guarding Raine

An Irresistible Man

McLain's Law

Rancher's Choice

Copyright © 2020 by Kylie Brant All rights reserved.

This is a work of fiction. Names, characters, organizations, places, events, and incidents are either products of the author's imagination or are used fictitiously. Any resemblance to actual persons, living or dead, or actual events is purely coincidental.

No part of this book may be reproduced in any form or by any electronic or mechanical means, including information storage and retrieval systems, without written permission from the author, except for the use of brief quotations in a book review.

ISBN: 9798649803458

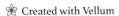 Created with Vellum

PROLOGUE

Two years earlier

The moon hung fat and low, barely skimming the jagged tops of the firs crowding the rundown home. The man moved stealthily from their shelter to the back door of the house. Because he was never unprepared, he'd first come a week ago when the place was empty. He had two entries already determined.

Last time he'd jimmied the back door with little more than a pick and a credit card. But a new deadbolt had been installed. A cheap one, likely. With enough time he could thwart it. But it was late and he was anxious to grab some sleep. Turning, he made his way to the front porch. Skirting the entrance, he stopped at the lone window. He withdrew the screwdriver from the pocket of his jacket and wedged it into the seam along the old wooden storm, prying it away from the frame. Gently, he leaned it against the peeling siding. Replacing the tool, he raised the inner window he'd left unlocked when he was here. Shook his head at the occupant's carelessness. To install new locks and not even check the windows? Sheer idiocy.

He peeked through the filthy blinds before holding them up and throwing a leg over the sill. Folded himself enough to ease inside. Then he straightened, drawing his weapon. Light from a TV screen spilled out of an open doorway. He quietly crept to the bedroom, letting the glow highlight him.

"You've disappointed me, Corbin."

The man in the bed froze. "Deacon." He licked his lips. Though his cell phone lay in his lap, one of his hands inched beneath the pillow next to him. "Been a long time."

"Stop." The command in his voice had Corbin freezing. Deacon was at the bedside in three quick steps. He took the handgun that was hidden under the man's pillow in one gloved hand and shoved it in his pocket. He mentally adjusted his original plan. One had to be flexible. "I understand you've been telling stories."

"No, I haven't said a word. Not to anyone, I swear." "Really?" Deacon's voice was soft. "Not even to a certain

assistant county attorney?"

His Adam's apple bobbing, Corbin croaked, "I wasn't going to keep that appointment. I won't."

"No. You won't."

Sensing the meaning in his words, Corbin made a wild lunge for the other side of the bed. Was caught by Deacon's fist in his hair. "Ease on back here, son, and I'll tell you how this is going to go."

There was the usual struggle. The pleading and tears. The false bravado before accepting the inevitable. In the end, he did as he was told. Not because Deacon didn't give him a choice. That wouldn't be fair. But because the alternative was worse. They always were.

Deacon returned the gun and kept his own weapon aimed as the man placed the barrel into his mouth. When his finger tightened on the trigger, Deacon stepped outside the room to avoid the spray. The sound of the shot echoed through the home.

He took a plastic bag from his pocket and scooped up the cell, dropping it inside. Then, because he wasn't a monster, he said a quick prayer for the soul of Corbin Fielding before leaving the place the way he'd entered, fitting the old wooden storm back into place and melting into the shadows. This wouldn't end with Corbin. He saw that now. It couldn't. The others would also have to die.

1

Deputy U.S. Marshal Cady Maddix surveyed the ramshackle apartment building through the night vision binoculars as her colleague, Miguel Rodriguez gave his report over the encrypted radio. "Four people inside. Three near the door spaced a couple of feet apart. Another is twelve feet away from them."

She lowered the glasses to study the diagram the property manager had drawn. The baby was likely in the bedroom, away from the adults. "Good. Keep moving." It took only minutes for the Range-R device to do its work, penetrating walls to detect the presence of humans.

"Already gone."

She raised the binoculars again to look out the van window. Miguel's report provided some verification for the tip she'd received earlier. Bobby Stallsworth had been identified this afternoon when he'd slipped away from an illegal poker game shortly before it was busted. Subject of a murder warrant, he hadn't been seen in the Asheville area in six months. If the witness was correct, he was currently visiting apartment 319 in the building down the street. The renter was one Sara Johnson, whose occasional boyfriend was a known accomplice of the fugitive.

Cady shrugged off a feeling of foreboding. Apartment buildings made for shitty entry points. Too many exits and citizens in proximity. A myriad of ways for a raid to go sideways. Meaning her planning had to be meticulous.

Unless Stallsworth made it easy for them and left first.

She glanced around. Like the rest of the neighborhood, the apartment complex was doing a slow slide into decay. Darkness couldn't completely hide the crumbling stone steps, or the cracked windows punctuating its exterior. Shrouded in shadows, it vaulted from seedy to sinister. She already knew the security was spotty. Most of the gates over the entrances were broken. There were no cameras.

The May evening was balmy, but Cady donned a jacket over her Kevlar, settling a USMS ball cap on her head and threading her braid through the back opening. Using the radio, she said, "We move forward. Four a.m. entry." Hopefully by then the city—and the occupants of the apartment — would be asleep. "Until then, surveillance." There was no way of knowing how long the fugitive would hide inside. But he wouldn't escape the net they had around him. She had a couple of people assigned to every exit, with one covering the rear. That doorway was boarded up, but the higher floors had a terrace overlooking the backyard.

Whatever the man decided to do tonight, they were likely in for a long wait.

CADY RUBBED at the cramp in her left quad as she raised the night vision glasses. There hadn't been an alert from the team in over an hour. None of the people entering or exiting the building had been identified. As long as that remained the case, Stallsworth was still inside. She pulled out her cell to look at the time. Twelve thirty a.m. Hours yet before the clubs closed in downtown Asheville.

"I've got movement in back." The voice belonged to Deputy U.S. Marshal Paul Chester.

"On my way." She lowered the binoculars and slipped her phone in one pocket and the radio in the other. Then picked up her Maglite and got out of the van. She headed in the opposite direction, crossing the street at the corner and continuing down the sidewalk. Raucous laughter came from a porch she passed, a reminder that for some, the evening was still young.

Cady turned, jogging now. She knew from Paul's earlier updates that the backyard was unkempt, a tangle of weeds and garbage. The rickety wooden fence enclosing it leaned drunkenly, its missing boards resembling absent teeth. She peered through one opening, scanning the area.

The slivered moon and scatter of stars overhead provided little light. She took out her radio. "I'm in the alley." Because she knew where to look, she made out a large shape crouched next to the Dumpster. Then she stilled, listened. There was a slight clatter. Not from the immediate proximity, though. Higher.

"One individual, late teen or adult. Third-floor terrace." Chester's voice over the radio was hushed.

"I see him."

An instant later, the figure was in the corner of the balcony, straddling the low wall edging it. He grasped the drainpipe in both hands. There was a rusty creaking sound as he swung over the barrier to shimmy down the side of the building. Considering the condition of the property, Cady wouldn't trust the rainspout's stability.

She heard a metallic shriek as the pipe pulled away. The man hanging from it jumped to the ground, rolled. Paul got up and ran toward him. "Deputy U.S. Marshals! On the ground! Arms behind your head. Now!"

The man beelined for a gaping hole in the fence perpendicular to her. She followed, hoping to trap him in the neighboring yard. "Unidentified subject fleeing on foot from the rear of the complex," she whispered into the radio. "All but west position hold."

Reaching the end of the fencing, she flattened herself to peer around the corner and switched on her flashlight. The building might have been a store once. The beam picked up the pockmarked siding, the sagging windows. Trash cans lined the alley, all spilling with waste. Cady kicked each to determine one wasn't hiding the stranger she sought.

She almost missed it. She'd already jogged by the overgrown brush growing close to the structure when something alerted her. She looked over her shoulder and saw the leaves of the bush shaking in the still night air.

She turned her light away. "He's in the—" Before she could finish the words, the stranger sprang from his hiding place and darted straight toward her. Cady raised the Maglite to catch his face in its glow. She dodged the metal garbage can lid he threw at her head before giving chase again.

"Bobby Stallsworth! Deputy U.S. Marshals. Get down on your knees. Hands behind your head!"

But the man was racing into the darkness.

"You got an ID?" Paul Chester's voice sounded behind her.

"It's him." His speed must be fueled by desperation. It was all Cady could do to keep him in sight as she ran after him. He bounded over obstacles in the alley and dashed through its mouth to the street beyond. "Bandit is heading west on Fleur Avenue. Request vehicle pursuit."

Her heart pounded with exertion and adrenaline. He headed down a road with only intermittent working streetlights, sailing over the occasional outstretched homeless person leaning against the cracked storefronts. When he disappeared around the corner of a dilapidated building, Cady took the turn wide in case he lay in wait. But then she saw him heading to the six-foot-tall chain-link barrier behind it.

She relayed the man's position, slipped the radio into her pocket, and gave a burst of speed. He was astride the fence when she reached it. With a leap, she managed to grab his ankle and climbed partway up, bringing her flashlight down hard on his thigh. He yelped and scrambled over the top, his foot slipping from her grasp. Cady scaled the fence one-handed. On the other side, she followed at a sprint, radioing updates on the fugitive's location. "No weapon sighted yet," she finished.

Her breath sawed in and out of her chest. Whatever Stallsworth had been up to in the last few months, he'd kept in shape. He led her several more blocks, dodging cars and the stray pedestrian. She recognized the Wall Street neighborhood they were entering. With a sense of unease, she predicted the man's destination an instant before he stopped at the front door. "We're at Grove's Motel." She trailed him into the seedy establishment. The business was a known haven for prostitutes and drug activity. She could hear the screech of a vehicle stopping nearby. Hopefully, a task force member.

The desk clerk barely glanced up as she rushed by. Stallsworth headed toward the back door. Searching her memory, Cady thought the place bordered Rat Alley. She burst out of the exit, the stench and sweaty heat enveloping her like a decaying sauna. She nearly gagged. The temperature notched up with every step. The passageway was enclosed, with a damp concrete floor. One side served as a rear entry to the businesses along Patton Avenue. The other was a solid brick wall, punctuated by grease traps, Dumpsters, and garbage cans, all potential hiding places. The single line of tube lighting hanging from the rafters above the block-long tunnel failed to pierce the shadowy corners.

She flicked the beam of her Maglite around the area as she updated the team. Unable to avoid the fetid stream of water down the center of the concrete, she crisscrossed the alley. She headed in the direction of a noise that sounded, hoping grimly that he'd tripped over some of the debris in the space. Preferably something sharp.

"We're across from Pritchard Park on Patton Avenue. We've got the other exit covered." Cady identified the voice on the radio as John Rossi, a Transylvania County deputy and member of the Carolinas Regional Fugitive Task Force. "It's still netted off, but it wouldn't take much to get through."

"Let's hope he tries," she muttered, squinting into the darkness. She heard a footstep behind her and looked over her shoulder to identify Paul Chester's large form. Four others followed him.

"Spread out. Check every garbage container. All building exits. I haven't seen a weapon, but assume he's armed."

She inched forward, playing her light over potential hiding spots as she searched. Unless he'd already dodged through a back entry, Stallsworth was contained in the area.

And she was well-aware how dangerous a trapped fugitive could be.

But when she reached the end of the alley, she encountered only the two team members on the other side of the plastic netting.

Cady turned, met up with Paul Chester a few yards back. "Either he's still in here somewhere, or he managed to slip into one of the businesses." She gestured for two of the men to check out the buildings and retraced her steps.

A pile of used lumber and cleaning supplies was stacked haphazardly against one structure. A pail was overturned, still rolling slightly. The doorway of the building had been covered by a piece of steel bolted to the brick exterior.

She crouched to inspect the heap of rubbish more closely. There was an eighteen-inch gap behind it. A hard knot of frustration formed in her chest when she saw a small metal door, no more than three feet by three feet.

Cady flattened herself against the building and sidled along until she could squat in front of the hatch. Screws had once held it in place, but they were missing now. She fit her fingers into the seam around it and pulled it off.

"Access?" Paul's voice sounded behind her.

"I'll see." She set the piece down and shone her light into the interior before wiggling inside. Moments later, she was in an eight-by-ten space. To her right was a door, up three rickety steps. She ascended the stairs and threw a shoulder against it, to no avail. A piece of tin plating had replaced the doorknob. There'd be no entry from this point.

As she backtracked, Cady heard the other marshal's voice on the radio. "What'd you find?"

"Nothing, yet." Ahead was a well of darkness. She inched closer. After several steps, her foot met only air. She scrambled back.

Paul joined her. "There's no way into the building through the entrance behind me," she murmured. "And the cellar staircase seems to be...ah." She glimpsed something in the corner of the opening and went for a closer look. "The steps are missing. There's a ladder here." It was old-fashioned, with narrow metal rungs in a wood frame. But it looked sturdy enough.

Dropping to her belly, she shined her beam into the dark pit below. Felt Paul crowd in next to her.

"Unusual for places around here to have basements. 'Course, I never figured on that hatch leading inside, either," he muttered.

She updated the team of their location before responding, "It might have been an old service entrance, recently reopened." Her grandfather's house had had something similar—a little area off the kitchen. Generations earlier the iceman could place square blocks of ice directly into an icebox.

Thoughts of her grandfather had her mind dodging the memories that threatened to follow. "I'll check it out." And hope like hell Stallsworth wasn't down there, waiting to ambush them.

"Give me your hand in case the ladder goes." Paul drew nearer.

Or in case someone below kicked it out from beneath her, Cady thought grimly. With one of her hands in Paul's hard grip, she began to descend. "Just a couple of rungs," he whispered.

She went down three, far enough to play her flashlight over the space. Cady could make out nothing but shadows and cobwebs. "It appears clear." When he released her, she went down a few more rungs before jumping lightly to the dirt floor. The space was cool and damp, a marked difference from the foul-smelling alley. She stabilized the ladder with one hand.

The cellar ran the full length and width of the structure above. Her light couldn't pierce the inky corners. As Paul reached her side, she moved away to check them out.

She found nothing but some piles of garbage, so she started toward her colleague, who was poking around nearby. But then she stopped mid-stride, something catching her eye. There was a door on the opposite side of the basement. Original to the building, she thought, approaching it. Oversized and made of wood, it groaned when she grasped the rusty handle and pulled it open to see a brick wall with something nailed below an archway. She reached out to touch the covering. Burlap.

She caught Paul's attention and gestured him over. They drew their weapons and positioned themselves at each edge. She flipped up the cover, and they swung around to face whatever—or whoever—was on the other side. But no one was there. A jagged opening yawned before them. For the first time, she noticed the fine dust lying on the floor in front of it.

Paul probed the gap with his flashlight. "More than a hidey-hole," he whispered. "It has some depth."

Cady radioed the two remaining team members in the alley to join them. Then, Maglite in one hand and weapon in the other, she bent to crawl into the claustrophobic space.

When she heard a soft curse, she looked over her shoulder and saw Paul hunched like a giant in a hobbit hole. She grinned. The man was broad and well over six foot. His shoulders filled the narrow area.

She'd gone about fifteen yards when she stopped, flicking her beam from one side to another. "It branches off here." She trained the light on the hole chiseled into the brick on their right. Cady exchanged her flashlight for the radio long enough to direct Rossi and Conway, who were trailing them, to take the turn while she and Paul continued forward.

They came to another hole that had been chiseled through brick. Stepping through it, they were in a passageway large enough to stand up in. Cady waited for Paul to join her. "What the hell is this?" she whispered, playing her light over the walls and ceiling.

"I'll be damned." He was silent for a moment. "There's folklore about old subterranean tunnels beneath the city."

That was news to her. "Folklore usually means untrue." They moved forward again.

"This sure wasn't constructed recently."

That much was apparent. The light-colored stone walls were cracked and stained. So was the ceiling. She eyed it distrustfully. Had a mental image of it caving in on top of them. The air seemed thick with generations of dust. But it was otherwise empty, except for random litter.

She bent to examine some of the rubbish. "I don't know how old this place is, but I'm guessing it predates McDonald's."

"This is a pretty cool find." Cady rose and looked at Paul. He shrugged. "Not the garbage. But I always heard stories when I was a kid. Never thought I'd get a chance to see one of the old tunnels my granddad used to talk about."

"Guess we've found where Stallsworth was holed up last winter." Asheville PD had searched for the fugitive for months before turning the warrant over to the USMS.

They walked another thirty yards before she slowed. "Watch your feet," she murmured. "It appears to end…" She played her light around. Holstered her weapon and knelt. "There's a drop-off."

She crawled out onto a stone ledge, shining her Maglite into a small chamber below. This was more room than tunnel, with a stench reminiscent of Rat Alley. An unrolled sleeping bag lay on a tarp in one corner. A few feet away sat a five-gallon bucket. From its smell, it served as a toilet.

Paul shoehorned himself in next to her, adding his beam to light the spac. "It's about three feet down."

"I'll go first. She secured the flashlight to her belt. "Give me some room." When he retreated, Cady turned, and, gripping the ledge, lowered her legs over it. When she was outstretched she let go, jumping to the bottom of the space and reached for her weapon.

Before she could complete the act, she was jerked off her feet. Her flashlight dropped to the ground. Rolled. She choked out a sound, but something unyielding was pressed tightly against her windpipe. A needle jabbed into her arm. As she struggled fruitlessly, she heard Paul's voice as if from a great distance. "Cady?

She was released, and her knees buckled beneath her as she gasped for oxygen. She caught a blur of movement from the corner of her eye an instant before something smashed against her skull.

2

Ryder Talbot rechecked his cell, already knowing it was in vain. There hadn't been a message from Cady. Not last night. Not early this morning. She must still be on the job.

He sipped his coffee as he watched the dogs race around his fenced-in yard. He'd brought Hero, her shepherd mix, home. They traded off canine duties when one of them got held up at work. Hero seemed far more at ease here than Cady ever had in the three months she'd lived with him.

If her house hadn't gotten shot up in the course of a case she'd worked last winter she wouldn't have moved in at all. He'd recognized that from the first. Had applied subtle pressure to convince her she'd never find a better place for her and Hero while she awaited renovations. The dogs' antics were lost on Ryder as he brooded. He'd thought proximity would succeed in bridging the distance Cady kept around her like an emotional moat.

He understood the events that had built her inner defenses. Knew she'd allowed him closer than she had anyone else. But since she'd returned to the acreage she rented, he was getting the slippery feeling that the few miles that separated them might as well as be thousands.

He should have pushed harder for her to stay. The thought circled, grew tendrils of regret. But he knew exactly how she would have reacted to a push toward commitment. She'd have backpedaled. Thrown up more walls.

Ryder wasn't so sure the result would be different from where they were now.

He whistled and both dogs bounded across the yard and up the deck stairs. He let them inside, and they paused obediently on the rug. Setting the coffee on the kitchen table, he crouched to wipe their paws with a towel he kept there for that purpose. He welcomed spring, but not the mud that accompanied it.

As he rose, his cell rang and the knot of apprehension in his chest eased. He took it out and answered quickly, one eye on the wall clock. "You must have had a late night."

He realized his mistake when a long pause followed his words. "Ryder... it's Miguel."

"Sorry. I hadn't heard from Cady, and thought..." The sentence tapered off as comprehension filtered in. The deputy marshal had never called him before. Had never had cause to.

"There was a problem with the warrant last night."

A problem. The oxygen froze in his lungs, making it difficult to force the words out. "Is Cady all right?"

"We're not sure. The thing is, she and Paul Chester are gone. We haven't been able to find either of them."

RYDER CALLED Miguel back when he hit the Asheville city limits and the man directed him to Court Plaza. He parked his official Haywood County Sheriff SUV and hurriedly got out of the vehicle. Rodriguez splintered from a small collection of law enforcement officers and headed toward him. "I need details," Ryder said grimly when Miguel drew nearer. The man's worried expression did nothing to calm the jitter in Ryder's gut.

"The bandit was holed up in an apartment complex and the team was in place. Either he was careful, or someone spotted us and tipped him off. He made a run for it."

The most carefully planned arrests could go wrong in an instant, Ryder knew from experience. "And?"

"Cady was on the guy's heels. Paul was behind her. They chased him into Rat Alley and the guy seemed to vanish. They discovered a hidden entrance to one of the buildings there." Miguel shook his head. "It's the damnedest thing I ever saw. You know all those stories about subterranean tunnels connecting parts of downtown Asheville back in the day?"

"I know that most of those tales are bullshit." Ryder was uninterested in the city's history at the moment. Urgency rapped hard at the base of his skull as he waited for the man to get to the point.

"Maybe." Miguel shrugged out of the zippered sweatshirt he was wearing. "But someone went to a lot of work to connect existing passages down there at the basement and sub-basement level." He folded the garment over his arm. "A sledgehammer and a pickaxe were found in one of the branches. We think the work was done by Bobby Stallsworth, the fugitive the team was chasing. He'd been working at Turk's Tavern before he decided to off someone. He's been at large ever since."

The facts gave Ryder pause. The bar contained a nugget of evidence for the stories about old Asheville's tunnels. A partial one existed beneath the building. "Did the tunnel connect to the tavern's?"

"He'd dug a branch to it. That's where Conway and Rossi found him hiding. When they hauled him out, they were unable to rouse Cady or Paul on the radio. They'd been communicating all along, so they knew the two of them had gone straight while they took the turn." He drew out his cell. Brought up some pictures and handed the phone to Ryder.

He swiped through them. They showed a gloomy enclosed area lit by some battery-operated spotlights. His stomach gave a hard lurch when he saw the single USMS hat. Then a close-up shot of a dark stain on the back of it.

He steeled himself to go on. The cap was Cady's. Its size alone told him that. Two radios were on the dirt floor. A flashlight. He paused over the next set of pictures. Wheel tracks?

Wordlessly, he held up the screen to Miguel. The deputy marshal's mouth flattened. "We think it was a four-wheeled cart of some kind. Had to have some sort of help to get Chester out of there. The guy's huge."

He was. Well over six foot with a sturdy body of pure muscle. If someone managed to incapacitate Paul, what had he done to Cady?

Because the thought could undo him, Ryder pushed it away. "Is Stallsworth talking?"

Miguel shook his head. "Lawyered up and hasn't spoken another word."

"Maybe he had an accomplice."

"He sure as hell didn't do all that digging by himself. We figure he might have had the cart down there to haul out the debris from the demolition."

Ryder looked at Miguel's phone again and flipped through the rest of the pictures. He paused when he came to several that appeared to lead from the chamber where Cady and Paul had been ambushed. "That looks like a storm drain."

"The final passage connects to one, yeah. It's fifty-four inches wide. We have one wit. A transient going through garbage cans. Says he saw a dark-colored cargo van backed up against the drain opening. He claims he's seen it there before, but this time a man loaded something into the back of it before driving off."

The details acted like a sucker punch. It took a moment for Ryder to beat back every dark and grisly thought that flashed across his brain. He'd been in law enforcement for over ten years. He knew kidnappings came with a running clock. And when the victims were cops, the stakes notched even higher. Hostage situations. Executions.

As if seeing from his expression where his mind had gone, Miguel quickly added, "Two missing deputy marshals means a massive outpouring of resources. We've got an aerial assist pilot looking for the vehicle and a BOLO out with a description of it. Federal, state, and local law enforcement entities are helping with this. We have an integrated incident command structure set up for communication with all the involved agencies. Allen wants your input about how to handle the news with Cady's mom."

He handed Miguel's cell back. "I'll speak to him about it." He was determined to play a more significant role than relaying messages to Hannah Maddix. He'd also talk to the supervisory deputy marshal about joining the task force. Ryder needed to be part of the effort to bring Cady safely back home.

3
———

Unconsciousness advanced and receded like a ragged wave in rhythm to the pounding in Cady's head. She wished the voice would go away. The one in the darkness repeating her name.

"Cady. Speak to me."

But talking was beyond her. It was all she could do to fight the nausea churning in her stomach. Rising to her throat.

"Cady." The tone was insistent.

She attempted to claw through the fog enveloping her. Ryder. He'd wanted to talk before she'd left on the warrant. But she knew what he'd say. That she'd disappointed him by moving back home. That he was tired of trying to break through her walls. The effort wasn't worth it.

Sorry. The word went unspoken. She couldn't be who he wanted. Didn't know how. The past had as much a grip on her as the hammering in her head.

"...he comes back."

Who? The question had her eyes fluttering open. She

could see nothing but blackness. The tunnel. The memory floated through her mind like a gossamer cloud. It was so dark.

A shiver racked her then as her senses began to awaken. Something rough beneath her cheek. Cold seeping into her bones. She moved her head. Groaned when the pounding there intensified. Gritting her teeth, she tried to push herself up. But her hands were bound.

Awareness speared through her, a quick blade of fear. Weakly, she fought to free herself.

"Look at me."

Her brain was fuzzy. But slowly, with great effort, she obeyed the voice. Not Ryder. Someone else. Paul?

"Tun...nel?" Her voice sounded drugged.

"Someone was waiting there, in the area behind the ledge. Grabbed you as soon as you went into that last chamber. Then knocked me out when I followed."

"Stallsworth?"

"I don't think so. The guy is only five-eight. This was someone bigger and a helluva lot stronger." For the first time she realized the other deputy marshal's voice was slightly slurred. "He must have injected us with something. Maybe more than once. I came to a couple of hours ago. I can't tell where we are. A cave, maybe. Probably a mine."

His words registered but comprehension was sluggish. "Drugged?" The nausea was sweeping over her in waves now. She wouldn't be sick. With sheer force of will she tried to control the sensation.

"...some sort of paralytic maybe," Paul was saying. "We have to figure a way out before he returns. Follow the chain on your manacles. What's it attached to? Can you pull it loose?"

Cady gritted her teeth as she finally managed to get her elbows beneath her and rise to her knees. Dizziness pounced then, swamping her. She stilled until it dissipated. Then she found the cuffs encircling her wrists, connected by about two feet of chain. She crawled forward on what felt like a canvas tarp, following the attached links. Four feet. Six. She stopped, wincing when her knee came in contact with something sharp. With hands thrust in front of her, she searched blindly. Cold walls. Stone. She brushed her fingertips along it until they met something jutting forward. Rough-hewn lumber. A thick metal loop was drilled into it. Still weak, she grasped the links and pulled with as much force as she could muster. It held fast.

"It's...secured. A timber of some kind."

"Yeah. Me too. How much slack do you have between your wrists?"

"Two feet or so."

"Less here. Maybe one."

A chill worked through her. Where the hell were they? She dropped on her haunches, suddenly exhausted. It took effort to control the heaving in her stomach. For the first time, she realized she was no longer wearing her holster, vest, or jacket. Which meant the kidnapper had removed them at some point.

"How far do you think... we are from Asheville?"

"Hard to tell." Paul's words were a rumble in the inky blackness surrounding them. "It's daylight. Maybe only barely. Look away from me. It's lighter at the mouth."

With a great deal of caution, Cady turned her head. The light seemed distant and didn't penetrate far into the mine. But it was there. She faced Paul again. "Stretch out as much as you can, feet first. I want to see how close we are to each other." She did the same and when she'd reached the full expanse of chain she swept one foot out searchingly. Her eyelids slid shut in relief when her boot met Paul's.

"If he gets between us, maybe we can rush him."

"He'll have to get close enough." For the first time, she wondered what their captor wanted with them. There were a host of reasons two deputy U.S. marshals would make high profile hostages. None of the possibilities were encouraging. "We'll have to make an opportunity." She didn't bother mentioning the obvious. Paul knew as well as she did how grim their situation was.

"We have to be practical. If one of us has a chance, we take it. Got it? If either of us breaks loose and can't get to the other, run like hell. Get help."

She immediately protested, "That's worst-case scenario."

His laugh was bleak. "Things look pretty desperate to me. I'm a bigger threat, which means he'll watch me more closely. Work on getting him to let his guard down with you. Take any opportunity that comes your way."

She pressed her lips together in silent mutiny. Paul's advice might be pragmatic, but it ran counter to every instinct she had. Sometimes one had to make their own opportunities.

If one presented itself, she'd take it. But she wasn't leaving here alone.

IT MIGHT'VE BEEN an hour later. Surely no more. Cady heard the sound of a vehicle moments before she saw a pickup back inside the mine. Lifting her pounding head, she stared. The truck blocked most of the daylight. A figure appeared.

Big. Likely male. She waited, eyes straining, but saw no one else. She released a breath she hadn't realized she'd been holding. "Showtime." His chains jangled as he shifted position.

"Remember what I said."

She didn't reply. Her focus was on the activity. The newcomer spent several minutes unloading the bed of his truck. Then he pushed a wheeled cart toward them.

"You're making a mistake." Paul's voice rang out as he approached. "We're Deputy U.S. Marshals. There'll be a massive manhunt to find us. You should let us go while you still have a chance. Before they track us here."

If the man caught the words, he gave no indication of it. He began unpacking the cart and then went back to the pickup, returning a few minutes later dragging a thick extension cord. She watched in silence for a while, still fighting the waves of sickness twisting her gut. He gave them a wide berth as he hauled something past their bodies, setting it on the ground on the other side of Paul. The stranger made several more trips with the wheelbarrow, seeming sure-footed even in the shadows. On the next trip he carried a flashlight, its beam splitting the darkness. With a start, Cady recognized it as a twin for theirs. He'd probably stolen it from one of them in the tunnel after the attack.

Crouching by Paul again, he muttered in singsong to himself as he worked. Moments later, a blinding light bathed the area, and she buried her face in her shoulder to shield her eyes. A spotlight.

Another one blazed, this one placed against the wall at Paul's feet. Trepidation began to thrum in Cady's chest. The man rose and retreated toward the truck. He was at least six-five and wide, obviously strong, although there was softness layered over the muscle. Frizzy brown hair stood up in tufts on his head, and he hadn't shaved in a couple of days. He wore dirty jeans, boots, and a hoodie, all the clothes showing signs of wear.

Her mind raced as she watched him return, carrying something. Their captor didn't look capable of masterminding the kidnap of two deputy marshals. Most likely he was tasked with keeping them secure until the pieces came together for whatever plan was in place.

"Looks like I'm his focus." Paul's whisper interrupted her thoughts. "If you get a chance…"

"…I'll take it," she finished for him. But not, as he'd advised, to escape alone. Her gut lurched again and Cady willed it to settle. She'd be no good to anyone if she got sick now. Upon the heels of that thought came an idea. And one that would take minimal effort to enact.

She turned to face Paul. Their kidnapper knelt beside him. Cady's heart stuttered when she recognized what was in his hand.

A syringe.

The sight had her stomach revolting and she gagged. This time she didn't attempt to control it. When the vomit rose she retched miserably.

Their captor gave a high-pitched screech. "No! Don't! Disgusting!" He rushed to her and kicked her in the side with his heavy boot, over and over. "No!" He dropped to his knees and grabbed her shoulder.

"Stop!" Paul roared. "Whatever you injected her with made her sick. If you do it again, you'll make it worse."

She lay there limply, emptied and gasping for air. Every breath was torturous. For long moments, she could feel him looming over her, as if considering Paul's words. Then he rose and headed to the front of the mine again.

When he was out of earshot, Paul asked, "Cady. You okay?"

She had to haul in enough oxygen to answer. "Yeah." There was a chorus of pain singing through her side. She clenched her jaw and tried to get to her knees. Caught her breath when the talons of agony clawed deep.

The stranger strode toward her. "Clean it up." Something hit her in the face. A towel. It occurred to her that her earlier strategy was working, if with an unexpectedly negative twist. She grasped the rag. Began scrubbing at the mess before pausing. "I can't manage with my wrists chained like this."

He cocked his foot threateningly, the warning implicit. She returned to the task. When she finished, she handed him the cloth. With distaste evident in his expression, he dug into his jeans pocket, withdrawing something. "Drop it." She obeyed and he came closer, yanking at the chain joining her manacles and fitting a key into the lock, releasing each cuff.

Then he picked up the syringe again. "Get it out of here. Throw it in the brush. If you try anything…" He moved to press the needle against Paul's throat. "I'll empty every drop of this into him. He'll be dead in minutes. You got that?"

The other deputy marshal was sending her a very different message with his eyes, but she ignored it. "Yes."

The difficulty she had rising wasn't an act. She stumbled toward the glimpse of daylight that promised freedom. Each step jarred the injury to her side. Worsened the hammering in her head. She slowed as she approached the pickup, looking at the license plate and committing it to memory before moving alongside and then past it. Into the blessedly fresh air alive with sunshine and the trill of songbirds.

"That's far enough!" The kidnapper's voice was incongruously high, like the whine of a power tool. She tossed the towel into the scrub brush crowding the rutted path the truck had followed. Her surroundings gave little clue of their whereabouts. Firs and deciduous trees punctuated the area, obscuring what lay beyond in any direction. "Get back here now. Or..."

His warning was clear. Cady turned around before their captor carried through on his threat.

The cool shadows that engulfed her as she moved deeper into the mine had her feet slowing. She knew she'd face Paul's recriminations. But she wasn't going to put the man's life at risk to save her own. There'd be another chance. She'd make sure of that.

When she returned to the tarp, the stranger set the needle aside and rose to grab her roughly. Clapping the manacles back on her wrists, he resecured them. Then he picked up the hypodermic again and bent over Paul.

"It's not too late." With effort, she kept her voice even. Persuasive. "You can still walk away from this. Believe me, you don't want to be around when they find us. You should leave now, while you can."

He ignored her, replacing the syringe with a large pair of scissors. Pulling Paul's shirt from his trousers, he cut up the center of it, struggling a bit when he got to the collar. Once it was in two pieces, he spread them wide, exposing the deputy marshal's broad back. His hum of approval as he ran his hand over the expanse of skin he'd bared had Cady's stomach turning again.

"Listen to her," Paul put in. "Walk out of here now." The kidnapper exchanged the scissors with the hypodermic and jabbed the needle into Paul's shoulder. When he withdrew it, she could see he hadn't emptied it into the other man and released a shaky breath.

"You're in charge here," she continued, drawing from every hostage negotiation situation she'd experienced. "We know that. We just want you to get away safely before anyone knows what you did. Or who you are."

"Who *I* am?" His shriek echoed and reechoed in the chamber as he lunged toward her. Slammed her head against the floor of the mine with every sentence. "I am a chosen one. You. Are. Nothing!"

When he stopped, her skull felt as though it were splitting in two. When she could form a cogent thought again, she realized that agitating the man was probably not in their best interests. She was beginning to think their captor might not be mentally stable. That would make their situation even more precarious.

Helplessly, she watched as he turned to a tray he'd set behind him. Selecting a gauze pad, he soaked it with something in a bottle. He wiped Paul's back before replacing the items and picked up what looked like sheets of paper. He removed a layer and then laid the piece carefully on the skin. Smoothed it out. Then he peeled the entire thing away.

Comprehension filtered in as she inched closer to look at the design. Cady had no personal experience with tattoos. But their captor's intention was obvious. The thought solidified when he affixed a contraption to his head, switching on its lamp before picking up a metal device and wrapping elastics around its tip. Then he brought out a small palette and emptied small colored tubes into the shallow cups etched onto it. After stirring each, he picked up the machine again, dipping it into one of the ink wells.

"If you move, even an inch, I'll hurt her," the stranger warned Paul. But she could see the increasing laxity in her colleague's limbs. The drug was already working. His flinch was barely perceptible when the kidnapper brought up the device and began applying its needle to Paul's skin.

Looking on in silent horror, she had no illusions. She'd be next. Even while chances of escape were slim, if they did manage to get away, they wouldn't do so without first being branded with their kidnapper's mark.

4

Ryder knuckled one bleary eye but didn't tear his gaze away from the screen in front of him. The incident command post had taken up residence in a hastily cleared conference area in the Buncombe County Police Department. They'd soon outgrow the space. More federal, state, and local volunteers arrived by the hour. The sheer volume of LEO turnout should have been reassuring. Their lack of results so far was not.

He shoved away the dispirited thought. Gathering more information and eliminating suspects were critical strides toward finding Cady and Paul. He realized that. He was also aware of the passing time. And the two of them had been missing now for—he checked the clock in the corner of the computer screen—nearly twenty hours. Each hour that ticked away was another nick at his heart.

He'd spent much of the day running down older model dark-colored panel vans registered in the state. Pairs of team members were checking out the most promising leads. It chafed that he wasn't on the action side of things, but given his relationship to Cady, he knew he was damn lucky to have a part in this at all.

"Ryder." Miguel dragged his chair closer and nudged his shoulder. "C'mon. You've been at this for twelve hours."

"And you've been here longer than that." He finally glanced up, noted the exhaustion stamped on the deputy marshal's face. "Any news?"

Miguel's dark gaze slid away. "Every avenue is being—"

"—investigated. Yeah, I know. Hell, I've said it myself. Save me the platitudes." Hearing the bite in his tone, he shoved away from the desk in frustration. "Sorry. Maybe you're right. Let new eyes take over for a while." Not that he expected to get any sleep until he knew Cady was safe. But he was useless to anyone if he wasn't mentally alert.

"Did you get in touch with Cady's mom yet?" Miguel stretched his booted feet out in front of him.

"No. I've tried her aunt several times. I have to run this by her first. She'll know best how much to tell Hannah." Both Cady's and Paul's phones were found outside the drainage pipe. "I'll give it another try on my way home." He picked up the sheet listing owner information of the vans he'd compiled. "There's an address on here I'm going to check out." He gave a thin smile when the deputy marshal cocked a brow. "It's over in my neck of the woods. I'll save you guys a drive."

Miguel covered a huge yawn with his fist. "Be sure and take someone with you."

Ryder opened his mouth to protest. Thought better of it. Jackson County was just southwest of his. He'd call a deputy from there to meet him at the address in question. He keyed the location into his cell and shut down the computer.

"Contact Allen if the lead amounts to anything." Miguel

rose and paused for a moment. "I know better than to tell you to get some rest. But we all need to be fresh tomorrow."

He knew the deputy marshal was talking as much to himself. And he was right about one thing. Ryder didn't expect to sleep. "See you then." The place was an hour from his home, give or take, and if he headed out now, it shouldn't be too late to make a stop.

The drive would even give him a chance to figure out what the hell to tell Cady's aunt.

"Alma." He squinted against the glare of an oncoming vehicle's headlights. "I'm glad I caught you. This is Ryder Talbot." A long pause greeted his words, so he added. "Haywood County—"

"—the sheriff." The woman's voice was flat. "Okay. Whaddya want?"

He wasn't surprised at her brusque attitude. He knew there was no love lost between Cady and her aunt, although she paid Alma a stipend to care for Hannah, who had early-onset Alzheimer's. "It's about Cady." He slowed to take the turn that would lead to where he was to meet Jackson County Deputy Harmon. "She was on the job last night. She and a colleague went missing. There's a large team of law enforcement searching for them. I just wanted to speak with you before contacting Hannah to make sure I don't upset her."

"She's asleep. And no need for you to talk to her at all. No news for her now, anyways, sounds like. You say they don't know where Cady is? She likely took something in her head and went off to check it out. Girl always thinks she knows best, no matter what others tell her."

A tight band of anger clenched in Ryder's chest. "I don't want to worry you. The search team—"

"—will probably find her. And then there'll be nothing to tell Hannah, will there? You call when you know more." Alma disconnected.

Ryder blew out a frustrated breath. No wonder Cady had her share of troubles with the woman. Her mom was the only one in Cady's family with whom she had a real relationship. No one else had given a damn about her. Not her vicious outlaw father. Not the emotionally abusive grandfather she'd been sent to live with at twelve.

And sure as hell not Alma Griggs.

No doubt all of that had gone a long way toward building Cady's fortress-strength defenses. He'd figured that out long ago. He'd just never come up with a way to overcome them completely.

Spying the deputy parked on the side of the road ahead, he pulled alongside him and buzzed down the passenger window.

"Sheriff." Wayne Harmon worked his shoulders tiredly. He had the muscular build of a devoted weight lifter. "I can provide a little background on the owner of the vehicle you mentioned."

A spark of interest nudged through Ryder's earlier frustration. "Frank Burgess?" The witness had described an older model dark-colored panel van. The team had concentrated first on the black and navy ones closest to Asheville and then branched out. Burgess's was burgundy.

"The same. He runs a game processing facility located twelves miles outside Bordertown."

"Bordertown?" Ryder had grown up in the next county and didn't think he'd ever heard of the place.

"It's not really a town. Just a bunch of shanties and

broken-down trailers, mostly. We get our share of calls to the area. Burgess cremates the carcasses. We've had run-ins with him over air permits and proper ventilation of the furnace."

His earlier anticipation deflated. "But no criminal history." He didn't need the deputy's corroboration. He'd checked himself before driving up here.

"Nope. But neighbors frequently call to complain about the noise and smell when the incinerator is running. I can lead you to the facility. He lives on the property."

Ryder buzzed up his window and put the vehicle into reverse, allowing the deputy to pull ahead of him. He followed Harmon's taillights as the road continued its climb up the incline. After a while, they turned onto a narrow, noticeably less well-maintained gravel. It was another twenty minutes before Harmon drove into a small clearing encircled by trees. He stopped in front of a shabby gray-sided building. Ryder parked next to him. He could hear a loud rumble coming from somewhere in the vicinity. Reaching for the Maglite under the seat, he switched it on and stepped out of his SUV. The van was parked near the low porch.

"What's that noise?" Smoke curled above the rear of the structure. There was a unique smell of decomposition and heated metal.

"Sounds like he's got that incinerator going." Harmon's voice was disgruntled. "We've warned him repeatedly about running it at night. When the wind's right, the sound carries fifteen miles or more. Pisses people off."

They walked toward the building. "Place looks dark." Stepping closer, Ryder peered through the grimy window in the splintered front door. "Wait. There's a light on inside."

Harmon tried the door and found it locked. A moment

later they heard a cell phone ringing. "Let's head around back. With the furnace going, he should be here. He's not supposed to leave it unattended."

The ground was as uneven as the road leading here had been. The deputy stumbled and Ryder threw out a hand to steady him. As they reached the other side of the locker, they saw a single closed overhead door and a regular entry. A security light burned outside the door, which was standing half-open. But it was the small brick addition jutting from the far corner that caught his eye. A loud rattling emanated from it along with a noise like a high-powered blowtorch.

"Burgess's incinerator is inside there." Harmon turned back to the structure, walked to the open door and banged on it loudly. "Burgess? Jackson County deputy. You in there?"

Ryder swept the interior with the beam of his Maglite. He spotted a free-standing double stainless-steel sink, some tables, and a station holding large electrical saws. The cracked concrete floor was split by a grate which, he assumed, caught the blood when the meat was cut away from the carcass. Doors flanked three sides of the area. One was half-open, with a wedge of light showing.

The deputy called out again. "Burgess?"

Something clanged somewhere within the building, perhaps a metal object striking the floor. A sharp yelp of pain followed. The two men exchanged a glance. "Hear that? Sounds like exigent circumstances," Ryder said.

"Someone could be hurt." They pulled their weapons and stepped inside. "Frank Burgess!" Harmon called loudly as he and Ryder crept closer to the lit room. "It's Deputy Harmon! We're coming in. Are you injured?"

There was no answer. The other man laid his fingers on

the doorknob and looked at Ryder, who nodded. He pulled the door open, and they both stepped quickly through it, weapons ready.

The cramped space held a rickety desk and a dented filing cabinet. Its only window was painted shut. Ryder led the way across the cutting room to an insulated door. A cooler, maybe. Burgess would need someplace to store the dead animals until he was ready for them.

They took up position on either side of the entrance. Ryder yanked the door open. The two of them rushed inside, their beams piercing the darkness. He switched on a light. Three carcasses were suspended from large hooks that attached to rollers on a ceiling track. The one closest to them was a bear minus its head. It wasn't in season. Burgess and his clients obviously weren't fussy about little things like poaching.

He brushed by it. The next was a deer. It was the shape of the third one that had a hard rap of adrenaline starting in his skull.

"Holy shit!"

He silently echoed Harmon's sentiment. The bruised and battered body hung from its bound wrists. Two things occurred to him in quick succession. The death hadn't been an easy one.

And the corpse was female.

5

The cool darkness enveloping Cady felt familiar. She drew up her knees and curled into a tighter ball beneath the scratchy wool cover. Odd. Her grandfather had never given her a blanket when he locked her in his root cellar. Those instances were carved in her memory, old scars that rose to throb anew when sleep pulled her under. She shifted position, battling the recollections that slithered through her unconscious. Earthen walls and floor. Chilly and damp. She'd crouch on the bottom step, amid the dirt and cobwebs and wait for the door to open. Usually, it was a matter of hours. But sometimes it was long enough for the day and night to twine together like a clenched fist.

Something grazed her cheek and she jerked upright. The chain on her wrists jangled as she brushed frantically at her face, recalling the colony of bats that had swept above them earlier, some striking her blanket, crawling over it. She shuddered, fully awake now. Not the basement at all. The mine. The tattoos. A captor that was surely mentally unstable.

And limited options for their survival.

The stranger had spent a long time bent over Paul,

bringing the scene on the template to vivid, violent life. When he'd risen, she'd hoped he would gather up his things and leave. Instead, he'd gone outside and remained there for almost an hour. But he'd returned and picked up the scissors again. Then it had been her turn.

The next few hours had been torturous as he'd begun a new tattoo on her. It'd felt like being caught in a swarm of bees. She'd made a small noise, and the man had reached up to slam her head against the ground. "You consider this pain? You have no idea what *I've* suffered!"

Cady hadn't made another sound.

Paul gave a mournful moan. Their captor had expended far more time on him. And he'd been injected again. Whatever the substance was, it left him sluggish and weak for hours.

"You awake?" she whispered. He didn't respond. They'd each been given a bottle of water along with a cold fast food sandwich and a bucket to use as a toilet. Obviously, the kidnapper wanted to keep them alive for a while. But once the tattoos were completed, what then?

Her mind skittered from the thought. She didn't want to be here to find out. Cady's brain spun furiously, plans half-forming only to be discarded.

The low rumble of Paul's voice split the darkness. "You made a big mistake. You should have run when you had the chance."

Guilt surged. Even if she could have brought herself to leave him, she was uncertain how far she could have gotten. The nausea coupled with the physical abuse had taken a toll. There was no point telling Paul what she'd seen while he was being tattooed. The peripheral glow of the spotlights had washed over the wall beyond their feet. Illuminated what she'd thought might be paintings or cheaply framed prints of some sort. Cady had crept as close as she dared to the edge of the tarp, her eyes straining to make out the subjects.

And when she did, horror slammed into her. She'd retreated rapidly, scrambling backward as far as the chains would allow.

They weren't pictures at all. The knowledge burned in her brain. Strangled her breathing. What she'd thought were yellowed parchments with colorful designs applied were actually skin.

Their captor wouldn't be content just branding them. He was going to remove the tattoo for his collection.

6

"There was no sign of Burgess?"

Supervisory Deputy U.S. Marshal Allen Gant had arrived minutes ago with a few members of the task force team. Ryder was taking him through the same story he'd reported to Jeb Redding, the Jackson County sheriff who'd gotten there earlier. "When we found the office empty, we checked the cooler. Burgess probably had gone out the front door."

Allen looked over Ryder's shoulder toward the shadowy line of trees rimming the clearing. "Hard to search in the dark."

"A K-9 unit is on the way. We're also waiting on a warrant for the house and vehicle. I did look through the van's windows, though. There's a large bloodstain on the cardboard covering the floor." He wouldn't let himself consider its origin.

"And the incinerator?"

Unerringly, Allen put his finger on the cause for the trepidation still churning in Ryder's gut. "The coroner shut it off. She said it would take hours to cool before she could examine the remains. She's focused on the corpse we discovered. Unidentified female."

But they didn't yet know what was in the furnace.

"Let's take a look." The supervisory deputy marshal headed toward the rear of the building, Ryder using his Maglite to illuminate the way. When they rounded the corner, he shut off the flashlight. The coroner had brought in spotlights. She was bent over the body from the cooler, which her assistants had loaded onto a gurney. Redding stood beside her, his hands shoved into his jacket pockets.

She looked up at the sound of their approach, irritation flickering across her expression. Her long gray hair was pulled tightly away from a lined face. She wore a white Tyvek suit, bonnet, and booties.

"Dr. Annie Paulsen. Supervisory Deputy U.S. Marshal Allen Gant."

"I was just telling Sheriff Redding. This one died unpleasantly. She's been dead at least twenty-four hours. Possibly longer, but not by much. The wounds were premortem. I'll have to get her in the lab to be sure, but probable cause of death is blunt force trauma."

"How likely is it that you'll be able to pinpoint the murder weapon?" Ryder asked.

"Interesting you should ask." She waved him closer and pointed at a wound on the corpse's chest. "See this?" She indicated another on the shoulder. "And this one? I counted seventeen of these. But here you can observe the relatively straight edges of the injuries. The damage inflicted. She was beaten by something with weight. Her head was probably bludgeoned with the same object. From the angle, I'm guessing the killer swung the weapon. I'll know more when I get her on the autopsy table. If we're lucky, I'll find remnants in the gashes." She shook her head. "Pretty brutal way to go."

"That's for damn sure," Redding muttered, staring at the body.

Ryder and Allen returned to the front of the building. A pair of headlights speared through the darkness as another Jackson County sheriff's vehicle pulled slowly into the clearing. "Let's hope that's the warrant."

"Covers the van, too."

He nodded, although the deputy marshal's words hadn't been a question. His gaze was fixed on Redding, who was striding toward the SUV. Two people were inside it. The one on the passenger side exited. A civilian. He went to the rear and raised the hatch. The K-9 team was here. The deputy opened the door and slid out from behind the wheel, handing something to the sheriff. Adrenaline sprinted up Ryder's spine. "Looks like we're in business."

"I'll join the group searching the van," Allen said.

"And I'll take the house."

THE RESIDENCE WAS next to the locker, one side perched over a sheer drop down the mountain. It was as dilapidated as the other building, sided in a dingy gray clapboard that hadn't been sold in decades. When Ryder and Deputy Harmon had approached the single-story dwelling earlier, he'd been worried he was going to put a boot through the rotting steps or porch.

The screen door hung haphazardly from the hinges. But the interior door had been replaced with a sturdy metal model. It took the deputy with the entry ram two tries to gain access. Ryder waited for the stream of law enforcement to enter before following them inside. He'd already ascertained that all the doors and windows were locked. Something told him that Burgess wasn't coming back.

With a corpse in his cooler, it wouldn't make sense for him to hang around the property once the law arrived.

But if the man had been the one to ambush Cady and Paul in the tunnels, there might be evidence here. As others searched the main floor, Ryder splintered off to join the two deputies heading down the rickety stairs off the kitchen.

It was more cellar than basement, with irregularly sized stone walls. He could feel a drop in temperature with each step he descended. He shone his flashlight over the spaces between the treads. Beneath the staircase would be the perfect place for an ambush.

But the space was empty and surprisingly clean, free of dust and cobwebs. The two men in front of him fanned out when they got to the bottom, and Ryder stepped between them. The area was small. The cellar would only be below the side of the house closest to the locker.

"Jesus." He took a couple of steps closer and stared. Heavy chains, mottled with rust, lay in a heap on the floor in one corner. They looked like the ones tow trucks used to lift and secure vehicles. But these were attached to sturdy rings drilled into the stone wall and ended in thick manacles.

The list of questions for Frank Burgess continued to grow.

"CRIME SCENE INVESTIGATORS are going over the vehicle now. The coroner tested the stains on the cardboard in it. The blood wasn't human. Any discovered evidence will be sent to the lab in Raleigh." Allen took his cap out of his jacket pocket and settled it over his shaven head. "Keys were in the ignition."

Ryder nodded. He'd noted as much when he'd peered in the windows earlier. "Doors were unlocked, too." If Burgess was apprehended, he could claim anyone had access to the van. Unless they found a witness who could place him in it at the time of Cady and Paul's disappearances, he could establish some reasonable doubt.

"You should call it a night," Allen advised. "You never made it home, right?"

"Neither have you." But Ryder already knew there wasn't much more to be done before daylight. The dog had picked up the man's scent in several different places in the woods surrounding the clearing. And Burgess had a two-hour head start.

"Did they find anything in the house to suggest a connection to my deputy marshals?"

"Nothing that stood out."

Allen blew out of breath. "Unless they do, we're done here. I'd advise you to do what I'm going to. Go home. Pretend to sleep. Return to command post tomorrow, ready to start over. I've got two people missing, and I'll be damned if I'll stop until I find them."

Ryder watched the other man stride away, his booted feet crunching on the gravel. It wasn't that Gant's words didn't make sense. He could feel exhaustion creeping in.

But he feared what awaited him once he did close his eyes. Every worst fear, each violent image that he'd successfully kept at bay would spring forth to wrap him in nightmarish tentacles and pull him into a pool of darkness.

And that'd be a walk in the park compared to what Cady was probably going through right now.

7

A low groan penetrated her sleep, but Cady couldn't fight free of the clinging tendrils of slumber. She was held captive by the familiar images that prowled the hem of her consciousness, ready to pounce when she lowered her guard.

Like an unwilling audience at a movie, she saw again the day she'd put an end to her grandfather's abuse with the screwdriver and flashlight she'd hidden in that damn cellar, so like the mine they were in now. The time she'd taken the door off the hinges and walked into the kitchen.

Try that again, old man, and you'll be the one locked down there.

The surprise in his expression, accompanied by his dry chuckle, like a breeze stirring dead leaves. *Well, maybe you got some grit in you after all, girlie. Not like your mama.*

The mental snippets shifted, reformed into an all-too-familiar technicolor montage. The warrant in St. Louis that had gone south. The kid—not much more than that—with a gun to the deputy marshal's forehead. Her shot. The shock on the young man's face before he'd crumpled atop her colleague.

The images went watery at the edges, melting away before congealing once more into a picture of another kitchen with peeling paint and cracked linoleum. Lonny Maddix laughing at her mother lying on the floor weeping, blood dripping from her face to soak the pretty flowered nightgown that matched four-year-old Cady's. The gun on the table. The weight of it in her hand. The shot splitting the night. Her father's crumpled body and her mother screaming, screaming, screaming...

Bolting upright on the tarp, she panted as she strove to shake off the nightmare, which was as oppressive as a shroud. Her heart hammered, its rhythm pounding in her ears.

It took a moment to sweep the fragments of memory from her mind, but Ryder's face remained stubbornly fixed there, eliciting a clutch in her gut. Outside of her mother, he was the only person she'd ever let close. And she knew what it said about her that she still hadn't managed to drop her defenses with him completely. Just two days ago, she'd had the sensation that something precious was slipping from her grasp.

Now she was grappling with the certainty that she probably wouldn't get a chance to set things right.

Dread anchored in her chest. She edged the scratchy blanket from her face and peered in Paul's direction. It was impossible to distinguish her colleague's large form on the tarp next to her. She could have been alone in the world. Certainly, she felt like it. There was something about facing death that had a way of encapsulating life, reducing it to moments, as if those instants defined the totality of years lived.

Her thoughts returned to escape. Their kidnapper kept Paul out of commission to eliminate the chance the deputy marshal would overpower him. He didn't see Cady as a threat. The realization burned, but it also had determination spreading inside her. His miscalculation could be weaponized against him. And she'd wield it when the opportunity arose. There'd been times in her childhood when she'd been helpless, but she'd always refused to be a victim. If she died in this damn mine, it wouldn't be without a fight.

As the sky began to lighten at the mouth of the cave, she settled on a plan. One that would decide how this nightmare was going to end.

And who would survive.

Because she was awake, Cady heard the truck before the kidnapper backed it into the mine. Then he busied himself with his equipment. The generator was positioned beside the pickup. He wheeled the spotlights, tattoo supplies, and electrical cords inside. She wondered why he didn't just leave the things here instead of hauling them away at night. If he were afraid they'd be stolen, it might mean the place wasn't as remote as she feared. There had to be a road nearby. Homes in the area. Occasional hikers.

Cady squelched the quick leap of hope at the thought. They couldn't count on being rescued. Their fate depended on her getting them free. Her palms dampened. Her muscles were tight in anticipation. She knew what she had to do. She'd only get one chance, and the odds seemed insurmountable.

Desperation may not fuel ingenuity, but it solidified resolve.

The generator roared to life outside the entrance, and the spotlights switched on. Their kidnapper approached, a menacing shadow.

He didn't speak, but then he rarely did. A shrill cry when he was angry or alarmed, and worse, his grating rhythmic humming while he worked over them. He was volatile, perhaps even mentally unstable. Last fall she'd gone up against Samuel Aldeen, a criminally insane fugitive and had barely escaped with her life. Did luck come in twos? She smiled grimly. She was about to find out.

He passed her to go to Paul, who remained motionless. Crouched between them. Cady rose to her haunches. Inched as close the edge of the tarp as she dared.

"I don't think he's doing well," she said. The stranger loosened the bandage he'd placed over Paul's partial tattoo and lifted it away, giving that eerie hum of approval when he bent to inspect his work. The sound had Cady's stomach twisting. "He hasn't moved since you left yesterday," she lied. "You must have given him too much of the drug."

As if he hadn't heard her, he took the familiar syringe from his pocket. Raised it in front of him as he eyed the contents.

"I think it'd be a mistake to—"

His backhand came with the speed and precision of a striking snake, his knuckles cracking against her cheekbone with enough force to have lights bursting behind her eyes. She bit back any sound of pain. She knew what to expect if she cried out.

"Get down and shut up," he ordered in that high thin voice. Cady obeyed, clenching her teeth against the throbbing in her face as she stretched out in a prone position. She waited for her surroundings to swim into focus. There was no sign of the syringe now. Had he injected Paul? The deputy marshal hadn't moved.

Their captor turned toward her. She felt him pulling the bandage away from her back. Heard his droning purr. Panic sprinted up her spine when he rose to fetch the tattoo supplies, sinking beside her to lay them out carefully.

He wasn't going to start with Paul today. Cady's escape plan, such as it was, would have to wait.

8

"Stallsworth still isn't talking," Miguel spoke as Ryder joined the huddle of USMS personnel in the conference room. "But early this morning, some task force members swept up a couple of homeless people sleeping in those tunnels. They had plenty to say. Last fall and winter a guy matching Stallsworth's description and occasionally another man would chase them out of there. But eventually, if they agreed to help dig, they were allowed to take shelter as long as they didn't tell anyone else about the place."

"Of course, he had assistance," Ryder muttered. His eyes felt as though they were filled with sand. He'd lain awake for hours, worry for Cady circling through his brain. It was worse when he had dozed; his anxiety would take on nightmarish levels, taunting him with his failure to find her. "What do you know about the other man who helped him?"

"Not much," Miguel said glumly. There were shadows beneath his eyes and like Ryder, he hadn't bothered to shave that morning. "They've made the rounds to other homeless encampments. With the milder weather, most people have moved outdoors. Altogether, a total of five people admitted to having been in the tunnels. All agree the second man was big, and somewhere between the ages of twenty-five and thirty. That's the common descriptor, although specifics differ. Height was reported from six-three to six-six, most skewing toward the larger end. Weight two-fifty or more. Everyone they talked to assumed he was just another transient who dug in exchange for a place to stay out of the cold. One claimed that Stallsworth called the man Coyote."

The fact sparked Ryder's interest. "Maybe it's an alias. That gives us a lead to track."

"We're running the description and partial name now through state and federal databases. We have more matching vehicles to investigate. Gant is handing out assignments."

For the first time, Ryder noted the supervisory deputy marshal across the room, his arms braced against a tabletop as he spoke to a small group of suit-clad people seated across from him. Brass, maybe. Here to be briefed, to give advice, and hopefully place resources at the disposal of the task force.

"I'm not sitting in front of that damn computer again," he said to Miguel.

"That chore is completed. We've matched all the van descriptions with owners and current addresses in North Carolina and surrounding states."

Ryder's brows rose. That'd encompass hundreds of vehicles, but he figured they wouldn't be sending task force members out of state. Instead, they'd rely on law enforcement in those locales to check on the motorists and report back, like they'd done yesterday with those located more than a couple of hours outside Asheville.

He caught sight of a tall thin man in the crowded room and paused. "Is that Deputy Marshal Quimby over there?"

He was another of Cady's colleagues. He and Paul split their warrant work with federal court duties.

Miguel's dark gaze followed his. "Yeah. He was on vacation, but once he heard the news, he hopped a plane as soon as he could."

"What about a forensic artist? And Stallsworth's known acquaintances?"

"On it. The artist will be here within the hour. Three of the interviewees agreed to stay at the Asheville PD to help with the sketch. Free coffee and cookies elicit a lot of cooperation. No one matching the kidnapper's description has popped on Stallsworth's acquaintances yet, so we're digging deeper."

"When it's finished, I want to run down possible suspects."

"Allen's handing out assignments," Miguel said noncommittally. But Ryder was already striding toward the supervisory deputy marshal.

A line had queued behind Allen, and the four people he'd been addressing at the table were gone. He made a motion for Ryder to wait while he dealt with the others.

When it was just the two of them, he said, "Dr. Paulsen called this morning. She thought the incinerated remains from last night were deer carcasses. But they collected debris from previous incinerations that had fallen into the secondary chamber."

A ball of dread formed in Ryder's gut. "What kind of debris?"

"Pieces of charred bone." "Animal or human?"

"Both the doctor thought. They've been sent to the lab for further analysis. I'm going to assume none of this has anything to do with Cady or Paul until we get proof otherwise. I suggest you try to do the same."

Good advice, Ryder reflected grimly. But it was difficult to shove aside the idea of those discovered cremated remains. To wonder... He slammed a mental door before his thoughts could go there.

Seamlessly, the other man switched topics. "Miguel has a list of vehicle owners to visit. You can accompany him."

"When that forensic artist is finished, I'd like to—"

"Everyone will be armed with the sketch when it's completed," Allen interrupted him, his focus already on someone or something over Ryder's shoulder. He walked away then, satisfied. He wouldn't be shut out of the most meaningful bit of information about the kidnapper once it was available.

And he'd use it to lead him to Cady.

Four hours later, Ryder and Miguel turned into the drive leading to a sagging two-story farm home thirty minutes outside of Durham. They were doing second-round checks on the suspect vehicles. When the local law enforcement couldn't clear the owner through the initial contact, task force members were assigned follow-up visits.

"There's the vehicle registered to Lee Vangard," Miguel murmured.

Ryder braced one hand against the dash as they bumped their way over the ruts, carved deeper by the spring rains. The van was parked in a ramshackle old corn bin, nearly as ancient as the house, open on two sides. It matched the DMV report. Black, fifteen years old, most of them hard ones given its appearance. He scanned the rest of the buildings on the farm site, his gaze lingering on the barn. There were doors on that building. And what looked from here to be a shiny padlock securing them.

His cell dinged. A second alert sounded on Miguel's. Simultaneously, they withdrew them from their pockets and opened the message to find a forensic sketch.

"That was record time," the deputy marshal murmured and enlarged the drawing with his fingers.

Ryder peered more closely at his phone, an odd flicker of familiarity niggling through him. "Recognize him?"

"Other than looking like a run-of-the-mill scumbag, nope. But I didn't expect to."

Neither had Ryder. He took another moment to stare at the sketch. There was something about the man pictured. He chased the mental snippet. Came up empty. In his line of work, it wouldn't necessarily be someone with whom he'd personally had contact.

"You think you know him?" Miguel asked.

Ryder gave the drawing one last look. "Sort of reminds me of someone, but I can't place him." The task force would be following up on the picture right now, sending out a crew to display copies in the area. Others would try to match the kidnapper's descriptors to information contained in Live Scan, a federal arrest booking database. The illustration would be sent to every law enforcement office in the state and beyond, but it was hard telling how widely it'd be dispersed from there. Two missing deputy U.S. marshals was a big fucking deal, but some smaller departments might feel detached from the urgency. Or overloaded with their own cases.

He quickly sent it to Jerry Garza, his chief deputy investigator, and, as an afterthought, added Stacy, who worked the front desk in his office.

Thumbs flying over the keys, he typed out a message to both recipients.

> Familiar at all? Arrested? Stacy-in files?

"Let's see if we can get a look at the vehicle before Vanguard realizes we're here." Miguel pulled to a stop next to the corn crib, and they got out of the truck.

They were walking toward the van when a shot rang out, kicking up dirt ten feet behind them. Ryder hit the ground, drawing his weapon with one fluid movement. A man was running from the house, a rifle aimed at them.

They'd found Lee Vangard.

THIRTY MINUTES LATER, they had the recalcitrant shooter disarmed and cuffed and were waiting for Wake County deputies to arrive with a search warrant. While Vanguard kept up a bitter running argument, Ryder half-turned away, pulling out his cell to check the message he'd received earlier. It was from Garza, and like the man, terse and to the point.

> Don't recognize. In our system?
>
> Unsure. No name. Stacy?
>
> On it.

He went to his contacts and sent a call to the woman. She answered on the first ring.

"Is this urgent or are you just impatient?"

One of his brows winged up. "Is that how you answer the phone now?"

"It is when I know who's calling. And what you want. That sketch? Seemed a little familiar."

Ryder quelled the immediate leap of excitement in his veins. "From where?"

"Well, for months you've had me double-check our paper records with those uploaded to Digi-Reel to make sure no more were missed. And my eyes don't thank you for that, by the way."

Tension crept into his muscles. "I recall." It'd been his dad, Butch Talbot, the former sheriff of Haywood County, who'd made the switch, although he'd retained the physical files. Ryder had discovered last winter that a handful hadn't been digitized. Conveniently, all were cases that reflected poorly on his deceased father. Hence Ryder's order for Stacy to compare the two sets of copies. He'd been through numerous drawers of case reports himself, looking for the ones he'd later discovered hidden in Butch's garage.

"The picture reminded me of a file I'd seen recently. I'm up to the last five years, so I sort of knew where to look. Digital format makes it quicker to flip through. I found the one I was thinking of, but side by side the mugshot and the sketch aren't an exact match. But there's a resemblance, for sure. Here. I'll take a screenshot and send it to you."

He opened the image in the text she sent. It showed a thinner man, several years younger. But the shoulders were just as broad, if without the added weight of the man in the drawing. If Ryder focused only on the eyes and nose…yeah. Definitely maybe.

"What do you think?"

He brought up the illustration, then looked again at the

screenshot she'd sent. "How long ago was the mugshot taken?"

"Five years. Joseph Wiley, aged twenty-one at the time. Aggravated assault." She was silent for a moment. "Looks like he had a job sweeping up for a garage in Clyde. Took a tire iron to the owner over a dispute. Put him in the hospital."

A cold ball of dread formed in his chest. "Was he sentenced?"

"Uh-uh." Stacy sounded distracted. Still reading, apparently. "It says here he was ordered to Rolling Acres Resort to undergo a forensic evaluation."

His earlier trepidation spread. The private residential psychiatric facility was on the eastern side of his county.

"There's an addendum dated three months later." A minute passed before Stacy's voice returned. "No prison time. His psychiatrist said it was a medication issue, which had been resolved. The judge ordered restitution for the victim's medical bills and three years' probation, conditional upon remaining under a psychiatric doctor's care. Like I say, not certain the pictures match, but worth checking out, right?"

"Yeah." His voice was flat. "Thanks, Stacy." He disconnected, his fingers clenching around the cell. He could have run across that same mugshot when he was looking through those files months earlier. That would explain the flicker of recognition that had hit him when he'd first seen the sketch.

Miguel drew closer and said, "We've got backup arriving in minutes. Then we can—" He broke off when he saw Ryder's expression. "You have something?"

"Maybe." He punched in Allen Gant's number while he filled him in on the conversation he'd just held, careful to keep any hint of emotion from his tone. "Might be nothing," he concluded. And found himself hoping he was correct. Because the little they did know about Joseph Wiley wasn't reassuring. A man with a history of mental illness and violence.

And Cady was at his mercy.

9

"Don't move."

Cady didn't need her captor's admonishment. He swiftly wiped her back with something and applied bandages. The hours she'd spent motionless as he'd tattooed her had rendered her muscles stiff. Her limbs felt wooden. She wanted to roll to her side. Bend her knees and arms. She didn't dare.

He'd taken breaks, getting up to stretch and to walk outside for a short time before returning. Once he was munching a sandwich. Any thought of food had vanished when he'd picked up that needled device and restarted. He could have tattooed the damn Sistine Chapel on her back in the long hours he'd spent hunched over her. The intense stinging, burning sensation stretched from one shoulder to the other, midway down her back. But the constant vibration of the device was gone, that feeling of a needle being dragged across her skin. And the continual drone of his humming, like a satisfied pigeon.

Cady hated herself for the relief coursing through her when the stranger picked up his supplies and turned away.

Finishing with her—at least for the day—just meant that Paul would soon be subjected to the same treatment. She thought of the frames nearby and shuddered. Maybe their captor had planned something special this time. A more elaborate addition to his collection.

Once he'd finished the tattoos, he didn't need them alive anymore. A blade of fear stabbed through her. Did he have to wait for the tattoo to heal before he removed it? She had a friend in college who'd gotten a rather unattractive tramp stamp. It'd taken weeks of care during the healing process.

They may not even have another day.

Surreptitiously, she bent one knee, focusing on the man now working on Paul. Then she flexed the other. Again and again, until the feeling returned to her lower extremities. Next, she wiggled her fingers and crooked her elbow with infinitesimal care, cautious not to jangle the chain. She winced when the skin pulled and stretched beneath the bandage.

The other deputy marshal didn't make a sound. She caught sight of the hypodermic then, on the floor beyond her tarp. Out of Paul's reach, but not hers, if Cady dared to stretch for it. It was half-full. She felt a flicker of sympathy. The kidnapper had injected Paul again.

She mentally counted down an hour and a half before the stranger took another break, heading outside. She moved her arms in earnest, bending and straightening them over and over. "Paul," she whispered, mindful of how noise would travel in the mine. "Are you all right?"

Her stomach sank when only silence met her question.

Then came, "...k..."

Hope leaped. "Try to stay alert." She kept the words low. Urgent. "I have a plan."

Moments later, she heard the echo of the stranger's

booted feet and she stilled, adrenaline and apprehension circling inside her. Timing was critical. She needed to delay until their kidnapper was totally engrossed in his work. Until he'd all but forgotten her presence.

She waited a half hour before awkwardly struggling to rise. Her muscles were stiff. Cady lurched to a crouch. Their captor stilled and slowly turned his head. And she knew she was out of time.

She launched herself at him, holding the chain between her arms taut. She struck his headlamp in her first attempt, slowing her movements. He let out a high-pitched screech and fought to stand. Cady kept her knees pressed to his sides, fighting to loop the links around his throat. And when she succeeded, finally, she crossed her wrists and pulled to apply more pressure.

He stood, his cry as piercing as a scalpel. The device clattered to the ground as he endeavored to loosen the ligature. She clung to him, maintaining the tension in it as he whirled in a frantic circle, punching her in the sides. He reached back to grasp her hair and yanked it hard enough to bring tears to Cady's eyes. He bucked and shook violently to displace her. Each movement jarred her injured ribs. Her throbbing head. Even as she readjusted her hold, her strength lagged.

But he was coughing and choking now, still attempting to wedge his fingers between the chain and his throat. Abruptly, he changed tactics. Spinning around, he stumbled toward the wall of the mine and turned to slam her against it. She ducked her head into his shoulder to protect it, but a chorus of agony sprinted through her body. He ran her into the stone again and again. Jarring her back. Her ribs. Fogging her brain.

"Don't...hurt...tattoo..." she panted.

He paused then, and with her last bit of strength Cady managed to keep the chain taut. But the past days had weakened her. She went limp, using her weight to pull the length of links tighter. The stranger fell to his knees, choking and gagging. Finally, he collapsed, facedown. And his movements stopped altogether.

Cady hauled in oxygen, trying to fight through the choir of pain to summon logic. She didn't think she'd killed him. It hadn't been long enough. She uncrossed her arms, urgency clawing at her. Either he was pretending or he'd genuinely lost consciousness. But she couldn't count on him being out for long.

She removed the ligature, hyperalert to any change in the man's position. But his muscles remained slack. Cady had to crawl over him to reach for the syringe. She brought it up and jammed the needle into his arm, depressing the plunger until the tube was empty. Only then did she shove her fingers into his pocket, desperation making her movements awkward. They closed around the key he'd pulled out that first day. Withdrawing it, she tried to fit it into the lock of her left cuff.

The sound of the click it made when it unlocked would have filled her with joy if it wasn't accompanied by a long, low guttural groan from their captor. He was alive.

And she was running out of time.

Paul was saying something. Had been for a while maybe, but she couldn't make out the words. Panic filtered in as she set to work on her other cuff. After unlocking it, Cady pulled the stranger's heavy arm down to try to secure the manacle around his wrist.

It didn't fit. Of course it didn't.

He stirred beneath her, coughing violently. Frantically, she rolled toward Paul. Found him nearer than she'd thought. Her hands shook as she strove to unlock the closest bracelet. The kidnapper flopped beside her as his limbs refused to obey the commands his brain was sending him. Finally, she got the cuff off her colleague and stretched it over toward the kidnapper. It wouldn't reach.

He tried to get to his knees. Failed. She grabbed his arm and dragged it over to the free manacle.

And the click as it locked around his thick wrist was the sweetest sound she'd ever heard.

Movements faster now, Cady got up and stumbled around Paul's form to unlock his other cuff. "Can you move away from him? Come toward me." She scooted to the opposite wall of the mine, the one beyond his feet.

The other deputy marshal's motions were clumsy and unbearably slow as he inched across the tarp. Not always in the right direction but at least farther from their captor.

Their one-time captor. They were free.

But Cady couldn't rely on them remaining that way. She hadn't checked the stranger's other pocket. What if the keys to the truck were there?

A harsh, garbled cry emanated from him. He was definitely conscious now, but not up. Not yet.

Leaving Paul for the moment, she rose and ran toward the front of the tunnel. She took a moment to tie the ends of her ruined shirt where they flapped behind her, before squeezing around the dilapidated pickup to the driver's door and opened it. It took more effort than it should have to climb inside far enough for her fingers to go searching for the ignition.

Only when she found the keys dangling from it did Cady let herself believe that escape was really possible.

If the stranger didn't have another key to the cuffs. *If* there'd been sufficient drug in that syringe to immobilize him for a while. *If* she could somehow figure out a way to take Paul with her.

She got out, raced to the bed of the truck and scrambled into it, hunting for something she could use to help move Paul. It'd be hours before he'd be fully functional again. Cady couldn't guess who might come looking for their captor if he didn't return at dark. She didn't know how long the bonds might hold him.

The truck bed was empty save for a heavy tow chain, so rusted it left orange dust on her hands when she touched it. But there was a thick hook on each end, which gave her an idea.

She shimmied from the pickup and hurried back inside the mine. Their kidnapper was more alert, but his struggles were weak. Hopefully, the narcotic would keep him out of commission until they were gone.

Her heart sank when she saw Paul. He'd moved only a foot or two in her time away. He wasn't going to make it the vehicle. Not without help.

"Go." There was more strength in the deputy marshal's voice than she would have expected. "Now. Go. Cady."

"I will," she promised as she passed him to turn the spotlights so they pointed toward the pickup. "If this doesn't work, I will." She wasn't sure how long they had before darkness fell.

She straightened and looked for the cart the stranger had used to haul his things. Found it several yards away. She winced as his low guttural cries filled the area. The damage to his throat had turned his high-pitched voice to a croak, but it still thrummed along her nerve endings, leaving anxiety in its wake.

The cart was homemade, with peeling weathered

plywood sides and bottom. But the handles were metal, and so was the axle. It might work. It *had* to.

Cady hurried to the driver's seat. Turned the keys to start the vehicle. Belatedly, she realized it was a manual and pressed the clutch pedal, trying again. When the engine coughed to life, she backed it deeper into the mine.

She stopped fifteen feet from the tarps. She didn't know how long the tow line was, but surely not much more than that. Climbing out again, she pulled on one end of the chain, crawling beneath the pickup to fasten the hook on the rear axle.

She was panting, as much from the rib pain as from the effort. She inched out again and got up to secure the other end to the rod under the wheelbarrow, and then stretched it out as far as it would go. The stranger was moaning and babbling as he tried and failed to rise. She pushed the cart to the edge of the tarpaulin before she was pulled up short.

Clenching her teeth, she headed back to the pickup. Unfastened the chain and moved the vehicle further into the mine. This time after resecuring the hook she was able to wheel the cart within feet of Paul.

"All you have to do it is get this far and climb inside. See?"

With difficulty, he raised his head. The whiskers and dirt on his face made him nearly unrecognizable from the man who'd followed her into that last tunnel. "Go. With...out..."

"No." All her frustration was loaded in the word. "Move your ass, Chester. Just to the wheelbarrow. I can pull you out of here." Then she had to figure a way to get him into the bed of the truck.

Urgency was battling with adrenaline. They were so close. But there was something building inside her that told her it could all fall apart.

And failure at this point was unimaginable.

Paul was moving. It was tortoise-like speed, but he'd made it to his knees, a monumental feat in itself. Inch by excruciating inch he headed in the direction of the wheelbarrow. A bat did a slow lazy swoop above them. Cady barely noticed. She'd shut out the pitiful noises coming from the stranger. She'd blocked everything but Paul's infinitesimal progress. She didn't think about what would happen if the chain broke. If she couldn't get the other man inside the truck bed.

Her only focus was escape. And damned if she'd leave alone.

10

"There are fifteen DMV listings for a Joseph Wiley." It'd been a long three hours and Ryder was on the phone with Supervisory Deputy U.S. Marshal Allen Gant. The man continued, "Only one looked anything like the sketch. The addy didn't pan out. We were able to track down his mother and sent a team to speak to her. She said her son didn't live with her. Claimed he's been backpacking in Virginia for the past week."

"Meaning she hasn't seen him for that long?" Ryder cast a gaze at Vanguard's farmhouse. The search of the home had turned up nothing, but one corner of the now-unlocked barn held crates of brand-new rifles. The guy had been hiding an arsenal in there, and he'd stopped talking once his stash had been found. They'd discovered no evidence in the van or buildings to suggest Cady and Paul had been here.

"A little longer. Nancy Wiley says she doesn't know where he's been staying. Oddly enough, she had no pictures of him there or on her phone. Says her faith forbids them."

Sects of the Amish believed that, Ryder mused. He

wasn't sure what other religions had similar customs. "What about the neighbors?"

"I've got people canvassing the area around her place and the old DMV address. Nothing yet. Of course, we can't be sure this is the right guy."

"His name...Wiley. One of the homeless men mentioned that Stallsworth called him Coyote."

Allen sounded puzzled. "So?"

"So...Wile E. Coyote? And the roadrunner?" Silence was Ryder's only answer. "You never watched Bugs Bunny reruns?"

"Oh, now I remember that character. Always getting flattened. I didn't know it had a name. Huh. Maybe..."

"Yeah. Maybe."

"Gotta go. Let me know when you're heading back to Asheville."

His phone buzzed as Gant was signing off and Ryder looked at the screen. It was an unknown number. Under ordinary circumstances, he wouldn't answer it. But nothing in the last few days had been normal.

"Sheriff Talbot."

There was a pause. Then a voice, female, laced with suspicion. "Anyone could say they was the law. Don't make it so."

He was already regretting answering the damn call. "Can I help you, ma'am?" Miguel headed toward him.

"What county you in charge of?"

"Haywood. Do you have the wrong number?" The deputy marshal was close enough to hear his side of the conversation and raised his brows. Ryder shook his head.

"Got someone here wanting to use my mobile phone. Planning to steal it, most like. But she said could I just make a call. Still don't know what to think. You really a sheriff?"

He went still. "A woman asked you? Who?" The breath trapped in his lungs as he waited for the reply.

"Katy something. She's out on my porch and yessir I got the door locked 'cuz she looks like the wrath of God. Clothes half falling off and face all beat up. She says the pickup she was driving died. Said the sheriff 'd send someone for her if'n I jist called this number."

THE HOSPITAL DOOR wouldn't fully open. Peering through the wedge of space, Ryder could see that the room was packed with law enforcement personnel. He squeezed inside by sucking in every ounce of breath. Then jockeyed around so he could see Cady, sitting up in the bed, her impassive expression masking how much she was surely hating being there.

His eyes slid shut then, and his knees went a little weak. He leaned against the doorjamb for a moment. Someone he couldn't see was saying, "What was your intention when you choked the suspect with the chain?" Ryder's eyes snapped open again.

"My intent was to incapacitate the kidnapper long enough to facilitate escape." Cady's voice was raspier than usual but its steadiness calmed something inside him.

"Were you trying to kill him?"

"Jesus Christ, Voight!" He recognized Allen's voice. "What kind of question is that, given the situation?"

Miguel gave Ryder a little shove and he straightened. He'd forgotten the deputy marshal was behind him. He wiggled farther into the room to allow him to enter.

"Her answer is required for the record," snapped the unseen man. "She also used a substance on him without knowing its identity or strength. In the event of a lawsuit, it has to be clear…"

Now there was a chorus of voices, most of them raised.

"My intent was to incapacitate the kidnapper long enough to facilitate escape," Cady repeated, once the noise level had dropped. "We were in weakened states. He'd been violent and unpredictable. He's a big guy. At least Paul's size. He also appeared mentally unstable. I was just hoping to decommission him so I could get at his key. To unlock our cuffs and get us out of there."

"And you did that, Deputy Marshal Maddix." He craned his head but couldn't see who was speaking. "Admirably."

"Perhaps we can return to that first day." It was the voice Ryder was already coming to despise. Whoever it belonged to had a major stick up his ass. "Explain again why you didn't attempt to escape the first time you were free."

"Wiley had the syringe at Paul's throat." There was a note in Cady's voice that he recognized. Exhaustion. But something else. Guilt? "He was threatening to inject all its contents into him if I didn't do as he said. I was also suffering from the aftereffects of the drug and unable to move quickly."

"Empty it into him, as you did to Wiley?"

"The hypodermic was full when he made that threat. Today it was filled halfway. He'd already injected Paul once. I'd requested that he not use as much as he had in the past, because I was uncertain of its effects."

"What was his response?"

She fingered the explosion of color beneath one eye. "He's not much for suggestions."

A ripple of laughter swept through the room.

"Fifteen minutes are up." The nurse beside the bed removed the pad she'd had pressed to the side of

Cady's head, dipped it in a container of water and wrung it out. Rivulets of red ran from it. "Doctor's orders. The patient will rest for an hour and if her condition is unchanged, there will be time for more questions then."

"First, I'd like to return to how you and Deputy U.S. Marshal Chester came to be captured." Just the sound of that voice had Ryder's fist clenching.

"In an hour," she repeated implacably. "And be aware that visitors aren't allowed past eight o'clock this evening."

There was a shuffle of feet and then people started drifting by Ryder and Miguel and out of the room. A man and a woman in suits drew nearer to Cady's bed. The male said, "Before we go, I just want to say again, damn fine job today, Deputy Marshal Maddix."

"Thank you, sir."

The woman echoed his congratulations, adding, "We're relieved that you and Deputy Marshal Chester weren't injured worse."

"How is Paul?"

Allen joined the two suits at Cady's bedside. "He's been airlifted to the medical center in Charlotte. They've got some toxicology specialists there." He smiled. "He was bitching and moaning about going, too. But I understand that he's going to be fine."

She tried for a smile. Didn't quite manage it. "He's got a right to do some bitching. He took the brunt of the drug. Talked the guy out of injecting me with more after it made me sick."

He patted her arm. "So you said. And you returned the favor by talking the asshole out of giving Paul a larger dose today."

Another guy with a briefcase brushed by Ryder on his

way out of the room. "Fucking lawyer," he breathed to Miguel, who was standing right behind him. "Figures."

"Probably from the federal attorney's office," the other man murmured. "But it's routine after something like this." He sounded like he was trying to convince himself. "There'll be a lot of hoops to jump through, getting the story straight for everyone."

The man and woman left then. Ryder thought he recognized them from the group speaking to Allen in the conference room earlier this morning. Then he forgot them as he got his first unimpeded look at Cady. His mouth dried. He strode to her side and took the hand she slipped through the bars of the bedrail.

"That old lady couldn't understand what the hell a marshal was but she seemed familiar with the concept of sheriffs." Her fingers curled around his and Ryder felt a weight lifted from his chest.

"Like I just said," the nurse started.

Miguel swooped in. "Don't worry, I don't have any questions." He leaned over and kissed Cady full on the lips. Then pulled safely out of range and grinned at her. "You had some of them a little worried. Not me, I've seen you survive explosions. Shoot-outs. Gunshot wounds. But the others were unaware of your superhuman powers."

She dropped Ryder's hand to drag her arm across her mouth and glared at her colleague. "Jesus, Rodriguez, like I didn't get enough germs from the bats in that damn mine."

Allen chuckled as Miguel blanched. Then the deputy marshal rallied. "As long as you didn't make out with any, your lips should be germ-free."

"Questions or not, everyone leaves. Now." The nurse crossed her arms. Allen took Miguel's arm and nudged him toward the door.

"We'll be back later."

When the woman aimed a stare at Ryder, Cady said, "He stays."

"The doctor—"

"Disregard the uniform. He's not one of them."

The woman studied them both, then reached for the pan of bloody water. "If you say so."

He waited for the door to swing shut behind her before recapturing Cady's hand and leaning down for a lingering kiss. Resting his forehead against hers, he murmured, "I don't know where to touch you that wouldn't hurt."

"It's not that bad."

He lifted his head. "Yeah? I got the rundown from the ER doctor. Three cracked ribs. Possible zygomaticomaxillary fracture—"

"X-ray showed no fracture," she put in.

"—six stitches to your skull, assorted contusions, probable concussion, dehydration and you received two injections for rabies—thanks to your flying friends in the mine. I believe she said there were three more shots in the series."

"Sounds like someone was a real blabbermouth." But her fingers curled tightly around his. And for the first time, a flicker of pain crossed her expression. "I'm not going to lie. Things didn't look good for a while. But this place is almost as bad. Promise you won't leave me here."

He brought her hand to his lips. "Baby, I can't do that."

"Figures. Guy sends the cavalry and thinks he's fulfilled his hero status."

Ryder's laugh was choked. All he'd done was make a damn phone call. Well, okay, a lot of calls and then he'd made Miguel drive like a maniac to get back to Asheville, with the strobe light flashing. Not much in the grand scheme of things. "There's only one hero in this room and it's not me. But I can promise I won't leave you alone. Is that good enough?"

She hissed out a breath. "Guess it'll have to be. I wasn't exactly sure where we were, even after we got out. I tried to mark the trail we took. How long did it take them to find Wiley?"

"You were over an hour away, off the beaten path in an old gemstone mine in the mountains of Madison County. Western North Carolina has a ton of abandoned mines and the state does shit-all to inspect them or keep people away. The task force needed the signs you left. It still took them a couple of hours." He didn't mention that many of the deserted mines in the region were shafts. Bodies could be dropped down them never to be found again. The thought had a chill creeping across his nape. It could have been far worse. "He'd stashed your weapons beneath the seat of the truck. But I don't think they ever found your jackets or vests."

She released his hand. Mindful of the IV in her other arm, Cady scooted so her back faced him. "First time one of these damn robes came in handy. Untie it. Then take a picture to show me."

The glimpses of ink through the opening in the gown had Ryder's muscles tightening. "Maybe that could wait..."

She sent him a fierce look. "For hours, people have been snapping photos of this and clucking over it. I should damn well be able to see what that lunatic did to me."

Because it was no more than the truth, Ryder reached out and untied the garment. Carefully parted it. Then stared in horrified fascination. Her previously unmarred skin had been branded with a scene straight out of hell. On Cady's right shoulder was a large bare circle enclosed by an intricate design of interlocking letters. But it was the vivid images that crawled over the rest of her back that held his gaze. Fire. The flames were so alive he could almost hear their snap and sizzle. There was some sort of structure being eaten by them and one fiery tendril curled around a person, devouring it the way a glutton inhaled a meal. A blackened tree was standing at the far edge of the scene. There was still a section of skin left bare. Wiley hadn't been finished.

"Bad, huh?" Cady's voice was flat. "I kind of got that impression from the reaction in the ER and the evidence tech. Maybe I should consider joining a freak show."

"He was... industrious." It was difficult to get past the impotent sense of rage billowing inside him. Even more than the injuries Wiley had inflicted on Cady, the travesty he'd wrought on her flesh had Ryder wishing there wasn't an armed guard stationed outside the man's room in the locked psychiatric ward. He'd be satisfied with a couple of minutes alone with her former captor to administer a fraction of the torture he'd subjected her to.

"The pictures?"

At her prodding, he took out his phone. She held the sides of the gown wide and he took several shots. Brought them up on the screen and then handed his cell to Cady. Tamping down the fierce cauldron of emotion, Ryder busied himself by drawing the garment closed, and tying it neatly.

"He's a decent artist. Who'd have guessed?"

Ryder's hands went to her shoulders and he pressed his lips to the back of her head as she flipped through the images, studying them intently.

"I never really considered what he'd drawn, but he spent the better part of two days, dividing his time between us. I couldn't see much of what he was doing when he worked on

Paul, but he will have gotten it worse. Wiley took more time with him."

"The guy makes a big canvas."

Cady made a sound between a snort and a sob and a vise squeezed his heart. "Right? I knew Wiley wasn't stable. I was pretty sure he was violently unbalanced. But this... the tattoo is a whole other demented dimension. What the hell *is* this?"

"An visible display of psychosis?"

Silently, she handed him back his cell. He could feel the shudder working through her. Ryder slipped his arms around her. In the next moment, she was flipping back the covers on the hospital bed and fumbling for the bed rail next to him. "Help me get this down."

"Are you supposed to get out of bed?"

"I'm going to shower. I want to scrub this damn thing off *now!*" Unable to lower the rails one-handed, she slammed a fist against them. "The ink is fresh. Maybe it'll wash off. I want it off." Her voice was tight but rising. The railing rattled as she began to battle it again. "I'm not going through the rest of my life wearing that sick fuck's brand."

"And you won't. But for now, it's still evidence." The word tasted sour in his mouth. "We'll ask in an hour when the crew comes back, okay? Then we'll get a doctor in here and discuss the best step forward. There are ways to remove a tattoo." None were easy, he knew. The process would be a long one and the results would be painful and imperfect. But he understood her reaction. And because he did, he lowered the rail. Helped her turn to her uninjured side facing him. Then he climbed in with her, taking care to keep his boots off the mattress. He rested one hand lightly on her hip.

"It's stupid," she whispered against his shoulder. One of

her legs moved to wedge between his. "I thought we were going to die. He had framed pictures of tattoos further inside the mine. Like he'd removed them from people, either before or after death. It was pretty easy to figure out what he had planned for us. We got away. This is nothing compared to his plan for us. But still..."

It was the first Ryder had heard about the frames. The news ignited an icy fury that was difficult to contain. She was here. She was safe. He whispered a kiss across her forehead. "Living with it isn't the price you pay for survival. He'll be locked away and you and Paul will return to your lives. That's a win."

Her voice was so low he had to strain to hear it. "It won't be a win until I erase every last mark he left on me."

11

Three weeks later

"I'm going to get spoiled, seeing you so often," Cady's mother teased as they climbed up the steps to Alma's cabin. "When's your vacation over?"

Vacation. She sent her mom a smile as they crossed the porch. "Pretty soon." At least she hoped so. The doctor had ordered the sick leave, but it'd been extended by a recommendation of the USMS Critical Incident Response Team. She grimaced at the memory. There were still hoops to jump through to prove her fitness to return to work. She was itching to do so. The days were long and outside of mandated appointments, tough to fill. May had melted into June, and the mild weather meant she could get outdoors. But her rib injury curtailed her activities. She could only go on so many walks.

According to Miguel, Stallsworth still wasn't talking. His association with a man who'd snatched two Deputy U.S. Marshals subjected him to extra scrutiny. The FBI had stepped in to handle the Joseph Wiley prosecution, so details were scarce. But Cady knew he was sitting in the Buncombe County jail. The thought was satisfying.

The door swung open to frame her aunt's girth. She studied Hannah carefully. But Cady's mom looked as pretty and refreshed as she had before their brunch, so there was nothing for Alma to chastise Cady over. That didn't exactly turn her visage welcoming, but she stepped back and allowed them to enter.

"Maybe you should rest after your morning out," she suggested to her sister as Hannah strolled by her.

"And waste spending a minute with my daughter? Not a chance." She laughed. "We had the best meal, Alma. I absolutely stuffed myself at the brunch buffet. I don't think I've been there before. What was the name of the restaurant we went to?"

Her stomach plummeted. "Jillian's. It's always been one of your favorites." Cady usually had only Saturdays to spend with her mom, but they went there often. She and her aunt exchanged a glance.

Hannah dropped onto the overstuffed sofa. "Well, we'll certainly return. Come. Sit for a moment." She patted the seat beside her.

"I have an appointment in Charlotte this afternoon, remember?" She wished she could forget it as easily. The psychologist she saw to satisfy the CIRT had an office there. She'd been twice already. The woman was taking her own sweet time releasing her for duty. Knowing that Paul had received a similar recommendation was little consolation.

At least she'd started the laser procedure for tattoo removal. It was unpleasant but it was vastly preferable to talking *feelings* with the therapist. Especially when a rapid return to the job hinged on the woman.

"She's gotta go. There's no reason you can't lie down for a while," Alma put in.

Cady crossed to her mom and bent to kiss her forehead. "I'll come by when I can." She was desperately hoping she'd be back at work soon. As much as she was dreading the afternoon appointment, it'd be worth going if it cleared her.

"All right then. Thank you for lunch, honey."

Alma followed her to the door. Through it. Once outside, with the door firmly closed, Cady turned to face her, braced for the usual rebuke. There was little about her that her aunt had ever approved of, and Hannah's health was an ongoing source of conflict between them.

But for once, Alma's concern wasn't centered on Cady's mom. "Been gettin' some traffic up here at night. Couple times this week. Maybe you could get that sheriff to send a car to watch the place. Chase off whoever's been snooping 'round."

The small cabin sat a quarter-mile off the road and was surrounded by trees and underbrush, making it nearly invisible. A passerby at night wouldn't even see the opening to the drive if he didn't know it was there. "What time is this happening?"

"After midnight. The headlights woke me the first time. Three or four days later, I heard someone on the porch." Alma crossed her arms over her formidable chest. "I got my shotgun and had it handy in case I needed it. Whoever it was went around to the back, too. Wouldn't be surprised if they was lookin' to break in."

Her aunt had a lot of less than admirable qualities, but fanciful she wasn't. "I'll let Ryder know. And if it happens again, be sure to call his office. If there's a deputy in the vicinity, he might be able to get here quickly."

"See that you tell him." Without another word, Alma

walked into the residence, leaving Cady with an all-too-familiar mixture of frustration and concern as she jogged to her Jeep. The cabin was isolated. The nearest neighbor was two miles away. It was plausible that a burglar had decided it would make an easy target, although it held little of value. But it'd be ballsy for one to make an attempt when the place was occupied.

She got in the vehicle and did a three-point turn in the small clearing, nosing the Jeep down the winding drive. Alma wouldn't hesitate to shoot at anything that moved outside the home, and that brought a different sort of worry. Cady would tell Ryder about the conversation later this evening. But right now, she'd spend the trip to Charlotte figuring out how to talk the psychologist into signing the release allowing Cady back on the job.

"So, how are you feeling physically?"

Dr. Yarnell was a petite middle-aged woman with a kind smile that belied her penchant for sandwiching incisive, scalpel-sharp questions between pleasantries. That habit of hers kept Cady permanently on guard.

"Fine. I was cleared by the doctor several days ago."

"How are the ribs?"

They sat in two comfortable chairs in front of a window with an uninspiring view of the next-door building's roof. That didn't keep her from looking out of it, to avoid the doctor's ever-watchful gaze.

"Better. I've had broken ribs before. They take time."

"The mind is the same way. It, too, requires time to heal."

She switched her focus to the therapist. "The difference is, my mind wasn't broken."

Yarnell gave her one of her soothing smiles. "Of course not. But in a figurative sense, it can be bruised, just as the body can be. If you have an injured knee, you start to stand or move differently, so you don't irritate it. It can impact the way you manage your duties. Emotional trauma works similarly. It can affect decision-making. The choices a person makes. That, too, can influence job performance, as well as relationships. And prolonged trauma or several instances of it can be even more impactful."

She tapped one pink-tipped nail on the folder atop the small table next to her chair and Cady's gut clenched. It was her personnel file. She didn't know every item in it, but obviously a summary of her personal history would be included. A psychological profile was required for every trainee before being admitted to the academy at Glynco.

And Yarnell always seemed as interested in the contents as she was in the kidnapping.

"You seem fixated on my personal history," Cady managed steadily. "But someone's past doesn't have to dictate their future." She'd said as much at the other sessions because the doctor kept returning to the same subject like a metal detector over an iron vein.

"We've talked about the tragedy that happened when you were four."

"When I shot and killed my father." Her gaze drifted to the window again. "I don't remember much of it. Just snippets of memory." She'd never been sure if they were due to actual recall or to others' retelling of the event. But the act had defined her childhood.

"He was a violent fugitive who was hurting your mother. You picked up the gun someone had left on the table. It wasn't your fault."

Something inside her tightened. Not everything would

be contained within the covers of that file. There were details she'd only recently learned herself. And she was still coming to terms with them. "I know that."

"Sometimes understanding facts isn't the same as accepting them emotionally."

Not for the first time, she was reminded of the hours spent while Wiley tattooed her. The drone of the machine. The sharp stinging sensation of the needle as it moved over her skin. The thought had her smiling inwardly. She was certain the doctor wouldn't appreciate the comparison. But also, like her former captor, there was no way to hurry the woman along when she was intent on her task.

"There's a USMS report in your file about another time your father visited you and your mother. Law enforcement arrived and he used you as a human shield so they wouldn't shoot while he escaped." Yarnell's gaze probed deep for a reaction. Cady was determined not to give her one. She resented—fiercely—the doctor's attempt to pry a response from her.

"Lonny Maddix wasn't a father in any but the biological sense. His failings have nothing to do with me."

Yarnell opened the folder. "What precipitated your being sent to live with your grandfather when you were twelve?"

She hesitated, trying to recall exactly how many details would be in there. "My mother couldn't take care of me anymore. Financially." That was true enough, only because Hannah's taste in men ran to good-looking guys with a glib patter and convenient morals who invariably took off with the rent check or drained her bank account. When they did, she and her mom would stay with Alma until Hannah got on her feet again.

"But you were living with your aunt immediately before

that point?"

Maybe the doctor was right earlier. Because it sure as hell felt like she was intent in finding every bruise in Cady's past and probing it for sensitivity. "I have two cousins. A few years older than me." When the woman's gaze lifted to meet hers, Cady had the feeling the psychologist already knew the facts and was just waiting to see if she'd verify them. "My mom didn't trust them around me."

"Were you raped?"

"I probably would have been. I grabbed a rock and split Bo's head open with it." The memory still brought a flicker of satisfaction.

Yarnell grinned. "Resourceful even then."

"You could say I have a deep-seated survival instinct."

"Your mother sent you to live with her father, a man she knew to be emotionally abusive. It would be natural to feel some resentment for that."

Up until that point, she'd forced herself to remain still, loathe to show any signs of agitation. Cady rose now, driven to move. "People's choices are limited as much by their abilities as by the options available to them. My mother is a lovely woman, but one who does best when she has someone to lean on. A man, when there was one in the picture. Her sister, when one wasn't. And if you placed a lineup of men in front of Hannah, she'd invariably choose the biggest loser. So, she knew it was likely she'd need to move in with my aunt again in the future." Cady strolled to the door and suppressed the urge to bolt through it before retracing her steps. "I had a crappy childhood. Lots of people do. You can pick through it for months like a crow on carrion, but that's behind me. I moved on."

Yarnell tapped her finger against the file thoughtfully. "We can't outrun our memories."

Didn't she know it. They caught up with her several nights a week when she slept. "We can't let them dictate our behavior, either."

"Are you experiencing flashbacks of your time in the mine?"

"No." When the psychologist pursed her lips, Cady shrugged. "Do I recall it? Of course. I was retelling every detail of the ordeal for days for the record. And I sometimes wonder if I did the right thing, not taking that first chance at escape. I played the odds, and luckily it panned out. But I don't stress about it. It doesn't make me anxious." Because that was a question the woman asked over and over. "I'm not worried about returning to duty, although I'd probably think twice before crawling into a tunnel for a while."

"It's not uncommon for people to carry post-traumatic symptoms from their childhood into their adult years. But focusing for the moment on the kidnapping, the indicators of PTSD may not be evident until you return to the job. Seemingly unrelated things could trigger it. Physical manifestations would be panic attacks, heart palpitations, feelings of extreme stress."

"I experience those every time I walk through your door," Cady countered, only half joking.

"Other signs are nightmares, depression, anger, avoidance, and fear of intimacy." The doctor looked at her expectantly. "You're not married."

"No."

"A support system can be invaluable for someone who's gone through a harrowing experience like yours."

Cady's mind flashed to Ryder. The distance that had yawned between them a few weeks ago had disappeared since her escape. He'd accompanied her home from the hospital and stayed, going to his house only to retrieve clothes and other belongings. They were back to where they'd been before she'd moved from his place back to her renovated acreage. Yarnell would probably insist they should have a discussion or something about it. They hadn't. But Cady was well-aware that in the seven months she'd known Ryder Talbot, he'd become the exception to her previous determinedly casual relationships. He was different. *She* was different when it came to him.

But she'd be lying if she claimed getting serious about a man for the first time in her life didn't still make her pulse jittery.

"I have... someone. And when you let me go back to work, I've got friends there."

The doctor was silent for a long time. Long enough to make Cady nervous. "Look. You can't foresee the future, so you have to rely on my past actions to determine my success returning to my job, right?"

Dr. Yarnell gave a slow nod. "That's the gist of it, yes."

"There's a lot in my history. And I overcame it. I went on. Paid for college on my own and made it to the academy. I've been successful in the U.S. Marshals Service."

"Your file makes that clear, as well."

"There's your answer, then. Want to know what's going to happen when I return to duty? I'll work the warrants. Make the arrests. Do the damn job. Because that's what I do, what I've always done. You talk a great deal about trauma, but everyone has baggage. I've never let mine control me. What happened with Wiley isn't going to control me either."

"I know you believe that."

"Because it's true. You can't get through things without moving forward."

Yarnell's lips curved. "I'll have to remember that one."

"Use it, it's free. You can even include it in the report

clearing me to go back to work."

"I might do that."

Cady stared hard at her. "You're releasing me?"

"I need to go over my notes once more and make a decision at that time."

"Because if you're greenlighting me you could give my supervisor a heads-up. That way he can start moving around assignments..." The woman's steady gaze halted Cady's words. "Or not." A grin crossed her lips when a tiny ding sounded from a timer on the desk. "It's been real, Doctor."

Dr. Yarnell rose and extended her hand. "I've been intrigued by our sessions. Do yourself a favor and be sure to reach out to someone if you experience any of the symptoms we discussed. PTSD can be one heck of a stumbling block, even for someone intent on moving forward."

Ten minutes later, Cady was out of the building and across the parking lot. She waited until she was safely in her Jeep before letting out a war-whoop. She hadn't been able to pin down the doctor but had good reason to believe she'd won the battle. That alone was worth the discomfort brought on by being beneath the microscope. Almost.

She was nearly home before she gave in to her urge and reached for her phone, pressing in Allen's number.

"Cady." His familiar voice was in her ear. "I was just going to call."

Passing a slow-moving tractor trailer, she said, "Did Yarnell contact you? Because I think she's clearing me to return to work."

He grunted. "The PC thing to say is take all the time you need to heal, your job will be here when you come back, yada yada. But I'm not going to lie, two deputy marshals short is a stretch, even with help from surrounding offices."

"I told her to let you know right away. So you could get a head start on shifting the assignments."

"If and when she releases you, there are protocols to be followed. I'll hear from the district headquarters and only then will you show your face around here, are we clear?"

Feeling slightly deflated, she said, "I know. But if you don't hear today, it'll probably be tomorrow."

"I'll let you know. And don't let me catch you camping out on the federal courthouse steps or I'll sic security on you."

"Pretty sure I can outrun them. You said you were about to phone me," Cady reminded him, slowing as a deer bounded out of a ditch and across the blacktop.

"About something else entirely. And I apologize in advance. I should have checked up on this sooner."

"On what?"

"That name you gave me last winter. Stan Caster."

The reminder of the surviving accomplice in her father's bank robbery three decades ago managed to pierce her earlier euphoria. "Right. You said he was being released soon from Butner. Did you hear from the warden?"

"No, because he had a heart attack last month and still hasn't returned to work. Caster got out ten days ago. I'm sorry about this, Cady. I made a note on my calendar to be watching for the warden's call and realized today I hadn't heard a thing. I didn't find out about it until I contacted the facility this afternoon."

Shit. Caster had landed back in prison to serve the rest of his sentence after violating the terms of his early release by harassing Cady's mother six and a half years ago. Upon the heels of that thought came another. What if the man was behind Alma's complaints about a trespasser at the cabin? It was a leap. But not impossible.

Allen was speaking again. "I spoke to Caster's parole officer. The ex-con is living with his mother in West Canton."

The town was in Haywood County, around twenty minutes from her home. Far too close for comfort. "Maybe I'll start asking around. It's not like I don't have time on my hands."

"I thought you said your return was imminent."

She smiled as she pulled up to the gates in front of her acreage. She parked to get out and open them, before driving through and stopping again to close them behind her. "Admit it, you miss me."

"I miss having five functioning deputy marshals. Seriously, if we get a release from the psychologist you're good to start as soon as possible. I've got warrants piling up and not enough hands to manage them."

Moments later they disconnected and Cady pulled to a stop in the drive next to Ryder's official car.

After the place had been shot up during a case she'd worked three months earlier, the renovations on the property had been extensive. Her landlord had modernized the entire house, added a third bedroom, and, most importantly, built a double garage in place of the previous carport.

She got out of the vehicle, wincing a little when she felt a twinge in her ribs. She had three more weeks before she could lift weights. Cady felt like her muscles were turning to mush.

No canines came racing across the yard to meet her, so she assumed they were inside with Ryder. Climbing the steps to the front porch, she went in the door and took off her boots. Hero, her German shepherd mix, got up from his sprawled position on the floor and came over to greet her. She got in no more than a couple of pats before he returned to the side of Sadie, Ryder's golden Lab and plopped down again.

Cady walked through the family room into the kitchen. Ryder was standing at the stove where he was stirring something sizzling in a pan. The smell explained the dogs' avid interest. She came up behind him, slipped her arms around his waist and hugged him. He smiled over his shoulder.

"Is that for finding a hunk in your kitchen or because said hunk is making you dinner?"

"Why can't it be both?"

"Tacos," he said by way of explanation.

"Perfect."

"You're just in time to make the salad."

She dropped her arms. "There's my impeccable sense of timing again." But Cady didn't mind. She was pretty worthless at cooking but adept at opening cans of soup or chopping vegetables.

"How'd the appointment go?"

"In terms of sheer hell, with my stay in the hospital a ten, it was a fifteen. Nothing like a head doc stomping around in your mind to help you work up an appetite. It paid off, though. The doctor was noncommittal, but I think she's going to okay my return to the job. Maybe tomorrow. I don't know how long it takes to get through the bureaucracy but—" She stopped, noting the rigid set to his shoulders. Realized what caused it. "It was going to happen sooner or later."

"Right." He stirred the meat once more, turned down the heat, and placed a lid on the pan before turning to face her. "Sooner's better."

"You're telling me." Cady took a knife from the drawer and veggies from the refrigerator. Between washing and chopping them, she gave him an abbreviated version of the meeting, leaving out the part about the effects of trauma on her personal life. She didn't need a therapist to recognize the source of her avoidance of intimacy. Her relationship with Ryder was uncharted territory.

"Oh." Belatedly, she recalled what Alma had told her. "My aunt wondered if you could send a car by her place at night for a while. She's had a couple of instances of a vehicle coming up her drive late at night and thinks once someone was prowling around."

He dumped some cheese in a dish. Reaching for the tortillas sitting on the counter, he placed them on a paper towel and warmed them in the microwave. "Once could be an accident. Twice, not so much. I'll put a call in later."

"And coincidentally, the incidents began after Stan Caster was released from Butner recently."

Ryder moved the pan from the heat and turned the burner off. "Caster. He was one of your dad's accomplices in the bank robbery thirty-odd years ago."

"The only survivor of the three."

"Right. I think it's been about six years since your mom filed a complaint about him when my dad was sheriff. He broke into her house, roughed her up. Made some threats."

Tension raked Cady's muscles. And she hadn't known a thing about it. Six years ago, she'd been assigned to the St. Louis office, a comfortable distance from her home state, which had held no pleasant memories for her. "He seemed to think she knew where the missing money from the robbery was. What are the chances he's given up that hope? I might pay him a visit. Get a feel for his intentions."

Hero rose and repositioned himself at Cady's feet. Eyed her hopefully. "You're not going to be happy with anything I drop, pal." He had a canine's disdain for vegetables, carrots, especially.

"Might be best to let the local law enforcement handle things, if you do get a line on him," Ryder observed.

"And say what? Welcome to the neighborhood? The police would have no reason to speak to him. He's completed his sentence. But I need to assess if he's still a threat to my mom."

"What's his last known address?"

Cady went in search of a bowl and placed the salad inside it. "He's living with his mother in West Canton."

He took out a couple of plates and fixed two tacos for each of them, carrying them over to the island. "If only you had an in with the sheriff of Haywood County."

She set the salad on the counter and sat down on one of the stools. "I hear he's pretty busy. Rescuing cats in trees and kidnap victims and whatnot."

"Mostly whatnot. And the rescue was unnecessary. I was little more than a conduit to a ride share."

Cady picked up a taco and bit into it. Wondered why food always tasted better when she didn't have to prepare it herself. "What I was saying. Sorta like an Uber app." She didn't quite manage to dodge the elbow he aimed her way. "You can rest easy. I promise I will never again let myself be captured by a crazy tattoo artist and chained in a mine."

"Very specific, but that works for me. I'm going to hold you to it."

It was a simple vow to make, Cady reflected as she polished off the taco and started on her salad. She'd visited Paul Chester again yesterday. He'd remain off work for far longer than her, having suffered complications from the drug cocktail he'd repeatedly been injected with. They'd had a close call. And even with their once-captor behind bars, she drew some comfort from never having to see Joseph Wiley again.

12

Stan Caster was surprisingly easy to find. Cady got out of her Jeep and surveyed the tiny home bearing the house number she was seeking. It was one of seven on the dirt road, all in varying stages of decay. It'd fared somewhat better than its neighbors. The yard appeared cared for, and someone had given the house a fresh coat of bright yellow paint. But the shingles curled on the sagging roof, and one of the front windows had been replaced with plywood.

A twenty-year-old Pontiac sat on a bare patch of lawn. There were no signs of life from the surrounding homes, but it was barely seven. Cady had wanted to get here before Caster went to work, if indeed he'd found a job.

Studying the house, she glimpsed movement behind the lace curtain of the remaining front window. She started up the ancient paved walk toward the equally cracked porch. Knocked on the door.

It was opened by a stooped woman who Cady pegged to be in her eighties. Her hair was neatly curled in a style fashionable five decades earlier, and she wore a bright printed blouse over white slacks. "Hello." Her smile was friendly, but she didn't unlock the screen door. "Can I help you?"

"I'm sorry to bother you at this hour, ma'am. I understand that Stan Caster is living here. I'd like to speak to him."

"Oh, dear. He's not an early riser, I'm afraid. He usually doesn't get up for hours yet."

"I didn't want to miss him in case he needed to get to work."

"Not today." She peered at Cady with shrewd blue eyes. "What did you say your name was?"

"Cady Maddix."

She blinked once, and at that moment, Cady realized the woman recognized her surname, although her expression didn't change. "Well, why don't I go back and see if he might be awake. If you don't mind waiting."

"No, ma'am."

The inner door closed, and she cooled her heels long enough to wonder if the woman was going to return. But after ten minutes or so, it reopened, this time revealing a man with long gray hair clad in jeans and a tee he was in the process of pulling over his head.

"Well, well." He unlocked the exterior door and came out onto the tiny porch, letting it bang behind him. "Don't need to see no ID. You got your daddy's look about you. It's like seeing Lonny Maddix's face on a woman's body."

Her eyes narrowed as he raked her figure with his gaze. "Sorry to interrupt your beauty rest. I'm sure it's a treat to sleep in after years of prison hours."

"Anything's better than that hellhole." He leaned a shoulder against the frame of the screen, which shuddered under his weight. "What'd you want?" The words were spoken around a yawn, as he scrubbed one hand along his unshaven jaw.

"I just came to introduce myself. And to let you know that my mother isn't as vulnerable as she was the last time you went to see her." She smiled thinly. "It'd be a mistake to visit her now that you're out."

"Heard you was a marshal. Guess you think that makes you something. All it makes you is a bitch with a badge."

"I'm a bitch who keeps her word," she corrected him. "Stay away from my mother or you'll deal with me."

He crossed one bare foot over the other and folded his arms across his muscled chest. The act made the dragon tat on his forearm flex and ripple. Her back itched just looking at it.

"What? Gonna kill me like you did your ol' man?" He shook his head slowly. "Damnedest thing I ever heard. Always wondered what something like that does to a kid. Lonny wasn't a bad sort. Sure as hell didn't deserve to die like a dog in his own kitchen."

"I'm sure the two of you had a lot in common."

"One thing we had in common was the take from that bank." His smile revealed poor dental hygiene and a missing front incisor. "Cops never recovered it. I got caught the first week. Lonny was loose for months. And all that money…" He made a gesture. "Poof. Like it went up in smoke. 'Cept that don't happen."

Her stomach clenched. Caster didn't sound like a man who'd put his past—and the missing cash—behind him. "I guess the answer died with him."

"Did it, though? You was just a little kid. You wouldn't know. But Lonny visited your place often, even when he shoulda known the cops would watch it. Your mama was always a looker, but he kept plenty of pussy on the side, so why would he risk it? Unless he wasn't checking on her, but the money he stashed in that house."

Apparently, the idea that Lonny had wanted to visit his only child hadn't occurred to the man. Perhaps Caster had known him well enough to disregard the thought. Cady had already concluded that her father didn't give a damn about her. That fact had been hammered home after learning that before he was captured, he'd once draped his three-year-old daughter over his shoulders and head as he escaped, using her as a human bullet catcher.

"Even back then banks were marking bills and utilizing dye packs," she said bluntly. "Forgive me if I don't believe either of you had the brains or the time to overcome those efforts. And neither would anyone who might have found the money. But it was never recovered or traced. That means it was likely destroyed."

"You're just like every cop I ever met. Think you're smarter than you are. Why you think we picked that bank in Black Mountain?" He leaned forward conspiratorially. "Lonny had someone inside."

His words stopped her cold. She'd never seen the police reports on the crime and because hers was a personal rather than professional interest, she wouldn't go looking for them. But she knew that would have been a lead exhaustively examined by law enforcement.

"You have a one-track mind where the bank take is concerned. I'm sure you've spent the better part of your time inside thinking about it." She smiled tightly. "Makes me worry about the rehabilitative nature of prison. But my mother has struggled financially all her life. There was never any sudden financial windfall."

"Maybe 'cuz she still has the money, ever think of that? You probably believe the feds, assuming he left it with his squeeze, Lily Prentice. All because she moved to South Carolina and bought herself a new car. They was all over her and still never found most of what we stole." His smile was ugly. "Likely 'cuz she never had it. Which means it's still out there."

This was news to Cady. But it didn't change her message for him. "My mom's off-limits. Stay away from her and we won't have a problem."

She was nearly to her Jeep when Caster yelled after her, "I ain't the only one knows 'bout that cash. Can't hold me responsible if someone else takes an interest."

She opened the door, bracing one hand on the roof before turning back toward him. "Believe me, if *anyone* bothers my mother with this, you're the first I'll come looking for."

"That was fast," Allen observed when Cady strode into the USMS offices that afternoon, fifteen minutes after his call. "I know you weren't camped out on the steps. What'd you do, drive here last night and sleep in your car?"

Her meeting with Caster had left her hyped-up with adrenaline and no outlet. She'd finally driven to Asheville and had lunch in a local mall filled with shrieking teens. When Allen had called, she'd bolted from the place like a racehorse out of the gate.

"Naw, she slept in those tunnels she got familiar with a few weeks ago." Miguel grinned hugely as he bounded up from his desk to wrap one arm around her shoulders in a quick hug. He held a sandwich in his other hand. "I hear they're cozy. Good to have you back. I'm tired of carrying the load."

"Now you know how I've felt for almost two years." But she couldn't keep a smile from her face as she went to her desk and opened the bottom drawer to drop her purse inside it. Then sent a pointed look at Miguel when she found it full of empty chip and sandwich wrappers. "Did the government outlaw waste containers in USMS facilities while I was gone?"

"Oh. Yeah." He ambled over and gathered up the rubbish and stuffed it in the nearest wastebasket. "I sort of spread out my workspace while you were gone."

"Spread out your trash, anyway." She checked for crumbs left behind. The last thing she needed was to find a mouse in her purse at the end of the day. "I was in the area," she answered Allen belatedly.

"You won't hear me complaining. I need you both in my office."

When they were seated in front of Allen's desk, he handed them each a file. "I'll be rearranging warrants as personnel gets reassigned," he said, "but this one is a priority. Frank Burgess. Jackson County reached out to us a yesterday. The press has been having a heyday with it. They're calling him The Cremator."

"Burgess. Why is that name familiar?" Feeling seriously out-of-the-loop, Cady flipped open the cover of the file and began reading.

"Maybe Ryder mentioned him." Allen's chair squeaked as he leaned back in it. "Those tunnels you chased Stallsworth into attached to a storm drain. A witness in the vicinity claimed to see a person loading something into a dark-colored van around the time you two went missing. Burgess owns a vehicle fitting that description, and Ryder followed up on it."

Now she recalled hearing the story. "This is the guy with

the dead woman in his meat locker, right?" A pretty gruesome tale and a reminder that there were worse fates than what she and Paul had survived. Not that Wiley hadn't had similar plans for them.

"Right. His incinerator was running and the remains inside were determined to be deer carcasses. But there was cremated debris in the second chamber of the furnace. That evidence was analyzed and the lab said there were remnants from both animal and humans."

Her gaze bounced up. "Could they tell how many different victims?"

"The last I heard, they were still working on that. Extracting DNA from cremated remains is dicey. And time-intensive."

"Did they ID the woman in the locker?" Miguel asked. "Ah." He turned a page. "Here it is. Deborah Patten."

Cady turned to the sheet he was looking at and scanned it. "Looks like she lived around Sylva until she was eighteen and then went to California, where she was imprisoned three years later for fraud." Upon her conviction, Patten's fingerprints and DNA would have been entered into federal and state databases. She glanced at Allen. "Wonder what brought her back to the area?"

"Turned out to be an ill-fated move," Miguel observed. "The ME classified cause of death as head trauma by a blunt instrument. But first, Patten was beaten with an unknown heavy object that had a sharp edge. Possibly a brick."

"The coroner did find minute clay particles in some of the wounds," Allen affirmed.

Cady studied photos of the body, her brow furrowed. "Any relationship between Burgess and Patten?"

"None discovered during the investigation conducted by the Jackson County Sheriff's Office. Her family left North

Carolina years ago and most of them are dead. Just a couple of cousins were found and questioned. They didn't recognize Burgess's name or likeness."

"There may not be a connection between them," Miguel pointed out. "Someone else might have killed her and Burgess was just the cleanup guy."

"Pretty slick way to get rid of bodies," she agreed, turning to another page. Stopped to skim when she saw the list of missing persons in the state. The report was depressingly thick. She did a quick check and determined Patten wasn't included in it. The thought that no one had missed the woman was disheartening.

"Ryder said there was nothing tying Burgess's van to Paul and my disappearance."

"That's the only reason you're on this warrant," Allen replied. "We got a handful of leads on van owners without alibis for the night you went missing, but no evidence was found in any of the vehicles, including Burgess's."

Mindful that it was already well past noon, Cady stood. "Miguel can fill me in on the rest of the file while I drive."

"Where are we going?" The man rose lazily. "And why are you driving? If I remember correctly, on our last day together—"

"Clean slate," she said crisply and retrieved her purse, which hopefully was rodent-free. "Three weeks apart means we start over on trading off driving."

"Even given a rule you just made up on the spot, why begin with you?"

"To show your delight in having me back?" But she was smiling as they left the offices. She was heading out on a new case while listening to Miguel bitch. It was great to be back.

"STILL NOT SURE what you hope to accomplish here."

Cady pulled to a stop in front of Burgess's locker and studied the building.

Miguel continued, "The Jackson County Sheriff's Office has been all over this scene. They had someone posted here for two weeks after the man disappeared."

"So you said." He'd read aloud from the file on the drive over. The search for Frank Burgess had been thorough. Cady didn't let the knowledge bother her. Many of their warrants were for fugitives other law enforcement entities had failed to find. "We have to start somewhere." She got out of the Jeep. Seeing where and how he lived could help them build a picture of the bandit. Knowing him was the first step toward predicting his movements.

Police tape still encircled the structure. Ducking under it, she approached the door and spotted the new padlock. Duplicate keys had been included in the case folder. She dug in her jeans pocket and, moments later, she swung the door open and walked through it, Miguel on her heels.

The interior was dated, with a couple of glassed-door coolers and a small chest freezer pulled away from the walls in the front area. Checking all of them, Cady found them empty and the units unplugged.

"Fun fact I didn't mention, there were assorted meat products kept in these." Miguel raised the lid to the freezer. Peered in, then slammed it shut again. "They were collected and sent to the lab to be analyzed."

Following his meaning, she grimaced. "Ensuring the ingredients were from animals and not humans?"

He lifted a shoulder. "Be another way to get rid of the victims."

"I assume they checked out."

"Yeah. That's one thing Burgess isn't guilty of."

The place had been thoroughly searcheded, Cady noted. The paneling was torn off. The carpet in the office she'd poked her head into had been pulled up. The drawers were sitting atop the desk, and the false ceiling tiles were stacked in a corner. The next room, with its saws and large sinks had been treated similarly.

"Like I said, nothing to be found here."

Moving more quickly now, Cady crossed to the cooler door and tugged it open. The room had a cement floor, ancient block walls, and a stained ceiling. She had a mental image of the crime scene photo of the body suspended from one of the overhead hooks and turned away. "Let's lock up and take a look at the house."

Similar disarray awaited them when they entered the home. Scanning the front room, Cady observed a sagging recliner, a small ancient TV, and a bookcase containing only a bible and some jigsaw puzzles. The covers to the heat vents were unscrewed and set aside.

She moved into the kitchen. The cupboards were empty, their contents sitting on the cracked vinyl counter. There were crumbs on the table, as if Burgess hadn't cleaned up after his last meal. Opening the door of the small refrigerator, she saw only a half a stick of butter.

"Not much in the bedroom," Miguel reported, rejoining her. "A couple of changes of clothes. A bed that should have been replaced twenty years ago. Pretty Spartan-like existence."

The description resonated. There was little to hint at the man's personality because the place was devoid of pictures or decorations of any kind. She studied the few dishes on the counter. The glasses were chipped and plain. But there was more rice than she would have thought any household needed. Five boxes, only one opened. Maybe that's what the fugitive had existed on, along with products from the locker next door.

Past the kitchen was a cramped hallway, with a door to the cellar on the left and a metal waste can to the right. She glanced in the container as she went by. Then turned to take another look, bumping into Miguel, who was following close behind her.

"I understand if you don't want to go downstairs. You wait here and I'll…"

Cady bent down to take a bread bag out of the can. Held it up. "Someone's been here."

"How would they get inside?"

"I don't know." She gave him a light shove, and he backed up so she could squeeze by him. "But there are crumbs on the table. See?" She pointed to the particles she'd noticed earlier. "The evidence team would have bagged the trash, so the sack is new."

"Someone could have picked up a piece of litter outside, dropped it in here on the second or tenth walk-through."

"Maybe." The deputies would have returned to the scene more than once. "But would they have dumped the remaining crumbs there before they threw the bag away?"

"Even after the sheriff withdrew the guard, there's no way to get in here without a key." He turned to head to the basement door again.

Miguel snapped on the light and proceeded down the steps, leaving Cady to follow in his wake. She shoved aside a sense of déjà vu. This was unlike the root cellar she'd often been locked in as a child when she was at her grandfather's mercy. Those walls had been earthen, not stone, and the room smaller. More claustrophobic. She rounded the staircase and mentally steeled herself as her gaze swept the area. But still, seeing the rusty chains and handcuffs attached to the wall had a frigid finger tracing over her nape. She took a deep breath. Blew it out, seeking to forestall the ghosts that threatened to swoop in.

"Not much to see." Miguel made an abrupt about-face and headed for the stairway.

"Relax. I'm not going to have a fit of vapors at the sight of the chains." Her voice was light. The smudge of memory that accompanied her words wasn't. The bruises from the manacles had faded. The recollection of how they'd felt would take longer.

She moved by him to check out the dark corners of the space. There was a grimy narrow window on two sides. Other than some old boxes and cleaning items in a pile against one wall, the place was empty. Cady turned and started for the stairs. Stopped when she realized Miguel wasn't following. She retraced her steps. "What's wrong?"

"Maybe nothing," he murmured, staring at the objects fixedly. "I could have sworn the pictures in the file showed that stuff heaped near the front wall and not the back one."

"Maybe it was moved during one of the searches," she said half-heartedly. But she could think of no reason to do so. Together they drifted toward the boxes stacked three high. "The report said the cartons contained only old paint cans and tools." She tilted her head at the stack. Each box was not quite square with the one below it. Balancing herself with a hand on the wall, she stepped on the corner of the bottom one. When it held her weight, she ascended the next.

"What are you..." The rest of Miguel's question trailed off as she crawled atop the third carton, where she had to crouch to avoid hitting her head. She could barely see through the filmy glass in the window. Running her hands over the rotting frame, she found it loose but was unable to pull it away. "Do you have a pocket knife?"

A moment later, he slapped one into her hand. "I don't get what you're going for here."

She pulled out the largest blade and began working it in the crack between the frame and its casing, prying gently. "Just trying to figure if... ah." The window tilted forward, and she caught it with both hands. "Take this, will you?" Carefully she handed it to Miguel.

Cady folded the blade into the knife and shoved it into her jeans pocket before propping her elbows on the crumbly concrete casing and leveraging her body into the opening, wincing as her ribs shrieked. Slowly she inched her way through until she was outside. Then she turned and peered at her colleague.

"Are you going to Houdini your way inside again, or was that the end of your act?"

"Funny guy. I'm saying again, someone was in this house recently who left the empty bread sack and the crumbs. And whoever it is gets in and out through here."

"Not Burgess." Miguel lowered the frame and leaned it against the stone wall. "He weighs close to two hundred. He wouldn't fit through that space."

"No. Not him." She reversed course. He reached up and guided her feet as she searched for the footholds she'd used for her ascent. She rapped her head on a rafter and swore. When she was halfway down, he handed her the window she'd removed and, not without difficulty, she worked it into the casing. "Maybe an accomplice of his has been coming and going since his escape."

"For what purpose?" he countered. "There was nothing

of value found here that first night or in any of the later searches."

He was right. But perhaps the intruder had been looking for something else.

They went back upstairs and out the front door. Cady relocked the padlock, then, as an afterthought, dug in her pocket for Miguel's knife. She handed it to him. "Always prepared. I bet you were a Boy Scout."

"Eagle Scout, actually."

Smiling, she jogged down the steps, genuinely amused. "Why does that not surprise me?"

She was still imagining her colleague with a chestful of merit badges as they got into the Jeep. She backed up and turned it around before attempting the narrow lane again. She slowed when she caught a flash of white in the rearview mirror.

"Don't turn around," she said to Miguel. "Do you see anything in that overgrown brush directly in back of us?"

He used the side mirror to look as she nosed the vehicle toward the drive. "No, what was I supposed to... ah." He was quiet until she turned down the rutted lane. "I got a glimpse of something light-colored. A shirt maybe. Close to the ground. Think someone's out there?"

"Let's find out." She cruised to a stop by a thick stand of firs. She got out and went to the back of the Jeep and opened it. Rummaged in her equipment bag for a pair of field glasses. Miguel joined her. They walked to the woods at the end of the lane and began circling back to the clearing. They didn't pause until they were parallel with the far corner of the property. Cady sank to her knees, raising the binoculars to peer through them.

"Anything?"

After a minute, she lowered the glasses and handed

them to him, shifting uncomfortably on the rocky soil. "It's a woman. Or a smallish man with long hair."

After a moment, he said, "Could be a teen."

"Maybe," Cady agreed. She hadn't gotten a look at the person's face. Just a general sense of her build. Light-colored top and dark pants, possibly denim. A slight figure. And she seemed to be waiting for them to leave.

"I'm going to try to come up behind her. Text me if he or she moves."

"Be careful. She may not be alone."

Cady rose, brushing the dirt from her jeans and then took off at a crouch, making sure to keep to the most densely wooded areas. Miguel texted once to tell her the figure was still there. When she finally got to the area she'd last seen the stranger, she responded.

> Changing course. Heading toward house now.
>
> Don't trip over her. C tall spindly pine? Keep it directly in front of you. She's behind bushes 5° N.

She dropped to all fours and began approaching more carefully. Using the top of the fir as her beacon, she inched closer until she saw the soles of tattered sneakers. She stopped, shifting position so she could follow the shoes to a pair of legs encased in ragged jeans. There was a long dark tangle of hair spilling down a narrow back in a baggy tee. Definitely female. And maybe as young as Miguel had guessed. The figure rose to her knees, then stood up, bending to brush at her pants before walking toward the home.

Cady straightened too, pausing long enough for the stranger to move several yards away before following again.

Her shirt caught on a bramble and she paused to yank it away, sending a shudder through the thicket. A bird fluttered out of it, squawking its annoyance. The female halted, then whirled around, eyes wide. Catching sight of Cady, she bolted. The stranger was no longer headed for the house but toward the edge of the cliff next to it. She followed. "Stop! Deputy U.S. Marshals!"

The woman put on a burst of speed. She wouldn't run that direction if she didn't think it represented escape. Maybe she knew of a trail down the steep slope.

She heard the crunch of gravel. Realized without looking that Miguel had joined the chase. The other woman had the advantage of knowing the area. Cady had the advantage of speed. She closed the gap between them inches at a time, ignoring the stabbing pain in her side. Then she was a yard closer. A foot. She could almost reach out and touch her. Almost.

Without a thought, she launched herself, hitting the stranger in the back and taking her down in a tangle of limbs. The other female fought wildly, and Cady's head rocked when she caught an elbow in the face. She grabbed one of her arms, twisted it behind her back until the stranger screamed silently, her face a mask of frustration and rage. With no little difficulty, Cady flipped her over, pressing one knee to the small of her spine as she subdued her. "Stop fighting! We just want to talk to you."

Miguel ran up to them. "What part of limited duty do you not understand?" He helped her pull the woman to her feet. She was older than they'd thought. Early twenties, maybe.

"Who are you?" Cady hated that she was panting. Three weeks of forced inactivity had taken a toll. And her ribs were screaming.

The female glared at her defiantly, giving her head a violent shake.

"Are you hurt?" Miguel gave her a concerned smile. "You went down pretty hard."

Her expression softened appreciably when she looked at Miguel's too-handsome face. Cady resisted the temptation to roll her eyes. But if his looks elicited more cooperation, she was willing to let him take the lead.

Shaking her head again, the woman pushed her long dark hair away from her face and yanked hard at the arm still in Cady's grasp.

"You can let her go. She won't run." He smiled again. "Will you tell me your name?"

The stranger reached for his hand and began tracing one finger over his palm. Spelling, Cady realized.

"R-I-N-A," he repeated. "Is it pronounced Reena?" She nodded shyly. "That's pretty. Do you have a last name?" She frowned and looked down.

"How do you know Frank Burgess?"

A shoulder bob was Miguel's only answer. "Do you live with him?"

Another nod, but she still didn't meet his gaze. "Are the two of you related?"

She gave a half shrug.

Cady studied the younger woman. The clothes she wore were well-used and swallowed her slender form. The jeans bore tears across the knees and were frayed at the hem where they'd dragged on the ground. The sneakers looked too large and were kept in place with safety pins instead of laces. The T-shirt was more of a dingy gray than white. Her gaze sharpened as she looked at the skin peeking through the rips. It was scarred in a way that puzzled her, mottled with tiny pockmarks. Most were white with age, but others were red and freshly bruised. She took out her cell and snapped a picture of the young woman.

Rina scowled at her. Slipping the phone in her pocket, Cady pointed at her injuries. "What happened?"

The woman caught Miguel's hand again and began spell-ing. R-I-S. When she finished, she seemed reluctant to drop it.

"R-I-S? What..."

"The rice," she murmured to Miguel, recalling the boxes on the counter. "Did Frank use it to punish you?"

Nodding, Rina folded her hands together and lifted her eyes to the sky.

"You had to kneel in it and pray," she guessed. Not so hard to believe that the man was a sadist, considering what else they'd learned about him.

Maybe a few hours in the dark will help you remember not to take what don't belong to you. The memory blew across her mind like an icy breeze. Abuse came in all forms. Recalling her grandfather's had her softening toward the other woman. "Are you able to talk?"

Rina shook her head, placing both hands on her throat. "Is your throat hurt?" Cady touched her own neck. The woman nodded.

"How long ago was it damaged?" Another shrug. Then Rina held her hand out, indicating a height to midchest. Meaning the injury had occurred when she was a child?

There could be many reasons for the condition, Cady mused, considering the young woman. Cancer. Head or neck trauma. But she couldn't quite push aside the thought that continuous choking often resulted in a damaged larynx.

"Is Burgess the one who injured your throat?" Miguel's voice sounded tight.

Frowning again, Rina shook her head. "Where is he now?"

She shrugged in answer to Cady's question. "Does he have another home?"

Rina looked confused at Miguel's question, but she lifted her shoulders again.

"Does he have family? Children?" he pressed. The woman didn't respond.

"Who did he chain up in his cellar?" Rina stilled, like a doe sensing a hunter. His voice softened. "You?"

A head jerk was his only answer. Then she gestured with her hands, turning them back and forth.

"Sometimes?" he guessed. She nodded again.

"Do you know any of Frank's friends?" Cady asked. When Rina looked puzzled, she tried again. "Did you meet anybody who did business with his locker?" Frustration surged when the woman didn't answer.

"We need to find Frank." Miguel's tone was sympathetic. "What can you tell us or show us that will help us learn more about him?"

Rina cocked her head, seeming to mull over his words. Then her expression brightened. She captured his hand and started toward the clearing again, tugging at him when he moved too slowly. Miguel raised his brows and shot Cady a look. She shrugged and tagged along behind them. She recalled the bread wrapper in the man's trash. The nearly empty refrigerator.

Her gut said the woman was yet another victim of Burgess.

Rina stopped and squatted in front of a thicket, pointing under it. Cady drew closer and dropped to her knees beside the woman who was filling her fist with dirt, then letting it trickle out, showing her grimy hand to Miguel.

"I don't understand. What is this?"

Silently echoing Miguel's question, Cady pushed back the closest branches and reached down to scoop up some soil. Then she jumped, dumping it out again. "Jesus!"

Her colleague looked at her like she was crazy, but Rina stirred her fingers in the debris Cady had released and held up what had first looked like a pebble.

But it wasn't a pebble. It was a partial human molar. And there were several others.

"Holy..." Ever fastidious, Miguel leaned away when Rina tried to give it to him. Cady sank down and moved aside more branches to see further inside the bushes.

"I don't think this is dirt or sand. It looks like ashes." And what she'd first assumed were rock and pieces of wood looked an awful lot like burned bone.

The other woman tapped her arm. When she had Cady's attention she slapped her chest then mimed carrying something heavy. Stopping and dumping it beneath the brush. Then she pointed in several other directions and sat back on her heels, looking proud of herself.

"You put this here?" She nodded.

"Did Frank Burgess tell you to get rid of the ashes?" Another nod.

"The whole property is a damn graveyard," Miguel muttered in disbelief.

Feeling a little sick, Cady scrubbed her palms on her jeans. "We're going to have to get cadaver dogs up here." She'd never considered what the man had done with the carcasses after incineration. But cremation didn't reduce an entire body to ash. She knew that much, although she'd need to inquire more into the process.

Rina mimed eating, then rubbed her stomach.

"There isn't a lot of food left at Frank's, is there?" Not

much more than the crumbs that Cady had noted on their walk-through. "Sorry. We don't have anything to eat."

She held out her hand in an unmistakable gesture.

"Take out some cash," Cady told Miguel.

"Why me?"

"Because my purse is in the Jeep." When he withdrew two twenties and a ten, she told Rina, "We want to know where Frank might go hide." When the woman shrugged, she jerked a thumb at Miguel. "He'll pay you if you can tell us about a place you know he's been before."

The woman eyed the bills avariciously. A moment passed. Then she used her finger to trace on Cady's arm. "T? I don't know what that means." Rina shook her head violently and traced the same sign. Then pressed her hands together and raised her eyes to the heavens. Understanding dawned. A cross. "Church?" Rina nodded. "You've seen Frank Burgess at a church?" Talk about the height of irony. "How long ago?"

Rina stretched out her arms. "A long time ago? More than ten years?" The woman nodded.

Cady looked at Miguel, who shrugged. "It's someplace to start, anyway. She'll have to take us there, though."

Rina got up and waved for them to follow her. Miguel shoved the money into the back pocket of his jeans. Regardless of whether or not the woman's tip panned out, they needed to feed her, Cady thought. And then convince her to voluntarily accompany them to the Asheville federal courthouse to do a proper interview with communication devices to make it easier to elicit information.

The three of them walked down the lane until they reached the Jeep. Miguel handed Cady the binoculars and she replaced them in her equipment bag before getting into the vehicle. He had seated himself in back with Rina, which might have been to make her more comfortable or to keep a closer eye on her. Either way, Cady approved. The woman was far too unpredictable.

They traveled no farther than eight miles before they were directed to a poorly maintained gravel road. But the journey had taken nearly forty minutes, as Rina had seemed uncertain of the directions she was giving Miguel. They'd backtracked and been re-directed so often that Cady was beginning to lose faith the woman knew where they were going. She glanced at Rina in the rearview mirror. Wide-eyed, she was turning her head from one way to the other as she took in the sights. Cady wondered how long it'd been since she'd been this far from Burgess's home. She gritted her teeth as the Jeep bounced over a particularly deep rut.

"Maybe you could try avoiding those," Miguel suggested helpfully.

"I'd have to avoid the entire road." She slowed, almost creeping along. The incline was getting steeper. If they failed to find the place this time, they'd head back to Asheville. It was already nearing five o'clock. Maybe the prospect of food would ensure the woman's cooperation.

"Turn right up by this bent tree." Miguel was interpreting Rina's directions. Cady did so, and now they were on a lane. One she hoped was going to take them to the church. Maybe there would be a pastor they could speak with. Records to examine. Or a way to track down other members of its congregation. Some of them would surely know Frank Burgess.

Cady could see a crooked cross on a steeple before she turned at the end of the drive into a small overgrown clearing that might have been graveled at one time. She stopped as the structure came into view. Recognition slammed into her. A vise squeezed her chest. She was dimly aware that she was breathing rapidly, struggling to get oxygen into her lungs, unable to tear her eyes off the nearby building.

"Cady? Cady?"

Miguel's voice didn't register. Neither did the fact that he'd followed Rina out of the vehicle. She concentrated on steadying herself. Dissipating the hammering in her heart. The moisture slicking her palms.

Her fingers clenched on the steering wheel in a death grip and still she couldn't look away. It was like staring into the eye of her nightmares. The church was dilapidated, with windows boarded over. Very little white paint remained, and only on the portion above the charred exterior. Someone or something had saved the building before the fire had devoured it.

And Joseph Wiley had faithfully re-created the church in the scene he'd tattooed on her back.

13

It was the shouting that finally broke shifted her focus. A man was heading toward Miguel and Rina, yelling and gesticulating wildly. She let out a shuddering breath and eased the Jeep closer to him. Then got out, closing her fists to still the trembling in her fingers. "Deputy U.S. Marshals," she called out, forcing herself forward on legs that felt wooden.

"I don't give a shit who you are." The man wheeled around and started for her. "This is private property and that building is a hazard. That's why it's fenced off."

She forced herself to glance at the church again, for the first time taking in the orange safety barrier fence staked around it. "What's your name?"

"Brian Morrison. I have a renovation and excavation outfit in Waynesville." His black cap was filthy but Cady could discern his business logo on it.

"Who owns this property?"

"Marc Ellis. He lives in South Carolina. He bought it six months ago. Hired me to demolish the structures on it."

The man looked capable of the latter. Forty-something, he had the build of a linebacker. Noting the bulge of his belly below the sledgehammer he cradled, she revised her estimation. Maybe one who'd been out to pasture for a few years.

"Place has been empty for years, and you can see what vandals have done." He waved his arm toward the church. "The stables were in worse shape so I started with them."

She looked beyond him to a partially cleared area. The buildings consisted of a series of three-sided stalls topped with a sagging roof. One such structure was semi-destroyed while the remaining two looked as if a stiff breeze would blow them over. A pickup and skid loader with his logo emblazoned on their doors were parked nearby. Two towering piles of debris had been formed. Another smaller heap was comprised of scrap metal.

"I'm to haul everything away after it's torn down and I have the right to keep anything of value."

"Like what?"

He shrugged a beefy shoulder. "Windows. Decent lumber. Truth be told, there's not much worth selling. The junk metal will probably fetch the most—lots of that in the old stables, with old hitching chains and rings. I'm getting paid regardless so... hey! Hey!" He broke off to shout at Rina. She'd climbed over the fence and was running toward the church. "Get out of there!"

The tightness in Cady's chest still hadn't completely eased. The property had a foreboding air, and it was infuriating to realize the sensation came from emotion rather than logic. The area was remote and encircled by woods. If she shifted a bit she could see an older two-story home in the distance. Rina had indicated that she'd met Burgess here at least ten years ago. From the disrepair of the structures, Cady suspected it might have been even longer than that.

She headed toward where Morrison stood conversing with Miguel. The other woman had turned back to walk toward the stables.

"...Ellis wants all the hazards removed as quickly as possible to avoid any legal responsibility for accidents."

"Who did he buy this property from?" Miguel asked as she drew even with them.

"You'd have to talk to him." The other man took off his cap and wiped his forehead. "That's all I know about the place."

"We'd like a look inside the building."

He shook his head at Miguel's words. "Can't allow that. Not unless you get a warrant that would let my client off the hook if you got hurt. Seriously, I've been in there. Hauled out some pews I thought I could sell for the wood. But anything not nailed down is long gone. What the last occupants didn't take with them, vandals made off with. Same with the house. Empty."

"Did you strip the home, too?"

The man nodded. "Pulled up the carpet and linoleum and removed floorboards and paneling that were still decent. I took out some windows I might be able to sell. I'll take it apart before bringing in equipment to knock it over. The floor joists and siding could be worth saving."

Cady turned to look for Rina. When she didn't see the young woman, she started toward the stables. Morrison jogged to catch up with her. "I can't have you enter the area I've been clearing. I don't want you messing with my system." It was the first time she'd heard anyone refer to piles of rubbish as a system but Cady shrugged. She narrowed her gaze, trying to imagine the space filled with animals and people caring for them. She couldn't summon the image. It was like someone had smeared this place with a sooty finger leaving it vaguely ominous.

"Cady!"

She startled at Miguel's voice as he caught up with her. "Have you seen Rina?"

"She went toward the stables." The sound of an engine starting followed her statement. "Dammit." Cady started running.

"Hey!" Morrison charged by them.

"Would she know how to—" Her half-finished thought was answered as Morrison's truck jerked forward, shuddered, and then roared out of the stable area and across the property, away from them.

As one, they veered toward the Jeep and got in it. Ignoring the red-faced gesticulating workman, Cady drove in the direction Rina had gone. When they reached the pickup, it was parked at the edge of the timber, still running. But with a sinking heart, she already knew the young woman was gone. Cady parked, and Miguel jumped out of the vehicle to check the truck. She ran into the woods, searching for a glimpse of Rina. But it was if the shadowy forest had swallowed her up. And it wasn't divulging its secrets.

"You had an eventful first day," Ryder observed after she gave him an abbreviated summary.

"A long one, anyway." Cady ignored the two canines gazing soulfully at her while she ate a leftover taco she'd reheated. "Rina admitted to hauling incinerated remains for Burgess and scattering them all over the property." She paused to take some more bites. "We spent a couple of hours looking for her. Even if it had been years since she was at that church, it was clear she was familiar with the area. It wasn't until after she took off that Miguel discovered the money he'd tucked in his back pocket was missing."

"She stole it?"

"Apparently. So she had no incentive to hang around. I put in a request for a forensic anthropologist and a cadaver dog so we can search the Burgess property for human remains. It's going to be a few days before the team can get here."

"Rina might have been feeding you a line from the beginning. Maybe she was an accomplice of Burgess's." Ryder leaned against the counter next to her, tipping a half-empty bottle of beer to his lips. She cast an appreciative eye over him. Barefoot, clad in jeans and a tee, he made an appealing picture. And not just because she'd spent the afternoon chasing after a mute, recalcitrant witness.

"I think she knows more than she communicated," Cady allowed. Finished with the first taco, she reached for the second. "She's young—no more than twenty-three or so. And I saw the scars on her knees. She also has marks that could be old wounds from the manacles." There was no way to know how long or often the woman had been imprisoned. "I get the feeling she wasn't allowed to complete her education, at least not after she went to live with Burgess." She was more intrigued than she wanted to admit about the woman's past.

"You feel sorry for her."

"Whatever connection she has to the fugitive, there's no discounting the abuse she's endured. So yeah, she's sympathetic." She chewed reflectively for a moment. "That doesn't mean I'm not going to hunt her down. Rina's the best lead we've gotten on the man." The only lead, she mentally corrected herself. "We've issued a BOLO in two counties. I don't see her running far, mainly because she doesn't have the resources."

He drained his beer. "There's the psychological aspect, as well."

Polishing off the taco, she swiped at her mouth with her napkin. "Exactly. It sounds like she was a child when she went to live with Burgess. The church where she said she saw him wasn't that far from his place. Her life has probably been contained within a few square miles." Add lack of education and abuse, and the woman would find it difficult to stray from her childhood boundaries. "Someone's going to know her, at least from her previous life. On the way home I called Marc Ellis, the new owner of the church property. He gave me the name of the seller. I'll contact him tomorrow." She hesitated, almost reluctant to bring up a change of subject. "I also stopped in and saw Stan Caster today."

She didn't need to possess any special powers of discernment to note his sudden stillness. "You went alone?"

"Broad daylight and his mother—a delightful woman—was home. We had a short chat."

Ryder's face was stamped with displeasure. But he didn't voice it, which was a point in his favor. "And?"

"He hasn't given up. He still has the money on his brain and my mom in his sights." She waved a hand when he would have spoken. "Not that he admitted it in so many words, but it was apparent from what he did say. He also tried to throw out a line about other people being interested in the cash, but I figure that's just a preemptive distraction. He claimed the FBI zeroed in on one of my dad's girlfriends back then when she made a big purchase without visible means to afford it. I looked her up, but she died ten years ago. She never went to prison, so even if the ex-con was telling the truth, the feds obviously didn't have enough to make a charge stick."

"I've got a car doing drive-bys at the cabin. Nothing to report on that end." He shook his head. "Caster has to be a special kind of stupid to think he can harass someone related to a deputy U.S. marshal. So, we can be fairly certain he'll have a frontman to mask any attempts he makes."

She told him about the man's claim that her father had a friend working at the Black Mountain Community Savings bank they'd robbed. He looked as skeptical as she'd felt at the news. "The FBI would have been all over that angle. Any relationship would have been tough to hide. I don't think of either Lonny or Caster as the discreet sort."

Cady got up and rinsed her plate before placing it in the dishwasher. To make up for ignoring the dogs while she ate — something Ryder was training her to do—she took out bacon doggy treats for each of them. While they snarfed them down, she surreptitiously pushed the clown doll her dog insisted on carrying everywhere under the lip of the cupboard. Even knowing Hero would retrieve it, she couldn't help hoping otherwise. The damn thing freaked her out.

Her palms went slippery when she recalled what else had freaked her out that day. Miguel would surely have seen the photos of the tattoos weeks ago, but he hadn't recognized the church today. And she hadn't mentioned it. Cady didn't know what it meant yet, but until she verified a connection, she was reluctant to bring it up.

She was almost sure the church had been the model for the scene tattooed on her back. But there was only one way to be certain. She schooled her expression to passivity before she turned to face Ryder again.

She was going to have to find a way to talk to Joseph Wiley.

∼

THE CELL ALERT wasn't hers, but it still brought her half-awake, searching the bedside table for her phone. Ryder's voice had her fingers stilling, and she rolled over to see him sitting up. She listened impatiently to his side of the conversation and then he disconnected, threw the covers back and slipped from the bed. "What's going on," she asked drowsily, propping herself up on one elbow. "Jailbreak?"

"No, thank God." He got up and started getting dressed with the aid of the flashlight app on his phone. "A camper went missing a few hours ago. A Phoebe Lansing."

"Maybe she realized how much she hated camping and found a hotel," Cady suggested, only half-jokingly. She enjoyed the outdoors but preferred a bed at the end of the day. She sat up, fully awake now.

"That's a possibility." Already dressed in his uniform pants and open shirt, he started searching in the closet for something. "Do you know where my hiking boots are? Dammit. At home," he answered his own question. "I'll stop by there on my way."

Ryder left the room then came back minutes later, freshly shaved, tucking his shirt into his pants. He paused to brush a kiss across her lips and then headed out the bedroom door. "Try to take it easier today."

"Good luck with the missing woman," she called after his retreating back. She had a flash of the female alone and afraid, hoping for rescue. Or maybe that was projection, based on her own recent experience. The memory darkened her thoughts. Since there was zero chance she'd be returning to sleep, she got up and headed to the shower. And began mentally preparing herself for facing her kidnapper again later that day.

14

"She wouldn't have just left," Ashley Perkins insisted again. She was scrubbing tears from her eyes, but her tone was firm. "We've planned this trip for weeks. We were going to take three days to hike the area. Cold Mountain and Black Balsam Knob for sure. Phoebe's an experienced hiker. We've organized an outing every month this summer to get in shape for doing a section of the Appalachian Trail in September."

"When did you notice her missing?" Ryder asked.

"About one thirty, when I got up to pee. I saw that her sleeping bag was empty and the flashlight was gone, so I figured I'd meet her coming from the restroom. But I didn't. And she wasn't there when I went in. I got back and she hadn't returned, so I woke up Tyler and Audrey Jensen." She nodded at the couple standing a distance away speaking to Ryder's chief deputy investigator Jerry Garza. "They hadn't seen her either. We looked around a little, then checked the vehicle." She pointed at the navy mid-sized sedan with a cargo rack parked in the single parking slot in front of their camp pad. "Her pack is still in the tent. From what I could tell nothing was taken from it. Her cell is under her pillow. I called her husband, Tim." Fresh tears sprang to Ashley's eyes. "Just on the crazy chance... but he hasn't heard from her since they spoke after dinner. Now he's freaked out and contacting everyone they know on the off-chance Phoebe phoned them."

Trepidation knotted his gut. His deputies' cars were parked with headlights on, splitting the darkness. He played his Maglite over the nearby wooded area. The private campground had two more public areas, but this space was on one of the more isolated loops. The other couple's tent was about fifteen yards away. Bushes and undergrowth provided a privacy screen between the tents and the lane for cars in back of the campsites.

"Show me the restroom." He followed her up the narrow road several hundred feet to the small brick building. Ryder was unable to make out the individual sites across the lane because of the dense vegetation.

"Do you know Phoebe's passcode on her cell?" When Ashley nodded, he said, "Let's go get it. I also want to see the rest of her belongings." As they made their way back to the site, he stopped for a moment to speak to Jerry.

"We'll need assistance canvassing the area." He was the oldest deputy in the office, a former colleague of Ryder's dad. But he was as canny a cop as Ryder had ever met.

"Call in another half-dozen deputies and reserves to help. I've sent a message to law enforcement in surrounding counties, too." Waynesville PD had already shown up to assist.

He was silent for a moment as he watched Audrey Jensen wrap her arms around Ashley. The four of them were from Sevierville, Tennessee. Ryder needed to talk to each of them individually. Learn their histories, the group dynamics. And then dive into Tim Lansing and his relationship with his wife. The man's alibi for last night.

The thoughts were automatic. You always looked hardest at those closest to the victim. Not that Ryder was sure yet that Phoebe Lansing *was* a victim. There could have been a fight with one of the others in her group. She might have hooked up with someone else in the campground. The possibilities were endless.

But he couldn't push away the memory of Cady's disappearance a few weeks ago. He had to follow protocol, but he wasn't going to waste valuable time on the hope they'd find the missing woman easily. "I'm going to request a SAR K-9."

15

Phoebe Lansing woke sluggishly. There was a light blinding her when she opened her eyes, so she threw up an arm to shield them. Then she realized three things simultaneously. She wasn't blindfolded. Her hands were free. And she was naked.

Panicked, she struggled to her feet and immediately whacked her head on something above her. Phoebe dropped to her butt again, the blow adding to the fuzziness. She was in a clear cube of some sort. Big enough that she could stretch her arms out and barely graze the ceiling and walls. Hope flickered. Glass was breakable. If she could only find something... She searched along her prison's seams. Found nothing. There were hinges and a latch in front. But the screws holding them in place were secure. The floor, though...there was some kind of grate beneath her, the slats too narrow to fit her fingers into. She spent long minutes trying to pry it out of its fittings. Failed.

Alarm welled, and she screamed. Lunged at the front of her cell and pounded on it. Threw her body against it time and again until she crumpled, winded, and crying great gulping sobs.

"Shh!"

Frightened, she pushed her fists against her mouth to stifle her cries while looking around wildly, expecting the person who'd kidnapped her. She hadn't seen a face, but from the size and breadth of his body she'd assumed it was a man. Had he come back?

"Be quiet."

Her eyes widened in horror. Not a man at all, but another woman next to her, in a cube like hers.

The stranger spoke again. "You don't want to wake them up. They'll hurt you. Save your strength. You'll need it."

"Who are you?" She tried to calm herself. Perhaps this person could help her. Maybe they could team up and escape together.

"It doesn't matter. It's easier if we don't know names."

Phoebe frowned. How could that make anything easier? "What is this place?"

"I'm not sure. They call it Life and Death."

16

"There's no reason in the world for you to ever get near Joseph Wiley again." Allen Gant's voice wasn't a shout, but it was louder than Cady had ever heard it before. "It's up to the federal prosecutor now, and we should steer clear."

She didn't remind him that if the time came for Wiley to stand trial, she'd be facing him in a courtroom. "A meet shouldn't taint the case if I'm asking him questions about an unrelated matter."

Allen looked to Miguel, as if for support. But he was gazing at the photos she'd requested from the kidnapping file. The ones showing the tattoos on her back. She knew from his silence that he'd recognized the church in the image.

"Wiley's refusing to speak to law enforcement. From what I hear, his attorney started squawking right away about resuming his medication protocol. He's going to pursue a diminished capacity case."

She doubted Wiley had been on meds when he'd ambushed and held them captive. His behavior had been explosive. But Ryder had told her about the man's past mental health history. She knew the hazards of medication noncompliance. Once patients were released, it became more difficult for their therapists to keep tabs on them.

"Who's the prosecutor?"

"Iden."

"I'll make you a deal." Cady paused to observe the flush mounting in Allen's face. "Talk to Iden, Wiley's lawyer, and his doctor. If any one of them don't agree, I won't mention it again." Recognizing the refusal on his lips, she added, "The church connects to Wiley and Rina, and according to her, it also links to Burgess. Wiley might be able to provide a lead on either one of them."

Allen stared at her unblinkingly. Without taking his gaze from her, he said, "Miguel. Give us a minute." When the door closed quietly behind him, Cady's supervisor spoke. "If you came to me with something solid, I still wouldn't like it, but I'd do everything I could to arrange this meeting with Wiley, because the job comes first. This..." He made a dismissive gesture. "You're on a fishing trip here."

"You know what they catch on fishing trips, Allen?" He looked away. "Fish. But first, you have to let me cast a line. I swear, if any of the others agree with you, I'll move on. And maybe they will. The doctor might think I'll be too triggering, or the attorney may believe we're trying to entrap his client or whatever. So, what's the holdup? Ask them and see. In the meantime, Miguel and I contacted Marc Ellis and got the name of the person who sold him the property. We'll be following up on the church and its members."

She hesitated, wondering whether she should press her luck. Forging ahead, she added, "I'd also like to see pictures of the other tattoos."

"How are those relevant to your warrant?"

"The one on my back seems to be. Fire. The burned church. According to Rina, that links to Burgess. Maybe there are other clues in Paul's tattoo. And the ones Wiley framed."

Allen slumped back in his chair. "You saw those?"

She didn't like to recall the moment she'd realized what they held. "Not closely. But when he had the spotlights angled to work on Paul, I'd get glimpses of them. It took me a while to realize they weren't just pictures."

Allen slicked a hand over his smooth head. "Well, that had to have freaked you out. I know they did DNA testing on the sleeping bag in the tunnel and some items left in the mine. It appears as though he was residing in both areas. Certainly, the investigation never turned up an address on him."

That would explain why he'd kept the frames in the mine, Cady thought. He had no permanent home. She wondered where he'd kept the other supplies he'd brought daily.

"I assume the tattoos were sent to the crime lab for DNA analysis." Although the only way they could be matched to a victim would be if the owner's DNA was in a federal database. Or if a family member had submitted samples to NamUs, the missing and unidentified person clearinghouse. "But you have pictures. And images in the digital file."

Allen stared at her for a long moment, expressionless. But she sensed the mental war waging within him. Finally, he sighed. "Fine." He opened his laptop and started typing commands. "I can trust your ability and judgment implicitly and still worry about you, Cady."

Something softened inside her. "I know."

"I'll present your idea to Iden straight-forwardly. But I'm praying she says no."

"I appreciate it." She got up and went out the door. As she went in search of Miguel, she didn't even know herself which answer she was hoping her supervisor would eventually have for her.

"Yes, this is the Mary Dornbier who sold a parcel in Jackson County to Marc Ellis recently." The woman on the other end of the phone spoke in clipped, no-nonsense tones. "I don't know how that could interest U.S. marshals."

Cady answered easily. "The property may involve a case we're working, ma'am. It would be helpful if we could discover the owner of the church for the period we're interested in."

"Well, if it was within the last eighty years or so, I can tell you. My father, Jeremiah Higgins. And his father before him."

A jolt of excitement worked through her. "Was your father a pastor?"

"He was, just like Granddad. Retired, oh... twenty years ago it'd be. No, twenty-five. Dad's ninety-nine now, and he moved down here to be closer to family when he was seventy- four."

"So... the structure was empty all that time?"

"Heavens, no. The property has been rented often. Dad was always so excited when someone wanted to take up the calling. He had a soft spot for that little church."

"I'm looking for records that might tell us who his renters have been throughout the time since he retired."

"You'll be disappointed," Mary said crisply. "Dad moved from a small house to assisted living. And for the past five years he's been in a nursing home. His dementia just got too bad for him to be left alone. Every time he changed residences, we downsized again. I didn't see the need to keep old records, so I could only tell you the name of the agent I listed it with and who they sold it to."

Cady's heart sank. "Surely there'd be bookkeeping. Rental payments made..."

"I threw all that junk out. There's not much space in a shared room in the care center. And I certainly couldn't keep everything."

She tried one more time. "Maybe if you ask your father..." Sadness entered the other woman's voice. "My dad's condition is advanced. Some days he doesn't talk at all. Others he's carrying on conversations with people I've never met. I'm sorry. Neither of us can help you."

Mentally agreeing with her, Cady said, "One more thing. Can you tell me when the fire occurred at the church?"

"Three years ago," Mary replied. "It was empty at the time, but it absolutely broke Dad's heart. That's one of the reasons I decided to get rid of the property. The structures would only decay more."

"Do you recall its address?"

"I lived there my entire childhood." She reeled off the information and Cady jotted it down. Thanking the woman, she disconnected, then looked at Miguel, who was propped against her desk. "Why can't it ever be easy?"

"I take it she couldn't help."

"It's been three years since the church burned. There were no property transfers for the last eighty years until the sale to Ellis," she replied gloomily, leaning back in her chair. "Only rental agreements, which aren't public records and the owner's family has destroyed their copies."

"And the owner himself?"

"Pushing one hundred with a bad case of dementia."

She blew out a breath and tried not to think of her mom's condition. To make comparisons that would only leave her anxious. "I could send in a request for information to the IRS. They should be able to pull up the non-profit status of a church functioning there ten to fifteen years ago."

"It'd be at least several days before we hear back," Miguel predicted.

Because he was right, she used her laptop to look up a number. "Why don't you fill out the request in case we strike out? I'll call the Jackson County Sheriff's Office." They would have responded to the fire, she figured. And someone there might be familiar with the church in question.

But the sheriff was gone and the deputy she spoke to was a transplant to the area. He could only relay facts from the incident report. She searched her contacts for Sheriff Redding's number and put in another call, slanting a glance at Miguel, who was at his computer.

"What'd you find out?" he asked, without looking up.

"Not much. I'm calling Jeb Redding, Jackson County sheriff." She knew the man from public safety regional task force meetings they attended quarterly "The deputy said the accelerant used was diesel—" She switched conversations seamlessly as Redding came on the line. "Cady Maddix, Jeb. I hope I'm not interrupting anything."

"No, I brought a couple of men to join the SAR operation in Haywood County." He was referring to Ryder's missing person, she realized. "What can I do for you?"

"You had an arson report at a rural church in your region about three years ago." She gave him the address. "I got the particulars from one of your deputies, but I'm wondering if you know the church's history. I'm looking for the name of the organization renting the building ten or twelve years earlier."

"It was vacant at the time of the fire, as I recall. Afraid I don't know anything specific about congregations occupying it before that."

"Maybe someone else on your staff might be more familiar with it."

"I'll mention it to them, and give you a call if anyone does. Is this about the Frank Burgess warrant?"

Of course, he'd make the connection. His office had worked the case before turning it over to USMS. "I'm not sure. Just a thread that came up in an interview."

"Well, I hope it plays out for you. I tend to think he found a way out of the area. Probably in another state by now."

After disconnecting, she filled in Miguel on both calls. "The arson investigation went nowhere. The fire marshal report said diesel fuel was the accelerant used, and there was plenty of it in the stables on the property. They attributed the crime to vandals."

"I take it Redding couldn't supply the name of the church."

When she shook her head, Miguel cocked a brow at her. "The IRS request might be our best bet after all."

"Maybe." She rose. "But I have one more idea."

17

Callie Godwin held Phoebe Lansing's toothbrush in her gloved hand. "Lexie. Take scent." The border collie sniffed the item for several moments and then lowered her nose. Ryder watched silently as the harnessed dog moved systematically across the two campsites occupied by Phoebe and her friends last night. The animal paused at the picnic table for a long time before moving on. Using ground and air scent, she worked the area methodically, following the missing woman's trail.

He already knew from his interviews that the camping party had eaten dinner at the table and had stayed seated there until after dark. Lexie returned to Phoebe's tent. Nosed her way inside. It was several minutes before she came out again. And this time the dog went down the incline to the car the group had ridden in. She circled the vehicle for a while, then continued to the spit of grass next to it, heading toward the lane Ryder had blocked off when he'd arrived.

Callie followed, leaving slack in the long leash. The canine crossed the narrow road and beelined for the small restroom. She was lost from sight as she moved inside the building.

"We finished canvassing lot A." Jerry Garza's voice was heard on the radio. "That's the whole campground. We've got a crowd of unhappy campers here, ready to get moving for the day. How's the scent dog coming?"

"We're not done yet. No one's released until we see what she comes up with." Lexie made her way out of the building and walked onto the road.

"You got it."

The canine moved a few feet down the lane and then stopped, returning to the area just outside the restroom and retracing the same path. Ryder felt his gut clench. He didn't need Callie to point out the obvious.

"Sorry, Sheriff. I think that's the end of the trail." He gave the handler a short nod. It was the worst possible scenario for them.

Phoebe Lansing had gotten into a vehicle.

18

"We're trying to find the name of a church that was active in the area ten or fifteen years ago," Cady told Walter Edsen, a Jackson County librarian in Sylva. He was a thin, bespectacled man who looked as old and dusty as the archives he tended. "All we have is the address."

He pulled at his lip in consternation. "That does present a bit of a dilemma. Let me look at some of the annals from that time."

He bustled away from the front desk and Miguel rested an elbow on it. "I hate libraries."

"Do they bring back memories of your misspent youth?"

"At my high school, detentions were served there and the nuns were unforgiving. The connection is forever etched in my psyche."

An alert sounded on her cell and she pulled it out to check her email. "The search for human remains on Burgess's property is set for Monday."

"Figures. Nothing about this case is coming together quickly."

She waited, but he said nothing else. And Cady had a

pretty good idea of what was bothering him. "You barely spoke a word in Allen's office earlier."

He studiously avoided her gaze. "Not my call."

"Bull. When he pulled the file and spread out the pictures of the tattoo, you recognized the church. I know you did."

"What do you want me to say, Cady? That I feel like shit for not realizing it yesterday when we went up there? Because I do. That I feel even worse knowing you did and didn't say a damn thing to me about it? Because that makes me feel pretty shitty, too." His mouth was a grim slash in his face. "Afterward, on the way back to town, you never mentioned a thing. Now all of a sudden, you want a meeting with the guy. I'm having a hard time following your thinking, because you're shutting me out."

A quick stab of guilt pierced her. "Seeing that church yesterday was a shock. I wasn't trying to keep it from you. I just... needed time to process."

She hated the flash of sympathy on Miguel's face. Almost as much as she hated the effect viewing the church had on her. "If there's a chance of getting any information out of Wiley, I can't let what happened scare me off from taking it."

It was bad enough that she was still wearing his brand on her back. The doctor had told her that newer tattoos were more difficult to remove. And as large as hers was, it could take more than a dozen sessions to do so. With appointments spaced six to eight weeks apart, it wouldn't be a speedy process. But getting rid of her former captor's mark would be worth it.

His answer was a long time coming. Finally, he said, "You don't have anything to prove. But I get it. As much as I can, anyway, having not gone through it with you. Given the shape that guy was in when he was arrested, I can't believe he's coherent, much less that he could give us anything of interest. I think we need to concentrate on finding Rina."

"Maybe he can assist us with that. They each have a link to the church." She looked up when she heard the tap-tap of the librarian's wingtips. "With any luck, we can do both."

"I think I found the information you wanted." Walter's creased face was wreathed in smiles as he returned with a large book. "This resource has a listing for all the churches in each township for the past one hundred fifty years." He set it down to face them and opened it to a place he'd saved with a handmade bookmark. Cady and Miguel peered at the page. The church's address frequently appeared in the section he'd indicated.

"The building housed several churches over the years," she observed. Mary Dornbier had said as much.

"That's not unusual at all," Walter piped up. "Congregations can disband. Some grow and need bigger quarters."

Miguel pointed to an item on the list. Life Church. The dates next to the name indicated that it would have been operational from fifteen years earlier until eight years ago. "Timeline's right," she muttered. Wiley would have been eleven to eighteen in that interval.

Cady smiled at the librarian. "At least we know more than we did when we walked in here today. Where would we find old records for churches that disbanded?"

"Hm-m." He pulled at his chin. "If a church simply moves locations, obviously the documents would travel with them. But when one dissolves..." He shook his head. "Possibly the former pastor or maybe even the secretary. But after this many years? I suspect they were discarded."

She managed a smile. "Thank you for all your assistance."

"It was my pleasure," the man said with an air of old-world courtliness. "I don't get a chance to dig into the archives much, outside of genealogical help. And as you can see, we're not busy during the summer. People have outdoor things to do when the weather is nice."

She thanked him again before she turned to follow Miguel out the door. "A name isn't worth much without access to its church records," he observed.

"There's got to be mention of it online." She slid into the truck next to him. "Local newspapers advertise their activities, right? We just need to check out Life Church's digital footprint." Cady booted up the dash laptop and turned its swivel mount toward her. She spent the next half hour on the task before raising her head, puzzled. "That's weird. There's nothing."

"What?" Miguel threw her a glance. "How is that possible?"

"It shouldn't be. I tried multiple search engines."

Cady called the Jackson County Library. When Walter answered, she said, "This is Deputy U.S. Marshal Maddix again. I was wondering if you have access to digitized newspaper archives."

"For the dates Life Church existed? I'll research it and compile any mentions I find and forward them to you."

"That would be extremely helpful." Cady gave him her work email. "I haven't run across any online trace of the church, which I found odd."

There was a short silence. "That is strange. Especially since it was still in existence eight years ago. I'd suggest checking the Gazette's newspaper morgue, but that building suffered a fire two or three years back. They lost all of their archived copies."

She stilled, her instincts humming. "How did it happen?"

"As I recall, they blamed it on the night custodian who had a habit of sneaking down there for cigarette breaks. At any rate, I should be able to find something, and I'll get back to you when I do."

Cady hung up and thought for a moment. "What are the odds that mentions of the church have been scrubbed from the Internet and a fire destroyed the local paper's old copies?"

"Helluva coincidence."

"Or not." Her cell buzzed, and she took it out of her jacket pocket. Even the lightest coat was too heavy in the summer months, but it covered her weapon. Her breathing hitched when she saw Allen's name. "Maddix."

"Cady. I can't say I've changed my mind about this, but you're about to get your wish. Iden has given her okay. You're to meet with the attorney and Wiley's doctor at the Buncombe County jail in two hours. Where are you?"

"Just returning from Sylva."

"You shouldn't have any trouble making it on time then." Allen hesitated before adding, "Good luck."

"Thanks." She disconnected and relayed the conversation to Miguel. His expression conveyed his concern better than words could have. Finally, he said, "You sure you want to do this?"

"Want? I don't know. But I think I need to."

"As I explained to Deputy U.S. Marshal Gant, your visit with Mr. Wiley is conditional." Reese Mennen, Wiley's assistant public defender, was probably still carded every time he bought alcohol and would be for years. Cady assumed his patchy mustache and goatee were an attempt to disguise his youth. "Dr. Hammond, an expert witness for the defense, will also be present and allowed to videotape the proceedings. Nothing said here can be used in the case he's charged in. You'll be required to sign an affidavit to that effect. Of course, it would be best if you stayed clear of the topic altogether."

"What if your client brings it up?"

The attorney looked nonplussed by Cady's question. "Ah... well, I'll steer the conversation away if you don't. Only Maddix will be allowed inside, per my agreement with Gant."

"Wiley's been violent in the past," Miguel put in. "Are you sure this is safe?" He pretended not to feel the kick she aimed at him under the table.

"There will be deputies outside the door," Mennen responded. "And there's a viewing window to the room. You're welcome to observe."

Dr. Hammond smoothed his thinning gray hair and gave them a tight smile. "Mr. Wiley has a long history of antisocial personality disorder, with a precursor of childhood conduct disorder. While cognitive-based therapy is the best long-term treatment for ASPD, Joseph does require medication for coexisting conditions of PTSD, anxiety, depression, and poor impulse control."

Cady cocked a brow. "*He* has PTSD? Ironic, given his inclination for causing others trauma."

"Without breaking confidentiality, I can say Joseph has experienced traumatic abuse, which is the origin of some of his compulsions. He exhibits a pattern of explosive behavior when things don't proceed precisely according to his plans. Like many people, he experiences thoughts, feelings, and behaviors that are actually in conflict with each other, which is another source of confusion for him. But he has resumed a medication protocol and has been cooperative in his sessions thus far. It's certainly possible that the sight of Deputy U.S. Marshal Maddix might be triggering for him. Or, it could lead to the sort of breakthrough we've been hoping for." The doctor brushed at something on his pale blue tie. "The truth is, we can't be sure."

"It's fine." Cady sent Miguel a pointed look. "Let's do this."

Mennen picked up his briefcase and set it on the table. Opening it, he extracted some papers, which he handed to her. She skimmed the document, which contained a bunch of legalese to summarize what he'd just told her. She took the pen he extended and signed where indicated, before returning the items. He briefly looked over her signature before replacing everything in his briefcase. "Well. If we're ready..."

With a mixture of nerves and adrenaline stirring within her, she stood. They followed Hammond and Mennen out the door and down the hall to another room with two deputies standing outside of it. One of them unlocked the door and Cady, the attorney, and doctor filed inside, while Miguel accompanied the second deputy to the viewing window.

Joseph Wiley was sitting at the table, shackles on his wrists and ankles. His hulk dwarfed the chair he was seated on, making it appear child-sized. His pale blue gaze moved over them disinterestedly. Until it settled on Cady. Her skull prickled.

"You hurt me!" he said accusingly.

She sat down across from him. "You hurt me first."

"I had to, in order to take my rightful place. If you had

obeyed, I wouldn't have punished you." His high-pitched voice was slower than she recalled, a bit slurred. Perhaps it was an effect of the meds.

"Who were you obeying when you kidnapped my colleague and me?"

His gaze slid away from hers. "Let's move on," Mennen said.

Cady switched topics. "I met a friend of yours."

"Who?"

She folded her hands before her. "Her name is Rina."

"Rina," he crooned. The sound sent a skitter down her spine. "She is a good friend. But she didn't speak to you. She can't talk."

"Why is that, Joseph?"

In response to Cady's question, he shrugged his massive shoulders. "Someone hurt her when she was a kid."

"She showed us the church. The one that had a fire."

"No!" He slammed his fists on the table, the chains clanking wildly. "It's gone. It burned down."

"Only partially. Someone bought it. It's being demolished."

That brought a flicker of a smile to the man's face. "Good. It was full of secrets. But when you kill a secret, it can't hurt you anymore. That's why everyone has to die. So the worthy can live."

A chill crawled over her skin. "Who has to die, Joseph?"

"Corbin did. He should have known better. 'Whoever keeps his mouth and his tongue keeps himself out of trouble.'"

Cady heard a murmur behind her and feared her time here would soon be over. "I'm worried Rina might be in danger. Where would I find her if she's hiding?"

"No one would hurt her. There's no reason to," he argued, frowning. "She isn't part of the plan."

"Whose plan? Yours?"

"Deputy Marshal." The attorney's tone held a warning.

Cady changed the subject. "She could be at risk if she doesn't have anyone protecting her." When his frown deepened, she added, "Can you tell me where to look for her?"

Joseph paused so long she didn't think he'd answer. But finally he said, "She likes the woods. He taught her how to live in them."

He. Frank Burgess? "What if Rina has money?" She was thinking of the cash the woman had taken from Miguel. "Where would she go to buy food?" It's not like the woman had access to a vehicle. She could hitchhike to town, Cady supposed, but she had a hard time picturing her in one of the big grocery stores.

"Sarah's Market," Joseph said promptly. He looked wistful for a moment. "She has the best caramel apples. I had one there once before she made me leave. The market didn't burn down, though. It wouldn't burn." He stopped then and his expression turned cunning. "I helped you. Now it's your turn. Show it to me."

"What?"

"My art. Let me see. It's mine, really. Let me look at it."

Revulsion rivered down her spine at the thought of the man looking at her, touching her again.

"All right, I think that's enough for today."

At the sound of the attorney's voice, Cady asked hurriedly, "Does Rina have a family? Someone she'd go to see?"

"Just her mom in Bordertown. But she won't go there. Rina hates her." His chair scraped as he pushed away from the table. Rose. "Just once. I want to see it again."

She stood, ready if he approached her. "It's mine. You gave it to me."

"Deputy! Deputy!"

There was a scuffle behind them but Cady's focus remained on her former captor. "You want me to show it to you?"

He nodded vigorously as he advanced. She backed up a step, keeping the table between them and lowered her voice conspiratorially. "Then tell me where Frank Burgess is." There was a long moment before the door opened and guards ran in.

"Wiley! Hands against the wall! Against the wall!"

The deputies flanked the prisoner and physically moved him away. Cady turned to follow Hammond and Mennen out of the room. As she waited for Miguel, she mused that while she hadn't gotten a verbal answer from Wiley about Burgess, she'd seen the expression on his face when she'd asked about the man.

Fear.

They were in the pickup, headed back to the federal courthouse before Miguel spoke. "I'm not going to lie. I had a bad moment there when he charged you."

"I wasn't in any danger," she reminded him. "It was different seeing him in jail. I wasn't powerless anymore." She'd survived Joseph Wiley. But facing him without reaction—or much of one—was satisfying as well.

He flashed a grin. "You proved you weren't helpless in the mine, too. Wiley seemed to hold a grudge. What do you think he meant when he talked about taking his rightful place?"

"I have no idea," Cady admitted. "Maybe it's related to something he said in the cave, that he was a chosen one."

"Both comments seem narcissistic."

"So does tattooing people against their will. Leaving his mark on us and believing he had a right to do so." The skin on her back itched at the thought. "Narcissism is one aspect of an antisocial personality. Did you see his face at the end when I brought up Burgess? He knows him. His fear of the man was stronger than even his desire to see the tattoo again. But we got a few other things from the interview. He mentioned someone named Corbin. And he gave us a couple of leads on Rina."

"Bordertown? Where he said Rina's mother lived? It's in the file. Jackson County deputies canvassed it looking for Burgess. It sounds more like a rural neighborhood than a town. It's about twelve miles from the fugitive's property."

"Rina gives us another channel through which to elicit information there." She stopped then, recalling something else Wiley had said. "When he was talking about that market, he said it wouldn't burn. There might be an arson report on it." She used her cell to check its location.

Moments later, she reported, "Sarah's Market is in Highlands, in Macon County."

"Not enough time to drive there today."

"It's only a little over an hour past my place. I can swing by after work." And afterward, she'd be taking a look at those images Allen had sent her. Despite her insistence earlier, she didn't look forward to the task.

19

Highlands was a picturesque town surrounded by the Nantahala Forest. Sarah's Market was a surprisingly bustling establishment a few miles west of its city limits. With its split log siding and rails around the small graveled lot, it blended into the woods rimming it. The parking area was full. Cady stopped behind a line of vehicles on the shoulder beside the property. She took a moment to scan the road behind her for the older model brown sedan that had followed her the entire way from Asheville. She'd first noticed it a block from the federal courthouse. It'd never been more than two car-lengths back.

Clearly not a professional, with those tailing skills. Cady waited until the vehicle drew closer. It slowed at the entrance of the market and then continued by. She jotted down the license plate before it disappeared. Something told her she hadn't seen the last of it.

Her cell pinged as she was getting out of the Jeep. Taking it from her pocket, she read Ryder's response to an earlier text she'd sent him.

> SAR K-9 lost trail on road. Working
> electronics and interviews. I'll be late.
>
> Stay safe.

She replaced the phone, concern for the missing camper rising. The dog losing the scent like that meant the woman must have gotten into a car. *Or been taken.* The errant thought whispered across her mind. Ryder would have cleared all the vehicles in the campground before allowing campers to leave. So the one carrying Lansing left before he'd arrived there this morning.

She studied the steady stream of customers coming and going from the store. The tourism season was in full swing, and there was plenty to keep visitors happy in western North Carolina's mountains.

A couple was leaving as she was about to enter and the elderly man held the door for her. Thanking him, she strode inside.

The place was more than a market and far less than one of the large grocery stores she usually frequented with the intention of getting in and out in the shortest amount of time possible. There were baked goods temptingly displayed in multiple aisles, which just seemed like a sneaky way to trick hungry customers into unplanned purchases. And as she strolled around, Cady noticed it appeared to be working. The fresh produce looked far more appealing than what she'd last bought. She retraced her steps to the entrance and picked up a basket. Maybe the owner would be more open to questions from a paying customer.

She'd filled the container half-full by the time she reached the front. It was a friendly place. Stores full of tourists usually were. Each time the double doors opened she turned, as if looking for an item. A wasted effort. She hadn't gotten a good enough look at the driver of the sedan to identify them.

The check-out counter was crowded, but two registers were going and the lines moved along steadily. There were also plenty more wares exhibited in the area. Her gaze passed, then bounced back to one small glassed-in case. Caramel apples.

She has the best caramel apples. I had one there once before she made me leave.

She left the line to get one and put it in the basket. Ryder had a notorious sweet tooth. The cookies she'd selected were for both of them, but this was for him.

"So good to see you again, Sarah."

Her head swiveled when she heard the words. They'd been directed at the younger woman working a register. Not so young, she mentally revised her estimate. Early forties maybe, which meant she'd been a fairly youthful store owner when Wiley had visited. Deliberately, Cady moved into her line, although the other was shorter. She waited patiently for her turn and then began unloading her items on the counter.

"Hope you found everything you were looking for," Sarah chirped cheerily. She had the same blond hair as the older woman checking, without the strands of gray weaving through it. Daughter, Cady surmised. The resemblance was there in the hazel eyes. And the smile.

"More, actually. Everything looked so good. Is this your place?"

Sarah made a head-tilt toward the other woman, who was engaged in a conversation about the benefits of home-grown herbs. "It belongs to my parents. They named it for me when it first opened, forty years ago. It wasn't much more than a glorified food stand at first. And now look at it." She flashed a sunny smile. "I'm buying it, though. They're planning their retirement, and, well, I've worked here all my life." She moved swiftly even as she chatted. "That'll be forty-two eight-five."

Cady pushed her jacket aside, showing the star clipped to her belt, before reaching into her purse for her wallet.

"Deputy U.S. Marshal Maddix. I'd like to ask you some questions if you have a few minutes. Or I can talk to your mother. I won't take up much time."

The woman froze in the process of bagging the groceries. "Oh my gosh. I don't know... Of course, I'll do it. But I have customers."

"Sure. I can wait." Cady helped the now-flustered woman sack the few remaining items and gathered up the bags. "I'll go load these in the Jeep first."

"Okay. I mean, I don't know how long I'll be, but..."

"I'll wait," Cady repeated before moving away. The place seemed no less busy than when she'd come in. She went to the Jeep and put away her sacks, before relocking it. Retracing her steps, she leaned against the rail bordering the front walk and scanned the parking lot. No brown sedan. She hadn't seen one when she'd taken the groceries to the vehicle either, so the car in her rearview mirror all the way here might have been a coincidence.

But she doubted it.

It was a little over ten minutes before Sarah came out of the doors, a worried expression on her face. Cady approached her. "How about we talk over here?" She led the woman to the back edge of the lot, onto the neatly trimmed grass that grew sparser near the woods.

"I'm so nervous. I've never even met a marshal before. I mean, my grandpa likes those old westerns, you know?

With Marshal Matt Dillon? I don't remember the name of the show, and oh my gosh, I sound like an idiot." She reached up a hand and pushed a tendril of hair behind her ear.

Cady smiled. "I'm not nearly as big a deal as Marshal Dillon, so there's nothing to be nervous about."

"I just don't know what the marshals would want with me. With us." Sarah twisted her hands together. "I'm sorry, I forgot your name."

"It's Cady Maddix." When she heard the crunch of tires on gravel she glanced toward the lot. Didn't recognize the car. "And I'm not here because of you or your family. I just need some history. You said your parents had this place for forty years."

Sarah nodded, shading her eyes as she looked over her shoulder at the store. "Yes. It's best you talk to me instead of my mom. She has a bad heart. Not that you'd give her a heart attack or anything, but... we try to protect her, my family and me. What is it you wanted to know?"

"I'm wondering if there's ever been a case of arson at your establishment."

"No, of course..." Sarah started to shake her head, then stopped. Her mouth made an O. "Well, someone tried to burn it down once. Geez, when was that?" She looked upward, as if seeking divine guidance. "I'd just had Janie. No, it would have been more than three months later, because I was back at work. So, twelve years ago. September or October."

Cady raised her brows. "That's specific. Do you recall the details?"

"Sure, something set off the alarm. My dad called me after he contacted the police. They sent a firetruck, but it didn't take long to put out."

Wiley's words replayed in Cady's mind. *The market didn't burn down, though. It wouldn't burn.* "Why is that?"

Sarah's smile turned mischievous. "You didn't notice? It's not constructed from logs, it's just made to appear that way. It's concrete. And the roof is tin."

Cady stared at the building, nonplussed. Now she'd have to take a closer look, because the siding had sure looked real to her.

"My dad was worried about all the timber around. There was a small fire when they'd first started their business. It began in the forest out back and spread to the store, but not to their house. Even though the damage wasn't extensive, he swore he'd never rebuild with wood." She lifted a shoulder. "He checked with builders all over the area. They advised a concrete log building so he went with that. They've remodeled and added on over the years, but always with the same product."

So, one part of Wiley's story had been true, Cady thought. "Do you recall if your mom had trouble with anyone in the store prior to that?" She could always check the investigative report, if necessary.

Sarah hesitated. "The deputies asked that at the time. But we felt sort of awful for listing people who'd been unhappy with us. I mean, every business owner has issues with customers at times, without any of them trying to burn down their store."

"Do you remember who the people were?"

She shook her head. "Not all of them. There was a Henry Caldwell. An older man who was... a bit unpleasant whenever he came in. Not just with staff," she hastened to add. "He was just a negative soul."

"Who else?"

The woman heaved a sigh, looking unhappy in the

retelling. "You know, the sheriff's office followed up with all the names. Some of the people never came back. Guess I wouldn't either, if someone all but accused me of attempted arson. There was Tally Orwell. She was a little light-fingered. My mom had spoken to her several times but had never turned her in. She was getting on in years and we thought maybe she had dementia. And once we had some tough-looking motorcyclists who were causing trouble and we had to call the sheriff. But they live out of state—"

"What about kids?"

"We don't have many unattended children here, but once in a while we get some on their bikes. Oh!" Her face brightened. "There was one teenager. Fourteen or fifteen, but he was really big for his age. He took out a caramel apple and just started eating it, right there in the store. He didn't have any money, and my mom made him leave. I don't know if that would make someone mad enough to come back for revenge. But I remember mom told the deputy about it, because there was just something about the kid. He was sort of spooky."

"I know what you mean." Cady pulled out her cell, scrolled until she found the picture of Rina. "Are you at the market every day?"

"Usually, at least for a few hours."

She held up the cell to show her the image. "Do you recall ever seeing this young woman?"

Sarah peered at the screen. "No-o. I mean, I don't think so. We get so many tourists... I really only remember the locals and people who are return customers." Her gaze flicked to Cady. "What's she done?"

"I just want to talk to her. Give me your number. I'm going to send you her picture so you can share it with your parents." Sarah reeled off her contact information and Cady sent the message. Then she slipped the phone in her pocket, pulled out a card, and gave it to her. "If she comes in, I want to be notified right away."

"Okay." The woman looked intrigued but didn't ask any more questions. "I'll tell my parents. You come back sometime. We have a pretty great old-fashioned ice cream you won't want to miss."

After promising to do so, Cady returned to her vehicle, sending another look up and down the road. There was no brown sedan in sight. She got in the Jeep and started it. She'd gone a half-mile before she spotted something. There. The fading sunlight glinted off something in the trees ahead to her ight. It took a moment to notice the drive all but hidden by the tall weeds in the ditch beside it.

She hadn't lost the tail. The driver was waiting for her to pass, before resuming it.

Without giving it much thought, she slowed then veered sharply to the shoulder, effectively blocking the car. It was time to end this. She had no intention of leading a stranger to her home.

Cady drew her weapon as she studied the person behind the wheel. Dark glasses and a ball cap pulled low shielded much of the face. The width of the shoulders could belong to either gender. But when the driver's door opened and a figure exited, she was still surprised to see a woman. The stranger approached Cady's vehicle.

Cady got out and aimed her gun over the top of the Jeep. "That's close enough."

The female stopped. "I just wanted to talk to you..."

"Really? You picked a funny way to start a conversation. Turn around. Place your hands on the hood of the car."

"There's no need for this. Like I said—"

"I'll determine whether there's a need." She closed the distance between them, and used her free hand to pat the woman down. Finding no weapons, she moved along the side of the sedan to look inside the front and back seats. A purse was on the center console. Cady opened the door, keeping an eye on the stranger, while she pulled the bag to the driver's seat, and searched for a billfold. When she glanced at the license, surprise punched through her. Nancy Wiley. Cady dropped the wallet, shut the door, and ordered, "Take off the glasses."

The woman obeyed, folding them and hanging them from the neck of her tee. Her brown hair was scraped back in a ponytail. The shirt and jeans clung tightly to her stout figure. "I'm Joe Wiley's mother."

Her face matched the picture on the license, and Cady could see the man in Nancy's broad forehead and deep-set eyes. "This is inappropriate. I can't help Joseph, so if you're here to plead his case, you're talking to the wrong person."

"It's not that. At least, not exactly." The woman clasped her hands together, twisting them nervously. "Joe's lawyer told me the people he took were marshals and that one was a lady. I been watching the federal courthouse for a while now, when I can. I never seen you before this week, so I figured maybe you was the one Joe hurt, just come back to work."

"You told the task force members who spoke to you that your son was hiking in Virginia."

Nancy's fingers clenched tightly. "A mother's got a right to try and protect her only kid. Truth is, he don't live with me and I don't know much 'bout his comings and goings. He's a grown man. Holds down jobs sometimes, least for a time. Makes his own money."

"What kind of work does he do?"

"He's been a janitor at a couple of places. He got some work as a tattoo artist more recent. But he was let go."

Hearing of Wiley's latest occupation elicited a flare of interest. "Why was he fired?"

"Joe has a thought and acts on it. He just can't think beforehand. That's been getting him in trouble since he was a kid."

Poor impulse control. Dr. Hammond's words from that-morning flashed across Cady's mind.

Nancy gave a weary sigh. "Tell ya the truth, he's always been two different people. Even-tempered, until something goes wrong. Then you never know what set him off. But he's better on medication. If he did what the lawyer says, he was off his meds." Sadness flitted over her expression. "I'm not excusing what he done to you or that other marshal. But I am asking you to find it in your heart to forgive him."

"Do you recall a friend of his named Corbin?"

The woman blinked. "Don't recollect one, no."

"Is Joe religious?"

"We weren't church goin'." Nancy's mouth twisted. "I got enough of that growing up. But he's got some mixed-up ideas 'bout religion, that's a fact. "

"What's his relationship with Life Church?"

Her eyes widened. "Now that's a blast from the past. There was an itty-bitty country church by that name, oh… twelve, fifteen years ago or so. I worked at the stable next to it for a time. Never heard of no church having a stable, but there it was."

"Can you tell me the name of the pastor then?"

"Don't think I ever knew it. I answered an ad. Interviewed with someone named Pam, I think. She was the one who gave me orders and paid me. Cash every week."

An unusual arrangement, Cady thought, but not unheard of. "Did Joe spend time there?"

"They was nice 'bout letting me bring him to work. I was mostly just feeding the livestock and mucking out stalls. And I thought it'd be good for him. They had horses, some cows, sheep, goats...all real gentle."

"Did you ever meet this young woman?" Cady dug in her pocket for her cell and brought up Rina's picture. Held it out to show Nancy. "She would have been a few years younger than your son."

Nancy peered closely and then shook her head. "There was always kids running around. Not sure I could tell one from the other, especially after all this time."

"Did something happen to Joe there?" He'd admitted to burning the church, and had tattooed it on Cady. The scene on her back was violent, not a depiction of fond memories.

"He stepped on a rusty nail in the barn once. Went right through his sneaker. Had to get a tetanus shot. But other than that..." She lifted a hefty shoulder. "There was a time a whole host of kids used to traipse through there. Boy Scouts. Class picnics. Even Rolling Acres Resort brought their patients out. Guess they thought the animals would be good therapy or some such."

Something clicked in Cady's brain. "Rolling Acres. Joseph spent time there."

It'd be impossible to miss the misery in the woman's eyes. "When I just couldn't control him no more, the doctors said he needed more than I could give him. I remembered that place 'cuz of them field trips. Thought maybe they'd know how to handle Joe, too. And they did. For a while. That's why I had to talk to you. To ask for your help."

Cady tensed again. Not because the woman presented a threat, but because she knew what she was about to say.

"Ma'am, I've already told you. I can't keep your son from facing justice."

"That ain't what I'm after. You think I want Joe to go free?" She smacked her hand down on the hood of her car in frustration. "You ain't been listening. I want you to speak up at his trial to make sure he don't. His best chance of getting better is in a place that treats illnesses like his, not prison. Wherever they put him, they'll see that he takes his meds. But he also needs therapy to get well. It's his only hope."

"You believed her?"

Cady'd called Miguel as soon as Nancy Wiley drove away. In the opposite direction this time. "She seemed credible, if misguided. Especially about her reasons for wanting her son to remain locked away."

"Attempting to tail a deputy US marshal is a cocky move."

"More desperate, I think." Cady relayed the rest of the information she'd gotten from Nancy.

"It would've been a break if she'd recognized Rina." He sounded disappointed.

"Breaks have been few and far between," she agreed. But once they disconnected, Cady had another thought worth pursuing. She might know someone who could verify part of Nancy's story.

She fed the dogs, then let them out before leaving again. The drive across town took fifteen minutes because the streets were still crammed with tourists and leisurely drivers enjoying the mountain view. When she finally knocked at the door of the residence she was seeking, Eryn Pullman immediately opened it.

She gave Cady a delighted smile and a quick hug. "I didn't expect to see you so soon after lunch last week."

"You might not be so happy when you hear I came looking for help."

The younger woman paused, looked at Cady's face searchingly. "You're back at work."

"How'd you guess?"

"It's in your expression. That scary sense of purpose." When Cady cocked a brow, Eryn laughed. "That was a compliment. I haven't forgotten it was your scary sense of purpose that kept Samuel Aldeen from killing my cousin and me last fall."

"You were well on your way to saving him and yourself," Cady corrected. "I just came in time for the last act."

A shadow flitted across Eryn's eyes. "Do you mind if we talk out here? I've been inside all day."

"A new painting?"

Eryn grimaced. "I'm not satisfied with it. We'll see if it shapes up tomorrow." She had exacting expectations for her artwork, Cady knew. They crossed the small yard to sit on a stone bench beneath a fragrant magnolia tree bearing yellow blossoms. "If you're working again, does this mean I get to assist with a case?"

"I hate to bring it up." Suddenly questioning the wisdom of her decision, Cady forced herself to continue. "I have a picture of someone who spent time at Rolling Acres. I know the chances of you recognizing him are slim, but..."

"It's okay. I want to help." But the young woman had sobered. The reminder of the years she'd been in the forensic psychiatric facility could hardly elicit pleasant memories. Especially when it had recently been proven that she hadn't killed her mother at age nine, as had been alleged.

Pulling out her cell, Cady flipped to Wiley's mugshot Ryder had shared with her after she'd returned home from the hospital. "This was taken about five years ago."

Eryn studied the image critically. "How old would he be now?"

"Twenty-six."

She shook her head and handed the phone back. "Even if we were at the facility at the same time, I wouldn't have come in contact with him. The wards are very age-segregated and they made sure we didn't interact with older patients. Each section had its own common and dining areas, as well. Even outside we were kept strictly separated."

Cady shrugged off a dart of disappointment. It had been a long shot, at any rate. "I recently learned that patients at Rolling Acres were taken on field trips."

"Oh, yes. We went somewhere weekly. Dependent on our cooperation in therapy, of course."

"Did you ever visit a stable with farm animals? There was a small church nearby."

Eryn made a moue of distaste. "I hated going there. It was smelly and sort of run down. The animals looked unhappy, too." A smile flickered. "I think I maybe visited three times. I refused to go after that."

"Let me show you another picture." She scrolled through her photos to find Burgess's driver license image that had been include in the file.

"Wait!" Eryn exclaimed. She took the phone from Cady and flipped back through the images until she settled on the one of Rina. "She was at the stables, once, too."

Everything in Cady stilled. "She was? Do you recall how long ago that was?"

"Ten years?" She shrugged. "I can't say. The only reason I remember is that we were around the same age, and someone said she couldn't talk. I always wondered why."

"Was she visiting, too?"

Eryn shook her head, setting her long blond hair swinging. "I don't think so. I figured she was a volunteer, because she looked like she was really working, not playing at it like we did. But maybe not."

Cady felt a quickening in her pulse. Nancy Wiley had said she'd been paid for her work, but perhaps the church had gone to volunteers after she'd left. She returned to the picture of Burgess. Saw the recognition on Eryn's face before she said a word. "You know him?"

"He was there once. He scared the heck out of me." She handed the phone back to Cady quickly, as if the memory was an unpleasant one. "I was bored with the animals, so I decided to go take a look inside the church. I was just about to go in when he yelled and started running toward me." She shivered. "One of the chaperones intervened but this guy was super mad. I guess I was trespassing, but I was just a kid. It kind of traumatized me. Since he and the girl made an impression, I sketched them a time or two."

"What was the man doing? Had you noticed him earlier?"

"He was mowing the lawn with this old push mower. I can probably find the pad containing the drawings." Her expression grew wry. "As my uncle continually tells me, I never throw any of them away."

But Cady knew that wouldn't be necessary. Eryn had already confirmed what Rina had indicated. She and Burgess were connected to Life Church.

20

"How long have you been here?"

Unsurprisingly, the woman in the cell next to Phoebe didn't answer. She'd said little since last night. Their cubes were identical. Fashioned not of glass, but sturdy acrylic. Small air holes had been drilled through them at random intervals. She'd thought perhaps those openings would weaken the overall structure, but hours spent kicking each wall hadn't even made a crack in one.

Her prison resembled a spacious homemade kennel for an animal. Panic, never far away, welled up again, a silent scream. She battled it away—this time.

An overhead light glared above both cells, but most of the room remained in shadows. She could distinguish what might be two tightly covered windows in the wall facing them. Only threadlike splinters of sunlight were visible in intermittent spaces around them. Near the ceiling, three tiny red dots winked.

If asked last week, she would have said the worst that could happen to her was to be separated on the trail from her group, without a map or GPS. But that was before she'd plunged into an unimaginable nightmare.

Tim would be frantic. And Emma... thoughts of her husband and four-year-old daughter were like a sharp blade to the chest. Would she ever see them again?

"It's been almost two months since he took me."

Phoebe jerked toward the other woman. Her face was emotionless as if the words held no meaning for her. Two months! A lifetime! No rescue. No escape. Desolation howled through her, clawing for release.

She hadn't even seen who'd taken her. The campground had been blanketed with darkness, the only glow coming from her flashlight. Phoebe had been half asleep, aggravated by the inopportune pressure in her bladder. Stumbling out of the restroom, she'd thought only of returning to her tent and getting back to sleep. But then a strong arm pressed around her neck. A hard hand clapped over her mouth. She'd felt a sharp prick in her bicep and her light clattered to the ground. Phoebe reached for more details, but they were blurry. She'd struggled, but she'd been so weak. Her limbs uncoordinated. And then, after she'd been dragged away, there'd been nothingness. Until she'd awakened here.

Great gulping sobs broke from her. She choked them back. She didn't want to rouse her captor.

"That doesn't help. Save your strength. You're going to need it."

With monumental effort, Phoebe forced the tears back and looked away. The other woman's ordeal to this point was evident. Her hair was matted. One eye was nearly swollen closed and her nose looked as though it had been broken. Her knuckles were puffy and scabbed. Two of her teeth were missing. There were older wounds visible on her nude body, in various stages of healing. The most terrifying was the long, ragged scar across her breast, dangerously close to her heart.

She hadn't answered any questions about her injuries, but Phoebe was very much afraid the kidnapper was responsible for them. Last night, her companion had issued directions in a monotone. *Use the grate to pee and poop. They'll make you sorry if they have to come in here. If you try anything during feeding time, they'll hurt you.*

There had been no food yet. No water. The lights blazing above turned the cells into saunas. Hunger and thirst could be another tool to control them, she thought bitterly.

She wedged herself into a ball in one corner of the cube, drawing her knees up and clutching them to her chest. She'd always thought she was emotionally strong, but now she was discovering she wasn't brave at all. Not really. Not when she couldn't be sure whether she'd see Tim and Emma again. Or her parents. Her sister.

Not when she didn't know if she'd die here.

"Don't do that," the woman hissed. "Sit up. They don't like it when they can't see your face."

Slowly, Phoebe unfolded herself and straightened. "You keep saying they. Is there more than one kidnapper? Are they watching us?"

"Everybody's watching us."

21

After leaving Eryn's, Cady drove out to the cabin. She liked to drop in unannounced sometimes. It gave her a clearer picture of how her mom was doing, without Alma's filter.

She parked the Jeep and walked up the steps, surprised when the door opened before she could knock. "What a nice surprise!" Her mom's pretty face was wreathed in smiles. "I was in my rocker and saw you from the window." She slipped her arm around Cady's waist and drew her inside. "I was going to call you anyway. We got the most exciting news!"

"What's that?" Cady looked around for her aunt. "Where's Alma?"

"Oh, she's weeding the garden. But she and I are spending a night in the cutest little bed-and-breakfast in Maggie Valley tomorrow. The view in the brochure is just spectacular. It may sound silly, but I'm just so thrilled. You know how much I love outings."

Cady smiled at her mom. "You sure do."

"And Alma's just the luckiest thing." Hannah continued

chattering as she dropped on the couch and patted the cushion beside her. Cady sat down. "She won the trip, can you believe it? I'm not sure how." A slight frown marred her brow. "Or maybe I've forgotten."

Before her mother could begin to fret about her memory, Cady guided the conversation back to the visit. "Tell me more about the B & B."

Hannah bounced out of her seat and hurried into the kitchen. She snatched up a bundle of documents and returned. "Here's the brochure. Isn't the house just charming? We're going tomorrow, which doesn't give me much time to pack."

Cady skimmed the glossy pamphlet, while surreptitiously looking the place up on her cell. It was legit. Mountain View Bed and Breakfast had been in existence for twelve years and the pics on the site matched the one in the brochure. Her brows rose when she saw the listed prices for a night. "It looks really nice, Mom. And there are a lot of shops and dining establishments in the area. You'll love that."

Hannah's focus veered to what she'd need to take along and the discussion was only interrupted by her sister's entrance through the back door twenty minutes later. "Alma," Hannah chirped. "I was just talking about your good luck."

"How'd you win the stay?" Cady asked her aunt.

"Some local giveaway that a bunch of the community businesses was involved in. Didn't even remember signing up, but maybe it's been running for a while." She washed her hands and wiped them on the towel draped in the door handle of the refrigerator. "Says it all in the letter."

Cady picked up the rest of the correspondence. There was a map to the destination along with a congratulatory sheet signed by the president of Haywood County's Chamber of Commerce thanking her for supporting local businesses. It listed three dates to choose from: tomorrow, next Monday or Tuesday.

She aimed another smile at Hannah. "You're both winners since you get to go along, too."

"No use going by myself," her aunt muttered. Her enthusiasm was considerably more muted than Hannah's. But Alma wasn't the excitable sort. Except when it came to her niece.

Cady glanced at the envelope in her lap. It bore one white typed label from the Chamber of Commerce and another with Alma's name and address. Her focus sharpened. What had looked like a smeary cancellation stamp on the postage didn't bear a date or a location.

Unease trickled down her spine, but she knew better than to say anything before checking into the matter herself. "I hope you both enjoy your getaway. The weather is supposed to stay nice."

"Oh, I wish you could come, Cady!" Hannah said. "It's too bad this didn't happen a week ago when you weren't working." From the grim expression on Alma's face, she didn't share her sister's sentiment.

Squeezing her mom's hand, she replied, "You can tell me all about it when you get back." A few minutes later she rose to leave.

Cady hoped for Hannah's sake that the contest was legit. But she had some research to do before her doubts were put to rest.

∼

Two hours later, her suspicions were validated. There was no information on the Chamber website regarding the giveaway. No news about it had appeared in the Haywood County *Gazette*. She'd called the bed-and-breakfast and verified the booking, so that part, at least, was real. If not for the strange markings over the postage stamp, she wouldn't have questioned the trip.

She sat back on the couch and absently petted Hero, who'd trotted over to lay his head on her knee, as if sensing her concern. It was also weird that the given dates for the stay were so specific. So immediate. What if the winner had a schedule conflict? What was the hurry? Trepidation swirled in her gut. If the contest was a sham, the only purpose would be to get Alma and Hannah to a desired location, or to ensure the cabin was empty for the night. And if the latter was true, it was impossible not to suspect Stan Caster.

She spent a few more minutes mulling the matter over, before giving a mental shrug. There was nothing more to be done now. She'd call the Chamber tomorrow, then plan from there.

Pushing her worry aside for the moment, she went to her email, brought up the images Allen had sent and arranged them on her desktop in a visual array. Wiley's unfinished tattoo on Paul appeared first, even more detailed than her own. Cady zoomed in to enlarge the picture and studied it more closely. Above a charred and blackened landscape, mythical winged creatures engaged in gory warfare. A moment later, she revised her assessment. The figures bore horns and wings. Angels and demons? Nancy's words from earlier this evening echoed in her mind.

...he's got some mixed-up ideas 'bout religion, that's a fact.

The framed images also featured violent scenes. Bloody

battles between two warriors. Kids getting eaten by fanged monsters. All brutal depictions from a damaged mind. She stilled when she came to the last image. The church again, this time painted a pristine white, stark against a sullen sky. Children filled each of the windows, their mouths opened in silent screams.

She had to look away for a moment, chilled. Cady had no idea what events had shaped Joseph Wiley's imagination.

But it was evident that Life Church figured into them.

She awakened early to find Ryder asleep beside her. She eased from bed and collected her clothes in the dark before going to the spare bathroom to shower and change. While eating cereal, Cady searched online obituaries for someone in the region named Corbin. Her hunt was rewarded when she found one for Corbin Fielding, dated two years earlier. The details were brief, with nothing to suggest a cause of death. The young man had been twenty-three, so he'd be Wiley's age. She was jotting down the information about his relatives and the funeral home when Ryder came into the kitchen, his hair still damp, buttoning his uniform shirt. She closed the lid of the computer. "Morning."

He rounded the island and paused for a lingering kiss. "Mm. You were dead to the world when I got in last night."

"When was that?"

He moved away to rummage in the cupboards for another box of cereal and a bowl. Carrying both to the counter, he went back for a spoon and returned to sit down. "A little after two."

"What's your working theory on Phoebe Lansing's disappearance?"

"The canvass at the campground was a bust. There were no witnesses. I remotely interviewed her spouse, parents, and sister. All swear up and down that Phoebe was an experienced hiker and looking forward to this trip. The rest of her hiking group says the same. Today, I'll take a couple of deputies and drive to Sevierville. Talk to neighbors and friends. The husband voluntarily relinquished all family electronics, and the police department there picked them up. I'll see if we can get more from them than we did from her phone."

"Her cell turned up nothing?"

He poured cereal into his bowl and doused it with the milk she'd left on the counter. "No suspicious texts or emails. Same with her social media. We should get the data dump from the provider today, so we can check for anything that's been deleted. And hopefully, we'll also receive the bank and credit card statements we requested."

The spouse's information would be as crucial as Phoebe's, Cady mused, shoveling in another spoonful of cereal. As much to eliminate him as a suspect, as anything else. When there was a possibility of foul play, police looked at those closest to the victim first. Statistics didn't lie.

"I hope for her sake, this was planned. That she'll show up somewhere, unharmed. But..."

"Yeah. But." Cady had a sudden flash of waking up in that dark mine. The burgeoning fear when she'd discovered the chains. Sympathy for the unknown woman worked through her. She knew Ryder would investigate both possibilities—an innocent disappearance, and a more sinister one.

He nodded toward the caramel apple sitting on the island near him. "Where'd you get that? And why'd you only get one?"

She smiled. "I bought it yesterday. For you."

He looked ridiculously pleased. "Really?"

"And there are cookies. You can take them on your road trip today."

"You know my weak spots. Thank you."

He didn't have many that she'd observed. His biggest one seemed to be regarding her, and the realization both warmed and baffled her. It had seemed empty here last night without him, the first time she could remember when she'd minded the solitude. Obviously, she'd developed a weakness where he was concerned, too. And the idea wasn't nearly as alarming as it would have been even a few weeks ago.

She recalled last night's conversation with her mom and asked him, "Do you know anything about a contest the county merchants were putting on? My aunt won something, but I couldn't find anything in the paper or on the Chamber website about it."

He shook his head. "I wouldn't necessarily, though. I don't pay much attention to that sort of thing. Why? What'd she win?" When Cady told him, he said thoughtfully, "That's a little odd. Why would the stay have to be scheduled so quickly? Most people wouldn't be able to juggle that into their calendar immediately."

She nodded vigorously, stabbing her spoon in his direction. "Right? That's what I thought. And the postmark seemed screwed up. Anyway, the Chamber opens at eight. I'll call them and follow up."

"Any leads on Burgess?"

"Eryn recognized him. From a long time ago." She summarized her conversation with the young woman.

"You've found a lot of ties to that church," he reflected.

"We just don't know what they all mean yet." Maybe that'd change today, and they'd finally find someone with a concrete idea of where Burgess could have gone.

"I DIDN'T REALIZE the place was this remote." Miguel's voice was distrustful. Cady didn't blame him. The lane leading to Bordertown was so overgrown and deeply rutted, she'd worried about damaging the Jeep's undercarriage. The neighborhood was notched into the mountains, appearing at the end of the drive in a clearing that looked as though the surrounding woods were stealthily inching toward it, until they eventually swallowed up the dwellings and returned the area to forest. The trail—because *road* was too grand a term— twisted through the space like a scar, with the residences scattered randomly along both its edges. It looked like a place people would come if they were hiding from society or the law.

Or if they had nowhere else to go.

Her cell dinged and she pulled it out to read Ryder's response to her earlier text message.

> Got the hotel and cabin covered.

Her thumbs flew over the keys.

> Great service.

> So you've told me.

Cady grinned. Smartass. It hadn't taken him long to get things moving after she'd messaged him about her phone call with the Chamber this morning. Unsurprisingly, the person she'd spoken to had emphatically denied any knowledge of the contest referred to in the letter Alma had received.

She put the cell away and scanned the group of homes

before them. It was a haphazard scattering of tar-papered shanties and run-down trailer houses. Old bathtubs, used applicances, and rusted out vehicles appeared to be the yard adornments of choice. A mangy-looking dog rested beneath a tree beside the nearest home, lifting its head to watch them without interest.

"The sheriff's office canvassed this place after Burgess spooked weeks ago," Cady noted.

"And no one claimed to know a damn thing about him."

"None that would admit it, anyway."

"What's our play this time around?"

"We focus on Rina and sneak in mentions of the fugitive in connection to her. We're concerned for her safety. Maybe she's still in contact with someone up here. I'd like to talk to her mother. According to Wiley, she lives in the vicinity, or did at one time."

Miguel nodded toward a man half-hidden by the hood of the old truck he was bent over. "Let's start with him. Try not to scare him."

Half-offended, Cady fell in step beside him. "I'm charming." When he slanted her a look, she amended, "I can be charming." Not that she thought charm was going to work up here.

They fought through a tangle of overgrown weeds to approach the man who sported a filthy tank and greasy jeans. The stranger didn't acknowledge them.

"Beautiful morning," she said cheerfully. Over the stranger's head, Miguel rolled his eyes at her. "We're looking for a young woman. Maybe you know her."

"Only people 'round here are as old and broken down as this piece of shit truck." The man's drawl was so pronounced Cady had trouble understanding his words. "This ain't no place a young woman would ever stay."

"We were told she lived here once."

His only response to that was a fluent string of curses. Miguel moved closer to the vehicle. "Need any help?" Cady's brows rose. She'd never observed him displaying an aptitude for anything mechanical.

Doubt sounded in his voice. "You know anything about engines?"

Miguel poked his head under the hood. "You trying to replace that spark plug?"

"Not having any luck. I can't get the threads to line up. Damn arthritis."

"Let me try."

Cady took advantage of the man's distraction by asking, "The name of the person we're looking for is Rina. Someone mentioned she once lived up here."

"The hell you say." The stranger straightened. His jaw was grizzled and his gaze suspicious. "What'd you want with her anyways?"

"We think she may be in danger."

He continued to study Cady while Miguel—she hoped — worked some magic beneath the hood. "She ain't been seen 'round here since she was a lil' girl. Goin' on twelve, thirteen years or so."

"Do you know where she went?"

Shaking his head, he said, "Heard things. I can't be sure what's true and what ain't. The one to ask is her good-for-nuthin' mama, but she'll tell a thousand lies before she speaks one truth." Disgust was stamped on his face. "Girl never got no chance with Selma Dierks for a mother."

"Does Selma still live around here?"

His only response was a finger jab toward the end of the road.

"What do you think happened to Rina?"

He leaned to watch Miguel for a long moment before answering. "Nuthin' good, I reckon. I remember hearing she got hurt bad somehow. Then she was gone. Never seen her again." He frowned. "But she must be alive, if you're lookin' for her."

"We've communicated with her," Cady affirmed. "We'd like to find her again and arrange a place for her to stay where she'd be safe."

He snorted at that. "Jail?"

"No, sir. As far as we know, she hasn't done anything wrong. But there's reason to believe she might be at risk from Frank Burgess."

"Bullshit!" He glared at her from watery blue eyes. "He wouldn't harm a fly and cops coming 'round these parts sayin' different are full of shit. Told that to the last ones asked 'bout him, too. He's a decent guy. A bit preachy, and I don't hold no truck with religion. But he'd have no call to hurt Rina and you're a liar if 'n you say otherwise."

His ire made his speech even more difficult to decipher, but Cady got the gist. "She told us that he's injured her before. Chained her up. Abused her. I believe her."

He searched her expression, and whatever he saw there must have convinced him. He sagged against the bumper. "Don't make no sense," he mumbled. "Not the Frank, I know."

"Sounds like the two of you were friends."

"Used to go fishin' with him. Not for a few years now, not since I busted up my knee, but we had us some times."

Cady glanced at his legs, but with the greasy denim encasing them, his injury was impossible to assess. "How long ago was it the last time you went?"

"Oh, let me see." He squinted. "Four years, mebbe. But almost every month before that, once the weather got nice."

"I'll bet you have some great memories of those outings, Mr...."

"Just Bill. And yep, we did. 'Nuff that I can say, what you're telling me don't make no sense."

"So, he never mentioned Rina to you."

He shook his head slowly. Beside him, Miguel picked up the ratchet wrench from the bumper and stuck his head under the hood again. "We talked most 'bout fishin', I guess. Can't help but wonder... if what you say is so, what'd he do with the girl while we was gone?"

"Did you ever use his business? His locker?"

Bill's expression grew guarded. "Some. Jist what was legal. What I couldn't do myself."

From his manner, Cady could only speculate that the opposite was true. That Burgess overlooked seasonal laws when accepting wild game to process. From the look of this neighborhood, the occupants lived a hand-to-mouth existence. She suspected that few possessed fishing and hunting licenses.

"Did he ever talk about Life Church?"

"Like I said, it was mostly fishin'. But I hope you find Rina. That girl deserves something better than comin' from this hellhole." He bent down to check on Miguel's progress. "Shit a'fire, what's taking you so long?"

"Finished." Miguel handed him the wrench and straightened.

Bill leaned closer to inspect his work. "Huh. Looks okay."

"Where are some of the spots you and Frank fished?" Cady sensed the man's cooperation was dwindling rapidly. "Were they mostly around here?"

"Not always. We had us a few trips when we took camping gear and spent a night or two. One time... hell.

When was it? Ten years or more. He took me to a spot right on the French Broad River. Madison County, it was, not far from Hot Springs. We stayed at his friend's home. Fancy place, an A-frame with a wall of windows looking right out over the water."

Interest sparked. "Do you remember the name of the friend?"

Bill shook his head, and looked as though he regretted mentioning it. "Don't think he said. It don't matter. We was alone there for three days or so." He began picking up the ancient tools at his feet. "I got packin' to do. Going to Wilmington to see my daughter."

"Did any of your neighbors know Burgess?" she asked.

"Probably none that will talk about it if 'n they do. Folks 'round here don't cotton to strangers, cops least of all."

They hadn't introduced themselves, Cady realized. She supposed they hadn't needed to. There wouldn't be many others asking questions in this area. "If you remember anything else about Frank or Rina, give me a call." She took a card from her pocket and handed it to him. Bill took it from her without a word and turned away, limping toward his decrepit trailer.

She and Miguel walked toward the small tar-papered home next door. "You've been hiding your talents. I wouldn't have guessed you had any mechanical know-how."

"I've got skills," he responded loftily. He kept his gaze trained downward as they strode through knee-high grass to the front porch. Checking for snakes? The thought had Cady moving faster. "Since his cooperation seemed to depend on my assistance, I didn't want to finish too fast."

"Uh-huh. And I was talking slow so I wouldn't rush you."

There was no screen, so Miguel hammered on the peeling front door. "You underestimate my abilities."

"I caught a glimpse of them a few months back when you couldn't manage a simple repair to a lamp," she reminded him.

"That was electrical." When no one appeared, he pounded again. "This was routine car maintenance. Some of my fondest memories are when my dad and I left the house to my mom and sisters and escaped to the garage. He taught me about cars long before I was old enough to drive one."

Cady fell silent. No one learned skills in either area without someone around to teach them. Her lessons had come at the hands of her grandfather, when he'd gotten too arthritic to perform them himself. Unlike her colleague, the memories brought her no pleasure. Nothing about her time living with Elmer Griggs did.

Suddenly, the door was yanked open. "What the fuck do you want?"

Cady blinked. The long unwashed blond hair could belong to either gender, but the bare chest put any confusion to rest. The man was thin to the point of emaciation. His jeans clung precariously to angular hip bones and his face was half-covered by a six-inch beard. "Deputy U.S. Marshals Maddix and Rodriguez. We're looking for a young woman who lived near here years ago. Her name is Rina."

"Shee-it, I wasn't around then, how the hell would I know?"

They'd obviously awakened him. Or... She peered more closely. His eyes were bleary, the pupils huge. She revised her earlier opinion. He was under the influence of something.

"What's your name?" Miguel asked.

"People call me... Charlie."

His pause suggested a lie, but Cady let it pass. "Do you know Frank Burgess?"

"No, and I told them other cops the same." His words were an eerie near-mimicry of Bill's. "I only been here a few months and I won't be staying once I find something else. This place is a shithole filled with losers and crack whores."

"Location, location, location," she murmured under her breath. Miguel's mouth quirked.

"Burgess has a meat locker about ten miles from here. Did you ever do business with him?"

The man glowered at Miguel. "Just said I don't know him, didn't I? Talk to that asshole across the way. He probably hunts. He's got enough guns to form his own militia. Not afraid to wave them around either. Asshole." The door slammed.

Cady preferred to believe the last reference was aimed at the neighbor and not them. She turned to look at the house in question. If anything, it was even more run-down than this one. Tattered blankets hung from the windows instead of curtains. The porch listed to one side. The only thing keeping the broken-down couch from sliding off it was the railing on the far end.

"C'mon." Cady strode toward the other residence. "Guess we're forewarned. Maybe we'll get a slightly warmer reception than Charlie would."

"Let's hope this guy isn't a Dirty Harry wannabe," Miguel muttered.

There was nothing resembling a walk up to the home. The dog responsible for the mounds in the patchy yard began barking inside the house at their approach. Avoiding the rotted holes in the steps, they climbed to the porch. A windowless screen covered the front door. When Miguel banged on it, the inner door shuddered as the canine on the other side battered it.

The site had her instincts quivering. The canine's relentless racket heralded their presence far better than Miguel's knocking could. Long minutes stretched before a voice sounded. "Shut the hell up!" The barking stopped on cue. She tensed as the door swung inward, framing a man. A naked man, Cady mentally corrected. Wearing only a scraggly beard and a holster, from which he'd freed a handgun.

She and Miguel drew their weapons and moved aside for cover. "Deputy U.S. Marshals. Lower the gun, now," she commanded.

"People come knocking on my door in the middle of the night," he screeched. "Man's got a right to protect himself."

"Set it on the floor. Slowly." She waited until he obeyed before she re-holstered her weapon. Miguel kept his drawn. "It's close to noon. We need to ask you some questions."

The man peered at them. Then his gaze shifted to something beyond them. "Think I don't know you set the law on me," he hollered. A door slammed behind them.

"We're speaking to everyone in the area. And your neighbor is the least of your worries. Threatening federal officers is a felony."

"Don't matter what kind of officers you are. I got nothing to say to cops."

"What's your name?"

"Saul Jonas. What's this about?"

The view afforded by the vacant space in the screen door threatened to sear her retinas. Cady kept her gaze firmly on his face. "We're trying to find a young woman who lived here when she was young. She might have been Selma Dierks's daughter."

"Rina?" His eyes darted up and down the street. "She back?"

"We don't know where she is. That's why we're asking."

Jonas reared away. "She got hurt bad here. She wouldn't return no matter how awful things got. What happened back then was probably Selma's fault. She's the cause of most trouble 'round here. Except for that fucking idiot across the road. I see you peeking behind the curtains, dumbass!" He yelled the last statement.

"Try to focus," Miguel advised. "How long have you lived in Bordertown?"

Saul shrugged. "Grew up here. This place belonged to my parents. They're dead, so it's mine now."

"Did you ever attend Life Church? It used to be in the area."

It was as though a mask had slipped over his expression. "Nope."

"Did Rina?" When he hesitated, Cady pressed, "Maybe you and she didn't go to church. Perhaps you just went to the stables there. Visited the animals."

"No. I never did."

"She could have started going after she began living with Frank Burgess."

The flicker of fear in his eyes was impossible to miss. "Don't know him."

His reaction said otherwise. "I think you do." Cady held out one of her cards. "If you're worried about your safety, we could help with that." When he made no move to take it from her, she let it flutter to the floor at his feet.

"You're wasting your time." Saul's voice was flat. "Everyone in this area is gonna tell you the same damn thing. There's not a bunch of churchy folk up here. Look around. If ever there was a place God forgot, it's this dump.

If you see Rina again, you tell her to run like hell. She's not safe 'round these parts. None of us are." He stepped back then and closed the door in their faces.

Cady and Miguel turned to walk cautiously down the steps. "Well, that's a first."

She nodded. "Gives a whole new meaning to going off half-cocked."

"I meant... he's the first to connect Rina and danger. We didn't tell him that. He came up with it on his own."

"Yeah." She turned at the edge of the dirt road and sent a contemplative look back toward the house they'd just left. "What do you suppose he's afraid of?"

"From the expression on this face when we mentioned Frank Burgess, I don't think it's a question of what, but who." There were at least a dozen more places scattered along the road. Not one of the occupants opened their door when they knocked. A few of them might have been gone. Or maybe asleep, despite the hour. But not all.

"The word's out," he said in disgust. "The rest either saw us or got tipped off that we're in the area."

"There's one more place we haven't tried." She pointed toward the home Bill had indicated.

"You think that's Selma Dierks's place?"

"Only one way to find out." As they strode toward it, Cady had the sensation of being watched. Their progress measured.

How had Rina left this place? she wondered. Had she run away or been taken?

Cracked pavers led up to the house. Its wooden siding was nearly bare, with only occasional yellow flecks of paint embedded in the grain. It was two decades past a needed roof replacement and the chairs that flanked the front door looked as though they hadn't been used for years.

She rapped on the window punctuating the door. The filthy blind covering it had once been white.

"I got a shotgun pointed right at you. Open the door, nice and slow. Let's see your hands."

Cady and Miguel exchanged a glance. Once again, they drew their weapons and moved to either side of the entry. She was closest, so she reached out to turn the knob. Pushed the door open. "Deputy U.S. Marshals, ma'am. Lower your weapon."

"Since you's hiding, think instead you should show me your badge or whatnot. Prove who you are."

Cady unclipped the star from her belt. Held it up in the wedge of opening. "Maddix and Rodriguez. Set that gun down slow and easy. We just want to ask you some questions."

A clatter sounded. "It's on the floor." A quick peek proved the woman right. The shotgun lay on the splintered wooden planks. Cady stepped into the doorway. An obese woman sat at a kitchen table. There was a lump beneath her apron that could be another weapon.

"Hands on the table, ma'am." She resecured her star as the stranger obeyed. Miguel was right behind Cady as she crossed to the woman and checked the deep pocket in the apron. Drew out a handgun that looked newer than anything else in the house. She set it on the chipped linoleum counter, out of the woman's reach. "What's your name?"

"You know my name," she snapped. "I saw that fucker Bill point out my place." When Cady just stared at her, the woman heaved a sigh. "It's Selma Dierks. You seen this place. Can't blame me for defending myself. Can't trust anyone up here, and that's a fact."

Dierks would tip the scale at three hundred pounds. Her

girth lapped over the sides of her chair. It was impossible to guess her age. Her stringy gray hair looked like it hadn't been shampooed in weeks. Her skin was the pasty white of people who only rarely ventured outdoors. Tiny piggy eyes squinted from a meaty face, and they were fixed on a spot beyond Cady at the moment.

"Can't say I ever had a guy looked like him 'round here. Hey, handsome. Wanna make twenty bucks?" She spread her legs.

"When's the last time you saw your daughter?" Cady rounded the table and nudged the shotgun farther away with her foot.

"I don't got no children. Men aren't interested in a girlfriend with a family. I've had my share of guys…" She preened at this and Cady felt a shudder of revulsion. "Kids—especially a girl—are bad news. Who needs the competition?"

"Is that why she doesn't live here anymore? She took too much attention away from you?"

Selma abruptly sobered. "Now why you wanna talk shit about Rina? My girl died in this house. Right here on this table." She slapped one broad palm on its chipped Formica top. "Went and got herself pregnant and who'd she come to for help but her mama. Couldn't save either her or the baby, and that's a failure that weighs mighty heavy on me, I can tell you."

Cady took the cell from her pocket and scrolled until she found a picture of the young woman. "This is Rina. And she's not dead."

Selma glanced at the image. Away again. "Looks like you saw her once. So why you need help finding her now?"

No apologies for her earlier dishonesty. Bill's warning echoed in Cady's mind. *She'll tell a thousand lies before she'll speak one truth.* "We're trying to find her because she may be in danger. I want to know why she can't talk. And where she went after leaving here."

"She's a mute. That ain't my fault, no matter what anyone else says."

"What happened to her?"

Selma jerked a shoulder. "She was a clumsy kid and I couldn't keep her to home. They brought her back once after takin' a fall. She never spoke again. Don't got nuthin' to do with me."

"When did she stop living here?" Since Selma had her gaze fixed on Miguel, Cady walked further into the home and poked her head into the next room. The place was tiny. A sitting area and one bedroom beyond that. She wondered where a child would have slept.

"She was ten or eleven. She got hard to control so I sent her to live with her father."

Cady refocused on the woman. "And who was that?"

Selma looked coy. "Someone who'd get her on the right path. Set a good example. His name is Frank Burgess."

22

"Burgess is Rina's father?" It took effort for Cady to keep the skepticism from her voice. Three weeks earlier, Selma had told the Jackson Sheriff's Office that she didn't know the fugitive. Was she lying then or now?

"He could be." Selma's voice was defensive. "He don't live too far from here. Has his own business, so Rina don't want for nuthin'. Sometimes a mother has to do what's right for her kid, even though it breaks her heart."

Selma didn't seem particularly devastated, Cady reflected. "How did you meet him?"

"Don't really recall. Rina's better off with him. He's a godly man." She nodded emphatically.

"What do you mean by that?"

"He's churchgoin'. I went for a while, too, but it wasn't my thing."

Miguel spoke for the first time. "Do you remember which church?" When she looked away, he continued, "Was it Life Church?"

She shrugged. "Might've been. Place wanted churchgoers to do all the work 'round there. I got plenty of my own to keep me busy."

"Do you recall the name of its pastor? Or anyone else who attended there?"

"Like I say, it was a long time ago."

Cady took over. "Frank Burgess isn't at his home or his business. Your daughter has no food. No place to go. Where would she hide if she was afraid?"

"Knows these woods like the back of her hand. She probably has men. Lots of men. Shelter in a storm, know what I mean?"

"You don't think she'd come to you for help?" She could already predict the answer to her question.

"Barely have enough food for myself, much less for a freeloader. She'll get by."

"Maybe she's with Frank," Cady suggested. "If you tell us where he went, we could find Rina, too."

"He wouldn't hurt her less'n he had to. She'll be fine."

The maternal instinct was strong in this one, Cady thought sarcastically. She banked the anger that threatened to rise.

"When did you last see her?"

Selma batted her lashes coquettishly at Miguel. "Don't quite remember. If Frank is smart, he'll have the girl tied up somewhere. Only way to keep her from running."

"I think you know more than you're letting on." He unleashed the charm. "A woman like you... bet you notice everything going on around here."

Selma looked pleased. "You'd be right 'bout that. I heard that Frank took off. Figured Rina was with him at the time. If not, she'll be in the woods somewhere. Probably in some cave she found. I was always having to pull her out of some dark hole. That girl ain't never been right."

Cady set her card on the counter before they turned to

retrace their steps to the Jeep. "Talk about a miserable childhood," she muttered. "I'm not sure who would have been worse, her mother or Burgess." Selma hadn't once shown a hint of concern for her daughter.

"Dierks isn't exactly a candidate for Mother of the Year," Miguel agreed. "It seems pretty clear that Rina would never return here, no matter how desperate she was."

They got in the vehicle and Cady turned around, heading back down the narrow drive leading them away from Bordertown. Halfway down the lane she met a sheriff's car. It stopped when she pulled alongside it, so she followed suit and lowered her window.

She recognized the man behind the wheel, but not the deputy next to him. "Jeb. Good to see you." Sheriff Redding was in his early fifties, with a receding hairline and prominent ears. His lean build was a studied contrast to the gym rat physique of the man beside him.

"Cady. Didn't expect to see you up here. My deputy, Wayne Harmon." Jeb jerked a thumb at the man, who looked a few years his junior.

"This is my colleague, Miguel Rodriguez."

Harmon pulled out a handkerchief to wipe his forehead. "Warm out today. And, as luck would have it, the sheriff's air-conditioning isn't working. We heard there were two marshals up here asking questions."

She cocked a brow at Jeb. "Someone called you about that?"

A brief twitch of his lips passed for a smile. "No, the call was the same sorta crap we get contacted about regularly. A spat between neighbors. These sorts of disagreements can get out of control quickly if we don't intervene, tamp down the tensions. The caller mentioned you were here, along with a long list of complaints about the fella across the road.

I accompanied Wayne because I'm short-handed today. I have a couple of guys out sick. We don't work this area alone. Lots of loonies in the area."

Silently, Cady agreed. "We ran into some colorful characters."

"Is this about your fugitive?" Harmon asked. Before she could answer, he went on. "I was on his property that first night with Ryder Talbot. We lost Burgess but discovered a dead body in his locker. Could've knocked me over with a feather. I've been out to his place before to investigate complaints. Never would have figured him for some sort of crazed killer. You guys get a lead on him yet?"

"Not really," Miguel said ruefully.

"Shit, he could probably live in the woods for months and never be seen if he didn't want to be."

"You seem to know the area well," Cady observed.

"Jeb and I both grew up around these parts. I lived the next county over, but that doesn't matter. I speak fluent hillbilly." Harmon grinned again. "Never would have guessed that would come in handy, but there you go."

"What do you know about a nearby country church that burned three years ago?" she asked.

"I spoke to my staff about it after your call," Jeb noted. He took a pair of sunglasses from the visor and slipped them on. "None of them were able to recall any specifics."

"I just knew it was there," Harmon put in. Cady wondered how his chattiness went over with the more taciturn sheriff. "Way I recollect it, the fire was set. We never had a suspect."

They'd learned as much yesterday. "We'll let you get back to work. Good seeing you again, Jeb." She nodded at the deputy, then carefully guided the vehicle down the rutted track to the road.

"Rina didn't indicate that she and Burgess were related when we asked," Miguel observed.

"It's hard to believe anything that comes out of Selma's mouth," Cady replied. "It might be true. Or maybe it's another lie to justify having 'given' her daughter to the man. She may not have even mentioned it to the girl." Sympathy darted through her. She knew from experience that abuse didn't always come at the hands of strangers. Sometimes family members were the cruelest.

"Next move?"

"The only tangible lead we got today was Bill's claim that he'd gone fishing with Burgess near Hot Springs." She turned off the rutted lane onto the blacktop.

He leaned forward to mess with the knobs on the dash. "He gave a decent description of the home."

"Really, Miguel? Eighty degrees? In June?"

He notched it down a little. "The passenger gets to control the temps and the tunes. You know the rules."

She did. She'd also learned that he had the circulation of a ninety-year-old woman and excruciating taste in music. Both of which he used to make her miserable when he wasn't driving.

Cady gritted her teeth and lowered the window. "We need to look at the places in that area for A-frame homes. Then track the owners of them."

"Shouldn't be too difficult to run title searches," Miguel agreed. He slouched more comfortably in his seat. "Swing through a drive-through on the way, will you?"

"Sure. If you set the temperature to seventy degrees."

His head swiveled toward her. "The passenger gets to…"

"Yeah, yeah. The passenger can also enter into a negotiation, if said passenger wants to eat today."

"You've got a mean streak, Cady."

"Don't I know it. I also know how hangry you get by mid-afternoon." She leaned closer to the clock on the dash. "One thirty? You must be starving. Oh, well. There's always supper."

"Mean," he repeated. "Seventy-four degrees is my best offer." He turned up the air conditioning. "It takes an unhealthy relationship with food, to weaponize it like that."

She smiled beatifically as the cooler air poured out of the vents. "We all have our flaws."

"There are worse ways to spend the afternoon than sightseeing on the French Broad." Miguel climbed out of the Jeep and stretched expansively. His mood, as usual, had been improved with nourishment. In this case, a twelve-inch sub sandwich. She'd guarded her six-inch religiously. Rodriguez didn't have boundaries when it came to food.

"Pretty," she agreed, scanning the row of five homes before them. The river twisted and turned on nature's whim, shifting between tree-covered shores and muddy beaches. The residences on this road sat on a hill, rising above the water like aerial sentries.

"A-frame." He pointed to the one that had drawn her attention. "We'll have to go around back to see if it has a bank of windows."

It almost certainly would have, Cady thought. What was the point of a scene if there was no way to view it? "We better knock first and introduce ourselves before we start traipsing over the property."

"Sure." He fell in step beside her as they approached the first home matching the description Bill gave. "Most of the homeowners are good about allowing fishermen access."

"We're not fishermen." And people might have a far different reaction when it came to welcoming deputy US marshals on their land.

As they drew closer, she could hear children's shrieks. A minute later one of the shriekers rounded the corner of the home and took up position in the bushes, ready to ambush his companion with a water gun of substantial proportions.

The ensuing full-frontal assault elicited more screams and an epic water battle that made her grateful they were out of range. "Hold your fire," she called out as they neared the front door. Both boys turned toward them. "Are either of your parents home?"

"Who are you?"

"Why do you want to know?"

"Is this about fishing?"

The questions pelted her faster than the water had bombarded the unsuspecting shorter child. "Deputy U.S. Marshals. Go get your mom or dad."

But the introduction just slowed things down as both came closer, jaws agape and eyes avid. "Do you have a gun?"

"Did you ever shoot a bad guy?"

"Have you ever been shot?"

"Do you have a badge?"

Head spinning by this time, relief filled her when an adult voice called, "Jimmy! Kevin! Get on in here!"

A woman was leaning out the front door, her gaze stern when it rested on the two youngsters and wary when it shifted to Cady and Miguel. "Can I help you?" she asked them. With barely a hitch in her voice, she told the boys, "Quit your dawdling and get inside!"

The kids ran to the house and through the door their mother held open for them. Cady was impressed. The woman had managed to shut off their questions as abruptly as turning a spigot.

"Deputy U.S. Marshals Maddix and Rodriguez, ma'am." Miguel took a step forward, then paused, because her attitude hadn't become less unwelcoming. "We wanted to ask you about your home."

"I don't know why." She came out onto the porch, which was just a square slab of concrete. "We pay our property taxes on time, twice a year, like clockwork." She was midthirties, attractive, wearing a tank, white shorts, and an attitude.

"This isn't about taxes, ma'am. We're interested in how long you've owned this home," Cady said. The place was in good condition, but possibly thirty or forty years old. The woman didn't look like someone who would be friends with Frank Burgess. Of course, only Bill had claimed that status.

"Seven years. No, wait. Seven years, three months and nine days."

Smiling, she noted, "That's very precise. Who did you buy it from?"

The woman folded her arms across her chest. "Why do you want to know?"

"We're trying to find someone, ma'am." Miguel's smile was as innocent as a choirboy. For once, it had no discernible effect on a female. "We understood that he spent some time in this area, in a home that looked a lot like yours."

That elicited a reaction. She bounded down the single step and approached them. "I doubt that very much. We bought this place from my husband's uncle when he moved to Arizona. I think he built it over thirty years ago."

"We'd like his contact information, if you have it."

Chewing her bottom lip for a moment, she said, "Maybe I should call my husband."

"Ma'am." Cady was losing patience. "Your spouse's uncle is not in trouble here. We're stopping by all similarly designed homes in the vicinity in the hopes that we can track down one homeowner from over ten years ago."

It took another few moments, but finally the woman said, "I have his number in the house. I'll get it for you." Turning, she went back inside and closed the door.

"You're losing your touch, Rodriguez."

"She's not a trusting sort," he agreed. "I'm going to look around back."

Nodding, Cady watched him walk away. She hoped it didn't take this long with all the houses in the area. If they could just find the owner who'd loaned the place to Frank Burgess, they might discover someone who knew his whereabouts.

The homeowner appeared again. "Here's his info. I also included other nearby houses that are similar to ours. We were looking at A-frames specifically, and my husband's uncle was taking a while to make up his mind. We began a list of alternatives."

"I appreciate it." Cady took the slip of paper just as Miguel was returning. "Thanks for your time."

"This person you're looking for," the woman called after them, once they'd turned and started back toward the vehicle. "Is he dangerous?"

"He's a fugitive, ma'am. But you don't have to worry." Cady turned to face her again. "We have no reason to believe he's in this area."

"The house was almost totally glass in the back. Great view," Miguel observed after they'd gotten in the Jeep. She scanned the note she'd been given and then handed it to him. It had six other addresses on it. "I'll drive around and make sure the list she gave us was conclusive," Cady said. "But you could get started on the online title searches now. Go back fifteen years, say."

"If we're in the right area, these few homes shouldn't be too difficult to trace," he said, with a rare burst of optimism. She shot him a glance, as he swiveled the computer toward him and booted it up. Deep dives into databases were rarely his favorite occupation. She had to figure that it being a Friday afternoon had more to do with his mood than a sudden love for research.

She drove slowly around the area, checking off addresses against houses matching the description. Cady found only one other missing from the sheet. Maybe it wasn't an A-frame exactly, but it seemed close enough in style that she added it, earning herself an evil eye from Miguel.

They were nearing Asheville when he finally looked up from his task. "Okay. For each of the homes we noted, I've traced all the property owners since the houses were constructed. When I narrow it down to the dates when Life Church was in operation, that's still seventeen names. I've got something going on tonight, but I can follow up with these tomorrow."

Belated memory struck. "I forgot to tell you, last night I found an obit for Corbin Fielding, aged twenty-three who died two years ago. I'm going to go inside when we get back, and see if I can get a lead on his next of kin." The obituary had noted Fielding's mother as living in Naples, Florida, but the father resided in Rosman, the same town as his son.

"Keep me posted."

After promising to do so, she dropped Miguel off at his vehicle and parked, continuing to their offices. Although not quite five, the space was deserted. She first checked databases to see whether either parent was in the system and got a hit on the dad. Adam Fielding had done fifteen-years for drug possession and distribution. He'd been paroled less than six months before his son's death. Mindful of the time, Cady immediately called the parole officer on the record and got the man's phone number and address. Rosman was just under an hour away. She wasted no time heading out to her Jeep again hoping that before the weekend was over, they'd be a lot closer to Burgess.

ADAM FIELDING WAS a fireplug of a man, short, squat and muscular. His head was clean-shaven, and he sported an eight-inch beard and a wary attitude. But when Cady said she was there to talk about his son, he visibly relaxed.

"We lived in Dillsboro when Corbin was little. He wasn't nine yet when I went inside. And a grown man when I come out." The words sounded more resigned than bitter. "His mom brought him to visit a time or two, but then she quit. Wasn't much later she quit me, too. Didn't hear much from either of them after that. But I had this hope, y'know? That maybe I could get to know my kid again when I got out."

Dillsboro was in Jackson County. So was Life Church and Burgess's home. "Did your family attend religious services?"

His beard wagged when he shook his head. "Not when I lived with 'em. Can't say 'bout afterward."

"Do you have a phone number for your ex?" Corbin's mother would have more details about her son's childhood.

Adam snorted. "Only contact I have with her is the

alimony I pay every month. I can tell you one thing. My son didn't commit suicide."

The obit hadn't alluded to cause of death. They usually didn't when people took their own lives. "Why don't you think so?"

He leaned a shoulder against the doorjamb. "They never found his phone. Just his laptop. These days, who doesn't keep their cell with them?"

There could be several reasons for it being missing, but she didn't mention that. "Did the police take his computer?"

Adam nodded. "After I raised hell about him not killing hisself. Took 'em forever to bring it back, too. They said they'd checked his social media accounts and whatnot. But he didn't have any. As far as I know, he only used the laptop to work on his drawings. Bet they never really investigated much anyways. They told me some doctor knew for sure it was suicide. Corbin was always a loner and not much of a talker. But that don't mean he offed hisself."

Cady stilled. "Was your son interested in art?"

His chest swelled. "You bet. Good at it, too." He stepped aside, pointing to an array of cartoons tacked to the wall above the couch. "He did those. Always was sketching, even as a kid. Used to make his own comic books. He wanted to be an animator. Guess there are sites where you can practice that stuff online."

"Do you have any other samples of his work?" Joseph Wiley's tattoos had told a violent tale, one she was still struggling to comprehend. She wondered what story his friend's art would tell.

"That's all I found in his house." Grief shadowed his expression. "There wasn't much else, other than his clothes and laptop."

"Would you be willing to let me take it for a while? I'd

like to look at his artwork on those sites you mentioned. I'd bring it back, of course," she added, when his eyes narrowed.

"What for?"

"I've seen the works of a friend of his. All art tells a story, doesn't it? I want to see if Corbin's expresses a similar one."

It took several minutes before she extracted an agreement from Adam. After filling out the paperwork documenting her possession of the laptop, she said, "I appreciate your help. And I'm sorry about the loss of your son."

He just nodded, and then, as if out of words, stepped back and closed the door.

She went to the Jeep and started it. She'd have to drive back to Asheville. Andy Garrett, one of their task force members, was a Buncombe County deputy and a whiz at computer forensics. Although it'd be Monday at the earliest before he could get to it, she was anxious to see if he could get her access to the sites Corbin Fielding had spent so much time on.

And whether his artwork had anything in common with Joseph Wiley's.

IT WAS after eight when Cady arrived at her empty home. She quickly texted Miguel a summary of her meeting with Adam Fielding. By the time Ryder walked through the kitchen door, she had the pizza and cheese bread she'd picked up warming in the oven. She went to the refrigerator and took out two beers and handed one to him.

"Your food surprises have been the best part of my day."

"Uh-oh." She twisted off the top of the beer. Collected

his and went to toss them in the trash. "That doesn't sound good. No luck today?"

"We got a lot more information." He paused to take a gulp, leaning against the counter. "But nothing on the bank or credit card statements immediately jumps out. We're still running down the data provided by the cell phone company. We've set up a tip line and Phoebe Lansing's face is all over the news in the tristate area."

She used two hot pads to remove the items from the oven, then loosened the foil on the pans containing the bread. Fine dining all around. Ryder loaded food onto the paper plates she'd put out and they carried them to the island. "Did her friends or neighbors have any insights?" She slipped onto a stool and lifted a piece of cheese bread to her mouth.

"All seemed shocked at her disappearance. A few were angry on Phoebe's behalf at the suggestion that she may have run off with someone. Tim Lansing's parents were staying with him at the time of his wife's camping trip, so he's alibied. At least on the surface." Ryder spoke in between bites of pizza. "We've started a list of all of her acquaintances. And I want to take a deeper dive into the electronics before sending them off to the lab. But my gut feeling? This is looking more and more like a stranger abduction. Wrong place, wrong time."

His words resonated. Just because stranger abductions were relatively rare, statistically speaking, didn't mean they didn't happen. She was a case in point.

As if he read her mind, his hand reached out to squeeze hers. "If it is a kidnapping, let's hope she has your guts and determination."

"And the opportunity," Cady murmured. Strength and cunning were worthless if there was no chance for escape.

Deliberately, she changed the subject. "What's the news on Alma's cabin?" Her aunt and mom had left this morning, and Ryder had had a car stationed nearby ever since.

"All's been quiet so far," he said, his mouth full. Swallowing, he added, "I didn't schedule anyone for tonight, though."

"No need." Cady took another sip from her beer. "I plan to park the Jeep down the road and wait inside the home for the night." The elaborate hoax of the phony "prize" made no sense unless its purpose was to leave the property vacant for a while. Just the thought of surprising Caster, or whatever lackey he sent in his place filled her with anticipation. "I'm looking forward to it, as a matter of fact."

He lowered the pizza. "As am I."

She cocked a brow at him. "I think I'm capable of getting the jump on a con man, especially when I have the element of surprise on my side."

"Well, then you'll be doubly effective with me there, too." His pronouncement brooked no argument. Cady opened her mouth. Closed it again. She figured the intruder would be alone tonight, but there was no way to know for sure. And she'd rather spend the long hours waiting with Ryder than by herself. The cabin held no pleasant memories for her.

She looked at him and smiled. "Having you there will make it the single best time I've ever spent in that place."

His expression was droll. "Why do I feel like that isn't an especially high bar?"

"Low self-esteem?"

"Never had that problem." He finished off the first slice on his plate and turned to the second. "No thanks to my dad." Butch Talbot. Cady's throat abruptly closed. She knew Ryder's relationship with his father, the former sheriff, had been contentious. She also knew why. Her hand reached out and covered his. He curled his fingers around hers, gave a squeeze.

"Hanging out in a dark empty house with a green-eyed strawberry blonde for the evening is actually the best Friday night plans I've had in a long time."

"Now I feel really bad for you."

"Don't." He swiped the rest of her cheese bread and took a bite. "Because I'm exactly where I want to be."

23

When two dark-clad figures entered the room, Phoebe scooted to the back of the cube. She turned to the woman next to her, searching her expression for clues. But as usual, the blonde watched the happenings without interest. Without hope.

On cue, Phoebe's body began to tremble. There'd never been more than one man here before. But she already knew the second man hiding beneath the monk-like robe and hood hadn't come to rescue them. It was difficult to keep track of the passing time, but she thought her kidnapping was almost forty-eight hours ago. They'd had no more than a single bottle of water since then. But each of the strangers held a foam food container this time and she began salivating, even while tremors of fear worked through her.

It was impossible to make out the men's features with the disguises they wore. The two were nearly equal in height. Thing One and Thing Two, she thought frantically. A malignant transformation of the silly creatures in one of the books Phoebe read to Emma at bedtime.

The first one chanted, "Bless these gifts and give thanks to the Lord for what you are about to receive."

The other woman ducked her head and repeated the words tonelessly, with Phoebe stumbling along.

The newcomer approached her cube, while the other went to her companion's. She shrank against its back wall. Perhaps he was the one who'd snatched her from the campground and denied her return to Tim and Emma. The thought had rage forming a tight hot ball in her chest. She wanted to attack him. To spring up when the top opened and rake his hidden face with her nails, to wound him in a flurry of blows. In her mind, she could see it. The pent-up fury of the assault. The man stumbling back, then falling. Her, surging from her prison—

The sound of the lock being unsecured had her flinching. And just that suddenly her fantasy evaporated like mist in sunshine. Even if she evaded one of them, she'd never avoid the other. The reality punctured her earlier fury, leaving her desolate. She reached up to take the foam receptacle he thrust at her, not even daring to look beyond the gloved hand extending it. Cowed. Completely intimidated.

Self-recriminations bloomed as the lid was refit in place. Noxious black thoughts that could cripple her if she let them. Rebellion was useless when she had no hope of escaping. But surely, they'd be let out of these cages at some point. Then. When there was a chance of success.

"Eat." The word was an order and she moved to obey. Opening the container, she stared in stunned delight. Pasta Alfredo. Two breadsticks. There was no silverware, but she was too hungry to care. She used her fingers to scoop up some noodles and ate ravenously. It was sticky and lukewarm. Food had never tasted better.

"You made the news. Your picture's plastered all over TV. But that won't help you. Nothing will."

Phoebe choked, unable to swallow. The other man had never addressed her, except to issue a command. She glanced at the woman beside her. She was plowing through the meal as if she hadn't heard anything. Perhaps she hadn't. Or maybe that flat, emotionless guard she wore was the result of repeated trauma.

She felt the heat of his focus like a laser and froze, afraid to even breathe.

"You might think the media coverage is a good sign. It's not. Just means the cops have nothing to go on. No one saw anything. That's why they're asking for help."

Mutinously, she tightened her lips. People were looking for her. She seized on that single fact and cradled it close, a precious glimmer of hope.

His voice turned cruel. "It was dark that night, wasn't it? And real late. You'll be news for a few days and then everyone will forget about you. This place will be your life now. And your death."

24

Ryder had different ideas for a stakeout than Cady. He insisted on stocking up on junk food at the convenience store on the way out of town. Amused, she followed him up and down the aisles, only drawing the line at Funyuns. "While onion breath might help fight off our intruder tonight, I have to be subjected to it, as well. So that's a no."

"Have to figure out some other way to put 'fun' into the evening, then," he deadpanned.

Rolling her eyes, she replied, "I'll leave you to it." She only required a couple of bottles of water to get her through the tedious hours of waiting. The fact that someone would show up tonight was indisputable. Getting Alma and Hannah out of the way guaranteed free access to the house.

Someone was blocking the cooler she needed, so she patiently waited until she could remove four water bottles and went back to join Ryder, who was now conversing with an older woman.

As she drew closer, the tenor of the female's voice had Cady's steps faltering.

"All I'm saying is, your father wasn't the man everyone thought. Not the force. Not the town. Certainly not your mother."

"You sound like you had a bad experience."

"You could say that." Her laugh was bitter. "He was a man to take advantage any way he could. I was grateful for his response when I had a break-in. But then he came back to double-check my safety. Wasn't long before he was making the kind of house calls no one expects from law enforcement."

"If you have a complaint to lodge, ma'am—"

"He's been dead nearly five years. Guess I should have reported him decades ago." She moved closer and lowered her voice. "Not a day goes by that I'm not ashamed of myself for falling under your father's spell. More than once I had a notion to go see your mother. Let her know the sort of person she was married to."

"I guess the question you have to ask yourself, ma'am, is if making someone else feel worse would make you feel better."

There was a beat of silence. Then, "Maybe you're not like Butch. If not, the world's more blessed for it. Living with the mistake I made with him is my own burden. Guess I've always known it."

She turned and brushed by Cady. She had a glimpse of a woman, pretty, midfifties before the stranger rushed away. Her gaze went to Ryder. His expression was inscrutable.

"You ready?"

"I am." She linked her free arm in his while they paid for their purchases and returned to the car. He was silent long after he'd pulled onto the road.

"I'm half surprised that hasn't happened before," he said

finally. I've known my dad was a serial cheater since I was a teen."

"Those hidden case files you found in his garage a few months ago..."

"Yeah. The only reason I could ever figure for them to be excluded from the Digi-Reel was that he had cause to hide them. They all involved an attractive woman as the complainant, so his motivation wasn't too difficult to fathom."

And Cady's mother had been one of those women. Being the estranged wife of the county's most wanted had landed Hannah Maddix squarely on Butch's radar. Cady reached out to lay a hand on his thigh, silently commiserating. The first time she'd seen the picture of the former sheriff hanging in Ryder's office she'd had a name to go with an old snippet of memory.

She'd been about six. Cold beneath the too-thin blanket that covered her bed. She'd slipped out of it and padded barefoot to the kitchen. She could feel the chilly plank floor under her feet. Still visualize the girl she'd been standing in the doorway. Cady couldn't peg which house it was. There'd been different ones every year, with enough similarities to meld together. Cracked linoleum. Sagging countertops. Unreliable appliances.

And that night, a man had been sitting in one of the chairs, with her mom on his lap. His uniform shirt was partially unbuttoned and his hand was inside Hannah's blouse. Shock and fear froze Cady in place.

Her mother had attempted to stand. His arm tightened around her, preventing it. "Go on back to bed, baby." Hannah had brushed the hair back from her face and tried to smile. "Get, now. I'll see you in the morning."

But she hadn't moved. Couldn't.

"You heard your mama. Get." The man's rumbling tone had held a command, one the child in her recognized and obeyed. She'd run back to her bedroom and dove under the covers.

She and Ryder were still grappling with what they'd learned about their parents' choices decades earlier. The consequences of those decisions could rise occasionally, like restless ghosts. "Think she'd bother your mom?"

He shook his head. "I hope not. It sounds like she's talked herself out of that for years. What would be the point now? No one's more surprised than I am that my mother has remained blissfully ignorant of Butch's activities." His tone turned bitter. "Hiding it so successfully from her might be the one decent thing the man ever did."

Because there was nothing to say, Cady stayed silent. Ryder was fiercely protective of his mother. Laura Talbot was a delightful woman, and her unawareness of her husband's proclivities was the lone bright spot in the whole sordid history.

He pulled his car behind the county SUV that was half-hidden on a wide shoulder beneath the low hanging branches of sweetgums. When the deputy got out to approach them, Ryder lowered his window.

"Everything's been quiet." Lanny Nygress's face was half-covered by the mirrored sunglasses he favored. His chin bore a recent shaving nick. "The occupants didn't even seem to notice me when they left for the day."

"Thanks. We'll take it from here."

The twentysomething officer grinned. "I'll let you have it then. I've got bigger plans for Friday night than a stakeout."

"Just make sure they don't interfere with your duties tomorrow," Ryder suggested wryly.

"A little beer. A little pool. A little dancing, to show the ladies what they're missing." He gyrated his skinny hips and grinned. "None of that will keep me from my shift, don't worry." He strutted toward his car.

"Why does that young man always make me feel so old?" Ryder murmured as he waited for Lanny to move out of the spot so he could drive into it.

"Because he's fourteen?" Cady watched the other vehicle leave as Ryder pulled even deeper into the trees. "Seriously, what are the age requirements in your office, anyway?"

"He's closer to thirty than twenty. But it's amazing what a decade on the job does to people."

Experience would help, Cady mused, but there were always those who managed to skip through life unscathed by the darkness others contended with. They got out of Ryder's car.

"You've got the keys?"

"A very grudging spare I obtained from Alma when I started paying her to take care of my mom."

"Then I'll grab the snacks."

Cady waited, noting that his navy Honda was even more indistinguishable than the SUV had been. When he'd locked it, she jerked her head toward the trees. "We can hike in."

The incline to the cabin was fairly steep but the fading daylight made their journey easy enough. Several minutes later they were on the porch of Alma's place. Cady fit the key into the front door. It moved stiffly in the lock, but eventually opened. She swung the door wide and ushered Ryder inside.

She relocked it after him and closed the curtains. No reason to make it easier on their would-be intruder.

He did a walkthrough. "Hard to know what kind of

information the guy is seeking. There's a small filing cabinet in the kitchen."

"Caster's focus is my mom." Cady crossed to Hannah's bedroom. "This is hers, although a stranger won't know that without searching both." She stuck her head inside. It looked like her mother, bright, pretty, and cheerful. It was meagerly furnished. An in-depth search wouldn't take more than ten minutes. Once again, she had to question Caster's intelligence. It'd be plain to the most cursory investigator that Hannah Maddix had never lived a life of luxury. She supposed a man locked up for thirty years living on the fantasy of finally getting his hands on his ill-gotten gains wasn't exactly dancing with reality.

After checking out the rest of the cabin's interior, Ryder said, "Where do you want us to be positioned?"

"I'll take the kitchen, around the corner. You can be upstairs. You'll have a good view from there." It felt strange for Cady to be in the cabin without Alma and Hannah. But it would be downright disturbing for her to while away hours in the loft bedroom that had belonged to her crass cousins. She'd learned quickly as a child never to let a Griggs boy corner her.

The memory was like an icy finger on her nape. "God, I hated the times we had to live here," she muttered. "Like we were some dirt-poor relatives hanging around for a handout. I spent way too much of my childhood living in someone else's space." She hadn't known what a freeloader was until her cousins had first hurled the term at her. "Whenever Mom's latest loser boyfriend would take off, I'd start keeping track of the dwindling groceries, knowing they wouldn't get replaced. She'd put on this sunny front that never quite hid her desperation." Hannah would wait until she thought Cady was sleeping to sit at the table, checkbook in hand, crying silent tears.

She wasn't aware of Ryder moving until he was at her side. "How long would the two of you stay?"

"Months, usually." They'd always stretched like years. "We'd leave when she could save up rent money again." But as Cady had grown older she'd realized it was a pattern on continual repeat.

He slipped his arm around her. Pulled her close. "Looks like the past tripped both of us up tonight."

She gave him a hug. "Yeah. The trick is not to let it suck us in." She took a deep breath, willed away the dark memories. "Now about those snacks..."

CADY SHIFTED in her seat again. She alternated between standing and sitting every thirty minutes just to ensure her butt didn't go numb. Darkness had descended long ago. She checked the time on her cell. Nearly midnight. The thought of spending several more hours like this tied her muscles into knots.

She stilled when she heard a creak outside. Someone expecting the place to be empty might drive right up to it, rather than plan a more covert approach. Ears straining, she waited long minutes but the noise didn't repeat. The property was heavily timbered, and hearing branches crack and snap was common.

Her phone chirped an alert for an incoming call. An unknown number appeared on the screen. She nearly ignored it, before reconsidering. She'd left cards with her contact information with a few people this afternoon. She answered, her voice hushed. "Maddix."

There was a pause. Then, "You're the lady marshal, right?"

"Yes. Who's this?"

"Saul Jonas. I been thinking 'bout what you said today. Maybe you can help. We should talk again. I'll tell you what I know. 'Bout Burgess. Deacon. Life and death..." His words were slurred, as though he'd been drinking. "But you gotta get me outta here. Somewhere they can't find me."

Excitement fired through her veins. "If what you tell us puts you at risk, we'll make arrangements for your safety. When can you meet?"

"Tomorrow. I don't go out at night. He watches sometimes. Thinks I don't know he's there, but I do."

He. Burgess? For the first time, doubt flickered. Cady hoped this wasn't alcohol-induced paranoia talking. "When and where?"

Saul named a discount store in Sylva. "Parking lot. 8 am. I drive a 2002 gray Chevy Silverado."

"Okay, we'll see..." she started. But the man hung up. Quickly, she texted the information to Miguel. Minutes later, she received an answering message.

> Changed his tune. Meet you there?
>
> Yes.

Another hour crawled by. The house remained quiet. She spent the time turning over Saul's words in her mind. What could he tell them that had 'life and death' importance? Could it have anything to do with the remnants of human remains found in Burgess's incinerator? Whatever he knew, his fear had come through loud and clear, both tonight and earlier today.

Her phone vibrated.

> Need more snacks.

Ryder's message yanked her back to their mission here the way nothing else could. She typed a reply.

> Guess you could have had Funyuns.
>
> We're far enough apart not to matter. Not later I hope.
>
> By the time this is over I'll be—

Cady's fingers stopped abruptly, uncertain what had alerted her. Something. Not in the back of the house either but... She cocked her head. On the porch? Another text arrived.

> Out front.
>
> Window?

She was half expecting the glass to smash. The last thing she anticipated was the door unlocking. Then easing inward.

She was on her feet now, weapon in hand. Cady sidled up to the corner silently. She wanted the intruder all the way inside so that retreat wasn't an option. She waited, thinking he'd turn on a flashlight, but instead the switch was flipped, flooding the front room with light. Bold son of a bitch, she thought, listening to the footsteps heading for her mother's room.

Cady tiptoed to the bedroom. She let him rifle through Hannah's things for four or five minutes before stepping through the doorway. "Stop right there. Arms up." Then she stopped. Stared. Because the man going through boxes of her mom's belongings was familiar.

But he wasn't Stan Caster.

"Fuck! Cady! What the fuck are you doing here?" LeRoy Griggs had jerked around at her words. Now he scrambled upright, spilling the contents of the cartons at his boot-clad feet.

"Waiting for a dumbass. And guess who showed up? Stop!" Her voice went steely as he took a step toward her. "You don't move unless I tell you. I can't wait to hear the bullshit tale you cooked up to explain this."

But it was blatantly apparent that he hadn't bothered to concoct one. His brother, Bo, had cunning, if a similar shallow intellect. But LeRoy was the follower, used to sticking to cover stories, not developing them.

He shifted from one foot to another. "I came to get something for Ma. I'm supposed to take it to her."

"Really?" Cady nodded reasonably. "She called and asked for a special delivery at—" She held out her cell. Checked the time. "One twenty-three in the morning? Must be a real emergency. What did she ask you to bring?"

"That's none of your business." Quick thinking had failed him, so he turned to attitude, of which he'd always had an ample supply. He came closer. "You're gonna wanna get the hell outta my way."

"Or I could call Aunt Alma right now. I'd like to hear first-hand what's so important she'd send you over in the middle of the night asking you to trash my mom's things."

His face turned ugly. "Fuck this. I don't answer to you."

"You're going to answer to one of us." Ryder's voice sounded behind her and the shock on LeRoy's face was gratifying. "It'll be a simple matter to check whether you're here at your mother's request. Once we get that out of the way, I have some more questions for you. We can do that here or at my office, the choice is yours."

LeRoy swallowed, his gaze going from one of them to the other. Back again. "This is my home. I gotta right to be here."

"Shoot, does that mean you gave up your luxurious living at Gracious Estates once Bo went to jail? Give it a rest, you haven't stayed here in years. I'm by often enough to know that."

"I didn't say I lived here, I said it's my home. Grew up here, which you oughta remember, since you and your mama sponged off us every chance you could."

She gestured with her weapon and he reluctantly backed up. "Who told you to come here? What are you looking for?"

He seemed to weigh the pros and cons of telling the truth. From the looks of him, the moral quandary was a weighty one. "Why was you here waiting?"

"Someone put an envelope in your mom's mailbox a few days ago. Told her she won a stay at a bed-and-breakfast in Maggie Valley. Don't suppose that was you?"

"So what if it was? That ain't a crime."

"As a matter of fact, mailboxes are for the sole purpose of delivery and retrieval of US mail. They're for items bearing postage and delivered by postal employees. Any other uses are illegal." Ryder's voice was confident.

LeRoy gaped at Ryder. After a moment, he glanced from him to Cady. "Shee-it, you made that up."

Her temples were beginning to throb. "No. He didn't. And doing so with the intent to defraud someone is a felony."

Her cousin finally looked concerned. "Now wait there, I just got this manila envelope in my door last week with a hundred dollars cash. Inside was this letter to put in Ma's mailbox. The note said I was to check when they was going away and look through Aunt Hannah's things for bank books or old records or something tracking her money. I was promised another hundred if I found something."

"How were you supposed to contact the sender?" Cady asked.

"He left a number to call."

Caster had known the ramifications for mail fraud even if LeRoy didn't. That'd be the only reason he'd solicited help. But the phone number meant they might be able to connect this to the ex-con, regardless. "Do you have the envelope and letter?"

"Yeah. I can show it to you."

"I'll take this," Ryder told Cady. "We'll drive your cousin's vehicle to his place. I'll have a deputy waiting there to meet us." She nodded and holstered her weapon. Since the cabin was in Haywood County, the crime fell under Ryder's jurisdiction.

"I'll clean up here and see you at home."

It took several minutes after the two had left for Cady to process the night's events. She'd suspected Caster was behind the phony winnings, but he'd surprised her by having the good sense to set up a buffer between him and the break-in. She went back into the bedroom and sighed. LeRoy had managed to make an unholy mess. She'd had no idea her mom had that much stuff stored in her closet.

She sank to her knees and started sorting through the items on the floor. Although Hannah used to be in charge of billing for a lumber company at one time, it'd been a couple of years since she'd been capable of handling her own finances. She didn't need to, with Cady home. She saw that her mother's disability check went to Alma, in return for taking care of her, in addition to a grocery stipend.

A spill of photographs had her halting in the middle of

her task. She picked them up and flipped through them. She hadn't seen any of the pictures before. One showed a much younger Hannah with a baby. Turning it over, she saw the words, *Cady three months* written in her mom's handwriting.

There were a handful more of her. Three of Lonny Maddix and her mother together. Cady lingered over those. Her dad had been handsome, but in him, she saw just a striking resemblance to Hannah's long string of losers. Cady found an empty envelope that the photos might have come from and slid them inside. There were some old bankbooks, she noted with surprise, but they were from a few years ago, not old enough to interest Caster.

She stacked things neatly into the boxes LeRoy had dumped. Cady picked up some loose sheets of paper and froze in place when she saw what was beneath them.

A gun.

Not just any gun, but *the* gun. The one that had been on the table that fateful night. Her stomach did a slow roll. She'd recently seen the crime scene photos from the incident so now she had an adult's perspective to add to the wisps of childhood memory.

She could see herself standing in the kitchen that night. Her father leaning against the door, laughing at Hannah on the floor. Blood dripped down her mom's face, staining her pretty nightgown. Cady reached for the weapon, the weight of it in her palm somehow familiar. *Squeeze the trigger nice and slow*. The sound of the shot had filled the small kitchen.

Why had her mother kept it? The question hammered at her. The police would have given it back after the investigation was over. Had she saved it for protection? Or from guilt? Her mind flashed to the upset Hannah had last winter. The sight of Ryder's official vehicle in the driveway had flipped an invisible switch in her, hurtling her fragile memory back decades. His uniform had completed the transformation. It wasn't Ryder her mom had seen when she'd run down the drive, but the former sheriff of Haywood County, Butch Talbot.

"You said you had a plan." She'd pounded on his chest, weeping. "You said it was the only way. I should never have agreed. She was just a little girl. And we turned her into a killer."

Cady and Ryder would never know for sure whether his dad had used his relationship with her mother to bring down Lonny Maddix after the marshals hadn't succeeded. But it sure looked like it and a few months earlier, a former employee of his had all but verified it.

A four-year-old girl. A means to an end.

She drew a breath, sought to shove the memories aside. Cady checked the weapon to make sure it was unloaded, then set it in the box, suddenly anxious to be gone. She collected the rest of her mom's belongings and replaced them without really seeing them. Her mind was trapped in a place it usually strayed only in her nightmares. Learning more details hadn't changed that. It'd only made them more vivid.

25

Something slimy and wet touched Cady's cheek. She brushed it away and shoved her face closer to the pillow. A snuffle sounded close to her ear, followed by a polite bark.

She tried to brush the item aside. When her hand came into contact with it, she opened her eyes. Then sat upright, sweeping it across the room. It was the clown doll Hero had taken a macabre liking to. She shuddered. The months it'd been around hadn't made her any fonder of it.

He returned with the toy and she rolled out of bed to avoid a game of fetch. The damn thing gave her the creeps.

Tossing a glance over her shoulder, she saw Ryder was still in bed. The dogs followed her out of the bedroom and she eased the door closed behind them. He'd gotten home long after she had, earning himself the right to sleep in. Blearily, Cady stumbled to the back door and let Hero and Sadie out before looking at the time. Barely six. She groaned. But it gave her a while before she was to meet up with Miguel and Saul Jonas.

Checking the coffee maker, she found a fresh pot

brewed. Ryder must have programmed the machine when he'd come home last night, which qualified him for sainthood.

She poured herself a cup and then let the dogs in, fed them, and released them to the yard again. When she'd imbibed enough caffeine to bring her fully awake, she looked in the refrigerator and took out the makings for breakfast. She had few skills in the kitchen, but it didn't take a four-star cook to fry some eggs and bacon.

Cady was just removing the bread from the toaster when Ryder, wearing only a pair of jeans, shuffled into the room. She paused in her task and poured him some coffee, shoving the mug into his hand before returning to buttering the toast. "Breakfast's almost ready."

"Bless you," he muttered, taking the coffee to the counter and pulling out a stool.

It took a couple more minutes before she had a plate in front of him with two eggs, two pieces of toast, and a mound of bacon. She followed that up with silverware and then loaded a dish for herself. Sat beside him.

"What time did you get in?"

"Four or so."

She looked at him askance. "Why are you up so early? You deserve to sleep until noon."

"How many of us get what we truly deserve?" He bit into a piece of bacon. Chewed with pleasure. "Although this comes close. If I may make one observation, your cousin clearly comes from the shallow end of your family's gene pool."

She smirked. "I've stepped in deeper puddles."

"God." His eyes slid shut in pained memory. "He makes a pile of moldy Jell-O seem smart by comparison."

"Did he have the correspondence?"

"Yeah. From the looks of his trailer, he hasn't thrown anything away in a year. The chances of getting prints off the envelope or letter aren't great, but they were at least handwritten, so we might be able to match them to Caster's handwriting."

Stupidity had a broad brush, Cady thought, unless the ex-con had someone else do the writing for him. "What's the plan? Have LeRoy set up a meet?"

"We'll get a warrant for the phone number first. It's probably a burner, but we could still ping its location and tie Caster to it that way. To lure him to a face-to-face meeting, we'll have to pretend your cousin has something pretty damn exciting." He shook his head. "Hard to imagine him believing the haul from the bank robbery is sitting in a lockbox somewhere. Or in an account, drawing interest for the past thirty plus years." He finished his plate and got up to reload it.

"Or he thinks something valuable was acquired with the cash, which he could steal or blackmail my mom for. The story just needs to fit with whatever he's envisioned, and he'll show up. You could manufacture fake account records," she suggested, as she polished off a pile of eggs. "Maybe showing small deposits at several banks in the area. Or some faked old receipts for large purchases like gold or jewelry. Either would play to his fantasy about that damn money."

Ryder nodded, plowing through the second plateful of food without seeming to take a breath. She topped off his coffee. "I have to meet Miguel. One of the guys we talked to in Bordertown yesterday called last night. He claims he has information on Burgess." She retrieved her weapon and a jacket from the front closet. Put them on. Grabbing her cell from the counter, she added, "Why don't you finish eating and go back to bed?"

"The suggestion lacks appeal since I'd be going alone."

Cady smiled. "This shouldn't take long. Then we'll have the rest of the day to do whatever." She headed toward the door.

"I reserve the right to define 'whatever'," he called after her. She smiled again as she shut the door behind her. After their late night, she looked forward to spending a lazy day with Ryder. However he defined it.

Thirty minutes later, she arrived at the discount store Jonas had mentioned, shortly before eight. Despite the early hour, the lot contained a few dozen vehicles already. She spied Miguel's pickup and pulled up beside him. Got out to join him in his truck.

"'Morning," he mumbled over the top of a go-cup. He sipped from it, then said, "I don't see our friend."

She scanned the area. There was no older model Silverado. "I wouldn't be surprised if Jonas were late. He sounded drunk when we spoke."

"Great. Yesterday, it was past noon when we woke him." He drank again. "Tell me again what he said last night."

"He wanted protection in return for telling us what he knew. He mentioned Burgess, deacon, and life and death. He wasn't making much sense." She wished now she'd thought to bring along more coffee. She was getting caffeine envy watching Miguel drink his.

"Is deacon another name? Someone else involved in Life Church? Or was he using it as a title for Burgess?"

"What do you mean? What kind of title?" She found the button on the side to lean her seat back a bit. Stretched out her legs.

He drained his cup. "Deacons can be ordained or

laypeople who help the priests or ministers with duties in the church."

"Interesting." Cady considered his words. "Although we're no closer to knowing whether Jonas was referring to a different person, or to Burgess."

"Hopefully he'll show up soon, so we can ask him."

But a half hour ticked by and the man didn't come. When his tardiness stretched to an hour, Miguel's patience frayed. "I'm not waiting until he finally rolls out of bed for the day. Let's go wake him up."

They were on the same page. She opened the door. "I'll meet you at his place."

Twenty minutes later, they were standing on Jonas's porch, pounding on the windowless screen door. "Déjà vu all over again," Miguel muttered. Like yesterday, no one immediately answered.

"Not quite. Hear that? No dog." She looked around the yard warily. The last thing they needed was for the beast to be loose outside. He knocked again and she went down the steps to the garage next to the house. She peered through a grimy pane of glass on the overhead door. A gray pickup sat inside.

She rejoined Miguel. "His vehicle is here. Maybe he's out back."

There was a bit more grass at the rear of the property than in the front, but Jonas wasn't in sight. Cady saw the dog, however. It was lying on its side near the open back door, whining piteously. Her hand crept to the butt of her gun as they moved closer. "It looks sick." Rabies was the first thing that occurred to her, maybe because of the series of shots she'd gotten weeks ago. The animal, a large pitbull mix, looked as if it was foaming at the mouth.

"I think it's been poisoned." Miguel maintained his

distance but crouched for a better look. "We had a pet that got into mouse bait once. It needs a vet."

But Cady was moving past him to the door. She rapped on it, making it swing in further. "Saul Jonas," she called. "It's Deputy U.S. Marshals Maddix and Rodriguez." Her only response was a distant drone of insects. Trepidation pooled in her gut. She turned back to wave Miguel closer, but he was already joining her. "Listen," she said, cocking her head toward the home.

He did so, instantly reaching the same conclusion she had.

"Shit." They drew their weapons and moved into the house, clearing it room by room. They followed the buzzing of the blowflies to the bathroom. Cady brought her arm up to bury her nose in the crook of her elbow.

Saul Jonas's body lay crumpled on the floor, blood and gray matter splattered around him. A handgun was at his side. They backed out of the room, so as not to disturb the scene. Guilt flared through Cady. "He was afraid," she murmured. "We saw that yesterday." And his fear had been verified by his call early this morning. "Something he knew got him killed."

"Possibly," Miguel cautioned. "It looks like suicide." He pulled out his phone and dialed 911.

But she didn't need an investigation to tell her what had happened. *I don't go out at night. He watches sometimes. Thinks I don't know he's there, but I do.* Saul's words rang in her mind. One sure way to lure the man outside, Cady thought grimly, was to wait until he let the dog out. When it didn't return, perhaps Saul went looking for it and a killer slipped inside. The open back door took on new meaning.

Evil finds a way.

"I agree, it'd be a pretty big coincidence if he killed himself after calling you," Ryder allowed when she filled him in on her morning. "But it's not inconceivable."

"I know." They were sprawled on the couch because that's where she'd found him when she returned home. "We waited until Deputy Harmon showed up. He brought a couple of reserves."

"Jonas's call to you helps peg time of death." Ryder reached out with the remote and turned off the ball game he'd been watching.

"Sometime between eleven fifty-eight p.m. and nine thirty-four a.m.," she agreed. The deputy had seemed singularly interested in the reason for the contact. Cady had been vague, only saying that it had been a follow-up of the conversation they'd had with the man the day before.

Nine and a half hours, give or take. That's all that'd stood between Jonas and survival. And their best chance for a lead in this case had died with him. "About the only good news we had was from the vet. He thought Jonas's dog would make it." Her cell rang and she stretched to retrieve it from the end table. "Maddix."

"Marshal?"

She recognized the voice. "Sarah?" Sarah Rayman from the market. Cady straightened to a sitting position.

"Yes. I wanted to call and tell you that the young woman was here this morning. The one you showed me a picture of."

Rina. Anticipation hummed. "How long ago?"

"It's only been a few minutes since she left. My dad followed her. If you get here soon, he'll be able to give you an idea as to which way she went."

Cady texted Miguel, but she didn't expect him to join her. Highlands was an hour west of her, and he'd never make it in time. Ryder accompanied her to Sarah's Market. When they went inside, the woman walked away from her register and made a beeline for her.

"They're in the woods, near Gleason's Point, Dad says."

"He's still trailing her?" she asked.

"He's familiar with the area around here. He's been hiking it most of his life." She handed her a receipt. "This is what she bought."

Cady glanced at it. Twenty-two dollars' worth of groceries, mostly fresh produce. They'd lost Rina three days ago. She hoped the woman had eaten before today.

"I wrote my dad's cell number on the back. Brad Sellers. He's trying to stay at a distance, but still keep her in sight. She's already walked further than he'd expected."

"That's over and above what I could have hoped for."

Sarah smiled. "He thinks this is the most exciting thing to happen since Luke Combs came by. Not that Dad's into the new country, but still, when he's in your store…"

"Thanks again for this."

"I hope you find her. Sorry. But we're really swamped…" She dashed away.

"Nice place," Ryder said as they made their way to the entrance. "Never stopped here before."

"We'll have to return." She pushed open the doors and pulled out her cell to call Sarah's dad. "I hear they have great ice cream."

It took longer than it should have for them to follow the instructions they got from Sarah's father to a meeting spot. Cady blamed their pace on sporadic cell reception and lack of sleep.

A sturdy sixty-ish guy wearing a ball cap and sunglasses strode over to them. "Deputy Marshal Maddix? I'm Brad Sellers."

Cady introduced Ryder and then said, "Your daughter says you can pinpoint Rina's location."

"I can show you where I last saw her. Your girl sort of zigzagged her way up here," he said, taking off his hat to reveal a bald dome fringed with gray hair. He wiped at his forehead with his arm. Cady handed him one of the water bottles they'd brought with them and he thanked her. "She seemed real familiar with the area. As much as I am, and I've hiked around here since I was a boy." He twisted off the cap of the bottle and drank.

Scanning the timber-studded terrain, she asked, "Do you know where Rina went?"

"Approximately." He took another swig of water. "I didn't want to get too close and scare her off. Follow me."

They walked through a copse of trees and across a clearing before the ground grew steeper. Fifteen minutes later Brad stopped. "After the incline you'll encounter plains, then more woods. But they end at that bluff up ahead." Cady followed the direction of his finger with her gaze. "She couldn't have traveled beyond it. It'd be a treacherous climb and if it's a hiding place she's looking for, she'll find plenty in those trees or the boulders behind them. There are some pretty places within. I figure if she's staying nearby, she'd probably stick close to fresh water."

"Thank you," she told Sellers sincerely. "This is a big help."

He grinned. "It was a thrill for me just to have a part. She looked sort of pathetic. Not like a hardened criminal."

"She's not. But she might lead us to one." And after what happened with Saul Jonas, Cady's concern for Rina had only increased.

"Glad I could help, but I should be getting back. You need directions when you're ready to return, you just call."

They may have to, Cady thought. She'd written all Brad's instructions down as he'd recited them because she honestly wasn't sure they'd find their way without them. She had a sudden idea. "Before you leave... Do you happen to remember hearing about a Life Church that used to be active in Jackson County? It had a stable on the property, as well."

"Sure, I seem to recall something about it. Just about what you said, though. I couldn't offer any other details."

"No idea who the pastor was?"

He gave a wry smile. "You get to be my age and remembering names is like trying to catch bubbles. They pop the moment you touch them. Not sure I ever knew it, to tell the truth."

"Thanks again for your help."

"That's still a lot of area," Ryder noted after Brad walked away.

"At least we're in the vicinity. How about we spread out twenty yards, and try to cover more ground."

"Make it twenty-five."

They split up and moved forward. Cady braced her feet to go down a slope. They were traipsing through a blanket of wildflowers, the land rolling gently in a series of knolls. The forest ahead was backdropped against a stony mountainside. When they entered the woods, their pace slowed. There were no visible trails. Fallen logs were obstacles to be crawled over or veered around. Sticks and rocks of varying sizes littered the ground. Cady stopped. Ryder was no longer in view. She pulled out her cell to call him. "I hear running water. I just can't figure out where it's coming from."

"Go west."

She brought up the compass app on her phone to guide her. It was easy to lose her bearings when the landscape changed so dramatically. What looked like a quick ten-minute walk took three times that, because it was impossible to move in a straight line. But the effort seemed worth it. They'd entered a sylvan scene. Slivers of sunlight penetrated the overhead canopy to dapple the forest floor. It looked like a fairy glen. The fanciful thought had her smiling—a moment before she slipped on a rock and turned her ankle.

Fairies be damned, she thought, sitting on a log so she could examine the injury. Weren't they the creatures responsible for luring unsuspecting people into the woods to their death? Wait. Maybe she was getting confused with mermaids.

Cady started at the sound of the voice coming from the phone she still held. "I can see a little waterfall and creek from here. Are you near it?"

"Are fairies and mermaids the same except for the whole fish thing?" she asked Ryder.

A beat passed. "Ah... they're mystical. Enticing, yet devious."

"I knew the little bastards couldn't be trusted."

"We seem to be having an entirely different experience, despite our proximity. Head northwest."

Gingerly, she set her foot down. It bore her weight, so she rechecked the compass app and followed Ryder's directions. It still took her ten minutes to make her way toward him.

"Oh." She stopped in delight. "That's pretty. But don't be lured into thinking it's all magical and stuff because that's how you turn your ankle."

"You're hurt?" He closed the distance between them. "Let me see."

"It's okay. Mostly." They must have reached the cliff Sellers had pointed out. She peered upward, trying to see the source of the water cascading down the face of the stone. It made a narrow stream that Ryder had to step over to reach her. No more than a couple of feet across, but deep enough to be a decent watering hole. The animal prints near it underscored the thought.

"Raise your foot."

Resting a palm on his arm, she obeyed. He probed her ankle. "It's fine. I've been walking without... ow!" She whacked him lightly. "Well, *that* hurts."

"It's swelling." He set it down gently. "You need ibuprofen." He dug in his jeans pocket. Took out a small tin and withdrew two white pills.

She gazed at them distrustfully. "Isn't there some urban warning about taking unmarked drugs from a stranger you meet in the woods?"

"Lucky for you I'm not a stranger."

She took the pills and swallowed them with a swig of water. "Rina's likelier closer to this place than where I was. Let's keep heading further in this direction and look for places that would provide concealment. And shelter."

They stopped when something crashed through a tangle of bushes and two deer bounded out. Ten minutes later, they could still hear the water but could no longer see it. They halted to investigate an overhang of branches curtaining the forest floor. Found only a nest of rabbits beneath.

"Selma Dierks told us she was always having to pull Rina out of some dark hole," Cady recalled. "We should look for caves. Or cutouts in the cliff."

They moved in tandem toward the face of the bluff ahead of them and spent fifteen minutes examining its unforgiving rocky face. While there were a few shallow openings, none would keep someone hidden for long.

She tried not to be distracted by the two fox kits chasing each other in a grassy area or the trill of the songbirds. Rina had covered a lot of ground by making her way to the market. She could have hitched a ride, but Cady couldn't see the young woman leaving the safety of the countryside for roads.

"What's behind that brush?"

"You'll have to be more specific," she said drily. Ryder pointed to a spot on the mountainside. She backtracked and followed him to it. Stared.

"It's a cave."

As they drew closer, Cady could see a pile of branches partially blocking the entrance. They'd been disturbed. The chamber was about five feet off the ground. She climbed up and peered inside.

Instantly she recognized that something was wrong.

"She's been here." She recalled the items on the receipt that Sarah had given her. Four oranges. Four apples. A length of deer sausage. Fresh string beans. The purchases were strewn about on the floor of the cave. Without a thought, she crawled in farther, struggling to get her cell out of her pocket as she did so. She turned on the flashlight app and lit up the area. And immediately the past grasped her by the nape. Gave her a violent shake.

Damp earthen walls enclosing all around her. *Maybe a few hours in the dark will help you remember not to take what don't belong to you.*

She sat stock-still as one flashback slammed into the next. The drone of the tattoo device. The hum of her attacker. The slab of cold stone beneath her. Surrounding her. And the near certainty that Cady wouldn't be leaving the mine alive.

"Easy." She didn't hear Ryder's voice behind her. Not then. Her whole body was shaking, she realized, as if distantly removed from it. How odd. "Just back up. And out." His hands were at her waist and he was dragging her more than she was moving herself because her muscles had gone to ice.

When she was in daylight again, it took real effort to haul in a breath, then another, to stop the raging in her chest that felt like the stampede of a thousand horses.

"Are you all right?"

She meant to nod but couldn't manage it. Not yet. Not until the shaking and gasping were over. "Shit. I hate it that Yarnell was right about something."

"I didn't think about it myself before you went inside." The self-reproach in his words was evident. "I should have."

"Well, if I didn't consider it, why would you?" It was easier now to speak, to breathe without that giant boulder of panic lodged on her lungs. "Damn embarrassing, I have to say."

He nudged a bottle of water into her hands. "Drink. More," he urged when she stopped after one sip. "Feeling better?"

"I will when I forget how I froze there a while ago."

His arm slipped around her. "That was just your mind

reminding you that you went through a hell of an ordeal a few weeks back."

"More like a slap upside the consciousness," she muttered. "Crude, but effective. Okay, though. I'm over it. Let's get a closer look."

"Stay put. I'll go."

She wanted to be offended. But Cady wasn't all that certain she wouldn't experience the same damn thing if she tried again. It went against the grain to have Ryder do it, but the point was she didn't have to. Not this time. She'd work on forgiving herself for that weakness later.

"The cave goes back about six feet, but the ceiling lowers dramatically. I'm on my belly here. There are some more soft firs inside. Maybe she bedded in here at night."

"Someone followed her."

"Or knew where to look." There were a few moments of silence until he rejoined her. "There's not much room in there. I'm guessing somebody found her shortly after she returned."

Someone had lain in wait and attacked Rina once she'd thought she was safe. The discovery, coming so close on the heels of Jonas's suspicious death, had guilt arrowing through her. She'd been too late. Again. Cady and Miguel had believed that the young woman could be in danger.

Now it seemed all but certain.

MIGUEL CALLED as they made their way back toward the market. "I've been trying to reach you. Why aren't you answering your phone?"

"Reception is spotty here. I got a tip. We've been looking for Rina."

"Did you find her?"

"Someone got to her before we did." Cady was beginning to believe that finding the woman came with a ticking clock. And the time was quickly running out.

"Damn. That's not good." He was silent for a moment. "But I think I have something on those properties along the French Broad. A friend of my mom's works for a title and realty business. She helped me trace all the owners of the houses on the list yesterday. I narrowed my search to the dates Life Church was in operation, and I've been reaching out to the former property holders. I've got two left to contact, and—get this—one of them is a Jeffrey Lord, who's part of an evangelical ministry outfit in Durham. It's called Covenant Leaders for Christ."

"Why is that name familiar?"

"Probably from the incessant radio advertisements. Its main spokesman is Lance Goodall."

"Ah." The name completed the connection, but it still meant little to her. She was not well apprised in religious matters. "Where is this Lord from originally?"

"Born in Tennessee, moved to North Carolina as a teen. He attended seminary in Wake Forest."

"Well, that has all the instincts humming."

"You're telling me. I'm going to see what I can learn about his employment history, but I may have found the pastor of Life Church."

"Great job," Cady said. "He doesn't own anything else in this area, does he?"

"None that I can find. But give me some more time. When I speak to him, want me to set up a meet for Monday?"

"We have the cadaver dog search and the anthropologist at Burgess's arranged for then. I'm not sure how long it'll take. I'm available tomorrow." Cady saw Ryder looking at her, his brows raised.

"I've got family commitments."

"It's okay if I go alone, isn't it? Let me know whether you get it scheduled."

"I'll get back to you when I have more information." Miguel signed off.

Disconnecting, she slipped the phone in her pocket.

Ryder was still eyeing her. "What?"

"I don't like the sounds of you meeting alone with anyone connected to this case."

They walked a bit faster. She had to admit that her ankle felt better after taking the pain relievers. "Nothing's been scheduled yet. But if you're dying to come along, you can."

"Yeah?" He bumped her shoulder companionably. "Is that an invitation? It's hard to tell with you."

"As much of one as you're going to get. But after today, I wouldn't blame you for turning it down."

"What, and miss all of this?" He gestured to their surroundings. They were nearing the spot where they'd met Sellers this morning. He caught her hand. Swung it. "Beautiful day, great scenery, gorgeous woman. A breakfast I didn't have to cook myself. Not breakfast in bed, of course."

"We both know how that would have turned out."

"We do. Tomorrow I'll linger in the bedroom and pray for a different result."

She laughed. "Hope springs eternal."

"Don't I know it." His gaze turned sober. "I realize the outcome wasn't what you would have hoped for today. But I still enjoyed spending time together. With our jobs, we don't get to do that enough."

Her stomach did a neat flip. "I never thought before about what it would feel like. To be part of a 'we.'" When his expression stilled, her palms slicked with sudden nerves. She desperately wished for a verbal rewind button. Because one didn't present, she plowed on. "Us, I mean. You and me. I couldn't imagine wanting that with anyone. But... I do. I haven't told you, but it's true."

The look in his eyes turned her brain to mush. He kissed her lingeringly and murmured against her lips, "Like I said. A perfect day."

THAT EVENING CADY stopped by the cabin to fill in Alma about last night's events. The conversation derailed quickly. "What the hell you sayin'?" her aunt hissed, her face shoved close to Cady's. "You blamin' this whole thing on your cousin?" She smacked the kitchen table with the flat of her hand, the sound traveling through the small cabin. "If that ain't jist the way. Ask fer yer help and you blame it on LeRoy."

"No use urging Mom to bed early this evening if you aren't going to keep your voice down." Her tone remained steady. Arguing with Alma was pointless. She'd expected this reaction. The minute one of her boys entered the discussion, the mama grizzly went deaf and blind.

"Can't let us have one thing, is that it?" She snatched up the envelope with the communications about their bed-and-breakfast win. "Gotta ruin it all, turn it into something it ain't."

"Stop!" Cady's patience was dissipating rapidly. "I'll go over it again. Try listening this time. I verified with the Chamber that there wasn't a contest going on. This—" she pointed to the letter purporting to be from them, "—is fake. Someone paid for your reservation, though, although we can't be sure who. I suspect Stan Caster, who has cause to want you out of the house. LeRoy said the envelope in his door contained cash and an offer of more if he'd come here last night and dig through Mom's things."

From the florid color in Alma's cheeks, her temper hadn't dissipated, but at least she seemed to be taking in the details this time around. "Well, he didn't know about this plot. He was jist trying to make an easy buck. If the boy had two brain cells he'd stop waiting to trip over money and go out and earn some the right way." Because she knew a hearty agreement would set Alma off all over again, Cady refrained from one. "No harm done. Don't like the fact that ex-con knows where my boy lives, though."

"He isn't blameless. LeRoy intended to steal anything that might be of interest to the author of that letter. I stopped him, but that doesn't change his objective."

Alma snorted, then they both froze when they heard a sound from the direction of Hannah's bedroom. After a moment, she returned her attention to Cady. "Don't know what he thought he'd find. Poor thing's only got a few boxes in her closet other than her clothes."

"Did you realize she'd kept the gun from that night?"

The shock in her aunt's expression was answer enough. "Why would she? Fact is, I don't know what's in her personal stuff, and no reason I should. Caster has something loose in the head if he thinks the money he and Lonny stole has just been sitting 'round for thirty years." She pulled out a chair and sank in it. "Joke's on him if he paid for that room. I don't think the smile left your mama's face from the time we went till we got back. She always was one to look past the storm clouds to see rainbows. Guess that's how she landed with your daddy to begin with."

"I'd like to take all the paperwork that came about the

contest. It likely has prints all over it but we may get lucky with the adhesives." Alma looked blank. "For testing," Cady clarified.

"Don't make no matter to me. How you plannin' to get Caster out of our hair? I know his type. If he don't get what he wants first time, he jist keeps comin'. Your mama ain't safe as long as he's out there, and that's a fact."

She didn't disagree, but she wasn't going to get into the specifics of a plan that was just in its development stages. "The sheriff's office is working on something."

"Just make sure it's over soon." Alma began stuffing all the correspondence into the envelope. "If Caster don't quit, one of these days, someone's gonna get hurt."

RYDER SPENT the time Cady was away on the phone with Jerry Garza, discussing a recent tip that had been phoned in and making tentative plans for LeRoy Griggs' contact with Caster.

"I've had run-ins with the Griggs brothers," the deputy noted. "Low on morals and brainpower."

"We'll have to idiot-proof a script for the initial phone call and then for the meet," he agreed. "You can spend time prepping him."

The older man swore. "It's the glamor of the job that keeps me from retiring."

Ryder laughed. For the next half hour, they roughed out details for the first contact, before Jerry had to take another call.

Disconnecting, he stretched out in the recliner and turned on the TV. Their talk reminded Ryder of the hours in the cabin last night. And Cady's gut-wrenching disclosure.

I spent way too much of my childhood living in someone else's space.

He'd known about her time staying at her aunt's and with her grandfather, of course. But when she'd decided to leave his place after renovations here had been completed, it'd taken him too long to connect her past with the slight uneasiness he'd sensed in her when she'd lived with him. At first he'd chalked it up to her innate emotional wariness and circumstances pushing her too far, too fast. But she hadn't objected to him staying here with her, so Ryder knew he'd misread the situation. He'd already realized she'd allowed him closer than she had any other man. But her words this afternoon had nearly undone him. *You and me. I couldn't imagine wanting that with anyone. But... I do.* The memory trailed warmth in its wake.

Up until now he'd deliberately refrained from voicing his feelings because he'd intuitively realized that doing so would send her running for the exits. He knew what her admission had cost her, and it gave him hope. Because he wanted more. He wanted all.

He changed the channel until he found a baseball game. Females didn't come more complex than Cady Maddix. But other women had long ceased to interest him.

In tandem, Hero and Sadie jumped to their feet and ran to the front window, heralding Cady's return. A couple of minutes later, the kitchen door opened, and she bent over the dogs for several moments before straightening to look at him. "Not joining in the canine chorus?"

Her smile hit Ryder like a sneaky left jab. Oh, yeah. A few complexities were worth it. "How'd it go with your aunt?"

She joined him in the family room, plopping down on

the couch before removing her boots. "It was trying. But she's eager to see the end of Caster's harassment."

Ryder turned down the volume of the game. "I spent a while talking to Jerry about the first contact LeRoy will make with Caster." He filled her in on the details. "And—we got a decent tip about Phoebe Lansing's disappearance from someone who called into the office. Serena Vance said she was going past the campground around two a.m. Thursday morning after working second shift when a vehicle turned east out of its front entrance. She said she had to pull onto the shoulder because it veered into her lane."

Cady's face was alight with interest. "Did she see anyone else in it?"

"No. She honked at the driver. Blinked her brights. But she said she noticed he'd been turned around to look at something behind him." Ryder shrugged. "She just caught a quick look. Older guy. Dark hair and beard. He was driving a dark-colored mid-sized SUV. She didn't get a look at the plates."

Her expression mirrored his frustration. "The timing is intriguing, but the description of the vehicle isn't going to get you very far."

"Just another in a long line of dead ends in the case," he admitted. It was too easy to recall the panic he felt when Cady was kidnapped. He didn't need the daily phone calls from Lansing's family to remind him of the passing time.

He already realized that every day the woman remained missing, the odds of finding her alive decreased.

26

"'Thus says the Lord, Behold, I set before you the way of life and the way of death.' You've yielded to sin without a struggle, but you must sacrifice blood to earn your place in eternity!"

The shout startled Phoebe from sleep. She jumped, scrabbling to the back wall of her prison. One of the robed men was back. And he seemed agitated. She looked at the woman in the next cube, searching for a clue. Saw her gaze fixed on the man.

He held his arms up and the voluminous robe pooled past his elbows. "Have you fought the devil who seeks to live in each of us? Or have you failed God with your weakness? Now is your chance to make yourself worthy. He smiles upon His warriors. In their final battle, they become deserving in His eyes."

As abruptly as he'd come into the room, he turned and left. The second man came in. The one who'd spoken to Phoebe before. He'd intended to frighten her, and he'd succeeded. She wanted to hope a search party would find her, but his words were an insidious whisper in her brain, sowing doubt. She couldn't be certain but thought it'd been three days since she'd been taken. And no one had come to rescue her. So perhaps he was right. Maybe she wasn't getting out of here alive.

She choked back a sob when the man approached her. He had garments over his arm and something in his hands. Opening the top of her cube, he dropped some of the items inside. He did the same to the cell next to hers.

"Put them on." Then he left them alone again.

She glanced at the other woman who was already moving to obey. Phoebe studied the outfit. It was more costume than clothes. A skimpy short fur dress with one strap that would leave her legs and most of her shoulders bare. A plunging neckline would reveal even more.

"What is this? What's it for?"

"You have to wear them or they'll hurt you." She reached for the remaining matching fur boots and drew them on. She looked more like *Tarzan's* Jane than a warrior. There was nothing remotely amusing about the thought.

Phoebe dressed more slowly. Anything was better than being completely naked. "What did he mean?" She pulled the dress up and hitched the strap over her shoulder. "All that warrior stuff?"

"They'll take us outside. The area will be lit. They'll have a camera, and we have to fight. And if we don't do what they say, they'll make us regret it."

She almost laughed despite the circumstances. Fight? Phoebe had gotten in a shoving match once after a basketball game in middle school. The memory was still humiliating. But the other woman looked deadly serious. "That's crazy. We can make it seem real, I suppose, without really injuring each other. Like those gals on the Roller Derby channel."

Her companion crowded to the side of her cell closest to Phoebe's. Pressed her face to the acrylic wall. "I won't be faking it." Her expression was dead sober, but her eyes... Phoebe shrank away. They were empty. Terrifyingly so. "And if you have any brains, you won't, either."

27

As it happened, breakfast in bed the next morning ended up including cold pancakes and eggs, because, as Cady had predicted, they'd been distracted from the actual meal. And, once their attention had returned to the tray Ryder had prepared, they discovered it was minus the bacon.

She looked at the crumbs on the plate and then at him. "Another excellent reason to let the dogs out for good after feeding them."

"That was rude," he told Sadie. His Lab pretended to be studying something on the other wall.

Cady considered Hero, who had his head on his paws, staring up at her. "Terrible manners. And it's no use pretending to be sorry when we both know you'd do it again in a minute."

Ryder draped a sheet over his lap and grabbed a cold pancake. Rolled it up and dipped it in syrup. Cady watched him without enthusiasm. "I think I'd rather have cereal." She slipped out of bed and pulled on her clothes.

"Ruining the view."

"Yeah, yeah." She snatched up her cell to carry with her to the kitchen. It rang just as she was taking a bowl from the cupboard. Checking the screen, she saw it was Miguel. What's up?" They'd been exchanging calls since yesterday afternoon.

"I've got the meeting set for today at two. Lord is definitely the same guy who started Life Church. I found employment records proving it. Before that, he served as an associate pastor for a year and a half at New Hope in Knoxville, Tennessee."

"What's he do at this Covenant Leaders place?"

"You'll have to ask him. All I can tell you is that he went there after his stint at Life Church. Here's the address of the headquarters in Durham."

She opened a drawer to pull out a pad of paper and a pen, jotting down the information Miguel reeled off. After their conversation, she was halfway through her cereal when Ryder tore into the room as if turbo-charged.

"Mom just called. She's got a broken pipe spraying water all over her kitchen. She and Dylan are mopping it up, but she was supposed to take him to Asheville to see his girlfriend today."

He was rummaging through the hall closet. Finally grabbed sneakers and jammed his feet in them. "I'm going over there. It's going to take a few hours. When do you have to leave?"

She looked at the clock. "Soon. But there's no reason I couldn't drop off Dylan on my way."

"That'd be a help." His last words sounded over his shoulder. He was already out the door. She guessed a broken pipe was the type of home improvement disaster that qualified as emergency status.

Cady carried her dishes to the sink and cleaned up the

mess Ryder's breakfast-in-bed prep had left before heading to the shower. If she were to get to Durham by two, she needed to imitate a measure of his urgency.

"Thanks for this, Cady." Dylan looked both guilty and relieved to be safely away from the monsoon in Laura Talbot's kitchen. "I mean, maybe I should have stayed and helped Ryder with those repairs. But Grace was really looking forward to today. We're supposed to go hiking in Pisgah Forest after she gets home from church."

"He appeared to have things under control." His mom's typically neat-as-a-pin kitchen would take longer to return to normal, but that would have to wait until Ryder got back from the hardware store with a more permanent fix.

Dylan Castle had gone through some subtle changes since his mom's arrest in the course of a case she'd worked last winter. He couldn't have landed with a better foster mother than Laura Talbot. He'd lost the lean, furtive look he'd had when Cady'd first met him, the perpetually on-edge appearance that had been honed from being on the run from a killer for five years.

He seemed relaxed and happy, and she knew the girl from his former school in Asheville had something to do with that. Cady'd helped out before, taxiing him over to see her.

"I've been wanting to speak to you alone, anyway." He sent her a quick look. "But maybe you don't want to talk about what happened last month."

She used her blinker and passed a slower car, then eased back into her lane. "It's fine. I'm glad to be back at work, though. The time off was tough." She raised her brows at him. "Apparently, I have no hobbies."

"Yeah. But was it hard going back to the job? I mean, after what you went through?"

"Not really." And she wasn't going to let the fact that she'd frozen in the act of entering a cave yesterday change her answer. "The other deputy marshal with me hasn't gotten a medical release yet. He was more badly hurt than I was."

"I'm not just being nosy," the boy assured her. "I'm going to be a junior this fall, and I've been thinking about what I might wanna do after high school. Like maybe work as a deputy. Or even a marshal."

"Really?" She managed, barely, to keep the surprise from her tone.

"Yeah." Somewhere he'd picked up a pair of reflective sunglasses, and she supposed he looked the picture of teenage cool with his shaggy blond hair, the tee emblazoned with the name of a band she'd never heard of, baggy shorts, and tennis shoes. "I don't wanna be stuck in an office all day, but I like the idea of a career that matters to people."

"Well, you know you can talk to Ryder or me about our jobs anytime."

"I thought about how awesome they were. I never thought about how you can get hurt doing them."

Ah. Here was the crux of the matter. "That's part of the deal when you wear the badge. Ryder hasn't been injured in his work as a sheriff, but he was once wounded when he was a Charlotte detective. Thousands of people in our fields are never seriously harmed. You assume some risk, but you can't do your job *expecting* it if you see the difference."

"Yeah. I guess you gotta believe it's worth it."

Leave it to a fifteen-year-old to boil it down to the nitty-gritty. Cady put on her own sunglasses. "I guess you do."

She got to Durham in plenty of time to look up all the properties affiliated with Covenant Leaders for Christ. The church was several miles from where she was to meet Lord. It took up a couple of city blocks, if one included the parking lots. Its style passed for modern architecture, Cady supposed, all wide angles with a roof that was a cascade of sweeping arcs. She started the Jeep again and drove to the headquarters. It consisted of another full block of structures and ramps, a small private hotel and a half dozen nondescript brick buildings, all three stories and painted blindingly white. She parked and walked up to the double doors. They were opened by someone standing inside. Cady took one look at the fortyish blond man in a neat light blue suit and said, "Jeffrey Lord?"

"Yes, ma'am." The smile he flashed revealed capped teeth as bright as the building's exterior. "I'm afraid I'm going to have to ask for some identification. Security isn't around on the weekend," he said apologetically.

Her star was clipped to her belt but she took her credentials from her pocket to show him. "Deputy U.S. Marshal Cady Maddix."

He looked beyond her. "I believe I spoke to your colleague on the phone yesterday."

"Rodriguez. He's unavailable today."

"Ah." He returned her credential case. "Well, please come in. I'll admit to being a bit confused about how I can help you. I'm not very familiar with your agency."

Cady followed him inside a nicely outfitted lobby area

and into a nearby elevator. "I got a look at your church as I drove by. Showy."

He bent forward to stab his finger at the button for the third floor. "It's lovely, isn't it? Such a remarkable testament to the generosity of our congregation. Part of our mission takes place under its roof. Another labors in buildings like these, taking care of a myriad of details for our international ministry."

The doors whirred open and they walked across brilliant white tile floors that were interrupted only by walls of solid glass. He led her through one such entry into a suite of offices with desks scattered about, some encased in their own smaller glassed rooms.

He escorted her to what she assumed was his inner sanctum. Here the panes had a smoky hue that allowed privacy. Cady gazed at the bank of windows that comprised one side of the room. "Is this the equivalent of the corporate corner office?"

"Oh my." He looked vaguely amused as he gestured her to one of a pair of leather chairs facing the modern glass-topped desk sitting in front of all that glass. "I can't say that I have much knowledge of the business world. Now. What is it that I can help the marshals with?"

"I'd like to talk to you about your time at Life Church."

"Life Church." Lord tipped his head back, as if contemplating something that gave him pleasure. "It was my first lead pastor role, you know. My only one, as it turned out, but what an exciting time in my life. My heart has always been with spreading Christ's words to those who might not otherwise hear it. Or learn to live it, as the case may be."

He stopped and looked at her expectantly. When she remained silent, he went on. "Simply put, I wanted to start my own church, rather than step into one where I was filling someone else's shoes. Having a ready-made congregation is, of course, ideal in many ways. But it comes with the parameters someone else set." He crossed his legs and folded his hands in his lap. "Starting fresh was a more daunting prospect, to be sure, but a thrilling undertaking."

"So, you rented a place."

"I scouted areas in both Tennessee and North Carolina. I was looking for a rural setting where people had a harder time reaching a church. One with a lot of shut-ins perhaps. And yes, I came across the property in Jackson County and it seemed perfect for my purposes." His smile grew quizzical. "I still don't understand why any of this is of interest to you."

"I wanted to ask you about a former member of your congregation. Frank Burgess."

"Burgess," Lord murmured. Then his eyes widened. "Frank! Yes, a wonderful man. He was a fervent believer and very giving. He was always right there if something was needed."

"You loaned him your house on the river once."

He looked taken aback. "Did I?"

"For a fishing weekend."

"Well, I certainly may have. We must freely share our gifts on earth if we want God to share with us the kingdom of heaven."

"Do you keep in touch with anyone from your old church?"

He looked embarrassed. "I always meant to of course. Such deep friendships form. But I'm afraid I didn't. And the congregation wasn't interested in finding another pastor when I announced I was leaving. That was a disappointment. You could say a failure on my part."

Cady eyed him. "How so? You said you hadn't wanted to work in a church that previously had a minister."

He made a moue. "Hypocritical of me, then. I liked to believe I'd made enough of an impression that they'd desire to continue what we'd started together. But the congregation was small. Maybe four dozen families. It simply dissolved."

"What happened to all the documentation once you left?"

"Goodness, I couldn't say." He looked perplexed. "I'm sure I gave the marriage, birth, and death records to the members to whom they belonged."

"And church membership records?" she pressed.

He gave a helpless shrug. "They were likely destroyed. If not by me, then by whoever was left once I'd gone who would have cleaned up such things. I really don't know. You mentioned Frank Burgess. Is that why you're here? Are you interested in him?"

"He's the subject of a federal warrant, yes."

He reared back as if slapped. "The Frank I knew was a gentle soul. Fierce in his love for God, but otherwise a simple man. I can't imagine... What does that mean? A federal warrant?"

Cady dodged the question. "He's a fugitive. I'm looking for any details you can give me about him." But that hadn't been all she'd been after. Lord had supplied some of the information she sought.

"Well, as I say, I have nothing current." He still sounded distressed. "Frank must have changed a great deal to have done something to bring him to the attention of the U.S. marshals."

"Had you ever been to his business? Or his home?"

"Not that I recall, but I may have. It doesn't stand out."

"What can you tell me about the stable? What did that have to do with your church's mission?"

He spread his hands. "I thought you were here about Frank Burgess. I'm finding all these questions about the church confusing."

The only confusion here, she thought cynically, was caused by his equivocating. "He was a member of your congregation. I understand he did a bit of grounds keeping. Maybe he helped with the animals."

"He probably did. Frank, like many of our members, pitched in where he could. We were quite poor in terms of money. People gave of their talents."

"How did a stable help with your church?"

He laughed with more amusement than Cady would have thought the question deserved. "The stables and home came with the rental of the property. Some of our members needed a place to keep their livestock. Others were donated. And we ended up with quite a collection, without really trying. We started charging a nominal fee for what was little more than a petting zoo and had a lot of children come from around the area on field trips and whatnot."

"And the fees went to the church's coffers?"

There was a flash in his eyes that might have been irritation. "More to offset the feed for the animals, I would think."

"I'd like to ask you about some children who may have been part of your congregation, or were perhaps seen at the stables. Joseph Wiley." Lord's smile stayed vague. "Rina. I'm not sure of her last name. Perhaps Dierks."

"The names don't ring a bell, but if they came to visit, there's no reason I'd recall them."

"Which ones do you remember?"

He blinked. "Pardon me?"

Cady stretched out her booted feet. The one ankle was

still a bit swollen from yesterday, and she hadn't thought to take anything for it. "You said you had four dozen families, meaning some had kids. Which do you recall?"

"Ah..." He appeared to be struggling. "It was such a long time ago."

"The very first church you started," she reminded him. "Memorable, certainly."

"Of course. There were the Whites. The Gordons." He seemed to have an excessive amount of trouble coming up with more. "The Finleys. I'm sorry." He caught himself. "I'm not comfortable sharing names of people that have nothing to do with Frank Burgess, since they couldn't possibly be relevant to your warrant."

She smiled. For someone who'd feigned bewilderment about her work earlier, he appeared to have gained sudden awareness. "Do you happen to know of any member of your congregation who was friends with him? People he might have kept in contact with?"

"No. Sorry." His tone didn't reflect the sentiment.

"Thank you." She rose lazily to her feet. "I appreciate you making time for me today."

"Your colleague indicated that this couldn't wait."

"It's a matter of some urgency, yes. I can show myself down."

"I'll accompany you. Security demands it of us, sorry."

They walked to the elevator. Then inside it. "Is your current position the one you left Life Church for?"

Lord shook his head. "No. I've been fortunate enough to have been blessed with more opportunities since my arrival here." When the elevator pinged and the doors slid open, they continued silently to the front of the lobby. There she stopped, as if she'd just remembered something. "What about Corbin Fielding?"

The flash of shock on his face was gratifying. "Who?"

"I was wondering if he and his mother had attended your church."

He lifted a shoulder. "I'm sorry. I just don't recall."

Cady nodded. "Thank you again."

"You're welcome. I serve in whichever way God shows me."

She left and walked swiftly to her Jeep. As she was pulling away from the curb, she saw Jeffrey Lord still standing inside those doors. Watching her.

Deacon picked up the phone, reflecting that even its ring held a tinge of hysteria. "Jeffrey."

"The marshal just left."

"And?"

"She was asking questions. About all of it. The church. The stable. Children."

He went still. Perhaps he'd silenced Jonas too late. What had he told her? Because he couldn't share his concern with Jeffrey, he assured him, "She's just fishing."

"Really? She mentioned Corbin Fielding. And Rina."

The first name brought a chilly blast of memory. "What exactly did she say about Fielding?"

"She asked if he and his mother were church members."

"Nothing else?" he asked sharply.

"No. It was at the end, and she was on her way out. She knows, Deacon. About everything. You promised to take care of it and a fucking marshal was on my doorstep!"

Jeffrey had always been prone to theatrics. He'd polished that quality in the pulpit. But Maddix probing the connection between Fielding and Life Church... that punctured Deacon's calm. "She's just kicking over rocks at this point."

"Like you've never been wrong? You said paying off the families that complained would keep them quiet. Corbin proved that was a lie. This should have all been over by now."

"And it will be soon. But until it is, we need to buy a little time."

Jeffrey took a breath. When he spoke, his voice was steadier. "They want Frank. Maybe you should give him to them."

A truly stupid idea, he thought, which was why Lord didn't make the decisions. Deacon just let him think he did. For now. "I still need him. But I have another way."

"Then get it done."

He disconnected. Slipped the phone in the pocket of his trousers. If the marshals had anything solid, Jeffrey would be in cuffs. But Maddix wouldn't have tipped her hand in the interview. She probably knew more than either of them would like.

Which meant she needed to be stopped.

"How'd it go?"

Cady turned up the volume on her hands-free phone app. She'd called Miguel to update him on the meeting, but there was so much background noise on his side, she could barely hear him.

"Are you at a heavy metal concert?" The screeching and high-pitched sounds couldn't possibly be human.

"My four-year-old nephew's birthday party," he yelled in

response. "Wait." It was several minutes before his voice sounded again. The din was more muffled now.

"What'd you do, hide in the garage?" she asked amusedly. She noted the car approaching behind her much too fast. She moved to the far side of the lane as he passed. It was Sunday, so westbound traffic was light, but steady.

"No, in my pickup. It's the safest I've felt since getting here. You have no idea how dangerous it is to be an adult male holding the piñata in a crowd of blindfolded toddlers swinging sticks."

She snickered. "Why not hang it from something?"

"The clothesline wasn't up to the task either. Seriously. Why not bag the candy and hand it out? I'm still hoping to have kids someday."

His aggrieved tone did nothing to lessen her amusement. "Even after this? Come up with a different plan for the piñata parties henceforth. One that doesn't involve you."

"You can never be ready for these things," he said gloomily. "My sisters get together and hatch the craziest ideas. It was this or dress up as a clown."

Her humor abruptly vanished. "Truly, you're doing humanity a favor dodging swinging bats instead. The world doesn't need another clown." It didn't need *any*.

"Easy for you to say. So. How was the meeting? I assume it's over."

"It was interesting. He wasn't what I expected. Though I haven't seen pictures of him from years ago, I'm guessing he's acquired some polish. Has the glib God speak down pat."

"I'm not sure what that means."

He wouldn't. Miguel had been an altar boy in his youth. "Capped teeth. Highlighted hair and what I'd lay odds is a two-hundred-dollar haircut. Fancy office. Not running things there by a long shot, but I'd wager he's on the fast elevator up. Haven't quite figured how he made the leap from Life Church to there."

"It doesn't matter for our purposes, does it?"

"Maybe not." But it'd fill in their picture of the man. Clearly, he'd risen in stature from the young pastor barely out of seminary who'd struck out on his own to start a new church. She'd had a hard time understanding his motivation for doing so but imagined with a bit of creativity his choice could be developed into quite a résumé builder. "He was pretty guarded. Professed not to remember people I asked about, although I did get him to admit he knew Frank Burgess. He had nothing but good things to say and claimed to be shocked about the arrest warrant."

"I'll bet."

"He didn't react when I asked about Joseph Wiley. Or Rina. And he struggled to come up with the names of any other families that attended his church. He cut himself off, saying it wasn't pertinent to the case. He was cagey, but I got three surnames. I'll start running those down." Deputy Harmon seemed to have his finger on the pulse of the area, she thought. And she'd ask Brad Sellers, too. Maybe his memory would be jogged by a name being given up front.

"Are you coming to the office first tomorrow, or meeting me at Burgess's place?"

It took Cady a moment to make the mental transition. The cadaver dog search. "I'll meet you there at eight."

"Sounds good."

"You heading back to the party?"

"Not yet. I brought my beer with me. I'm hiding out until someone finds me."

She disconnected, still grinning. She wasn't without sympathy for her colleague. Ryder's two nephews lived in

Greenville. The one time she'd met them, they hadn't stopped running or yelling the entire afternoon. They'd exhibited their affection for their uncle with non-stop wrestling matches and armed assaults with couch cushions and pillows. Yet even their aggressive combat play had been preferable to facing a smiling two-pronged interrogation from Ryder's mom and sister.

She rolled her shoulders at the memory. Cady had enough trouble navigating her own family dynamics without adding in Ryder's. But she'd gradually grown fond of his mother. It was hard to maintain a guard against someone who was just genuinely nice.

Glancing in the rearview mirror, she saw a slick dually pickup behind her. Ahead, a small compact with the diagonal sign in the window proclaiming a baby was on board maintained a steady pace.

Her thoughts returned to the case. She made a note to check with the crime lab about test results for the remains found in the bottom of Burgess's incinerator. It'd been nearly a month since they'd been discovered.

A dump truck in the on-coming lane drifted well across the center line. Cady was already in the right lane, but she hugged the edge of it and honked her horn. The dually in back of her was still approaching at a good clip.

Defensive driving measures were useless against the bigger vehicle. It outweighed her by tens of thousands of pounds. The scene snapped into slow motion. She was trapped. There was no way around the larger truck, and the driver in back of her showed no signs of slowing. On her right was a steep embankment above Spruce Creek.

Disbelievingly, Cady watched the dump truck veer sharply toward her. The first impact sent the Jeep spinning. She fought to right it. The truck approached again, and this time, she turned the wheel violently to the right, her foot on the brake. She'd be taking the embankment either way. It may as well be on her terms.

The terrain was rocky, the incline hazardous. The bottom sped up to meet her. She downshifted, braking as she bounced in her seat. Her descent slowed, but not enough. The vehicle hit the base of the slope hard. There was a loud blast as the airbag deployed. The Jeep sailed over the bank into the creek bed, sliding several more feet before shuddering to a stop.

"Do you think it was intentional?" Allen demanded.

Cady winced at the decibel of her supervisor's voice while she buttoned the clean shirt Ryder had brought her from home. "The driver could have been sleepy or drunk, but I don't think so. He didn't just drift over into my lane. He deliberately trapped me between vehicles and tried to force me off the road." She'd said as much to the trooper who'd arrived at the scene before she'd been bundled away in an ambulance she didn't need, courtesy of Ryder. She threw a sulky look in his direction.

The nurse bustled inside the curtained ER cubicle then, and applied some ointment to the friction burn on Cady's face. "This will help with the pain. The doctor will write you a prescription for it. Let me see your palms."

Cady obediently turned them up. All told, she'd gotten off far more lightly than expected. Although she hadn't tried getting off the examination table yet. Moving might open a fresh new hell.

Stoically, she withstood the nurse's ministrations and continued her conversation with Allen. "I couldn't get a view of the driver when he was next to me, but his DOT number and plates were smeared with mud. Like he might have come from a worksite."

"Or he blurred them deliberately," Ryder put in grimly.

"Well, yeah, that occurred when he tried to run me off the road." She lifted a shoulder, winced a little at the resulting twinge. "I was going down the embankment one way or another. I took what I thought would be the easiest path. If I battled him a few more moments, I'd have gone through the guard rail and almost certainly flipped the Jeep." Finished, the nurse moved away and a doctor came into the area.

Looking around, he observed, "Crowded in here."

Pointedly, Cady retorted, "It won't be when you dismiss me."

He pinned the X-rays he carried side by side on the film illuminator on the wall. Switched it on. "By some miracle, it doesn't appear as though you've re-broken your ribs. That doesn't mean that the jarring you got today isn't going to make them more painful. In fact, you should count on it. You'll be one walking bruise tomorrow. I'd suggest taking it easy for a while." He went on to talk about the friction burns and abrasions. She knew she'd gotten off damn lucky. Struggling out of that creek it had been her ankle she'd noticed more than anything. But then, she'd been running on adrenaline at the time.

"Fortunately, I have a slow day tomorrow."

"You'll need it. Listen to your body. Don't overdo things." The doctor handed her two prescriptions and left.

Ryder moved to her side. "The trooper said three witnesses stopped. The driver of the car in front of Cady and two who saw the incident from the oncoming lane of traffic. One of the wits was an off-duty cop. He said Cady's defensive driving was the damnedest thing he'd ever seen. Couldn't figure out how she didn't overturn the Jeep."

"Just how badly did your interview with Lord go?"

Allen's tone was joking, but Cady considered the question seriously. "He certainly wasn't happy with my questions, but I didn't leave with proof he's still in contact with Burgess. He's come a long way from a simple country preacher, that was obvious. I got the feeling he didn't enjoy having me poke into his past, but that wouldn't be reason to try and end me."

Allen stared at her long enough to make her uncomfortable.

"What?"

"This probably has nothing to do with anything," he started.

"I've never trusted conversations that began that way," she muttered.

"But early this morning, Joseph Wiley was taken to the hospital with chest pains."

Trepidation surged. "And?"

"His cuffs had to be removed for some tests they were running. I don't have all the details, Cady. But somehow, he got away from his guard. He's escaped."

28

Phoebe leaned miserably against the back wall of her cell. Her muscles sang a chorus of aches. The slightest movement hurt. Vision in one eye was blurred. When she gingerly touched it, she discovered it almost swollen shut. Blood remained crusted beneath her nose, and her lips felt unnaturally thick and cracked.

Last night, the first man had run the camera. He'd called it a rehearsal. For what, she didn't know. He'd introduced them as if to an unseen audience as Foxy Frieda and Guerilla Greta. The other stranger had held a gun on them, to prevent them from running away.

The woman next to her was still and quiet. Phoebe didn't look her way. She didn't want to recall the transformation in Greta. It'd been immediate and shocking to watch. Terrifying to experience. She shuddered as her mind played a mental clip from hours earlier. The woman hadn't seemed like a warrior. She'd been an animal.

And before it had ended, Phoebe had been just as savage.

And that terrified her even more. Was that the purpose of the dehumanizing treatment?

After the fight they'd been returned to their cells. The glare of the spotlights overhead pierced the darkness, but left blankets of shadows across the rest of the space. The tiny red lights high on the wall near the ceiling reminded her of the eyes of animals. Of predators stalking their prey.

And that was exactly what she and Greta were to the two men in this place, she realized. Prey. And once they'd served their purpose, they'd be discarded.

The thought was accompanied by a wave of fear. She wanted to go home. The need welled up inside her, a powerful surge of emotion. She longed to hug Emma. Needed to feel Tim's arms around her again.

But a newfound survival instinct had her blocking the memory of both. Thinking of what she'd lost weakened her. It blinded her to the reality of her situation and solved nothing.

She was going to die here, unless she managed the impossible. Phoebe knew that from the little Greta had told her. She turned her head and met the gaze of the woman in the other cell. The necklace of purple marks imprinted on her throat made Phoebe so nauseous she had to look away again. To take deep breaths to avoid throwing up.

It was hard to say which sickened her most: the image of the violence she'd been capable of inflicting on the woman. Or the prospect of what awaited her if she didn't do the same the next time.

29

It was well past the time she should have slept. But despite the events of the day—or maybe because of them—Cady was wide awake. She didn't want to move lest she disturb Ryder.

Her Jeep had been towed, of course. Hopefully, it wouldn't be a total loss because it'd just been assigned to her a few months ago after her last vehicle had gotten shot up. Ryder had been abnormally quiet during the ride home and all through the quick meal they'd thrown together. Afterward, she'd taken a long hot soak, hoping to stave off some of the stiffness tomorrow was sure to bring.

She wouldn't blame him for trying to figure a way out of this relationship. Cady had never before made it beyond a casual few weeks. Had never wanted to until Ryder. But even she knew that a significant other constantly getting herself bashed up probably wasn't swipe right material on any dating app. Not that she'd ever use one. But still.

"Can't sleep?"

She jumped. "I thought you were."

"I can't." He sat up, plumped the pillow behind him, and

rested against the headboard. "Your thoughts were too loud."

"Yeah? First time I've heard that, but it makes an odd sort of sense. They're ricocheting around in my head pretty hard."

"Could've knocked something loose today." He was close enough to catch the elbow she jabbed toward him before it found its mark. He set it gently aside. "Let's hear it. What's going on in there? The warrant?"

Burgess would be a perfect deflection, Cady thought, as she eased herself cautiously to a sitting position. Work. That's what she usually seized upon. But instead, she heard herself asking, "On a scale of one to ten, how bad was the phone call today?"

"I'm having a problem with that ranking system." His voice was pensive. "Let's say a ten is you calling to tell me you're being shot at from the neighboring property and a hundred is hearing that you've been kidnapped. This afternoon, given the fact you phoned yourself and sounded okay? A five. Might've jumped to a seven once I got a look at the Jeep, but you were also upright at the time so it settled back down."

"You were quiet."

"I was working hard at not saying any of the stupid things bouncing around in *my* head at the time."

"It wouldn't have made a difference if you'd gone with me to Durham. Or Miguel." She knew him well enough to be sure he'd considered the idea.

"It wouldn't have, which doesn't mean the thought didn't occur and require some restraint to avoid voicing."

She smiled, shifting closer to him. His arm snuck around her waist. "Restraint can be an admirable quality."

"It might have also occurred that you seem to have a knack for causing people to wish you bodily harm."

"Hard to believe, right? With my sparkling personality and all."

He laughed at that and something in her chest eased. A tight coil of tension she hadn't even been aware of.

"This is the job." His voice in the soft veil of darkness was a low rumble. "No one gets that better than me. Tomorrow the shoe could be on the other foot and you could be the one getting that call. But I could do with a break from the bodily harm incidents for a while."

"We have a pretty quiet day planned for Monday."

"Good to know. Although it's the unplanned that causes me some bad moments."

"I couldn't blame you for hunting for an escape clause."

He bent his head to kiss her shoulder. "Nope. I'm sticking."

Such simple words to finally still the chatter in her brain. "I'm glad to hear it."

Getting out of bed in the morning took some strategic assistance from Ryder. Cady took a long shower with a punishingly hot spray to pummel her muscles into something approaching submission. The bruising had started, a sullen rainbow of navies and reds that she knew from experience would soon settle into an even more colorful mosaic. Holding her arms up for the amount of time it was going to take to put her hair in its usual braid was out of the question. She settled on a ponytail she could pull through the back of her ball cap. Taking two extra-strength over-the-counter pain relievers felt like capitulation. She knew it was the only way she'd make it through the next couple of days until the stiffness dissipated a bit.

Ryder's gaze was knowing when she walked woodenly to the kitchen. "Why don't we have a hot tub?" she asked. "Seems like it would come in handy and there's plenty of space."

"The idea has merit." From the gleam in his eyes she knew they weren't thinking of the same advantages. "But you don't put that sort of expense into a rented property, and something tells me Dorothy isn't planning any more updates after the last renovation."

Getting her vehicle and house shot up a few months ago had brought on the remodeling. And Ryder was right. Cady's landlady wouldn't be doing more work. But if it *were* her place, she'd add a damn hot tub. Or a live-in masseuse.

"Are you leaving without eating?"

She strapped on her weapon with a slowness that had her gritting her teeth. "I'll grab some cereal bars." She crossed to the closet and took out a navy jacket with U.S. Marshal emblazoned on the back, already knowing she'd have to ditch it later that day when it warmed up. Not without effort, she slipped it on. Returning to the kitchen, she dug in a cupboard for the bars and dropped them in her pocket along with her cell.

"I want to get an early start. My car isn't as sturdy as the Jeep. The drive up to the Burgess property is pretty rough."

"It is." He left his bowl of cereal long enough to get up and cross to her, brushing a kiss across her lips. "Remember your promise."

For a moment, her mind went blank. Then she nodded in understanding. "An uneventful day."

"I'm holding you to that."

"Not sure I'm up for anything more."

While driving, she called task force member Andy Garrett at the Buncombe County Sheriff's Office. When he answered, Cady asked, "Have you seen the paperwork for the computer I brought in Friday?"

"Good morning to you, too. Yeah, I've got it here in front of me. Your note said you're interested in Fielding's online activity, but the history is empty."

"I'm looking for specific sites that allow people to draw cartoons or do animation. You can still find them, right?"

"Everything someone does on a computer leaves a trail. And the laptop hasn't been wiped, so it shouldn't be a problem."

"Good. If you find any of those sites, I'd like a copy of his activity on them."

"I'll get back to you."

Satisfied, Cady disconnected. She had no idea if there'd be anything worthwhile on Corbin Fielding's laptop. But she'd get a quick response from Andy unless his other duties called him away.

It took nearly twenty minutes longer to reach the Burgess property than it should have, because she had to inch her car up the drive to avoid all the bumps and ruts. She used the time to contact the Raleigh crime lab. When she arrived at the place, there was already a truck with a small enclosed trailer being unloaded and a van parked next to it. The forensic anthropologist was here.

"Cady Mado." Dr. Traci Odell left her supervision of the equipment transfer to approach with her hand outstretched.

"Good to see you again." She returned the woman's bear-like grip. Tall, blonde, and long-limbed, Traci would look more at home on a California beach than in the field where she spent much of her time.

"Likewise. You do run into intriguing cases."

"Nothing quite like this before. Or," she corrected herself, scanning the property, "what I think this is going to turn out to be."

"I brought some of my lab grad assistants from the department's program. Judi, Todd, William, Melinda, Lynette."

She gave a wave in their direction, having no idea who was who.

"Any updates on the remains found last month?" Traci asked. Cady had told her when they'd spoken earlier about the discovery in the second chamber of Burgess's incinerator.

"I called on the way over. Bad news, I'm afraid. All of the human bone remnants were too small and damaged to extract DNA. Hoping you'll have better luck with the ones today."

Traci nodded. "About those specimens you discovered last week...how burned are we talking? Because there's a range of results possible, depending on the degree of preservation."

"I'll let you judge for yourself. Except for me picking up a handful before knowing what they were, the site hasn't been disturbed." She led the anthropologist over to the brush Rina had pointed out to them. Squatting was impossible, so she slowly got to her knees.

Traci studied her. "I hope you acquired that soreness in a pleasurable way."

Grimacing, Cady admitted, "I was forced off the road yesterday. Landed in Spruce Creek."

Eyes widening, she said, "And you walked away? You were born under a lucky star."

She'd certainly never thought so, but maybe adding up the events in the last few months alone should change her mind. There were only so many times a person could hope to cheat death.

"William, bring me a trowel, a sieve, and two trays," Traci called out. She got down on her belly and Cady held up the lower branches so she could see better. "Oh, yeah. We've got some molars there. A couple of phalanx bones. Burned black. Hopefully, not all of the samples we find are this degraded." She peered closer. "That's interesting."

"What?"

"The heat from a cremation retort reduces a body to gases and bone fragments. Afterward, most crematoriums use an electric processor to convert the remains to ashes." Traci pulled a pair of nitrile gloves from her back pocket and drew them on, before stirring her index finger in the pile.

"Nothing like that appeared on the property's inventory," Cady said surely.

"I'm not surprised. These fragments haven't been pulverized completely. I'm guessing your guy settled for a large mortar and pestle. Or a heavy mallet of some sort."

A lanky young man hurried over with the supplies Traci requested and Cady moved away, allowing them space to work. A disturbing image floated across her mind, of Frank Burgess removing cooled remains from the incinerator and hammering them to smaller pieces. When she walked back to the locker, Miguel had arrived and so had the handler with the cadaver K-9.

"Scott Morgan." The balding man dressed in jeans and boots wearing a backpack greeted her. He was unloading a German shepherd from the kennel in the back seat of his car. "This is Lucy. She's my human cremains detection dog. That's cremains—cremated remains." He snapped a leash to the dog's harness, and then straightened.

"Cady Maddix. Miguel Rodriguez." She jerked a thumb at her colleague, who was approaching them. "The forensic anthropologist's team is on site. I showed her to the one set of cremains that I knew of. The witness indicated there are several more on the property, but I have no idea how many are human."

"No problem," Scott responded cheerfully. "Lucy will know. You mentioned on the phone last week it might be a complex site." He beamed at her, petting the dog that sat at his side. "Our favorite kind."

"Then it won't matter if the human and animal bones are dumped together."

"Not at all." He scanned the area. "Human cremains have a distinctive odor, easy for trained dogs like Lucy to identify. We worked the wildfires in California a while back. Also, Colorado. She's got lots of experience." He patted his backpack. "We'll put down evidence markers at each detection site so the anthropology team can follow up in the order we find them. Who do we have today?" He craned his head to read the signage on the trailer. "Traci!" he said with genuine pleasure. "She's the best in the state. And in great demand. You were lucky to get her."

"We're fortunate to have both of you," Cady responded.

"Well." He looked modest. "I welcome the chance to help out." Shifting his focus to the dog, he said, "Lucy. Ready to go to work?" He unsnapped the chain. "Search." She bounded off across the lot, taking time to sniff here and there before continuing on her journey. Scott ducked into his car and took out a tall to-go cup before ambling after her.

"You want a coffee? I picked up two."

Cady's brows skimmed up at Miguel's offer. "I hope this isn't pity coffee. That's usually bitter with unspoken guilt."

He went to his truck and came back with cups, smaller than the one Scott held. He handed her one. "Why can't one colleague do something nice for the other?"

She sipped. Nearly closed her eyes and wept at the first taste of caffeine. "No reason. I brought you something, too." She reached in her pocket and pulled out a bar, handing it to him. "Breakfast on the go today." Withdrawing the other, she used her teeth to peel the packaging down far enough to bite into it.

"It's not why I bought you coffee." Miguel managed to hold his cup steady while stripping the wrapper off his bar. "But I do feel guilty."

"It wouldn't have made any difference if you'd been with me yesterday."

He correctly interpreted the narrowed look she shot him. "The outcome might not have been different, but better my pickup bit the dust than your Jeep."

Silently, she agreed. The USMS kept a fleet of federally confiscated vehicles at the courthouse. Deputy marshals often needed to blend in, so there was a variety. But none were as nice as the almost new replacement Jeep she'd gotten a few months back. If she knew any prayers, she'd send up one that it wasn't totaled.

"You did your penance yesterday. The birthday party."

"Even so, I'm probably in better shape than you are, after that ride down the embankment." He eyed her knowingly. "How bad is it?"

"I'm sore enough that I'm going to keep moving around so I don't freeze in one place once my muscles stiffen."

She relayed what she'd heard from the crime lab earlier that day and he nodded. "I suspected as much. Hopefully, today's samples will be less damaged."

"That would be a break." She headed toward her car. "I'm going to make a couple of calls."

Miguel had already devoured the bar. He wadded up the wrapper and shoved it into the pocket of a jacket identical to hers. "To whom?"

"Those family names Jeffrey Lord mentioned? I want to run them by Sellers, the owner of Sarah's Market. He and his wife have lived around here for decades, and they'd see return customers from several different counties as well as tourists. If you want a job, you could try tracking down Doris Garner, formerly Fielding, Corbin's mom. She lives in Naples, Florida."

"Good girl!"

Cady's attention jerked to where Scott was petting Lucy, praising her lavishly. He took a red ball out of the backpack and threw it down the drive for her to fetch, which she did. Over and over.

"There's two," she murmured. Even expecting it, the reality was a jolt. Two unidentified victims. As the handler set the dog to work on another search, Cady wondered bleakly how many of those markers would be strewn around the property by day's end.

She finished the coffee and breakfast bar as she went to her car and sat in the passenger's seat with the door open. She called the sheriff's office and asked for Wayne Harmon. Was told he wouldn't be in until this afternoon. Cady left a short message requesting he call her back and hung up before scrolling through recent numbers to find the one belonging to Brad Sellers and contacted him.

"Mr. Sellers, it's Deputy U.S. Marshal Maddix."

"Good morning. I've been wondering about the young lady you were looking for. Did you find her the other day?"

"No. She'd gone when we got there." There was no

reason to tell him that she believed someone might have forcibly removed Rina from her hiding place.

"I was going to call you today anyway. I asked my wife about that pastor you asked about—the one at Life Church. We finally landed on the name. Jeffrey Lord."

"Thank you for giving it some effort. I was able to speak to him yesterday." She watched as Traci came into view. The woman motioned for her assistants to carry the covered trays to the trailer while she walked over to examine the site where Scott had laid the marker. "He mentioned some families with kids in his congregation. The Whites. Gordons. Finleys. I wanted to run the names by you and see if any of them are familiar."

"Hm-m. Let me think." Several moments passed. "I know some Gordons, but their children are young. And they aren't from around here originally. But I'm friendly with a Richard Finley. His family used to attend a rural church when he lived near Cullowhee. They moved away, but he returned six months ago. He and his wife divorced, and his ex is dead now, I'm sorry to say. I know he had some trouble with his daughter stealing and running off. She doesn't have anything to do with him now. I can contact Richard if you'd like. See if he'd talk to you."

"Please do." Cady disconnected moments later and eased to her feet. Slammed the door and headed back to Miguel.

"Good girl!"

She winced a little as the sound of Scott's praise floated through the air. Lucy had found another set of cremains.

By noon, the K-9 had added three more sites to her find list, bringing the total to six, counting the one Rina had shown them last week. Each had Cady's gut knotting tighter.

"I predicted the whole damn area would be a cemetery," Miguel muttered as they both sat in his vehicle.

"These locations are closest to the house. Maybe it'll slow down when the dog has to move further afield."

He looked at her, askance. "How many are you thinking are out there?"

She shook her head slowly. "I honestly have no idea." But from what they knew so far it appeared likely that Burgess was a serial predator. With human cremains on his property and a dead woman in his locker, it was easy to believe the worst. And given the state Deborah Patten's body had been in, perhaps all had been subjected to torture first. Cady just didn't know why.

But she remained convinced it had something to do with Life Church.

Deputy Wayne Harmon returned her call a few moments later, and they spoke for several minutes. He promised to look into families with the surnames in question who'd lived in the area during the time Life Church operated. She hung up, not expecting much. Most of the names were common.

But it was a thread and maybe it'd lead to someone with knowledge of Burgess.

While she waited, she called Walter Edsen, the librarian. He apologized profusely for not contacting her earlier. "Truth is, I've had no luck at all, and that is truly puzzling. Digital newspaper archives aren't complete, but I should have found some mention of the church."

"We've discovered the identity of the pastor through other means. I appreciate your efforts, though." After Cady disconnected, she summarized the conversation for Miguel.

"I know businesses that offer to scrub the Web to clean up people's reputation," he mused. "But those digital archives would have to be hacked to remove unwanted mentions."

"Someone went to a lot of effort to erase Jeffrey Lord's history here." That and the man's spotty memory pointed toward someone with something to hide.

A half hour later she received a call from Sellers. "I did speak to Richard and he agreed to talk to you—his afternoon's open. But fair warning, he probably wants to pick your brain about his estranged daughter, Michelle."

"Ask if he can meet me at your place in thirty minutes." After agreeing, they hung up. "I'm going to speak with a former member of the church," Cady informed Miguel.

"You're supposed to be taking it easy. 'Don't let her lift a finger,' Gant said."

"That doesn't sound like Allen."

He waved a hand. "Something to that effect. I'll go. And I'll hit a drive-through, bring back lunch."

"I know where the market is, and Finley is expecting me. I can buy the makings for sandwiches, though. Chips. And I'm told their caramel apples are great. If you don't whine, I'll get you one."

"Get two," he advised, leaning against his pickup to keep an eye on the activity. "I'm feeling malnourished."

30

Richard Finley looked significantly older than Brad Sellers, although Cady suspected his creased and rosy visage could be blamed on something other than age. She noted the slight shake of his hands when they sat down on a bench outside the market. Observed the broken capillaries across his nose and cheeks.

"I appreciate you meeting with me," she said.

"Not like I got anything better to do. I fish some. Hunt a little. Do some trapping. Got permits for everything," he added hastily.

"Mr. Sellers says the two of you knew each other when you lived here before."

"Yeah. Years ago." He looked off in the distance as if mind-traveling back to that time. "I can see now that was probably the beginning of the end of my marriage. But it got better for a while, before it got worse again."

"I understand your family were members of Life Church."

"Brad said he told you. Can't imagine anyone caring.

Little bit of a place clear out in the country. These days they have them big fancy churches with movie theater seats and coffee shops and cafeterias in them." He cocked his head at her. "You believe that? Life Church was barely big enough to hold fifty. And it was never full. But my ex-wife, Diana, she had a friend who went and she insisted that was what we needed to work out our problems."

"You had marital issues?"

"We was drinking, both of us. It was a tough life for Michelle, our daughter. Richie, my son—I moved back here to live with him—he was a lot older. Twelve years between him and his sister. He was out of the house by the time it got real bad."

"Did the church help?"

He rubbed the side of his nose with a crooked finger. "Seemed to, at first. I don't hold much with religion, but maybe it was just going along with Diana that helped. She and Michelle liked it. Couldn't tear that girl away from the horses at the stable when she was ten or so."

"What was your relationship with the pastor, Jeffrey Lord?"

Richard shook his head. "We spoke a few words after service once or twice. I'd compliment his sermon because that's what folks do. Truth was, he was long-winded and once he got wound up it was all brimstone and hellfire." He flashed a grin. "I nodded off a time or two during it and my ex gave me hell for that, too."

"You never saw him outside of church?"

"Nope, I never did. And I started making excuses not to go on Sunday, although Diana would still take Michelle. Some folks would bring picnic lunches and make a day of it. They was always having activities for the kids. Seems like the two of them was running up there daily."

"Do you recall the name of the friend of your ex-wife who attended there?"

"My memory ain't the best. And she wasn't someone I knew well."

"What about Frank Burgess? I understand he was active in the church. He may have volunteered as a groundskeeper."

"Burgess," he muttered, frowning. "I remember a guy who cut the grass. He and another man always got the people fired up, shouting out agreement during the preaching. The hotter the pastor got, the more they liked it. The one—Burgess? He usually had a kid with him, a girl. She and Michelle took to each other. Don't recollect her name, except she couldn't talk."

Cady quizzed him a while longer, but Richard didn't know anything else about the fugitive, including where he lived. "Did you know any of the other members at Life Church?" When he shrugged, she pressed, "The Gordons? The White family? Deborah Patten?"

He shifted position on the bench. "Like I said, Diana stuck with it a lot longer than I did. I never got friendly with anyone up there. And the place got to be a bone of contention between me and my wife. For some reason, Michelle didn't want to go anymore."

Interest spiking, Cady asked, "When did that happen?"

"Oh, she was twelve or so. That's about the time we began having more trouble with her. First were the nightmares, screaming fits in the middle of the night. Then she got to stealing. From us and anywhere we went shopping. It got so bad one of us had to stay in the car with her." Misery filled his expression. "Diana figured the girl needed more church, not less. That became one more battle between us, and meantime, Michelle started running off. Don't know how many times the police brought her back until they finally stuck her in juvie."

"When's the last time you saw your daughter?" Cady inquired gently.

"Six years ago. Right before her eighteenth birthday. She was gonna get out then. Too old for the system, I guess. And she told us both she never wanted to see us again." His eyes went filmy. "Harsh words to hear from your child. But I see it now. We'd lost her long before that." His tone turned pleading. "Maybe you could find her. Might be she could tell you more about that church. I'd like to know where she is. If she don't wanna see me, well... still would be good to know she's okay."

"I'd like to talk to her, but if I locate her, I won't be able to share her contact information without her permission," Cady said, not without sympathy.

He pulled a folded piece of paper from his pocket. Handed it to her. "I've had plenty of time to think about all the ways we done that girl wrong. There's no reason in the world she'd want to speak to me, but if she ever does, that's my number."

"That'll have to be her decision."

Richard gave a slow nod. "Fair enough. Just knowing she's out there, doing all right, would be enough."

Cady thanked him for his time and headed into the market. The conversation had darkened her mood. Traumatic childhoods came in an array of scenarios, and not everyone escaped their pasts. She found herself hoping Michelle Finley had.

She stocked up on the supplies she'd promised Miguel, adding extra because she didn't know whether Traci's team and Scott had come supplied. She got a case of bottled water, and, after a moment of contemplation, caramel apples for everyone.

By the time she returned to the Burgess property, there was yet another yellow marker in front of a heath thicket. She talked with the group about breaking for lunch. The response was enthusiastic. And while the others had brought their own food, all were on board with the dessert.

Thirty minutes later, the teams were back on the job and Cady was finishing up the last of her sandwich in Miguel's truck while using the laptop.

"There are lots of ways to drop out of society if someone has a mind to," he was saying, from the driver's seat. "Look at the people living in Bordertown."

"Some there are likely still paying property taxes," she murmured. Michelle Finley wasn't. She'd already checked. "But I may have found her. At least the age is right. She's working at a grocery store in Knoxville, Tennessee." Cady fervently hoped this was Richard Finley's daughter. It'd be a relief to find her alive. "If it's her, she didn't get far." The city was less than two hours from Asheville. "She's got a sheet. Bad checks. Shoplifting. Hasn't done time. And her record stopped five years ago."

"She hasn't gotten caught since then?"

"Maybe." Cady switched to another database. Found nothing else. "I'll start with this. If I strike out, I'll look further from home."

She got out of the pickup and strolled to the far side of Burgess's house where it looked out over the mountainside. Keying in the number to the store, she asked for Human Resources. Was finally connected to a Sandy Wagner.

"This is Deputy U.S. Marshal Cady Maddix," she began. "Do you have an employee by the name of Michelle Finley?"

"Ye-es," the woman said slowly. "She's here now. What is this regarding?"

"She isn't in trouble, but I'm hoping she can help me with some background for a case I'm working. I'd like to talk to her."

"Just a moment."

Cady cooled her heels for several minutes. She spent the time scanning the view below. The rocky cliff side descended at least a quarter mile until it vanished into a canopy of trees. A thought occurred, was quickly banished when someone came on the phone.

"This is Michelle."

Cady repeated her introduction and said, "I'm looking for the daughter of Richard and Diana Finley."

There was a long pause. "That'd be me, I guess. I haven't seen my parents in years, so if this is about one of them..."

Adrenaline sparked through Cady's veins. "It's not. I'm just verifying that I have the right person. I'm working a federal warrant on Frank Burgess, and I'd like to speak to you about him."

"Oh my God." The woman's voice was a whisper. And Cady didn't think she'd imagined the hint of fear in it. "What's he done?"

"He's wanted for murder." At least one, she added silently. The number was multiplying with the search taking place on his property."

"Now, that doesn't surprise me." A thread of bitterness sounded. "Who'd he kill? Rina?"

"No. But we believe she may be in danger."

Another long pause. "I don't like to dwell on that time. But she was my friend. My only one until I got out of that hellhole. What do you want to know?"

"I'd like to meet with you." She glanced at Miguel, who was standing nearby watching the activity. "With my colleague. We won't take up much of your time."

"I don't want my family getting wind of where I am," she said bluntly. "You have to promise me you won't share my whereabouts with them."

"I do."

"It can't be tonight. But I open here tomorrow, so I'll be off at three."

"That works. Just give me your address."

"I'd rather we met somewhere public." She gave Cady the directions to a local park. "It'll be closer to three fifteen before I get there. I'll meet you at the fountain." After seeking reassurance once more that Cady wouldn't share her information with the Finley family, Michelle hung up.

Miguel ambled over as she was slipping the cell into her the pocket of her jeans. "From the length of the call, I assume you landed on the right person."

"Yeah." She briefed him on the conversation. "She *really* doesn't want this getting back to her father. She didn't appear to realize her mother died."

"Some families are toxic. You have to cut ties for your own mental health."

Cady glanced at him, a little surprised at his insight. Miguel's family was close. Sometimes people who didn't grow up in dysfunction couldn't truly understand its lasting impact. "You're right about that, which is why we'll keep her location to ourselves. Know what else I've been thinking about, standing here?"

"I'm not sure I want to guess."

"Why did Rina run this way when we were chasing her that first day?"

"Well, that's random." He'd shed his jacket, long before she had. "What difference does it make?"

"Maybe none. But she could have turned around and headed back for the woods. Or tried running past us, across the parking into the tree line along there. Or to the side…"

"I get the picture. This way was closer."

"But it's a drop-off. Look." His reluctance to follow her was apparent. She went to the edge of the cliff. "She must have known this direction offered an escape. Which means there's a way down. At least far enough for her to get out of sight."

"I'm starting to see where this conversation is going and I can't say I like it."

Not without difficulty, she got to her belly and peered over the edge. "I can see a ledge. Yesterday we found she'd been sheltering in a cave. Maybe there's another one below."

"There's no way in hell you're going to check it out."

She stuck out a hand and he helped her up. Masterfully, Cady stifled the groan that threatened to escape. "I took the equipment from the back of my Jeep before they towed it and transferred it to my car." The look he sent her was not promising. "I've got rope. If we secure it to my belt, with the other end to the bumper or something, I should be able to walk my way down the side…"

"Right," he scoffed. "You can't even get up by yourself, but you're in shape to scale mountains. If you return to the office with another scratch on you, Gant will have my head."

"Okay." Miguel looked shocked at her easy acquiescence. He shouldn't have been. He was right. It'd been a chore just to get up again. "You do it."

"I'd respect you more if you'd just come out and asked me to begin with."

"No, you wouldn't. You'd have still bitched. But I'm willing to try it myself."

"Because you don't have the sense God gave a gnat." He craned his neck to look over the cliff. Shuddered. "Tell me again what I'd be looking for."

"An escape route," Cady reminded him. "One she thought represented safety."

"You don't think she's down there now?"

She shook her head. Sometimes Miguel could be deliberately obtuse. Especially when he didn't want to do something. "No. But she could have a hiding place that she's run to before. Somewhere she might have left something we could use to help us find her now."

He looked over the side again. "I don't have mountain goat abilities. I'm not going down there without a rope."

Cady made sure her smile didn't show. "I wouldn't expect you to."

Twenty minutes later, they had a visibly nervous Miguel roped up and making his way down the face of the bluff. They'd pulled the truck as close as possible and secured the other end tightly to the bumper. He picked his descent carefully, choosing his approach before taking each step. He was ten feet down when he looked up at her. "It's not too bad, actually. I haven't had to scale. There's a steep path and lots of toeholds."

"Then you want me to untie the rope?"

"On the long list of your annoying qualities, Cady, your sense of humor is at the top."

She grinned. "What's at that ledge?"

"The one I passed? Nothing. Barely big enough to stand on."

Another few minutes went by before he was standing on

a larger shelf jutting out from the cliff. "This might be something."

"What?"

Miguel didn't answer. He sidled along the mountainside and disappeared behind a large boulder. "There's an opening here," he called up.

She impatiently waited for him to reappear. After ten minutes, she shouted down, "Do I need to send the cavalry?"

He finally showed himself, lugging something with him. "I found a box. I'm using the rope on it so you can pull it up."

"Good girl!" The words sounded in the distance. This time Cady barely noticed.

"I'm ready."

"Get one of Traci's kids to help you."

"I don't need—" She snapped her jaw shut. Every muscle in her body hurt. Depending on how heavy the case was, she couldn't be sure she'd be able to raise it on her own. She fetched the lanky assistant, William. He followed her with alacrity and managed to pull the load up with an ease Cady knew would have escaped her.

"What's in it?" he asked her as they untied the wooden box.

"I'm not sure." But if it was something as inconsequential as the young woman's rock collection, she'd never hear the last of it from Miguel. She tossed the free end of the rope back down to her colleague and then dragged the container a few feet away from the edge. It was old. Not more than eighteen inches wide by ten deep. The hinges were rusty, as was the clasp lock on the front. Cady started to open it, then thought better of it.

It was another fifteen minutes before Miguel reached the top, huffing a little. "What was inside?"

"I waited for you."

His expression brightened as he untied the cord from his belt. "Thanks."

"Well, you did the work." She pushed it over to him and let him do the honors. He had to use his pocketknife to pry open the lid. There was a dark blue cloth covering the contents. Once he removed it, he and Cady stared, nonplussed.

"DVDs?" She pulled a pair of nitrile gloves from her back pocket and put them on before drawing one out. There were stacks of them inside the container, and nothing else. All were labeled only with dates. A quick flip through them showed they were from the time Life Church was in operation.

She said as much to Miguel, cautioning, "Not that we can be sure these have anything to do with the church."

"Maybe Burgess was burning bodies even then and filmed his incinerations," he said darkly."

"Where did you find it?"

"I wouldn't call it a cave. The hole only went back a couple of feet. But it's not visible from here. I had to climb behind that boulder. And there were a bunch of rocks piled in front of the opening. Rina could have been headed there when she ran from us. She'd have been out of sight if she got past that stone. There's a shelf above shielding the ledge. I'd guess she's used the area for shelter before."

To escape punishment from Burgess? she wondered. The saddest thing about the thought was that Rina had had nowhere else to run. She couldn't seek safety with her mother. Selma had given her to the man. The girl had been trapped, victim to Burgess's temper. To his abuses. The pang of sympathy Cady felt was personal.

"Let's load it up," she said. "When we get back to the office we'll take a look at some of them. See what we have."

Miguel flipped the lid closed and picked up the box. "I'm going to go out on a limb and say they're not someone's vacation footage of Disneyland."

She was silent. Because there had to be a reason for hiding the DVDs. And she couldn't think of one that wasn't sinister.

Traci's crew had packed up at five and headed for a motel. Lucy had hit on ten cremains that day, and there was no way of knowing if the search was complete. Scott had promised to bring the dog back first thing in the morning. After seeing them off, Cady texted Ryder that she'd be late before heading back to Asheville with Miguel. The offices were empty when they got there. But the conference room held all of the electronic equipment, including a DVD player.

"Should I start with the one labeled with the earliest date?" he asked. They both wore gloves in case they needed to have the whole lot fingerprinted.

"Just pick one." Her gut was in knots. It seemed to take him an inordinate amount of time to select a disc and slide it into the compartment of the machine. Press play.

There was static. It cleared, but the screen remained shadowy. Slowly it lightened to reveal a room. There was some sort of banner on the wall and a mattress on the floor. Two naked figures were on it.

"Ah, shit." Miguel rubbed his eyes, as if seeking to expel the sight.

Cady swallowed hard. From the angle, it was impossible to see faces. But from the size of the people, she could hazard a guess that the offender was adult. The victim much younger.

"Put in a different one." Silently, Miguel did so. They sat through a couple of minutes before again changing the discs. After watching parts of five of them, Cady leaned back, revulsion snaking down her spine. "If this has anything to do with Burgess, with Life Church, we're going to bury those bastards."

"Every last one of them," Miguel agreed grimly.

31

The monotony of the passing hours was a double-edged sword. Phoebe welcomed every moment without their captors in the room. It meant she was safe, for the time being. The robed figures came and went, but the first man was here the most. She thought he might even stay in another part of the house some of the time. But she and Greta were brought food and water only sporadically.

The tiny red lights near the ceiling winked malevolently. Did the men watch them that way when they were absent? If so, she wondered why they bothered. There was no way out of their cells. She'd tried.

There was a quiet moan beside her. She restrained herself from looking at her companion. Knowing she'd hurt the woman—that Greta bore wounds Phoebe had inflicted — made her sick to her stomach. The pain that still radiated from her own injuries felt like just punishment. Never in her life had she imagined she could strike another person. To set out to purposefully wound them. The guilt was paralyzing, even knowing if she hadn't defended herself, she would have been injured far worse.

She drew up her knees. Buried her face in them. Maybe this was what hell was like. Losing her sense of identity, everything she'd thought she'd known about herself. Placed in limbo at the mercy of monsters intent on shredding her humanity, one strip at a time until the darkness that lay within was revealed. The rot at every human core.

Tears streaked down her cheek, and impatiently Phoebe wiped them away. They solved nothing. Any emotion that didn't result in her escape was a waste.

A rhythmic pounding began again. Soon it'd resound in her temples, reverberate through her head until she wanted to scream. She covered her ears. She hadn't realized how much she'd grown accustomed to silence until this racket had started.

But after several long minutes of the repetitive thudding, she finally turned around to look at the woman in the cage the second man had hauled in earlier that evening. She was slight, wiry, but she reminded Phoebe of something feral, wild, if not dangerous. Her long dark hair was tangled and matted, the ends jagged. Her eyes were wide and fearful.

Phoebe spoke to her for the first time. "You need to stop. You don't want to bring them in here. They'll hurt you. Save your strength. You'll need it."

32

Cady pulled into the parking lot of the Swain County Sheriff's Office when dawn was spilling over the horizon. Grabbing the wooden box Miguel had found from the seat beside her, she got out and headed to the front doors. Because she'd texted last night to set up this meet, Deputy Ben Trettin had arrived early and was waiting for her.

He buzzed her inside. "Beautiful day."

"You might not feel the same way after you start looking at these DVDs."

The Carolinas Regional Fugitive Task Force was comprised of select law enforcement officers who assisted the U.S. Marshals Service. They were chosen for their unique specialties. As the most talented cybercrime officer in the region, Ben Trettin's expertise would be invaluable.

She followed him to a room located deep within the building that contained an array of electronics. Two large tables held computers and oversized monitors, printers, and more devices than Cady could name. She set the box on the first free space she could find. Opened it. "We hope to have them all fingerprinted when you're done."

Ben looked more high school teacher than cop, with a mild manner that belied the cyber genius within. "Of course. All these discs have footage on them?"

"We only checked a handful. And only a few minutes of each. Here." She pulled a list from her pocket and handed it to him. "There's some sort of sign or banner on the wall. I only caught a glimpse of it, but if there's a close-up, I'd like a still of it. And photos of the faces of the victims and offenders."

"It'll depend on the angles," he said, and she nodded.

"I'm hoping someone made some mistakes along the way. Also anything that would hint at where this took place. Basement? Bedroom? Any descriptors will be helpful."

"Got it. How soon do you need this?"

"You can send me results as you get them."

He went to a bookcase and withdrew some gloves from a box there and pulled them on. Then he returned and took out a disc, placing it in a freestanding DVD player hooked to one of the computers. "If you have a quick timeline on this, I can farm some of it out. I've got some guys in the area with cyber skills. I've joined up before with Wendell in Cherokee County. Redding in Jackson."

"I know Sheriff Redding. Haven't met Wendell. Why don't you just see what you come up with in the next couple of days and we'll figure how much more help we'll require."

Ben nodded, already intent on the images on the screen. "That I can do."

"Thanks." She showed herself out of the building and was almost to her vehicle before her cell buzzed. Answering it, she slipped into her car. Buckled her seat belt.

"I'm beginning to think you're avoiding me."

She smiled at the sound of Ryder's voice. "You were the one who was late last night." Cady had gotten home around seven-thirty after first swinging by the Buncombe County Sheriff's Office. Andy Garrett had performed his magic and had retrieved not only the art sites Corbin Fielding had frequented most, but the passwords for each. She'd spent hours going through graphic novels he'd created online. She hadn't been quite sure what she was looking for, but she'd run across nothing alluding to Life Church.

"I had to drop off the discs we found with Ben Trettin." She'd told him about the find on Burgess's property during a brief phone call before he'd headed out for the evening.

"Ah. Then Trettin has a far worse day ahead of him than my night was."

She pulled out of the lot. "Do tell."

"My great-grandma had a saying. 'Two heads are better than one, even if one is a sheep's head.' Your cousin puts lie to that, but the initial contact was made and a meet set up. We had LeRoy threaten to keep his findings for himself if he isn't cut in on the operation."

"Caster might be stupid enough to believe that bank robbery money is still sitting around, but there's no way he'd agree to share it."

"He might pretend to in order to get what he wants. And if we can get that conversation on tape, we'll have all we need to put him away again. The contact will take place at ten tonight at The Place." He named a local Waynesville bar. "We'll be outside. You can listen in if you want."

"I'd like that."

He paused. Then said, "Pretty sad that this will mark a hot date for us."

She laughed again. "I'm going to let you make it up to me."

"I'll hold you to it."

Cady was still smiling when they disconnected. She had

a feeling her light-heartedness would be long gone after she spent a couple more hours on the Burgess property.

ALLEN GANT PULLED into the small rutted parking lot shortly after noon. He got out and stretched before heading over to Miguel and Cady. "Any more hits this morning?"

She nodded to where Traci's team was working several feet inside the stand of trees at the southern side of the property. "Three more today. The dog is still searching. That's thirteen sets of human cremains so far."

He muttered an oath, taking a USMS ball cap from his back pocket and settling it on his head. "This could go on for days."

"I hope not. We appreciate you coming to stand in." When she'd spoken to him last night, Allen had immediately offered to take their places while they went to Knoxville. Her supervisor in St. Louis had been more of a bureaucrat. Allen was a working deputy marshal. It wasn't unusual for him to help them out when they needed it, even joining arrest operations at times.

Her cell signaled an incoming text. A spark of excitement ignited when she saw it was from the Swain County deputy. There were attachments. "From Ben," she told the others. The two men crowded in to see better.

> More later today. Can you stop by after work?
>
> Might be six or seven.
>
> Let me know. I'll wait.

Cady opened the first photo. Her stomach did a slow

roll. It was the room they'd seen in the clips yesterday. The image focused on a dirty white banner hanging above the mattress. Printed in Gothic-type font, it read Life and Death.

"What's that supposed to mean?" Miguel muttered. "Did the offender threaten the victims if they told anyone?"

But she didn't hear him. Her gaze was fixed on the lettering. Life and Death. *L&D*. The letters and font were a match for those forming a circle on her shoulder.

"Cady, is that..." Allen started.

"I think so." Her voice sounded raspy, so she cleared it. "The letters," she said for Miguel's benefit.

"One of the tattoos he did on you. Yeah, I see it now."

She tapped the next attachment. "Burgess," Both of the men said simultaneously.

In the following image, the adult's face was blurry. But two teens were also present. One she recognized. "Joseph Wiley," she muttered, unsurprised. Dr. Hammond's words replayed in her mind.

I can say Joseph has experienced traumatic abuse, which is a source of some of his compulsions.

Wiley had said something similar in the mine. *You have no idea what I've suffered!* Now, they did—at least some of it. "So is this what motivated him?" she asked. "Do the tattoos serve as a testament to his suffering?"

"More likely, they're a rationalization for his actions," Allen responded, his tone bitter.

But human nature was complicated, Cady mused. She thought both could compel Wiley's behavior.

She half expected the face in the next picture to be Rina's.

But this girl was blonde. Pretty. Sort of familiar, but not. "That looks like it could be a younger Deborah Patten,"

Allen said, studying the image. "I'll see if I can dig up a high school photo online."

Cady's throat was tight. She put her cell away. "Thanks. We'll stop to see Ben on the way home from Knoxville later today." She glanced at Miguel. "We're getting close. Let's see if Michelle Finley can get us closer."

THE PARK WAS a rolling expanse of green lawn, shaded by maples and gnarled old oaks. The fountain was in the center, a small splashing monument to someone named on the plaque beneath it. They waited ten minutes past the agreed-upon time. But then a female with frizzy, long brown hair and dark shades came down one of the paved paths toward them.

"Michelle Finley?" When she nodded, Cady said, "Deputy U.S. Marshals Maddix and Rodriguez. Thank you for coming today. I know this will stir up some unwanted memories."

"I almost didn't show," Michelle admitted. They began walking with her. "But I have a four-year-old daughter. Maura. She's the reason for all my choices these days. This is what I'd want her to decide, if she ever had to. Do the hard thing. The right thing."

Cady and Miguel exchanged a glance. The child might explain why Finley's short-lived record had come to an end. "Tell us what you know about Frank Burgess."

The woman inhaled sharply. "He's a monster. That's a fact. He acted all religious, but he abused Rina something terrible. She told me—you know she can't talk, but we could communicate—he beat her. Chained her up. I don't know what all else. But I knew even then that he used religion the way my parents used alcohol. As an excuse for every bad choice they ever made."

"Sounds like you gained some understanding."

Michelle snorted. "If you knew the hours I spent in group therapy. Youth homes," she added, by way of explanation. "Some of them were pretty scary places. After a while, I stopped fighting the system. I graduated high school with enough college credits to count for a full semester. But then when I got out I sort of spiraled."

"Until your daughter," Miguel guessed gently.

"Yeah. Until my purpose. Now I work as often as I can. Our apartment's a dinky place over a garage, but the landlady is older and real nice. She watches Maura for me and I do her shopping and help with her yard. I'm saving for something better." Her mouth went tight. "Something more than Rina ever got a chance for, I'm sure."

"What can you tell us about Burgess and Life Church?" Cady asked.

The breath exploded from her. "*That place.* I still have nightmares. At first, I liked it. Not the services so much, but the stables had horses. They were old, but really sweet and we could ride them. I would help out because Rina was there and together it was fun. I'd beg my mom to go to every dumb activity they came up with, just to be with Rina, and the church was my only chance." She stopped at a bench beneath a densely leafed maple. Sank onto it. Cady and Miguel took seats on either side of her.

"We'd ditch work and run off more often than not." A smile flickered. "That girl knew the forest like she was born there. She taught me a lot. How to mark my way so I could find the path back. What berries could be eaten and when." She wrinkled her nose. "The only thing I wouldn't do is follow her into caves. Rina couldn't pass a hole without wanting to crawl inside it."

Her expression clouded. "She wanted to show me something once. I went with her, ready for an adventure. Except it was really far in the woods. I couldn't even say how long we walked. We finally came to this house surrounded by big firs and something inside me knew… I didn't want to go closer. She took my hand and pulled me. Told me to be quiet and we tiptoed up to a window." Her jaw snapped shut then, and she swiped angrily at her eyes. "Burgess and Pastor Lord were there with some of the teenagers. The men were… at the time I didn't have the words but they were sexually assaulting them."

"Do you remember the names of any of the teens you saw?"

"I only looked for a few seconds, but I saw the pastor with Holly Travers. I was shocked and scared so I turned and ran. I didn't know how to get back to the church. I just had to be anywhere but there."

Cady made a mental note of Holly's name. The scene Michelle was describing mirrored the clips she and Miguel had seen on the DVDs. "That had to have been terrifying."

"I had nightmares about it forever. Rina made me go back once more. She needed me to see. She was trying to get me to tell my mom or dad. I think so they'd call the police."

Realization dawned. "She was attempting to stop the abuse."

Michelle nodded miserably. "I tried to tell my mom a couple of times. She accused me of making things up. I admit, I'd started getting into trouble by then. Lying was the least of it. The second time she slapped me hard across the face and threatened to drag me to Pastor Lord and repeat all the lies to him." Her voice tapered to a whisper. "I was terrified she'd make me talk to him. And he'd do to me what I saw him doing to Holly. That's the first time I ran away. And as many times as they dragged me back, I'd run again." She was crying in earnest now. "But after all this time, I just think about those poor kids. I didn't get help. Maybe I could have somehow, but I didn't. So what happened to them after was my fault."

Cady felt a twist of sympathy. "The responsibility lies with the abusers. You were a child. And you tried. So did Rina. You're helping now. More than you know."

Michelle wiped her face again, looking exhausted. "It doesn't seem like much. After all this time and what they suffered, I wish I could do more."

Cady hesitated. Then said, "Maybe you can."

"I THINK it could be too triggering for Michelle." It was the third time Miguel had raised the issue on their way to the Swain County Sheriff's Office. He pulled into its lot and parked.

Cady texted Ben that they'd arrived, and opened the door of the pickup. She'd left the USMS replacement vehicle she'd driven home from work yesterday at Burgess's. The five-year-old Buick Enclave was a twin for the one her elderly landlady drove. Not for the first time, she hoped the Jeep was salvageable. "It's a long shot," she responded belatedly. "But she might be able to find that house again. Without her, we'd have no chance of locating it."

"She seemed traumatized at the thought."

She had. Unease stirred inside Cady as they walked to the front doors. Which meant the woman probably wouldn't agree. "It'll have to be her decision. Her story ties Lord to this thing. I knew the slimy bastard was lying." She just hadn't been sure what he'd been covering up.

Ben let them in and led them to the same room Cady had accompanied him to earlier today. "I didn't get through as much as I would have liked this afternoon, after sending you the first batch of stills. I got sidetracked, but I found what I was looking for. I wanted you to take a look."

Puzzled, they exchanged a glance. "Okay."

"The thing is, you do this job long enough and you see a lot of stuff you'd rather not. Especially on the Dark Web, which is a snake pit of illegal activity." He rounded the table and sat in front of a computer with an oversized monitor. "Navigating it is a challenge. Think of the Internet at its inception, before everything was indexed and search engines were limited in their capabilities. Browsers exist, but it's difficult to keep up with the shifting landscape. I might land on a site one day and not be able to find it the next."

He paused to take another gulp from a cup of coffee sitting nearby. Grimaced before hastily setting it aside. "I work mostly cyber fraud, but I'm on a state-wide team that focuses on online sexual exploitation of minors. It was the banner that rang a bell for me. Life and Death. I finally figured out why. I'd run across it last year, but I had the devil's time finding it again today. At least three sites bear that name. One's a pretty gruesome video game. Another was a service where a person could hire a hitman. My buddy has spent over two years trying to track down its owner. The one I wanted to show you has been operational for two years. The FBI has been monitoring it because it seems to be a snuff site."

"You mean movies?" Miguel asked.

"Right. Sexually deviant videos abound on the Dark

Web, most of them poor quality. But these films have gotten surprisingly professional. They look real. You'd swear the woman—or occasionally man—is dead at the end. The feds have received tips from Hollywood to help them spot the fakes. And even then, it's not always a sure thing. Long story short, they still aren't certain whether the deaths on L and D are genuine or not."

Snuff movies. Cady shuddered. "And you think it has something to do with what's on those discs?"

"That's just it, I don't know." He tapped at the keyboard. "I'm just saying, it bears the same name I saw on the sign, and the font for the lettering is similar. I'm going to show you a video that posted recently. It's very indicative of what the site has been producing." A glare of lights split the screen. When Cady's eyes adjusted, she could make out a tree line. Was there a shadow of mountains? It was difficult to tell. And the background could be edited in later, at any rate.

Two blonde women walked into the lit area. Although they were dressed in what looked like fur, much of their skin was bare. Cady noted one of them shivering.

A chyron flashed across the bottom of the film. Three-time champ Guerilla Greta. The shorter of the pair burst forward, striking poses and flexing non-existent muscles. Was she wearing a wig? Cady studied her. If not, she was unkempt. Fading injuries were visible on her face and limbs. But as Ben had noted, it was impossible to tell if they were real or manufactured for an audience.

The chyron changed, as did the focus of the camera. New challenger Foxy Frieda. The taller woman stumbled forward, as if pushed. She looked bewildered. Terrified.

Greta tripped Frieda then leaped astride her, punching

furiously. Frieda raised her arms to shield her face in a feeble attempt to ward off the blows.

"I took a video of what appeared on screen with the sound off, so it's missing the narration from someone using a voice changer, and music," Ben said.

Cady winced as she continued to watch. "Foxy Frieda" was getting beaten badly. Her attacker stood and began kicking her.

"New bouts appear randomly. Sometimes every week or two, and then there will be a time of varying duration with only reruns. Several days before a match, the film starts showing two people in what appears to be clear cells of some sort, twenty-four seven. Hard to say whether the video is on a loop or if they're really jailed that long." Frieda grabbed Greta's chained foot and pulled her off balance, sending her crashing to the ground.

Ben continued, "Based on what I've seen before, this fight is the prelude to the main event that follows within a few days. Viewers can place bets on the winner of the life or death bout, and even bid to win the right to name the weapons used. It gets bizarre. They've fought with medieval flails, those poles with two spiked metal balls. Scythes. Sledgehammers. Bricks."

"Bricks," Miguel murmured. Cady nodded. The coroner reported finding clay particles in Deborah Patten's wounds. Cady's throat dried as she watched Frieda on top of Greta, choking her. "You said they don't always use women?" She had to force the words out.

"No. There have also been male/male and male/female matches. All are pretty brutal fare. And like snuff movies, impossible to be certain whether the death of one of the parties is 'real' or not. All I know is, they *look* genuine. Whoever runs the website goes by the name of lcwarriors."

"Could you do still shots of the women's faces in this film?" Cady asked.

In less time than it would have taken her to turn on a computer, Ben had two-by-three-inch squares lined up on the screen, each with an image of one of the women.

"The younger one looks sort of familiar," Miguel murmured.

She studied the pictures, recognition flaring. "It's the camper who went missing in Haywood County last week. Phoebe Lansing. Ryder's still investigating her disappearance."

Ben turned from the computer to look at them, his expression excited. "That could put a regional slant on this. If one of these women was kidnapped from near here, either the site may originate from somewhere in the vicinity..."

"...or the kidnapper might," Cady finished. She went silent, mulling the possibility. She reached for her cell and brought up the picture of Deborah Patten's mug shot from the case file. Showing it to Ben, she said, "If you can go back through the older videos and find this woman, we can connect the website with the fugitive we're hunting. They might have been fighting with bricks." She told him about Ryder discovering Patten's corpse in the locker. "It would have been a month ago. Maybe slightly longer."

"I remember that one. First, let me print these off for you." He pressed a command. One of the printers began to whir.

Cady's cell dinged. A message from Allen. She opened it and saw a high school graduation photo of a young woman. She showed it to Miguel and then Ben.

"That looks like one of girls in the close-ups I sent you today from the DVDs," the deputy said.

"It is." They waited twenty minutes for him to find the fight video where Greta was swinging a brick at Patten.

"Bingo," Miguel breathed. "She was abused by Burgess as a teen. Years later, her body shows up on his property. That connects him to lcwarriors."

"If he's targeting former victims, Wiley could be in danger since his escape." Cady recalled Saul Jonas's words in their phone call. *'Bout Burgess. Deacon. Life and death.* Did the man's 'suicide' have something to do with all this? The puzzle was taking shape, but they were missing some vital pieces.

"We'll need still photos from the scene with Patten." Cady straightened, slightly sickened. "This is huge, Ben. Thank you."

"Glad to hear my tangent wasn't a waste of time. I'll get more from those discs tomorrow."

"It wasn't," she assured him. Frank Burgess. Life and Death. The rape videos. Deborah Patten. Phoebe Lansing. All seemingly disparate, but with threads linking to the same thing.

Life Church.

"This feels very clandestine." Cady scrambled into the back seat of a dark sedan a block down the street from The Place. "Do you have LeRoy ready to go?"

Ryder looked up from the laptop he was balancing on his knees. "Jerry's at the motel giving him last-minute instructions."

"What'd you wire him with?"

"You'd swear the microphone was a nickel. Same size and appearance. A little heavier."

"Nice." Gone were the days that an informant wore bulky wires under their clothes to transmit conversations to law enforcement with receivers parked nearby. Now the transmitters could fit in buttons, pen caps, or—in this case —a fake coin.

"Is the search finished at Burgess's place?"

"Yeah." They'd touched base with Allen on the way home from meeting with Ben. "Fourteen sets of cremains altogether. Dr. Odell took possession of them. She'll coordinate with the crime lab." She hoped the forensic anthropologist's specialized training would speed up results. "I brought you something." Cady took out her phone and showed him the stills the deputy had taken from the Life and Death videos. "Recognize her?"

Ryder peered at her screen. Frowned. "That's Phoebe Lansing. Why do you have her photo?" In lieu of an answer, she scrolled to another. "And that looks like Deborah Patten. Where'd you get these?"

Cady summarized Ben's findings, then flipped through the rest of the images pulled from the films on the web.

Stunned, Ryder just stared at her for a moment. "This proves Lansing was kidnapped. Nothing else made sense. But I've been all through the family's history, and as far as her husband and parents know, she hadn't been near western North Carolina until fairly recently. She's not linked to Life Church."

"Patten was on one of the DVDs filmed in a room with a Life and Death banner on the wall when she was a teen," Cady replied. "Years later, she appears as a captive on a Dark Web site entitled with the same words. She's beaten with a brick and her corpse winds up in Burgess's locker. Now the website shows Lansing. Maybe she isn't connected to the church, but the bearded man Serena Vance saw driving out of the campground could have been Frank Burgess."

"I've had officers poring through the state DMV database all day, looking at owners of dark SUVs. That's a long shot." Ryder's expression was grim. "But if Burgess is the driver, it's unlikely he obtained the vehicle himself. Maybe we should start checking rental companies."

While they spoke, his chief deputy slipped into the front seat. "Jerry," Cady said in the way of a greeting. "Condolences for having to work with my cousin."

His voice was pained. "Let's just say there's a reason the guy isn't working for NASA. Or, a million of them." She grinned. "I think he has his part down. Problem is, he's not great at ad-libbing. We'll have to see what happens from here. Or listen to it," he said, nodding toward the laptop.

Ryder picked up a radio from the seat beside him. "Everyone in place?" Two different voices replied in the affirmative. As an aside, he told Cady, "I've got Uetz in there. Kalachek is out back." The men were two of his deputies. "We're covered. And... here's LeRoy."

She recognized her cousin's slouched walk beneath the watery glow of the streetlights. He stopped in front of the bar then sent a furtive look around before ducking inside.

Ryder turned up the volume on the computer. She could make out the clack of pool balls, a buzz of indistinct conversation, and the wail of a country music artist. Then came LeRoy's voice. "Yeah. Um. Gimme a Bud bottle."

They listened to the transaction with the bartender. Then long minutes stretched with only background noise. Ryder had Cady summarize for Jerry the information she'd discovered about Phoebe Lansing.

Ryder's radio came to life. "Target at rear entrance."

She straightened. There was another long pause before

she heard a voice she recognized as Stan Caster's. "Let's take this to the free booth." A minute later, the ex-con spoke again. "You and me had us a friendly business proposition. You got a lotta nerve, son, trying to change the rules."

"I ain't," her cousin whimpered. "I got what you asked for. Just seems to me, I had two choices. I could send it on to you or go after the money myself."

"Thoughts like that could get a man killed."

"Hannah's my kin."

"Think I don't know that?"

"You got me breaking and entering, burglarizing my aunt and for what? Two hundred dollars. Uh-uh. Something wrong with that. Especially knowing what I know now."

"I didn't make you do shit."

"Guess that Franklin was for nuthin', then. We must be done here."

Garza turned to look at Ryder, brows raised.

"The fuck we are." Caster's voice was ugly. "I paid you a hundred and you get another for results. You sent me a sample of what you found. That's the only reason I'm here. I don't take kindly to blackmail. You're lucky I don't gut you right now."

There was a definite quaver to LeRoy's voice. "You're gonna wanna put that away before people notice."

"Atta boy," Jerry muttered. "Remembered that much."

"I know where you live, remember? I can get at you anytime. You or your mama."

"You're a fucking ex-con. Guess the cops would be plenty interested if 'n I was to tell them about all this."

Several minutes ticked by. Finally, Caster spoke again.

"You're right. I don't need cops sniffing around and you don't want to be looking over your shoulder for the rest of your life. Give me what you got. Then we can discuss terms."

"How 'bout I show you?"

Faintly alarmed, Cady glanced at Ryder. If LeRoy revealed the false evidence now, there'd be no reason for the ex-con to have anything further to do with him. He'd have what he wanted.

Ryder caught her look. Correctly interpreted it. "He's following the script."

She listened as her cousin apparently showed Caster pictures he'd taken on his phone of the phony bank statements he'd claimed to have discovered.

"Don't worry, we changed the date on his cell to coincide with the night he broke in," Garza said over his shoulder.

An argument erupted between the two men, one Cady had predicted. "Listen, fuckwit, I don't have to pay you another dime. You already showed me the fucking proof I wanted. Get outta here before I start slicing off little pieces of you and send them to your cow of a mama."

"Okay, you can be that way." She assumed the shake in LeRoy's voice was genuine. "Just remember, you can't get at that money. Only Hannah can. And who has access to my aunt? It sure the fuck ain't you."

Even knowing the conversation was based on a pretense, Cady's blood went cold. The threat to her mom was all too real. And Caster would be even more lethal if the imagined cash wasn't available.

"Now, I don't know what you got in mind." LeRoy paused to emit a juicy burp. "But you need Hannah to get at the money. Figure I'll get to it faster than you could."

"Sit your ass down." Caster was silent for a moment. "Say you're right. Can you get her alone?"

"Shee-it, you kidding me? Me and Hannah is like this. I take her out couple times a month for lunch and shit. Wouldn't be too hard to talk her 'round. Drive her to the bank. Make her think she's getting out some money for a good reason. Hell, she'll forget about it before we get home. She's got that brain disease. She's loonier than a bed bug."

Cady's nails bit into her palms. Consciously, she uncurled the fist she'd made. "Like I'd ever let him anywhere near my mom," she muttered. And she wasn't only referring to Caster.

"Let's work out the details." For the next hour, they listened to the two men debate how LeRoy could get at the money and then to a more contentious argument over what his cut would be.

"Caster believing that the robbery take is still out there untouched and accruing interest in banks makes him an even bigger dumbass than my cousin," she muttered.

"You never go wrong when you play to these guys' basest instincts," Jerry replied. "That's a tidy imaginary sum your mama accrued. Just over a hundred thousand dollars. Savings accounts don't pay much interest. But we figured money markets would be way over Caster's IQ. Plus harder to liquidate."

"Sounds like the meeting is breaking up."

At Ryder's words, her attention returned to the audio. He spoke into the radio. "Target exiting."

They got out of the car and strode to the front entrance. As they neared it, the door flew open and LeRoy burst out. Jerry pulled him aside. Fast-walked him in the direction he'd approached the bar from. Ryder's radio sounded. "Suspect in custody."

Cady and Ryder walked through the establishment and out the back exit. She could hear Caster's stream of curses as Kalachek placed him in the back of the county SUV he'd driven into the alley after the man had entered the building. Caster broke off when he saw Cady. "You fucking bitch. I shoulda known. This is entrapment. I'll be out again by tomorrow."

She moved toward the open back door of the vehicle. "You're grossly underestimating how damaging your recorded conversation was." She turned to Ryder. "Sheriff, what charges will you be bringing against Mr. Caster?"

"We've got solicitation for breaking and entering. Conspiracy to commit fraud, and the amount in question bumps that up to a felony. Of course, with these new offenses so quickly after your parole and your previous record..." Ryder shook his head. "Afraid you're going away again. Can't say I'm sorry to see it."

The man's face went ugly. "Think this means your mama's in the clear? She ain't. Plenty of people in these parts haven't forgotten that our take from the bank was never found. Your own cousin will probably steal it from her."

"Don't you get it? There. Is. No. Money," Cady enunciated. "The 'proof' LeRoy showed you? Faked. You've created a fantasy about your heist. And it's sending you back to prison."

He began cursing and she stepped away so the deputy could close the door. Uetz and Kalachek got in the front seat. Started the SUV and pulled away.

Garza came jogging up then. "I sent LeRoy back to the motel for another night. It'll probably be safe to let him go home tomorrow."

Ryder nodded. "You can call it a day. I'm going to the office for a while."

When he turned to Cady, she said, "See you at home."

"I shouldn't be too late."

"I'll be up. I've got work."

She'd made it back to her car, buckled up, and was

about to leave when her cell alerted her to an incoming text. She pulled out the phone, her heart speeding up a little when she saw the message was from Michelle Finley.

A person has to be able to live with herself. I got someone to cover for me tomorrow. Meet you at nine at Central Park in Sylva.

See u then. Thank you.

Cady quickly texted the news to Miguel before pulling away from the curb. She wouldn't allow herself to feel guilty about what Michelle's assistance might cost the woman. Not when it represented their best chance to find the place where the footage on those DVDs had been filmed.

IT WAS NEARLY midnight when Ryder came in. Cady turned away from the computer, rubbing her eyes. He came up and looked at the screen. "I didn't know you were into comics."

"I'm not. And this is a graphic novel, although I had to look up the difference."

He went to get a glass and poured himself some water from the refrigerator before returning to peer over her shoulder. "Why are you looking at these?"

She told him about Corbin Fielding. "He was a friend of Joseph Wiley's. Lord reacted when I brought up his name, so when I heard he was an artist..." She nodded toward the laptop.

"...you figured maybe his artwork was as dark as Wiley's?"

"I thought it might tell a similar tale," she admitted. "So far it hasn't. Although the drawings are clever. Miguel hasn't had any luck getting a call back from Fielding's mom, and his dad was in prison, so I'm not sure whether Corbin had a link to Life Church. Look here." She went back to some pages she'd bookmarked. Pointed at a frame.

Ryder leaned closer. "Hard to tell in the costume. But looks like Wiley."

Cady nodded. "I thought so, too. His character is Ink Man and Corbin is The Vindicator. They work together to bring down the villain, Two-Face."

"Original."

She lifted a shoulder. "Fielding's strength was the illustration, not the storyline. I'm finding that a bit difficult to follow. There are hundreds of pages in this thing. And I haven't even started on the animation sites yet."

"We're both sleep-deprived. This can wait." He finished his water and set the glass in the sink.

That's why everyone has to die. So the worthy can live.

Joseph's words rang in Cady's mind as she powered down the laptop. She wondered if he'd been including Corbin in that declaration.

And whether Adam Fielding had been right to doubt his son's suicide.

33

"You had no call to bring Rina in here, Deacon. She's not involved in this."

Phoebe straightened in her cell and strained to hear. The two robed figures had gone through a side door. To a garage, maybe. Or to the next room.

"I'm not having this conversation every fucking time I come here. Were you planning to leave her tied to that tree out back forever? I noticed the branches shaking when I was editing the film we shot, so I came back to check it out. If I hadn't found her, you probably would never have told me you'd caught up with her again."

There was a scuffling noise. Then the first man—Frank — spoke, sounding subdued. "It was too dangerous to take her back to my place."

"Well, at least you're smart enough to realize that. But I've been thinking the last couple of days. If you kept Rina secret, what else have you kept from me?"

"Nothing, Deacon, I swear."

"Maybe. Or maybe you lied about destroying those DVDs two years ago when I said to."

"I burned them, just like I promised. How many times do I have to tell you that?"

"See what lack of trust does to a person? It makes them doubt."

"I've done everything you said all along!"

"Perhaps. But I'll be asking Rina about them all the same."

At first Phoebe had been relieved when the men ignored them to leave the room together. Anything to have their focus off her. But now she began to consider what would happen if they fought between themselves. What if they killed each other and she and the two women were left to slowly starve to death? Would that be worse than the quick vicious end they had planned? Just considering the thought made her stomach twist.

Phoebe glanced at Greta. She wore no expression. Not curiosity. Not fear. She sat facing forward, as lifeless as a mannequin.

"This has nothing to do with Rina. You leave her alone!"

"I'm not going to hurt her. Take the rental and go hunt for Joseph. You'd know better than me where to look."

She turned around and looked at the new woman. Recognized the fear in her eyes. As if it were a virus, Phoebe could feel Rina's fright take root in her own system. Lick up her spine. Rage through her veins. When Rina trembled, Phoebe felt an answering shudder work through her own body.

She heard a rattling sound. Of an overhead garage door opening? And then the start of a vehicle. Moments later, the noise repeated. Then the inner door opened. He'd sent Frank away so it must be Deacon standing there, his face hidden by the oversized hood of the robe. He started toward them, and she shrank away, curling into a ball in the far corner of her cell. But he wasn't interested in her. He stopped at the acrylic cage holding Rina. He reached out gloved hands to rack back the lock. Fold back the lid and stretch inside, yanking her to her feet and out.

"You can make this easy, or you can make it hard." He gave her a shove, and she stumbled to all fours. Grabbing one arm, he dragged her to the door he'd just come through. Phoebe wiped away the tears of relief streaming down her face, hating him. Hating herself.

And pitying the newcomer for whatever was in store for her.

34

Michelle Finley barely spoke a word when Cady and Miguel picked her up at the park and drove to the old Life Church property. "If you're having second thoughts at any time, you just have to tell us," he told her.

"I'm going to try my best. This time, I have to know I did everything I could." She was quiet again for several more miles. After Cady finally turned off the county road to the gravel, she looked back to see Michelle twisting her hands in her lap. "I remember the way," she whispered as if to herself. "Stupid that just thinking of seeing it again has me reacting like this."

"It's a normal response to a traumatic memory." When Cady had attempted to explore Rina's cave, her involuntary physical response had frozen logic. Paralyzed her muscles. "I meant to ask you yesterday if you remember any of the names of other church members."

"Not really. There was a deacon who gave sermons sometimes when Pastor Lord was gone. But I don't recall a name."

Jonas's words replayed in her mind. *Deacon. Life and death.*

"You mean Burgess?"

"No, it was another guy."

Cady tried again. "Were there any other kids you played with?"

The woman's mouth twisted. "A lot has happened since then. I was friends with a girl named Megan. And Sally somebody. But I only ever saw them at church, and I spent most of my time with Rina."

When they pulled into the clearing, Cady noted that the stables were completely razed, although towering piles of rubbish still dotted the area. Mentally steeling herself, she looked at the church. Morrison was currently working on deconstructing it. The steeple was missing, as was much of the roof.

"It's mostly gone," Michelle whispered. "I can still see it, though. The way it used to be." They got out and Cady and Miguel hung back, allowing the other woman to set the pace. She walked to where the stables had once stood. Gazed at it for a long time. "I was happy here as a kid. For a while at least." She turned toward the church and shuddered. "I'd help tear that down, if I could. There's nothing I'd love more than to run a bulldozer over that place."

Morrison had caught sight of them and headed their way. "You again. Now what?"

Miguel looked at Michelle. "Which way?"

She raised a shaky index finger to point. He told the man, "We're going to the woods. I don't think we'll be bothering you."

His words didn't stop the workman from eyeing them suspiciously as they strolled past him and across a large grassy area, where Michelle paused again. "We'd have events here sometimes. Races and games and such. But more often than not, Burgess would have the kids play warriors." The word jolted Cady. "They'd use sticks for swords. But it usually turned into a fight. Whoever got knocked down had to recite a bible verse before they'd be let up again. It finally stopped, because parents were complaining their children were getting hurt."

"Lcwarrior," Miguel murmured. Cady nodded. Maybe the website name had originated from the faux battles Michelle remembered.

She led them behind the farmhouse but her footsteps slowed when they approached the trees. Finally, she stopped in front of one. "Rina and I climbed this all the time. We'd pretend we lived up there, like princesses in a castle." Her smile flickered for a moment before disappearing. She walked past it and through the woods, her pace quickening when she found a familiar landmark. Several times they had to backtrack. Each time she'd apologize.

"I'm sorry. It's been so long."

"It's fine. Just take your time," Cady told her. Because it was approaching noon, she passed out the premade sandwiches and bottles of water she carried in one of the market's shopping bags. They ate on the move. After a while, Michelle broke the silence again. "You didn't tell my dad I'd be here today?"

"No. I did call him this morning and told him I'd spoken to you. He was happy to know you're okay." She reached in her pocket and withdrew the note the man had given her. "He wants you to have his number."

Michelle fingered the slip of paper before shoving it into her purse. "Did he mention my mom?"

There was a pang in Cady's chest. "I'm sorry."

The other woman's gaze flew to hers. Then her eyes

moistened. "She's dead? I don't know what I expected. I haven't forgiven either of them. But a part of me hoped someday..." Her voice trailed off. It was several minutes before she spoke again. "There's a house up ahead."

"Does it look familiar?" Cady asked.

Michelle swallowed. "The one Rina took me to was single-story like this one. It had three windows in the back." Her words weren't quite steady. "There were firs all around it. Unless they've been cut down since."

Miguel took the notebook from his back pocket that he'd been jotting down distances and directions. He noted the location of the property and said, "Let's keep going. Maybe something else will jog your memory."

His words were prophetic. In the next couple of miles they came across a line of four more homes. Two of them had evergreen windbreaks. "I don't think it was any farther than this," Michelle said finally. "I mean, I know I said we walked forever to get there but we were children."

"We've done some backtracking, though, too, which adds to the mileage." Miguel pulled out his phone and did some calculations, toggling between the GPS, compass, and calculator apps. "I estimate we've come five miles, not counting when we retraced our steps. That would have felt like a long way to kids."

It felt like a long way now. Cady's ankle had begun to twinge and her limbs were stiffening. But a thread of excitement filtered through her veins as she studied the house before them. At the very least, a title search would tell them who'd owned the properties at the time Life Church was operating.

The owner of the home where the rapes occurred had a lot to account for.

They watched Michelle Finley drive away from the park before Cady started the vehicle. "We need to dig into the property owners for those houses she led us to."

"Since I just finished doing title searches for Lord's former home, I'd probably be faster at it." Miguel turned the laptop to face him.

She turned out of the lot and rubbed her quads with one hand. The doctor had said the the muscle aches would last for a few days. She should have demanded that he define 'a few'. Then, because she hadn't heard from Ben, she called him. He answered on the second ring.

"Cady." He sounded harried, but there was a note of excitement in his voice. "I know, I know, it's been all day. But I got sidetracked again. I'm just sending you some stills. I got one different man. Three more kids."

"What distracted you this time?"

She drifted to the far side of the lane when a semi passed her. Tried not to be reminded of the dump truck driver who'd attempted to run her off the road.

"Hear me out. Wait. Are you with your colleague?" When Cady answered in the affirmative, he continued, "You might want to put this on speakerphone." She did so, setting the cell on the center console. Miguel looked up from the laptop. "Okay."

Ben started again. "I got to thinking about your fugitive's link to the discs and the Life and Death website I showed you. I tried to determine whether the same staging location was used for both. The videos on those old DVDs were almost always filmed in daylight, or at least twilight, so I was able to take dimensions of the area. I'd estimate it at twenty by twenty. It could be a good-sized bedroom. Or maybe a living room."

His theory made sense. "Okay."

"There are two windows across the back wall. The camera always points that way. So, while I could figure out some measurements, I obviously can't predict how big the entire house is, or how many rooms it has. Given the angle of the sun, I'm guessing the rear of the structure has southern exposure. I got close-ups of the windows. The curtains were sheer. There's a wall of evergreens beyond the house. Mountains in the distance."

"Treeline. Mountains." Cady thought for a moment. "That's all I could make out of the background in the films you showed us from the Dark Web site. I figured it could be edited in, though."

"If it is, the exact same backdrop was chosen for both the DVD videos and the Life and Death movies." She'd never heard the mild-mannered Ben Trettin so animated. "The movies are shot outdoors. I was able to get at least partial views of three shuttered windows on the home. It's single-story—I caught a glimpse of roofline in a few of the films. And a back door. It's impossible to be certain, but I wanted to tell you, I think there's a distinct possibility—"

"That the rape videos and Life and Death battles were filmed at the same house," Cady murmured, her mind spinning.

"I can't be sure," he stressed again.

"But now we're aware of the chance," Miguel put in. "Thanks, Ben. This is major."

"Well." He sounded pleased. "I hope it'll help if you ever find the place."

"Working on that," she said. "And your description and dimensions will be beneficial as well."

"Good to know. I'm going to send you those stills. I'll get back at it tomorrow."

Thanking him again, Cady switched off the phone.

Glanced at her partner.

"Full circle," Miguel noted.

"That's what I was thinking. I keep thinking about something Michelle said today."

"About the warriors?" His focus had turned back to the laptop.

"Right. This much coincidence makes me antsy."

"Because maybe they aren't coincidences at all," he replied grimly. "They might just be the same vicious bastards, fifteen years ago and now."

Her cell began pinging. Ben was sending the images. "Open those, will you?"

Miguel picked up the phone and opened the attachments When he stared without speaking, she demanded, "Don't keep me in suspense. What is it?"

Silently, he held up one of the photos for her to see. The subject in it was younger. Not as blond. And far from the polished man she'd met in Durham.

But it was unmistakably Jeffrey Lord.

SHE'D BEEN LATE GOING HOME AGAIN. When she finally left the office, it was already six. Ryder had texted that he'd be tied up for a few hours, without going into detail. Cady decided to swing by her mom's. It was past time to put Alma's mind to rest about Caster bothering them again.

But a female was standing across the street when she drove out of the lot. Recognizing her, Cady pulled to the curb in front of the courthouse.

Then she got out and approached her. "Security watches for people hanging around, Ms. Wiley. This is a good way to get yourself hauled in for questioning."

"I been watching for you." The woman was dressed much as she'd been before. But now she wore a mask of quiet desperation. "You heard they lost my boy?"

"I was told he escaped, yes."

"What kinda cops we got in this town, they can't even hang on to their prisoners?" She paced on the sidewalk. Back again. "Are they close to finding him?"

"I don't know. I'm not involved in his case."

"According to my son's lawyer, Joseph took you from some tunnels downtown. Maybe that's where he was living. They oughta check there."

Helplessness swamped her. "Ma'am... Nancy. I'm sorry. I can't help you."

"He'll want to get back home," she muttered. "Not my place, but he could live in them woods. He'll try to get back to what he knows."

"You should tell the police that."

"They won't listen to me. But you could call. And tell them to check the forest behind Life Church. Or around that market you stopped at. He knows both of them areas real good. They should look there. It's dangerous for him to be loose."

Remembering the image of a teenaged Joseph Wiley in one of the rape videos, Cady asked, "Who do you think he's in danger from?"

"Hisself, of course." Nancy didn't meet her gaze. "Bad things happen when he's not on his meds."

That's why everyone has to die. So the worthy can live. Did Joseph think he was fated for death, or for life? Either way, his mother was correct. It was a danger for him to be free.

But perhaps not for the reason she thought. "I'll pass on your tips."

The woman stared at her, as if gauging her sincerity. "You promise?"

"I do."

"Thank you for that." She turned to walk away. "Might be, you'll save his life."

Cady got back in her car and put in a call to Iden, the federal prosecutor, leaving her a message before pulling away from the curb. Hanging up, she reflected on the irony of the person terrorized by Joseph Wiley being expected to act as his savior.

When she reached the cabin nearly an hour later, her mom was sitting out on the porch in one of the rockers there. "Cady!" Hannah's smile was bright as she came to meet her. "What a nice surprise. You're just in time for dinner."

She stopped to hug her mother and then slipped an arm around her waist. Walked with her up the steps. "You haven't eaten? It's almost seven."

"Not yet. Alma's busy in the garden. Still slightly confused, Cady opened the door and they went inside. Immediately, her gaze was drawn to the kitchen. The strainer was on the counter, dishes neatly stacked in it to dry. Given her aunt's ferocious neat streak, she doubted they'd been there long.

Hannah had forgotten she'd had dinner.

Worry streaked through her. Other people could have occasional moments of mental blankness. But with Alzheimer's, each new instance was a measuring stick. Were the bouts more frequent? More severe? Everything was carefully documented to keep track of the disease's progression. The doctor had already switched Hannah's meds to treat a moderate, rather than a mild stage. With every new example of forgetfulness, Cady was acutely reminded of the passage of time. It might only be a few short years before her mother no longer knew her. The thought was heart-wrenching.

The back door opened then and Alma entered, pausing in the doorway for a moment when she saw the two of them. Then she shut the door behind her and came inside. "Hannah. Did you show Cady what you bought her in Maggie Valley?" When her sister looked at her blankly, she reminded her, "The necklace?"

"Oh!" Hannah clapped her hands. "You're just going to love it. We have matching!" She dashed into her bedroom.

Alma drew closer and lowered her voice. "You done anymore 'bout that Caster feller? 'Cuz the longer he's out there free, the more nervous I get."

"He was arrested last night. He'll be going back to prison."

"And LeRoy? He shouldn't have no trouble to deal with over this."

She mentally rolled her eyes. "Because of his assistance, there won't be any charges against him."

Hannah returned to the room. "There was a shop that painted our names on these little stones and strung them. Aren't they the sweetest things?"

She admired the necklaces her mom held up, obediently turning so one could be fastened around her neck. She saw Alma sink heavily into a chair. She must have been more worried about her son than she'd let on. Cady would like to think he'd learned a needed lesson from the whole episode. But somehow, she doubted it.

Ryder still wasn't home when she got there, but there was a note saying he'd fed the dogs, which was more information than his text had contained. Mentally shrugging, she fixed herself a sandwich and then turned on her laptop. She hadn't had time yet to look up Holly Travers. Michelle had named her as one of the teens she'd seen being sexually abused. Cady was prepared to dig for a while. People moved away. Women got married and changed their names. Or some dropped out of sight completely, living with someone or renting. Not working, or paying taxes. She started with some secure government databases.

When she had enough identifying details to be reasonably certain she had the right person, Cady checked employment records. Found that Travers hadn't held a job in almost two years. Unless it paid cash.

She switched to a search engine. Social networks were often goldmines of information. But she didn't get that far. Because there were plenty of hits about Holly Travers of Colorado Springs.

Her stomach plummeted as she skimmed them. News articles about the mysterious disappearance of a twenty-four-year-old woman. Media clips featuring her teary-eyed fiancé describing how she hadn't come home from work that day. Pictures of the *Have You Seen This Woman* flyers posted around the city. The stories were daily at first. Then they'd dwindled before tapering off to articles on the yearly anniversary of her disappearance.

Cady sat back, her mind racing furiously. Deborah Patten had been kidnapped from another state and ended up on the Life and Death movies. What if Travers had too? She searched for both women on NamUs, a national clearinghouse for missing and unidentified persons. She got a hit only on Travers. Of course. She had siblings. Parents. A fiancé.

She reached for her cell. Called Miguel. "What are you doing?"

"Working. You?"

"Same." Cady told him everything she'd found on Travers.

"Interesting. I've been running down Gerald Edwards."

"Who?"

"Didn't you check your email? We got a word from the crime lab a couple of hours ago. They have a DNA match to one of the framed tattoos found in the mine."

Cady opened her email but didn't find the message in her inbox. Searched further then breathed out a curse. "It's in my junk folder." She quickly skimmed it. "What was Edwards doing in CODIS?" The federal database was a compilation of DNA profiles taken from crime scenes and convicted offenders.

"He served thirty-five months for robbery. The feds have already called Edwards's mother and delivered the news. Gerald was raised in Wilmington. He was an addict, supporting his habit with forcible purse snatching. He moved to Asheville after his release and the last contact his mother had with him was five months ago. But I don't see anything in his past that would link to Life Church. He spent his teenage years living near the coast."

"Phoebe Lansing doesn't seem to have a connection either, but she's in the fight movie," Cady reminded him.

"She was snatched from the region."

"So maybe Edwards was kidnapped from Asheville." She was thinking out loud. "We can't be certain yet how many kids from Life Church were abused. So far there have been six in the pictures Ben sent us. Michelle named another victim, Holly Travers, so that'd be seven." And she'd be shocked if Saul Jonas wasn't found somewhere on those discs. "But he's only halfway through the DVDs. What if the abuse victims are being silenced in the most final way possible?"

"You think Lord is behind this?"

"He'd have reason to be. He has lots to lose, beginning with his fancy office. We can be sure Burgess is involved, since Patten was discovered in his cooler."

"Edwards is only connected to Wiley at this point. Patten is the single victim we've seen in both the old videos and on the Life and Death site. Lansing's involvement still doesn't make sense."

"Stay with me. What if Lord wanted to get rid of the victims permanently?" Cady thought for a moment. "The site on the Dark Web became active a couple of years ago." It didn't escape her that the timing coincided with Corbin Fielding's suicide. "They had to search far to find Patten if she was still in California. In the meantime, it's to their benefit to keep the Life and Death site going. That brings in cash." The words tasted bitter. Benefiting from the victims' deaths after victimizing some of them earlier in their life was almost too evil to contemplate. "Every fight has one loser. Which means they need a replacement for the next bout."

"Are you saying they snatch people at random to fill in?" Miguel sounded skeptical.

"It would explain Lansing, who had no ties to the church." The dogs started barking outside. She set the laptop aside and went to the window. Ryder was home.

"That sounds like a lot of maybes."

"Yeah, it is." She couldn't disagree. "The only way to be certain is to catch these guys and question them. But I'm going to reach out to USMS in Durham. Have them monitor Lord until we finish this thing." Miguel agreed and then they disconnected. Cady sent a message to an acquaintance in the Durham office with a photo of Lord with a victim. She added an explanation of where they were in the investigation. The door opened just as she hit send.

Two canines burst into the house with Ryder following much more slowly. Cady eyed him. For a normally even-tempered man, he didn't look happy. He wore a tee with the sleeves ripped out, jeans and sneakers. The grass clinging to his denim-clad legs was evidence of what he'd been busy with.

"Mowing?"

He grunted in answer, moving to the refrigerator and taking out a bottle of water. Twisting off the cap, he guzzled from it. He lowered it long enough to say, "Lawn care at three different properties sucks."

"No reason I can't help with that." She went to the kitchen. Leaned against the counter.

"When?" He cocked a brow at her and drank again. "You're not home any more than I am. I was teaching Dylan how to use the mower at Mom's, so hopefully that'll be one less job. But I still had my place to do after. And soon I'll have to mow here, too."

"Why don't we hire a service?"

"Because it's dumb to keep two places anyway." He finished the water. Tossed the container in the recycling bin. "I can never find stuff I need because it's scattered between both our houses. You get that, I know, because you lived the same way for a while."

There was a clutch in her gut that she couldn't identify. "What are you saying?"

"Maybe we need to look at a more permanent solution.

Sell my house. Pick out something together. Dammit, Sadie, give me that." The dog had deftly jumped up and snagged the bottle cap he'd set on the counter. He bent to take it out of her mouth. Threw it away. "Something to think about, anyway. I'm going to take a shower."

Cady slumped as she watched him stroll away, all casual. As if he hadn't just lobbed a verbal hand grenade. *Permanent.* The suggestion had wings of panic fluttering in her chest, even couched as it'd been in logic.

It didn't help that she understood his point. When she'd lived at his place while the renovations were being done here, she'd never felt quite at home. She hadn't been certain whether his offer to stay there would have been made if necessity hadn't demanded it. And her past made it challenging for her to live in someone else's space.

She'd been happy to have him here after she left the hospital, and the hypocrisy was a bit difficult to swallow. She knew how it felt to have belongings divided between two places. They could hire someone to take over lawn care, but there were still other ongoing house duties to be fulfilled.

Cady didn't need Dr. Yarnell to help her figure out what lay at the root of her avoidance of intimacy. She'd never lived with anyone before. Hadn't dreamed of meeting someone for whom she'd give up that much independence. But now she had, and if she was honest with herself, she wasn't willing to go back.

The question was whether she was willing to move forward.

∽

DEACON PARKED at the end of the road and made his way toward the house. Darkness did the home a small favor, hiding its decay and lending it a shroud of dignity that dawn would strip away. A glow shone behind the closed blinds. He continued to the back of the residence and saw a light there, as well. Returning to the front, he banged loudly on the door, then ran to the rear again, taking out his picks and penlight.

Kneeling before the door, he clenched the light between his teeth as he worked on the lock. In a couple of minutes, the faint sound of success reached his ear. He replaced the items in his pocket and laid his gloved hand on the knob. Turning it, he eased the door open a crack.

He could see the woman standing at the window, peering through slats in the blinds. Deacon slipped inside and moved out of her line of vision. It was nearly fifteen minutes before she gave up her post and walked to the kitchen. He stepped from his stance at the sagging counter. "Hello, Nancy." He enjoyed her start and the flash of fear in her eyes more than he should. "Sorry to break in on you, but we need to talk about Joe."

"He ain't here," she stammered.

"But you know where he is. Fact is, you were talking to the marshals about him just this afternoon."

The guilt was easy to read in her expression. "That's a lie!"

"You were in Asheville by Otis Street today. The federal courthouse and the FBI are near there. Which did you visit?"

A minute ticked by. Finally, she said, "I waited for that marshal. I hoped she'd have heard something about the search from the cops."

Maddix. The name echoed in his mind like a curse. "What'd she say?"

Nancy lifted a shoulder. "Says she don't know nuthin'."

"We both want the same thing here." Deacon went to stand in front of her. "To find Joe."

"Yeah, but I want to keep him alive!"

"A little late to be pretending maternal instincts, isn't it? You were always more interested in what you could snort up your nose than you were in raising a kid."

"You trying to say I'm the cause of all his problems? Fuck you. Maybe I should tell the marshal what happened to Joe when he was younger. Bet she'd find that interesting."

He tamped down the flare of fury her words ignited. "You seemed happy to be bought off at the time. Maybe it wasn't enough." He withdrew a wad of cash from his wallet, handing it to her. When she was intent on counting the money, he took a step closer. Put one hand on her chin, and the other on her head. A belated sense of danger had Nancy stiffening, but it was too late. With a quick twist he snapped her neck. The bills fluttered to the floor as she crumpled. It was all he could do to wrestle the body to the cellar door. He opened it and turned her face forward. Then shoved her down the steep stairway.

Switching on the light, Deacon descended the first few steps, ducking down to see the space. It was cramped, only large enough to hold the furnace and water heater. He went back to the kitchen and picked up the money, shoving it in his pocket before doing a walk-through of the house. It was empty. He exited through the back door, first securing the lock. When he got to the drive, he paused at the left rear side of Nancy's car and stuck his hand under the fender, his fingers searching. The GPS tracking device he'd attached Sunday night was still there. Detaching it, he dropped it in his jacket pocket and headed for where he'd parked his vehicle.

He'd hoped that tracing her movements might lead him

to Joe. But it'd divulged even more critical information. Not knowing what the woman had told Maddix was a threat to their entire mission.

And the only way to deal with a threat was to eliminate it.

He pulled out his cell and called a contact. When the man answered, Deacon said, "Remember that favor you owe me?"

Silence. Then, "Yeah."

"It's pay-up time. I want this done tonight. This is how you'll do it."

35

Phoebe came upright, shielding her face defensively. When a blow didn't come, she lowered her arms, blinking in the bright overhead light that shone around the clock. She wasn't sure what'd awakened her, but she listened carefully until she was certain she and the other two women were alone.

A rhythmic scratching sounded from below the red lights. It continued for a long time. She glanced at Greta. The woman also seemed to be listening. After several minutes of silence, there was a rapping noise. Then the sound of breaking glass. She cowered, thinking one of the men would come running. But Phoebe saw no one until a large form appeared from the direction of the wall and loomed over her cell. She scrabbled to the back corner, cowered there. It was a man. He was whiskered, and wearing clothes that were a little too small. He crouched down to look at her and then moved away to the next cube. Repeated the action.

Phoebe shoved a fist against her lips. Nothing about the stranger was reassuring. Did he represent rescue, or yet another threat? She turned when she heard his whisper behind her, curiously high-pitched for such a big male. He was beside the cube belonging to the third woman. When Deacon had brought her back, she'd been beaten badly. One of her eyes was ringed in purple and bruises bloomed all over her body.

"So that marshal was right. You *were* in danger, Rina, and you shouldn't have been. This is wrong. The plan was *perfect*, but you aren't part of it." Something in his voice made ice trickle down Phoebe's spine. "Who brought you here? Who can't be trusted? Frank?" He tapped once at the cell. "Or Deacon?" He knocked two times.

Rina didn't respond for a long minute. Then she rapped twice.

"Joseph! Get away from her."

A light flipped on and a man was standing there with a rifle aimed at the intruder. Phoebe stared. She recognized Frank's voice. His robe was crooked, and a dark beard partially showed through the opening in the hood.

"You and Deacon lied to me." The newcomer approached the robed man, as if unconcerned about the weapon. "You said if I helped you, afterward we'd finally start the church you always promised. I'd be an elder. You've told me since I was a kid that I was chosen for an elevated position before God. But it was all bullshit, wasn't it?"

Frank held the gun, but it was Joseph who seemed to dominate. "I've always been honest with you. It's Deacon. He betrayed us both. He brought Rina here. He means to kill her, I know it. When we're finished, I'm not so sure he don't mean to get rid of me and you, too. But I've got a way for us to have that church we always talked about." He lowered the rifle. Motioned the younger man closer. They withdrew deeper into the home, and try as she might, Phoebe couldn't make out their words.

But their earlier conversation had trepidation twisting through her. She'd like to believe that dissension between the men might open up an opportunity for her and the other captives. She turned to look at Rina and saw a fatalistic certainty reflected in her expression.

The appearance of the third man would change nothing for them. They still weren't leaving here alive.

36

Hero scratched at the door and Cady slipped from the bed to let Sadie and him out of their room. They'd raised a racket earlier this morning with their barking and Ryder had locked both dogs in the bedroom with them. The canines had remained unsettled, awakening her whenever she dozed off. Next time, she promised herself grimly as she fed the animals and then shooed them outside, they'd be kept in one of the spare bedrooms.

The sky was just beginning to lighten, but she wasn't in the mood to appreciate dawn's approach. She poured herself a mug of coffee and drank half of it before silently gathering her clothes and getting ready in the second bathroom. Then she went back to the kitchen and topped off her coffee before turning on her laptop.

She spent an hour skimming Corbin Fielding's drawings again, before stopping short and rereading what had caught her eye. The villain Two-Face had an alternate persona and it was named for the first time. Deacon.

Saul Jonas had mentioned the name. Michelle Finley said a man served that function at Life Church. Cady flipped through several more pages of the graphic novel in hopes of seeing a drawing of Deacon's face but didn't find one.

Ryder came in minutes later, buttoning his shirt. "Are the mutts outside or did you give them away?"

"It was tempting," she said darkly, and reached for her coffee again. At that moment, the canines started baying. "Maybe I'll buy some muzzles today."

Ryder grinned. "Lack of sleep makes you cranky. They've probably treed another opossum."

"I'll check on my way out." She loaded up her laptop and downed the rest of the coffee, before retrieving her holster and weapon from the closet and buckling it on. The dogs were in front of the house. Cady stepped out onto the porch, nearly tripping over something sitting next to the door.

A box. She crouched for a closer look. It bore the markings of a retail giant with a typed label addressed to her. A sense of unease filled her. She shopped as rarely as possible and not at all recently. "Did you order something for me?" she called through the door to Ryder. "There's a package out here, and I didn't send for it." He joined her, stocking-footed, and took a look.

"No. Maybe your mom or aunt."

"Neither would have a clue about online shopping." She recalled the ruckus their pets made last night and a slow chill worked down her spine. "I didn't see this yesterday when I got home. Maybe it was brought after we went to bed and that's why they went crazy." There were security lights on the front door and the garage, but their bedroom faced a different direction.

He guided her inside the house. "Take Sadie and Hero to my yard. Text my mom and let her know so she can have Dylan check on them later. Then you may as well head to work." He collected his weapon and boots and went out the door with her. "It's probably nothing. I'll keep you posted."

Cady whistled for the pets and herded them into her vehicle. "Nice try. I'll be back in a few minutes." She forestalled his objection by adding, "Best case scenario—we're over-reacting." But her gut said otherwise. After being run off the road days earlier, a suspicious package had alarm bells going off.

CADY SUMMARIZED the events of the morning for Miguel over the phone while she watched the response efforts in progress. When she'd returned from taking the dogs to Ryder's, the street fronting the acreage was already blocked off. His deputies were establishing a perimeter and evacuating neighbors. She'd been allowed access and directed to the property across from hers.

Her colleague gave a low whistle. "I hope there's an innocent explanation for the package. But if not, it proves Sunday's 'accident' wasn't a one-off. Have you spoken to Allen?"

The memory of that call had her wincing. "Yeah. If this situation doesn't end well, he'll be calling in a USMS counter-surveillance team again."

"That's some kind of record. What's it been, three months since they put one in place after John Teeter shot up your house and vehicle?"

"Just over."

"Maybe they need to assign you your own permanent protection detail."

"Don't even joke about it," she replied feelingly. "Have you heard from Fielding's mother?"

"She hasn't responded. Local police in Naples are supposed to try to make contact. I'll finish up the title searches on the houses in the area Michelle took us to. Keep me posted."

"Okay." Ryder strode by with Jerry Garza as Cady disconnected. She hurried to catch up with them. "What's the timeline?"

"Asheville PD bomb squad will arrive in an hour," Ryder said over his shoulder. "We'll be set up over here."

She stifled a sigh. She went to the Enclave parked in the neighbor's drive, booted up her laptop, and brought up Corbin Fielding's graphic novel. She might as well pass the time constructively.

A moment later, her cell rang. The message on the screen read NC DPS. She answered. "Maddix."

"Deputy Marshal, it's State Trooper Hank Thornton. I was at the scene last Sunday when you were run off the road. I hope your injuries weren't serious."

"Hello. Yes, I'm fine. More sore than anything."

"Glad to hear it wasn't worse. Reason I'm calling is to update you on the investigation into your incident. We think we've tracked the vehicle used. It was abandoned twenty miles from your scene. We traced it to a private company in Webster. The truck was stolen from their lot that afternoon. We processed it for prints, but we've haven't had a hit on the latents yet."

"Really?" When she hadn't heard anything, she'd figured tracking the dump truck was a lost cause.

"They did find black paint on its fender. We're in the process of trying to match it to samples from your Jeep. I'm afraid that's all I have for you. If we find out more, I'll contact you again."

"I appreciate it. Thanks for calling." Cady hung up,

mulling the information. It didn't sound like fingerprints would identify the thief. He'd probably worn gloves. But Webster was in Jackson County, a half-hour from Waynesville. If the vehicle went missing Sunday, its driver almost certainly had one express purpose: to head toward Durham with the intent of ambushing Cady.

Her gaze went to the scene playing out in front of her house. And if that had been the plan, it meant whoever had arranged the incident knew which road she'd be on and which way she'd be headed.

Because he'd known where she lived.

RYDER STOOD next to the Asheville PD's bomb squad van, watching one of the explosives specialists huddle over a computer to operate the disposal device remotely. Images from its cameras filled the screen. The robot had been equipped with an X-ray machine attached to one of its arms. It climbed the steps and approached the parcel. The technician manipulated the robot so the machine was centered over the package, then toggled the controls to perfect the scan.

"Pipe bomb, looks like," he said after taking pictures from every angle. "No way to be certain what the energy source is, but it's often black powder. Very volatile." He studied the images more intently. "They'll frequently explode upon contact. The fact that someone handled it enough to get it to the porch without leaving body parts behind makes me think it might be a bit more stable. Maybe the package is set to detonate when opened." He took several more X-rays before sending the robot back to the trailer. "We should have no difficulty disarming it with the PAN Disrupter."

"The water cannon?" Ryder had seen one used when he'd been on the force in Charlotte. It'd disarm the IED and allow the specialists to gather evidence faster and safer, with minimal damage to the home.

The man nodded and began speaking over the radio to his colleagues. After he'd finished his conversation, he looked over at Ryder again. "My buddy just reminded me that we encountered several of these IEDs over this way five years ago."

"That was before my time, but I don't remember hearing about cases like that here."

"We worked with the Jackson County Sheriff's Office on them. All were similar enough that we thought they came from one source. Once we disrupt the bombs, we send the pieces to Quantico. The sheriff over there probably has their report handy."

"Thanks. I'll contact him." Ryder pulled out his cell and put in a call to Jeb Redding. He waited a short time until the man came on the line and briefed him on the morning's events.

"I had something similar happen over here a while back," Jeb said. "We found several pipe bombs over six months. Some detonated. Deputy Harmon headed up the case, but the way I recall it, the bombings stopped before we ever landed on a suspect. We always figured the bomber moved out of the area. I hope like hell he isn't back."

"I'd like a copy of the federal lab report, if you have it."

"I'll have my staff send it to you. It'll be interesting to see if Quantico can determine whether the same guy constructed your IED."

"It will be. Thanks, Jeb." Ryder hung up, then called

Cady to relay the information. "Jackson County again," he concluded grimly. "Everything circles back to there."

"It seems like it." She briefed him on the trooper's call earlier. "And before you overreact, Allen is requesting a counter-surveillance team. They'll probably get here tomorrow."

"None too soon," he said feelingly. "Do you think Lord's behind these attempts on your life?" He watched the bomb squad's water tanker lumber down the road toward them.

Her answer was slow in coming. "My gut feeling is yes. He's had years to cover his tracks, but he has to know we're getting close. He doesn't have what it takes to make a direct attack on me, though. He'd send a goon. Maybe Burgess."

A boulder had settled on his chest. "I don't want to lose you. Or what we have."

"Me either." Her voice was soft. "That's a pretty big incentive for both of us to be careful."

The tanker was slowing next to the trailer. One of his deputies was waving him over. "I have to go. Stay safe." He strode away, slipping his phone into his pocket. And tried to shove aside the mental image of what that bomb could have done to Cady this morning.

IT WAS early afternoon by the time Cady and Miguel got started checking out the properties Michelle had led them to yesterday. Cady's road was still blocked, so he met her at Ryder's house. She updated him on the events at her acreage and the trooper's call as he drove them to Jackson County.

"Well, I'm glad they're sending a security detail," he said feelingly. "They'll probably suggest you move again."

She considered the idea unenthusiastically. "We'll see what they recommend."

"What'd the bomb squad find in the IED fragments?" Miguel was onto another topic. "Was it like the ones Redding's office dealt with years ago?"

"There were similarities. Black powder was used as an explosive. The same type of caps attached to a metal pipe. There were nails packed in this time, though. And the package had fake bar codes on it. It'll be a while before we get a report." She shrugged, but the thought of the damage the shrapnel could have done sent a shudder creeping down her spine. Deliberately, she changed the subject. "I took another look at those images of kids Ben texted yesterday. I think the second one might be Saul Jonas."

She took out her cell, brought up the pictures, and showed them to him.

"There's a resemblance. Hard to be sure with the beard he wore."

"It's something in his eyes. And his coloring. Maybe he thought the arsenal he compiled would save him."

Miguel drove them to a gravel road perpendicular to the blacktop fronting the homes Michelle had shown them yesterday. He slowed to a stop, parking on the shoulder. The tiny residence at the end of the drive was only slightly bigger than the coop and chicken run next to it. Chickens were pecking desultorily in the dirt. They approached, but didn't have the opportunity to knock. An elderly whiskered man came out, holding a flat pan filled with feed and headed for the pen. When he saw them, he scowled. "You two are trespassing."

Cady tapped the star clipped to her belt. "Deputy U.S. Marshals, sir. We wanted to ask you a few questions."

"Ain't promising to answer." He set the pan on the ground.

"Do you know any of your neighbors around here?"

"Nope. And I don't want to."

He'd be right at home in Bordertown, Cady thought. But she kept her voice pleasant. "How long have you lived here?"

"Ten years. Bought the property because it was the only place on this road. Then I got people moving in next door, building a big damn house for their big damn family. Kids and dogs spilling out in all directions." She'd obviously hit a sore spot. "I have a right to shoot anything that comes on my land."

"Not necessarily, sir." She pretended not to hear what he muttered under his breath. "Did you buy the place from the former owner?"

"Nope. Realtor said they found him stiff as a board in his bed. No telling how many days he'd been dead." He repeated the words with relish. "Price was cheap because of it. Didn't bother me."

Somehow that didn't surprise her. "Thank you for your time." She and Miguel headed back to his pickup.

"We can skip the home he mentioned. County tax records show it's only been there four years." Their pace quickened when they saw a sheriff's car pulled alongside Miguel's vehicle.

The driver got out of the SUV. "Deputy Harmon." Somehow Cady wasn't surprised to see him. He seemed to pop up everywhere.

"I stopped to see who was parked there. It's unusual for ol' man Timmons to have company." He waited expectantly, but when they remained silent, he went on. "Meant to call you anyway, but now I can just give you the list you asked for."

Cady's expression must have looked blank. "The names you called about?" He drew a small notepad from his back pocket and flipped it open. Then tore off three sheets to hand to her. "I hope this helps."

The church members Lord had mentioned. Gordon. White. Finley. The list the deputy had put together was depressingly long. Scanning it, she saw Richard Finley's name near the bottom. "I appreciate this. Thanks."

"No problem." He started back toward his vehicle.

"How's the investigation proceeding into Saul Jonas's death?" Cady asked.

Wayne faced them again, pulling a handkerchief from his pocket to wipe at the back of his thick neck. "The autopsy is scheduled for tomorrow. But Jonas had a permit for the gun found by the body, and his prints were on it. I'd like you to come in and fill out a formal statement about your conversation with him. You might have been the last person to speak to him."

After she promised to stop by the Jackson County Sheriff's Office the next morning, he returned to his SUV and continued on his way. Cady and Miguel got in the pickup. He turned around in the drive.

"Did you know that Corbin Fielding died the same way Saul Jonas appeared to?"

"Over half of suicides involve a firearm," he pointed out.

He was right. And suicide attempts were three times more likely for people who had experienced sexual abuse as children. But those facts didn't douse the doubts circling in her head. When Jonas called her, it had sounded as though he had information on Burgess and the mysterious Deacon, who'd also appeared in Fielding's drawings. But if the young men had been silenced, why fake suicides? Why hadn't they appeared in the Life and Death videos?

It was past time, she thought grimly, to make an arrest and put some of her questions to rest.

They went a mile down the road before getting out again to check the first of the remaining five houses. "You can't see any of the other homes from here," she noted as they walked up the drive. The property was heavily wooded, with a few evergreens but mostly deciduous trees. When she knocked, it was only a moment before a woman with a long gray bob answered the door, smiling at them quizzically.

"Are you lost? We get that a lot around here."

"No, ma'am." Miguel flashed a smile and Cady watched the woman melt a little around the edges. Seriously. The man should come with a warning sign. "Deputy U.S. Marshals Rodriguez and Maddix. We're checking out some homes in the area. Wondered how long you've had yours."

"Oh, my, going on thirty years now. We bought the place when the boys were small and they're grown men now. I'm Peg Gibbon, by the way. My husband and I moved to Florida six years ago, but we come back three or four times a year to escape the heat." She smiled. "Or for the peace and quiet. There's plenty of that."

"Do you know who lives in the house next to yours?"

"I sure do. Some very good friends. The Munsons. We usually time our visits for the same dates, but they had other plans. They live in Baton Rouge."

"When's the last time they came?" Cady put in.

"We both spent Thanksgiving here last fall. Stayed for nearly a month."

"Do you know anyone else on this road?" Miguel asked.

"I'm afraid not. We don't socialize much when we're here. And all the places are so isolated, you rarely see a soul when you drive by."

Thanking her, they returned to the truck. "That means we can skip the neighbor's home."

"Sounds like it," Miguel agreed. "What she told us matches the owner on the title search information."

The house two doors down looked deserted. It was a one-story with a single stall attached garage.

When no one responded to their repeated knocking, Cady said, "Let's take a look out back."

"We just saw it yesterday."

"But that was before we heard Ben's theory comparing the homes where the DVDs and the Life and Death footage were filmed." Without waiting to see whether he'd follow, she rounded the garage. Firs grew close to the structure. She had to wait for a break in the tree line to get to the yard.

It took Miguel a moment to catch up with her. "This looks like it could be the scene of those fight videos," he noted.

Silently, Cady agreed. Three windows punctuated the back of the house. All were covered with heavy wooden black shutters. "This is one of the two Michelle thought was familiar."

"It's also one of the two with the owner listed as an LLC. The other is two more doors down. Let's take another look at it."

They retraced their steps and drove past the next home. It was an A-frame and the title search had shown that it'd changed hands four times in the last twenty years. Miguel stopped at the house on the other side of it. It was the first one Michelle had thought she recognized yesterday. Another ranch style, it was brown, rather than navy. And the garage was a double. Matching shutters were closed over the front window. They didn't look as though they'd been open anytime recently. Towering pines surrounded the home.

Cady pounded on the door. Waited several moments before knocking again.

Miguel leaned forward to hammer at it. Still nothing. He turned away.

"Listen." She pressed her ear against the door. At first, she thought she'd imagined the earlier noise. But then it came again. A rhythmic thumping. She waited, but no one came. They walked to the drive. "There's something in there," she insisted. "Twice after I knocked, I heard a sound."

"It might have been an echo." When she just looked at him, he shrugged. "Or, it could've been made by a pet."

Her mind flashed to Ben's description of the caged females on the L and D site. "Or maybe someone's in there. Someone who isn't free to answer." She pulled out her cell and checked the time. Nearly three. She was surprised Miguel hadn't started whining about food yet. "Let's check out back."

The rear of the property was eerily similar to that of the home a couple of doors down. It was secluded by a wall of firs.

"What are you thinking?" Miguel asked.

"Surveillance."

He sighed. "I knew we should have eaten before driving up here."

37

The wave of hope was so powerful it was dizzying. Phoebe waited in vain for another knock. When it didn't come, she brought up both feet and began kicking her cell. Someone was out there. *Don't leave us!* A silent shriek of desolation streaked through her. She aimed another kick at its side, then listened hard. Heard only silence.

That ended all too soon.

Phoebe had no idea where he'd appeared from, but a dark-robed figure was bearing down on her like a sinister specter of death. She scooted to the back of her cube and shielded her face with her arms.

He unlocked her cell and yanked her to her feet. "'The Lord will fight for you, and you have only to be silent!'" he hissed. His hard fingers wrapped around her throat as he shook her brutally.

She reached up and tried to loosen his grip. Phoebe couldn't draw a breath. He was killing her! Her lungs were starved for oxygen. Knees weak, she went limp. And only then did he release her. She wasn't aware of the lid closing again. She could only frantically gulp air as the room did a kaleidoscopic spin.

Long minutes passed. She lay there, crumpled. Broken. Worse than no hope was to be extended a tenuous ribbon of it, only to have it snapped.

For the first time she understood Greta's blank expression.

It was far easier to feel nothing at all.

38

Cady's butt was numb. She'd been sitting for hours, concealed between a couple of huge pines. Shifting position relieved the muscle stiffness only briefly. The text she'd sent out to the task force had elicited several offers of assistance. She'd selected two, John Rossi and Keith Pritchard. The men had brought more equipment and enough food to keep even Miguel happy.

She raised the binoculars again. It was nearly six thirty. Only one vehicle had gone by since they started surveillance. Watching sloths would have been more exciting. She alternated between staring at the property and using her cell to scroll through pages of Fielding's graphic novel. Neither activity was particularly stimulating.

"I'm falling asleep out here."

Cady smiled as Miguel's voice sounded through the radio. He was stationed at the rear, in the corner opposite her. The other two team members watched the residence two doors over.

"I've got a cramp in my left butt cheek and I'm pretty sure I'm sitting on an anthill," she responded.

"That'll keep you awake. I just want to note, if this stretches until after dark, these trees are probably full of bats."

She hissed in a breath. After her experience in the mine, the thought was disturbing. "You had to say it."

A half hour later, Cady was squirming again. They'd been here long enough for her to question what she'd heard inside the house. To doubt every conclusion she'd drawn in the case.

Earlier, Ben Trettin had texted images of four different teens with the same three adults. Burgess and Lord were recognizable in several photos but there was never a good angle for the third man. She suspected that was by design.

She studied the house for several minutes, before refocusing on her phone. Cady had lost track of the developing storyline, but she stopped scrolling each time the character Deacon was featured. The alter ego of Two-Face.

Her cell vibrated in her hand. "Allen." She'd texted him earlier about their planned surveillance.

"Just a head's-up, the counter-surveillance team will be in place tomorrow morning. They recommend you find another place to stay."

Cady mentally sighed. She raised the field glasses with her free hand. "I'll tell Ryder. We can go to his place."

"A hotel would be better. Whoever sent that explosive knew where you live. Which means they may also know about your relationship with him."

She cursed silently. "You're right. We'll have to figure out something for the dogs, though."

There was a beat of silence before Allen went on. "I talked to him earlier and he filled me in on the bomb's components. Jesus, Cady. If that had gone off..."

"It didn't."

"Right. And with the team's protection, the sender won't get a second chance. Keep me posted if you get action tonight."

She agreed and hung up. As promised, she texted Ryder before observing the house for a while. Minutes later, she glanced at her phone again, flipping faster through the comics.

She almost went by it. Had to back up to look again. The title of the segment screamed at her. "Two-Face Unmasked!" Cady stared at the section's pictures more closely. All showed Deacon's face for the first time.

It was a clever caricature. But a sick sense of recognition twisted through her. She took screenshots of several of the drawings, sending them to Miguel.

> Look like anyone we know?

As she waited for the reply, she gazed at the home again. A bird flying from its roof was the most action they'd seen since they started.

Her phone alerted.

> Maybe Corbin knew him. But not proof he's involved in this.

Cady didn't respond. She searched for a web address and texted it to Michelle Finley.

> Click on each personnel photo and let me know if you recognize anyone.

Ten minutes crawled by. She was about to contact the woman to make sure she'd seen the text when Michelle called.

"I don't understand," she said without preamble. "What

does the deacon of Life Church have to do with the Jackson County Sheriff's Office?"

Excitement thrummed in Cady's veins. "Did you see that man depicted on the site I sent?"

"Well, yeah. I went through all of the employee pictures like you said. But everyone just called him Deacon when I was a kid. He never wore a uniform or anything to services."

She named the man she'd recognized, and Cady thanked her and hung up. But her mind was racing. A person holding a position of authority could instill a lot of fear in former victims. He could also slant investigative findings. Or illegally use law enforcement databases to find people who'd moved out of the area.

Her spine shot with steel. Burgess wasn't going to be the only person she took down before this was over. She picked up her radio. "I've got an update."

IT WAS NEARING eight o'clock when Cady wiggled farther into the stand of firs, raising her binoculars. A midsized dark-colored SUV came into view. As it drew closer to the property, she got on her belly, ignoring the twinges in her muscles as she squirmed for position to keep the vehicle in sight.

It pulled into the driveway. Two passengers. Cady strained to make out the driver. When she did, adrenaline shot through her veins. The garage door opened and he drove inside. The door closed again.

She exchanged her glasses for the radio. "Visual of Frank Burgess confirmed."

They'd pulled back to the house two doors down. Cady had texted several more members of the task force and reinforcements were on the way with more equipment.

She was going over the entry plan with Rossi and Pritchard when Miguel's voice came over the radio. "There are five people in the house." He was operating the Range-R device that detected human presence inside a structure.

Cady's head snapped up. "Five?"

"Affirmative. I've double-checked. All adults. Three close together in the room nearest the front door. The other two are in the east side of the home."

Her pulse sped up. "This has to be where they're keeping the fight victims."

"Likely they're the three in the center of the house. Not a lot of movement coming from them."

"The possibility of hostages changes things." John Rossi noted.

Cady nodded. "It ups the risk. So, we'll devise several different ops. Be ready to switch plans as our intelligence evolves. Remember that Frank Burgess's accomplice inside could be a member of law enforcement." A sense of urgency built in her as they brainstormed options.

By the time the other members arrived, they needed to be prepared to move.

39

"It has to end quickly. We've run out of time."

Phoebe straightened in her cube and strained to hear the murmured voices.

"I've told you before, Deacon, it must be done in a holy manner."

"You've had it your way for long enough. That marshal is too close. It's over. Tonight is the last video. We round up the others, kill them and burn the bodies."

"Never known you to leave money on the table."

"Jeffrey will give us plenty when we've completed the mission. You just need to find Joseph. I've already taken care of Jonas."

"What? Without telling me? I guess you think you're making all the decisions now."

"Don't you get it, Frank? He was a powder keg waiting to go off. And so's our operation here. I'll get you new ID. Return the rental and buy you a vehicle. You'll be free."

The words grew muffled. She could only hear a word or two. It didn't matter. She didn't care about what they had planned.

She only cared about tonight.

Phoebe and Greta had been forced to shower earlier and then were relocked in their cells. The men had ignored Rina. Phoebe wrapped her arms around her waist and rocked rhythmically. She knew they were being prepared for another film. A fight to the end.

Urgency sprinted through her. Unless they figured something out, one of them wouldn't be alive in another few hours. She didn't know which she feared more—death or survival. To live knowing she'd been the cause of another's demise would be a whole new hell.

Phoebe pressed her face against one of the air holes on the side of her enclosure and whispered to Greta. "Listen to me." She tried to keep her voice low enough that it wouldn't be picked up by cameras. "We can take them by surprise. Rush them once we get outside. We grab weapons and then—"

The woman slowly turned to face her. "It doesn't matter. I told you. They'll kill us if we try. One way or another, one of us is going to die today." She paused a beat before adding, "And it isn't going to be me."

40

"We've got company." Rossi's voice sounded over the radio. "One individual. Likely male, from the size. Heading toward our positions from the woods."

The full task force had arrived, four of them situated at the rear of the property. Cady thought quickly. It was dark, but the team had the advantage of night vision goggles. "If he gets close, Rossi and Pritchard, take the subject down. Tompkins and Garrett, assist as needed." It wasn't unusual for things to go sideways on a raid, but the timing couldn't be worse.

"Roger that."

Seconds stretched into minutes. Tompkins whispered, "Arrest in progress."

A short time later, Rossi's voice was heard. "Unknown subject in custody. No ID."

"Take him to base and send me a pic." Their vehicles were hidden at the house two doors down. "Cuff his wrists and ankles."

It was another ten minutes before her cell vibrated.

Shock spiked through Cady when she saw the image Rossi had sent. Their party crasher was Joseph Wiley.

She texted an ID. If this house were the place where the teens had been assaulted years ago, he'd undoubtedly know its location. But there was no reason for him to be here. Unless he knew the men were inside. Or was aiding them.

Time crawled as she returned to surveillance. Her phone signaled an incoming message. She glanced down at the text from Rossi.

> Wiley says Burgess left gun for him under tree. Plan was to overtake Deacon later tonight.

The back door opened and her attention bounced back to the house. She exchanged her cell for the radio. "We've got activity in the back yard."

A figure wearing a long-hooded robe was carrying something. He approached the trees Cady was using as cover and set his load down. She peered closely. A spotlight. The man made a couple more trips before returning to switch on each item. Light beamed inward toward the residence.

Her mind raced. Were they planning on filming another fight video? If so, the team's options suddenly narrowed. Having victims in the area increased the danger exponentially. But the women were at even graver risk without an intervention.

She got to her feet, fading well back into the shadows before raising the radio to her lips. "Prepare for plan C."

41

Their cells opened. "Get out. Put the outfits on."

The fur garments they'd worn before were on the floor in front of their cubes. Greta was already scrambling to obey Deacon's order. Phoebe followed her lead, her fingers awkward with haste.

"This might be your lucky day. Whoever's the winner will go free."

A spear of hatred stabbed through her. If she hadn't heard him talking with Frank earlier, she might even have tried to believe him. But she knew there would be no "winner." Death awaited all of them.

A wave of despair hit her. It grew stronger when he flipped on another light in the room, and left briefly, only to return carrying some metal instruments. "These are your weapons."

Phoebe drew closer to look at the strange items. They had long handles like tongs that ended in wickedly spiked claws. The man lunged at her, clacking the ends together, raking her bare shoulder with the teeth. She cried out as blood welled up from the gash he'd inflicted.

"Now you know how they work. Next time duck away, or it'll be the shortest match in history. They're breast rippers. You aim for the chest and go deep." Phoebe clapped one hand to her wound, resolve hardening inside her. It wouldn't be Greta she'd attack if given a chance.

Frank entered the room and raised his arms high. "Sin is the wild beast living in all of us, and it can only be cleansed by blood. To survive, you must fight or perish. Blessed are God's warriors who die fighting in His name. Follow me."

He turned and led them through the side door, down the hall and out to the back yard. Knowing what awaited her made Phoebe's knees go to water.

The spotlights had her shielding her eyes as she stumbled outside. Deacon carried a rifle. "Go stand in one corner of the spray-painted square."

But Phoebe moved past the area he indicated toward the dense line of evergreens surrounding the yard. Her muscles tensed as she poised to run.

"Get over here!" That quickly, her moment of opportunity vanished. Frank ran to yank her by the arm and drag her back. "Follow directions."

The weapons were in the middle of the square. When the two women took their places, Deacon said, "When I give you the signal, you rush to pick up your breast-ripper and begin the match." He moved several feet away, cradling the rifle. "On three. One, two... three."

They raced to the center of the rectangle. Greta got there first and kicked Phoebe's weapon away. She was diving for it when more lights split the air. Loud bangs sounded. A disembodied voice called out, "Deputy U.S. Marshals. Drop your weapons. Get on the ground."

Phoebe was confused. Was this part of the video? But in the next moment she saw Frank lower the camera, swiveling his head from side to side. Deacon sprinted away from the house, heading for the row of firs on the side. Black-garbed creatures were bursting from between the trees, running toward them, with rifles raised.

"Hands behind your head. Now!"

"Suspect on the run. Northeast corner of the property."

Frank raced back into the house.

"Everyone on the ground!"

Panic warring with bewilderment, Phoebe dropped her weapon and knelt. Waited for one of the black-clad figures to pull her to her feet, and lead her away. But it wasn't until they walked through the border of trees that the truth hit her hard in the chest.

It was over. She was free.

CADY KEPT her position between the drooping branches of the evergreen. The suspect rounded the house and headed right for her. She let him close half the distance before stepping out. "Lower your weapon. Hands behind your head."

He stilled. Pivoted.

"Jeb Redding. Drop it now!"

Two more team members ran toward them. She never took her eyes off the man still hidden by the oversized hooded robe. The adult who'd figured in Corbin Fielding's final artistic works.

"I'm not going to repeat myself." She approached him, her rifle level.

"Cady. You've misread the situation."

"I misread *you*. That's over. The gun."

He set it on the ground. One of the task force members kicked it away. Another lowered the man's hood. Even given her earlier certainty, the sight of the sheriff was a gut punch. "On your knees," she repeated. "Hands behind your head."

"You got this all wrong. I've been looking for Burgess all along and followed him here. I was in disguise..."

With two members still covering Redding, she cuffed him. "Your disguise was your uniform. It hid an accessory to murder. A child rapist." Because there wasn't a doubt in her mind that he was the third man in the church videos. "You belong in a cage. I hope you spend the rest of your life in one."

42

Frank Burgess sat in a cell in the federal courthouse, his head in his hands. "'Avenge not yourselves, but rather give place unto wrath, for it is written, vengeance is mine; I will repay, saith the Lord.'"

"He can take care of the vengeance." Cady eyed him steadily. "The US government will mete out justice. We know about Life Church. We have the videos."

His head swung up, his eyes wild. "The pastor told us to get rid of them years ago, but we knew he'd turn on us if we didn't keep proof he was involved, too. After Fielding died, Deacon changed his mind and told me to burn them. I meant to, but they had disappeared from a box in my cellar." His gaze dropped. "I figured Rina must have taken them, but she denied it. He beat her, trying to find out what happened to them."

"Which adults are in them?" It took effort for Cady to keep her voice level.

"You know if you watched them. Me. Jeffrey Lord. Deacon—Jeb Redding."

"How did Redding earn that name? Was he studying to be a pastor?"

Burgess snorted. "We was considered elders of the church, him and me. Lord called him Deacon, 'cuz he'd step in when Jeffrey had to be gone. Did some of the preaching, too. He just wanted a title to go with his high opinion of himself. He was only a deputy back then, but still thought he was something. Some of us serve God without needing recognition."

"Were you serving him when you raped those kids?" Miguel's arms were crossed tightly across his chest, as if to stop himself from lunging at the man.

Burgess's mouth twisted. "You both sit there and judge me? God alone determines my repentance. I did good, too. I took Rina in. Didn't know if she was mine or not. Didn't even care! Selma Dierks is wicked and evil flourishes around her. One of her boyfriends near killed the girl for stealing a dollar from his wallet. I introduced her to the holy word and raised her right. And I never laid a hand on her in lust."

"You don't get points for the kids you *didn't* molest." The disgust Cady felt for the man nearly choked her. "Who owns the residence we raided tonight?"

"Redding. He bought it twenty years ago. Put it in one of them things that hides the owner." The LLC, Cady interpreted. "No telling what he did in there before I ever knew him."

"Tell us about Life and Death," Miguel put in. "We know the fight videos are on the Dark Web. You're making money from them."

"Not me. Redding." He raised a shaking hand to wipe his forehead. "We had no choice. Two years ago, he discovered

Corbin Fielding had an appointment with an assistant county attorney. That would have ended all of us."

"Who killed Corbin? You or the sheriff?" Because there wasn't a doubt in Cady's mind that Corbin's father had been correct. His son hadn't committed suicide.

"That was Deacon. Jeffrey made us realize we were living on borrowed time. They weren't kids anymore to be held off with threats. Even 'fraid as they was of Deacon, someone was bound to talk. So they had to be silenced. But I insisted it be done in a godly way. Allowing people choice over their own life or death makes them worthy in the eyes of God."

"They had to die so the worthy could live," she said, para- phrasing Joseph's words.

When the man nodded, Cady drew a deep breath. Sought control. There were no limits to what some people could rationalize. "How did you find all of the victims? Some of them didn't even reside in the state anymore."

Burgess waved a hand. "Deacon tracked them. Cops have ways."

Miguel's expression hardened. Cady knew what he was thinking. Redding had used his legal authority for his own sick ends.

"Who forced me off the road after I went to see Jeffrey Lord?" she asked.

"He insisted we do something. Deacon knew where I could steal a truck. I left it so it could be returned to its owner," he added, as if that wiped out the small fact that he'd tried to kill her.

"How many child victims were there?" Miguel queried.

"Twelve. With Jonas gone, ten have already died."

"Who killed Saul Jonas?" she asked.

"Deacon. He did them all. Fielding. Jonas. Nancy Wiley."

Cady and Miguel exchanged a glance. He got up and left the room.

"Why was Joseph's mother murdered?"

"She knew what happened to Joe back then. She and a few others. Jeffrey paid them to stay quiet." Frank scratched his jaw. "Deacon found out she was talking to you, though. We couldn't trust her not to say too much."

The news had her stomach twisting. Miguel came back in the room and she saw the corroboration in his expression. Whoever he'd called had verified Nancy Wiley's death. "She just wanted her son safe." The woman's concerns might well have sprung from more than one source, Cady acknowledged. She could have also suspected what end the two men planned for Joseph.

"We found the burnt remains of fourteen people on your property."

Burgess looked startled at Miguel's words, then resigned. "Rina. I could never break her of her laziness. She was supposed to take them into the woods, far away from the house."

"If Deacon killed Fielding and Jonas, eight of your former victims died in the L and D deaths. Why were there fourteen sets of remains?"

"All he thought about was money. He set up the website. He profited from it. I participated only as a way to purify my sins in the eyes of the Lord. But if we only had one of the former church members..." He shrugged. "He wanted videos. So, we needed participants."

Participants. The word brought a sour taste to Cady's mouth. "And who found them? Who kidnapped Phoebe Lansing?"

"I was in charge of finding extra competitors. But often Joseph..." His voice gentled. "I indulged his weakness and he was eager to help. He believed we'd start our own church once we finished our mission. He'd take my van. Like the night you met up with him." He smirked. "I always cleaned it real good after. Deacon said how you never got no evidence from it."

If they hadn't escaped, she and Paul had been destined for the Life and Death matches. A chill worked down her spine. "Joseph hunted victims if you let him tattoo them first? A compulsion that was likely rooted in how you victimized him as a teen." The man looked away. "We arrested him tonight," she continued. "Outside the house where we found you. He said you and he were going to punish Deacon."

"Because he was going to kill Rina. That wasn't part of the plan, and Joseph was as angry as I was."

She handed him a legal pad and pencil. "Write down the victims who appeared on the rape videos. Then make a list of those in the L and D films. Don't forget to account for Holly Travers." They sat in silence as he obeyed. When he'd finished, she said, "We know Phoebe Lansing and Rina. But who was the other woman there tonight?"

"Greta. I mean, Kelli Sinwell."

Cady recalled the woman's blank expression as the medics checked her. She had a long recovery ahead, emotionally. All because of three men attempting to escape accountability for their actions.

When he finished, Burgess gave a heavy sigh, as if the act had exhausted him. "What's going to happen now?"

"I also want the names of any other members of Life Church you haven't listed. When we're done here, you'll be taken to a federal detention center to be held for trial. And hopefully, you'll spend what's left of your life behind bars." Cady tamped down the emotion that wanted to surge. There was no adequate punishment for the trauma and brutality he'd inflicted.

But there'd be justice. And if the survivors were willing, they'd have a hand in meting it out.

It was nearly nine a.m. before Burgess had been taken away and they'd summarized the events for Allen. He shook his head sadly. "Hell of an ending. You did a good thing, exposing these scumbags."

"We're not done yet," Cady said. Miguel nodded.

"You could turn the rest over to the deputy marshals in Durham," Allen suggested. "Or wait until you get some sleep." Seeing his answer in their expressions, he said, "Have it your way. I'll facilitate on this end. Go finish this thing."

43

"Thank you again, sir." Jeffrey Lord smiled broadly as he walked Damon Phillips, his immediate superior, to the door. "I promise you won't regret offering me this opportunity."

"I know you'll do us proud in whichever mission country you're assigned." The older man clapped him on the shoulder. "You've done good work here. We expect more of it in the future."

When he'd gone, Jeffrey barely restrained a fist pump. Everything he'd worked for all these years was about to come to fruition. Damon hadn't told him which overseas mission he'd be assigned to, of course, but a man could dream that it'd be in a country with excellent fishing and lax consent laws. He sat in his chair, arms behind his head, and allowed himself to visualize it.

When his door opened without a call first, he straightened, instantly indignant. "Sable, how many times have I told you—"

But his lovely soft-eyed assistant wasn't framed in the doorway. That marshal was. The one Deacon had promised to get rid of. The one whose eyes had called him a liar, no matter what he'd told her. Three men accompanied her.

He rose, smoothing his tie nervously. "Deputy Marshal Maddix. This isn't a good time. I have meetings for the rest of the day."

"I'm afraid they're canceled." Two of her companions stepped forward and cuffed him.

"Stop! What is this? Sable! Call security!"

"Jeffrey Lord, you're being charged with twelve counts of sexual assault of a minor. Accessory to murder. And conspiracy."

He took a step back as she recited the Miranda, wincing when the cuffs pinched his wrists. "What on earth are you talking about?"

"Do you need to view the videos to be reminded?"

The bottom fell out of his stomach. His throat dried. "I... don't know what you mean." Frank had sworn he'd burned those DVDs.

"Don't worry. The jury will see them. Take a good look at your office. It's a far cry from the six-by-eight cell you're going to be living in."

44

One week later

Cady raised her brows when Ryder disconnected his call and went to the kitchen, opening one of the cupboards to grab both the pets' leashes. "Are we going for a walk?"

"You get to stay home. Dylan and I are taking the dogs to the dog park. It's man-time."

She smiled, genuinely amused. "Don't tell Sadie."

He came over, propped himself on the arm of her chair. "I think he wants to talk to me about my job."

"Ah. I had a short conversation with him about that a little while ago. He's thinking about a career in law enforcement."

"So I gather. What were you telling me before he called just now? About the women. Rina and Michelle."

"Oh." Remembering gave her a glow of satisfaction. "They've reconnected. Rina is in a woman's shelter right now in Asheville, and the social worker is trying to find her a place in a sheltered workshop. That's vocational training for people with disabilities. She's also lining her up with a device that will help her communicate. Michelle drove up and took her to a meeting with the federal prosecutor today. They're both going to testify against Burgess, Redding, and Lord." Cady hadn't heard anything about Kelli Sinwell—except that she was still in the hospital. The woman had a long battle ahead after her recent trauma. "I understand that Phoebe Lansing has also agreed to give testimony about her experience."

His face went pensive. "It'll be tough on them to relive it, but hopefully they'll get some satisfaction from seeing their abusers sentenced. What are you going to do tonight?"

She rose, and they walked to the door together. "Probably go see my mom. She's got a summer cold." It was likely nothing, but Cady had felt hypervigilant since Caster had targeted Hannah. Delusions, she reflected as she went to the garage, could be dangerous things.

BUT WHEN SHE got to the cabin, her mother wasn't sitting in her usual chair. Her bedroom stood partially open, with light spilling from it. Cady sent a quizzical look at her aunt, who'd answered the door.

Alma just shrugged and continued past her to the sink, where she was washing the dishes. "She's in a snit this evening. Couldn't find something in her room and now she's tearing it apart. Like as not, she's already forgotten what she was looking for."

Cady peeked inside and had a feeling of déjà vu. Drawers were hanging out of the dresser. Hannah was on the floor, with the contents of the boxes strewn all around her. "Mom." She crouched down next to her. "What are you doing? Can I help?"

"Oh, thank goodness you're here. I can't find it anywhere."

"What is it?" Gently, she stilled Hannah's hands and drew them from a box. "Tell me."

"My favorite nightgown. You remember. You had a matching one when you were little. It was white, with pink rosebuds and a ribbon threading the neckline. I've been searching for hours."

Cady reeled inwardly. She recalled the garment, but the last time Hannah had worn it was that night over thirty years ago, in the kitchen of an unmemorable house. Blood had dripped from her face, staining the gown. And Lonny Maddix had stood over her, laughing.

The sound of the remembered gunshot echoed through Cady's mind. "Mom, you haven't had that nightgown for ages. I bought you a turquoise one not long ago. Let's see if we can find that instead." She found the nightie hanging in the closet and laid it across the bed.

Hannah looked distressed. "I've made such a mess. I can't sleep in untidiness like this."

Cady guided her out the door and into her chair. "It's too early for bed." She used the remote to scroll until she settled on a favorite show. "You enjoy some TV. I'll clean up your room."

It didn't take long to pick up the clothes, fold them, and set them neatly inside the drawers. But all three boxes from the closet shelf had been dumped in the center of the room. For the second time in days she sorted through pictures, matchbooks, papers, souvenirs... and of course the gun. The scattered detritus was a sad summary of a life.

In an attempt to organize the stuff this time, she

collected all the sheets to go together. They were different sizes, and as she transferred them to a box, smaller scraps fluttered to the floor. She picked up one, saw it was written in her mom's handwriting and stopped to read it. Reggie Carlson. Rent. Trust. Cady taken care of. The last words were underlined twice. Frowning, she turned it over and saw Alma's writing on that side. A card was paper clipped to it.

Reggie Carlson Real Estate Attorney Property Transactions

The company on the card had a Charlotte address. Her aunt's notes were more copious. Trust - 5000 seed $$$. Lily P. Wait 2 or 3 years to rent. Those $$$ pay taxes. Acct w/extra $$$ 4 cash.

There was more, but her head was spinning. She got up and went to find her aunt. Found her scrubbing the old gas stove.

Her voice pitched low, she asked, "Who's Reggie Carlson?"

Alma never paused in her task. "Who?"

Cady held up the sheet with the attached card. "Why would Mom be interested in a real estate attorney?"

"She squirrels away the damnedest things."

"This is your handwriting."

Finally, her aunt stopped and turned to look at the note. "That's the company we rent this place from, is all." A burner flared behind the woman, and before Cady could react, Alma snatched the sheet away with her free hand and held it over the flame.

"What are you doing?" She grabbed at the paper.

Alma blocked her until the note ignited and curled. "Step away now or you'll get burned." Then she turned the gas off and carried the fiery remnant to the sink. Dropped it inside and ran water over it. "Just got done cleaning that stove," she muttered darkly.

She gripped the woman's arm. "Why'd you do that? What are you hiding? Who's Lily P.? Lily Prentice? Was she the one who found five thousand dollars after Lonny died?"

Shutting off the faucet, Alma faced her and folded her arms over her chest. "Sounds mighty lucky, if so."

Cady stared at her, half-formed thoughts bouncing through her mind. Caster had told her about Prentice—how the feds had thought the woman might have gotten some of the bank robbery cash. *Seed money*. To cast suspicion in another's direction? "The card says the attorney does property transactions," she said slowly.

"You don't need to be looking at me with your cop face, missy. The name of that company is the one I've paid rent to for most of thirty years. I welcomed you and your mama here whenever you needed a roof over your head, don't go forgettin'. No idea what else you're runnin' on about." Alma's expression was closed. "First Caster, now you. Seems to me, trouble has a way of findin' a person, without them lookin' for it."

HERO AND SADIE came dashing into the house, both heading for the water dishes and lapping from them as though parched. Ryder followed, snapping on the light. Then stopped when he saw her in the family room.

"Why were you sitting in the dark?"

"I guess it matched my thoughts."

He set the leashes on the counter and approached her. "What's going on?"

"Let me spin you a story." Her voice was flat. "What if Stan Caster was right all along? He said they had someone inside the bank they robbed. Someone the feds never discovered. That's why the bait money wasn't in the bag. And what if he was also correct about someone finding the cash?"

He looked perplexed. "I thought we were in agreement that was all a fantasy."

She laughed without amusement. "He told me one of my dad's girlfriends was suspected of having some of the money. She bought a new car with it and caught the FBI's attention."

"So, that was true?"

"I hate to live in a world where the man is right about anything. But I'm sitting here trying to think of a different explanation for how this played out, and I can't."

Ryder just looked at her for a moment. Then he set something on the floor and lifted her out of the recliner. Sat and repositioned her on his lap.

Annoyance edged through her black thoughts. "After the last seven months, one thing you should have learned about me by now is that I'm not a lap sitter."

He slipped an arm around her waist. Drew her closer. "Don't think of it that way. Consider yourself an anchor to keep me from slipping off the chair. Why don't you start from the beginning."

She relayed the scene at the cabin, the words on the note, and her conversation with Alma. "I looked up Reggie Carlson. He does property transfers, real estate transactions, and more. Do you know what a land trust is?"

"Vaguely."

"Theoretically, if you find the right lawyer, a client can give him a bag of cash and have him buy a parcel of land. If an irrevocable trust is formed, it's almost like an LLC, its own entity, so the taxes and title would be in the attorney's name as well." The research she'd done had gone a long way toward fleshing out her earlier suspicions. "I expect there are even ways to use checks ostensibly written for rent that the lawyer really uses to pay taxes." She knew there was no way Hannah could have come up with such a plan on her own, but she'd been aware of it. *Cady taken care of.* How? shewondered sickly. By arranging a safety net for the two of them?

"So, if I'm following... you think now that your mom did discover the money. Even though the two of you lived in poverty all your life?"

She remembered the bare cupboards. The dwindling supplies of food. The rebound—again and again—to Alma's. "My aunt would have come up with the idea. And being her, she developed a strategy from which she'd benefit, too. She pays cheap rent, and my mom has a place she can always fall back on. Lifelong security, without ever drawing suspicion from the FBI."

He only had to consider for a moment. "You mean the cabin?"

She nodded. "After Alma destroyed the one note I discovered, I looked through the rest of my mom's things." She'd set aside any consideration for Hannah's privacy. Had skimmed every piece of paper she'd found, including the contents of a single sealed envelope she'd run across. "My mother and aunt granted each other power of attorney thirty years ago. I discovered copies of the documents from the same lawyer."

His arms tightened around her. "Tell me again what the note said. The one in Alma's writing." After she did so, he was quiet for a long time before saying, "I agree. It's possible. What do you want to do?"

"I have to report it. To the FBI, I guess. They could investigate." The thought made her want to weep.

"Investigate what? A cryptic note that no longer exists? They could never get a warrant based on supposition, no matter how certain you are."

His words punctured her conclusions with reality. There was really no way to know whether or not her worst fears were true. And somehow that was worse.

"Even last year, I would never have fathomed it." She let herself lean against him. Just for a moment. "But then a few months ago we found out—"

"—that my dad, as sheriff, very likely coerced your mother into keeping a handgun in the house. Readily available. He probably showed you how to shoot it. He didn't give a damn how Lonny Maddix got dead, as long as he did."

Pull the trigger back nice and smooth. The words sounded again in her mind, but she'd never been able to pin them to a specific memory.

"What we've pieced together from things your mom and my dad's former investigative officer have said isn't evidence. Like your notion about the land trust. All we have are guesses."

"You didn't see Alma's face. From what she wrote, I can figure exactly how they did it."

"It makes as much sense as any other explanation." One of his hands was rubbing her spine in rhythmic strokes.

After being sent to live with her grandfather when she was twelve, Cady had missed years with Hannah where she might have gleaned more details about her past. Instead, she was left to discover remnants for herself, stitching them together in a dark patchwork of family history. The weight of it was suffocating. It'd drag her down if she let it.

"You had a crummy childhood," he said. "You're a walking testament to resiliency."

A compliment from someone who was all too aware of the ways her past had shaped some of her emotional responses. Her mind flashed to all the victims in the case she'd just finished. As she'd told Yarnell, plenty of people had endured worse.

There was little she could do about her suspicions. She couldn't share them with her mom. That would undoubtedly elicit an episode. With each one, Hannah's grasp on the present loosened a fraction more.

Hero padded over and nosed something on the floor by the chair. Cady looked down at him. "What's that?"

"What... oh." Ryder reached over and picked something up. Rolled it tightly in his hand. "Bad timing. It's nothing we need to discuss tonight."

It was a newspaper brochure of some sort. She took it from him and turned some pages, her stomach flipping when she realized it advertised properties for sale. "Ah."

"The dogs and I drove by a couple of places on our way home," he confessed. He took the booklet and opened it to a black-and-white photo of an acreage. "Closer to town than this one, but on the opposite side. Not as much land. Sadie thought the house needed a little work. Hero approved of the yard."

She was silent for a long moment. Cady felt like she was teetering on the brink of a cliff, arms wheeling. Now was the time to pull back. Or jump.

"What are you thinking?"

She felt the sticky tug of her past. Drew a breath and

reached for a piece of the future. "I have to trust the female on this one. But maybe the interior is more impressive."

His smile was a promise. "We should take a look."

She looped her arms around his neck. Took the leap. "We should."

ACKNOWLEDGMENTS

Research is almost as much fun as writing. Okay, it's often *more* fun than writing, especially when I'm under deadline. An author needs a lot of information to credibly write even a couple of sentences of description about a topic. I'm endlessly grateful to Deputy U.S. Marshal Robert S. for your help throughout this series, answering questions about USMS procedures and operations. I so appreciate your time and knowledge.

Thank you again to Dr. Gary Keller for your in-depth answers and for brainstorming about my mentally ill character. Your details are always as fascinating as they are helpful.

When it came to incapacitating my bad guy to facilitate my heroine's escape, DP Lyle, MD, offered excellent suggestions. I appreciate your input.

Harry Marsh, Attorney at Law, not only filled me in on trusts but conceived several devious plans my characters could enact. I think you have a future as a suspense writer!

Barbara Kemmis, Executive Director, Cremation Association of North America, supplied details about older model furnaces and cremation procedures. I appreciate your assistance.

On my first trip to Asheville, a bartender told me about the tunnels that existed under the city generations ago. I vowed then to have them figure into one of my books. I'm indebted to Vance Pollock of Asheville, whose knowledge of the city's history helped me devise details for my first chapter. I'm sure I didn't do credit to your information.

A thank you to Christine Williams, Uzzell Wild Game Processing, Goldsboro, NC, for explaining procedures, regulations, and sharing pictures of the facility. It was so helpful.

Dr. Brooke Rosonke filled me in on medical procedures necessary for my poor character held captive in a mine full of bats (my nightmare!) She and I are grateful.

James L'Etoile, crime author and nationally recognized expert on prison and jail operations, helped with my parole questions. Thank you for offering your expertise!

As always, any errors are the fault of the author.

ABOUT THE AUTHOR

Kylie Brant is the author of more than forty novels, including *Cold Dark Places* and *Down the Darkest* road in the Cady Maddix series, the Circle of Evil Trilogy, and the stand-alone novels *Pretty Girls Dancing* and *Deep as the Dead*. She's a three-time RITA award nominee, five-time RT Award finalist, and two-time Daphne du Maurier Award winner. Brant is a member of the International Thriller Writers, Novelists, Inc., and Sisters in Crime. Her books have been published in thirty-five countries and translated into nineteen languages.

Printed in Great Britain
by Amazon